The Pain of Strangers

Killing them since 1987

Andrew Barrett

The Ink Foundry

© Copyright 2022

The rights of Andrew Barrett to be identified as the author of this work have been asserted in accordance with sections 77 and 78 of the Copyright, Designs and Patents Act 1988. No part of this publication may be reproduced, stored in a retrieval system or transmitted in any form or by any means electronic, mechanical, photocopying, recording or otherwise without the prior permission of the copyright holder.

Published in the United Kingdom by The Ink Foundry.

For rights and copyright enquiries, please contact:

permissions@andrew.barrett.co.uk

This book is a work of fiction. Any names, characters, companies, organizations, places, events, locales, and incidents are fictional or are used in a fictitious manner. Any resemblance to actual persons, living or dead, or actual events is purely coincidental.

Contents

Dedication	VI
Praise for The Pain of Strangers	VIII
Preface	IX
1. How it Began	3
2. How it Ended	6
3. The Robbery	13
4. One Last Kiss	16
5. Back in the Tent	18
6. Use Your Eyes	25
7. Late Again	29
8. The Promise	32
9. Making a Stand	39
10. The Dominance of Pigeons and How Life is Shit	46
11. Swilling the Leaves	52
12. Spinning Circles and The Baseball Bat	56
13. Common Sense and Spontaneity	59
14. Blowing Smoke	63
15. A Funny Taste	69
16. A Major Application	77
17. A Need to Meet	80

18.	A Nasty Bastard	83
19.	Climbing the Ladder	89
20.	The Sixth Cigarette	93
21.	A Circle of Shit	100
22.	Hopping Mad	105
23.	A Crying Shame	111
24.	The Beginning of the Argument	114
25.	A Closed Throat	120
26.	The End of the Argument	122
27.	Eyes Half Open	127
28.	An Innocent Corpse	129
29.	Life's a Drag	135
30.	Ridge Detail	137
31.	The Hammer	142
32.	A Friendly Visit	147
33.	Tea and Biscuits with an Iron Maiden	150
34.	The Knock	157
35.	Sleeping With a Madman	163
36.	Flattery but no Quality Street	170
37.	The Punk and the Pianist's Finger	176
38.	The Gothic Behemoth's Scullery	181
39.	The Scene Examination	187
40.	The Thumbscrews and the Samaritan	190
41.	An Honourable Arsehole	197
42.	Dry-humping Cynthia	201
43.	The Faraday Cage	208
44.	It Could be Beautiful	211

45. Norton Bailey and the Great Flaps of Justice	217
46. To Want Something Too Much	222
47. And the Jaguar Purred Across Crumbling Bridges	226
48. The Tattoo with Pointy Teeth	233
49. Hyde Park in the Rain	237
50. The Art of Delusion	240
51. A Tin of Biscuits and Dreams	244
52. Inside the Faraday Cage	253
53. The Killer, the Thief, and the CSI	255
54. Fire and Bluetooth	259
55. From Green to Red	267
56. No Room for Justice	271
57. When the Fire Went Out	280
58. Promises, Promises	282
59. Epilogue	289
Afterword	292
Acknowledgments	296
About the Author	298
Also by Andrew Barrett	300
Reader's Club	302

This book is dedicated to Lottie Rose

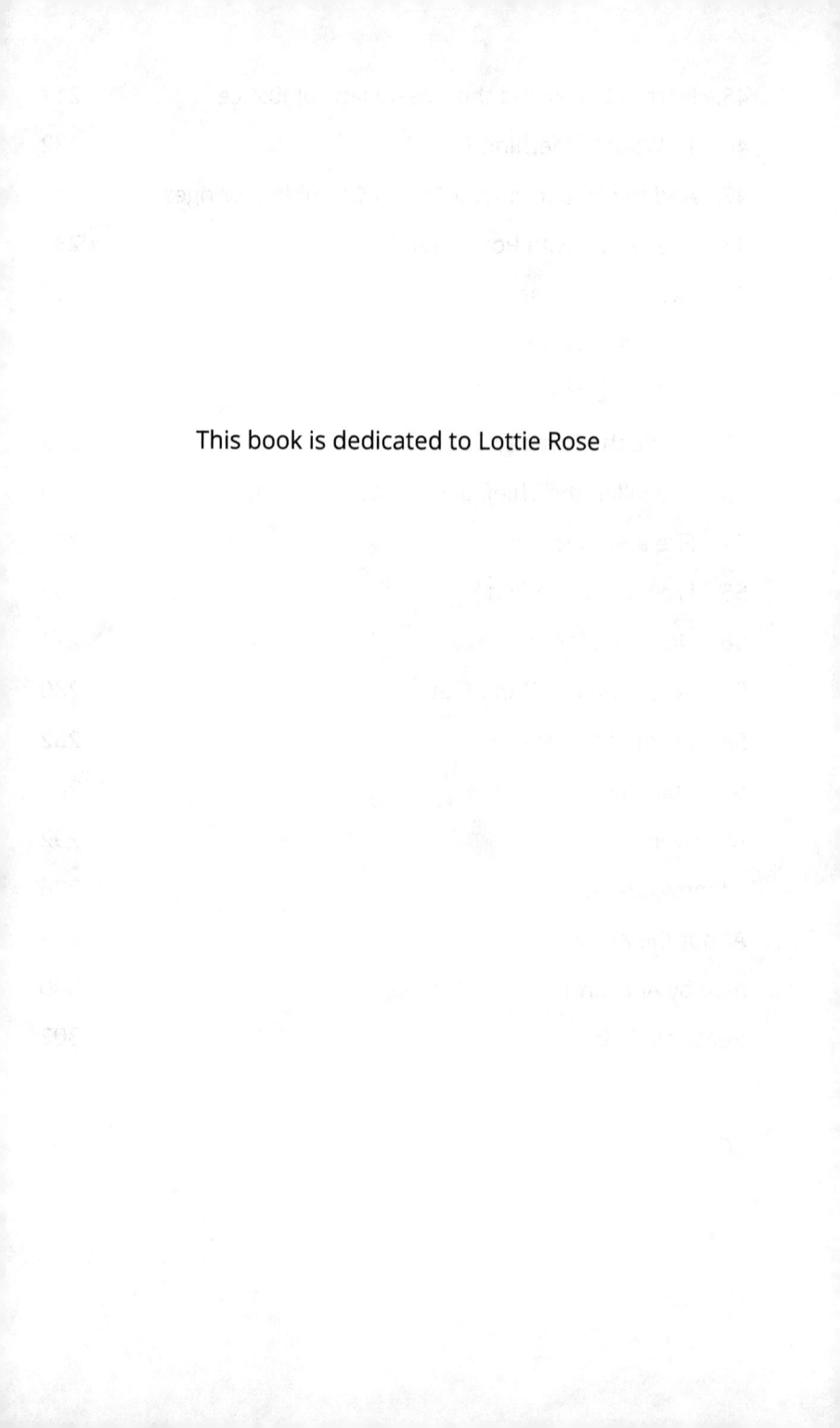

Praise for The Pain of Strangers

Make sure you have your seatbelt fastened because you won't want to put this book down.

Blood, gristle and dour Yorkshire humour infused with a twist of shock and horror. This book should have a cocktail named after it.

Murder, mayhem, mystery and Eddie's inimitable dark humour make this a must read!!

It was a great read and I laughed lots throughout. I squirmed a bit as well.

My new favourite Eddie Collins book! Read in one sitting; laugh out loud moments, yuck - teeth clenching bits n of course read fast n don't breathe moments! Perfect.

The Pain of Strangers was brilliant and had everything you need in a crime book.

A clever, psychological thriller from the supremely skilled author, Andrew Barrett.

This story is the new beginning of the Eddie Collins series and pulled me in right from the start. There's lots of action, plenty of nastiness, loads of dark humour, and much agonising.

This mystery is a classic good guys vs bad guys, except that we are never sure who is good and who is bad.

Barrett is simply excellent at putting the reader by the side of the character

When characters are speaking to each other, my head nearly turns from person to person as they speak

Eddie is his usual rude and sarcastic self, to the point I'm sometimes cringing at what he says!

As usual, the forensics are really interesting to read about and held my appeal.

Yet again, the author weaves his magic in his words.

Lots of forensic work, plenty of blood, a danger for everyone, and a great plot with wonderful characters.

Preface

Proud to swear in British English

Chapter One

How it Began

1980

Maureen Bailey hurried through Leeds city centre; a see-through umbrella kept the drizzle away but it couldn't shield her from the nerves she felt. Her face was pale, the lips she licked constantly looked like ones stolen from a corpse, and her heart threatened to stop working right then and see her drop to the wet pavement like a sack of—

"Mummy, slow down."

"Mum, is this really necessary?"

Maureen stopped dead and stared at her children. She took a breath, and shut out the noise of the crowds and the noise of rain pummelling the umbrella. "I can't slow down, Libby. I need to be somewhere in," she flicked her sleeve up her arm and glanced at her watch, "fifteen minutes. I have an appointment." She stood a little straighter, a little taller and her gaze met Norton's eyes. "I don't know what you think you know, but this is very important. To me, I mean. And it's important to you, to both of you; it's for your futures, so you need to cooperate; yes?" She glared at them both. "And you need to keep this to yourselves."

"Keep what to ourselves?"

"Judging by the smirk on your face, I'd suggest you have a pretty good idea of what I'm planning. If you wreck the plan, you wreck my future, and you wreck your future, and you wreck Libby's future. Is that clear?"

The smirk did not disappear. "I don't think you have the right—"

"This is not a debate. But yes, yes, I do have the right. So step aside, Norton, let's get through the day."

The smirk developed into a barely hidden smile. "Very well," he said. "Libby, keep up."

They set off walking again, and Maureen wondered what had just happened. "I'll get some cash, and you two will go to the market, find a cafe, get a hot drink and a bacon sandwich. I'll be with you in about an hour. Buy some flowers for the parlour from Rene's, alright? And don't engage in conversation with strangers and ragamuffins. Is that clear?"

The bank was on George Street. It was a Midland bank and it had one of those novel Automatic Teller Machines in the wall. Amazing. She still considered them a marvel – you could get money from a machine; it was like having a secret, she thought. But it wasn't like the kind of secret she clasped in her bag today.

She swallowed, waited in the queue, fingers tapping the umbrella handle, Libby holding her other hand tightly like she always did – scared to let go. And Norton said, "Gonna look in the model shop, okay?"

Maureen nodded, "Off you go, keep an eye out for us."

She faced front and the queue had dwindled; the crowd of pedestrians milling around outside the parade of shops, crossing the road to the markets, and heading across town towards The Headrow was enormous. Saturday in Leeds: why did she choose a Saturday? "Midweek would have been better," she whispered to herself. She felt the eyes of the world upon her, she felt as though her bag was as see-through as the umbrella, and the whole world knew what she was doing.

"What did you say, Mummy?"

She stepped closer to the machine, and gave thought to Norton and his horrid smirk. Did he really know what she was planning? And could she trust him not to go running and tell his father? She bit her lip and could only pray that asking for his silence would be enough. If Dennis found out...

"Mummy?"

Maureen saw there was no one in front of her, so she stood before the machine, and swallowed again. She shook her hand free of Libby's grasp, and took out the ATM card and a slip of paper. The paper had her personal identification number written on it. They said you weren't supposed to keep it written down, but really, how else could you remember it? "This is all very Doctor Who," she said.

She put the card in, squinted as the screen told her what to do next. She carefully pressed the numbers onto a keypad and waited, lips dry again, heart fluttering. She had an awful feeling about all of this, and wondered if she might not just forget the whole—

The card presented itself and the machine whirred. As she reached for the money, she could see her fingers shaking. Why would they—then Libby screamed.

Maureen turned around and saw Libby on the ground, pushed aside by a skinny thug with a skinhead haircut. The thug reached for her bag, but Maureen turned away, and took a step back. "Here," she said, "take the money. Twenty pounds."

The thug grinned and snatched the money, rammed it in his jeans pocket but still had hold of the bag. She pulled, and he pulled. She yanked and screamed, and the thug yanked harder, and before long, part of the crowd had peeled off and was gathering around them like black clouds rolling in a storm. Libby was still screaming, and the thug's smile had gone – just anger left.

"Get off me!"

There was movement to her right and she caught a glimpse of Norton coming to rescue her. The thug pulled harder, teeth bared, frantically trying to get the bag from her, his urgency now inducing a more violent approach. And no sooner had that thought crossed her mind, when something profound did happen.

Maureen found herself on the ground. All the strength seemed to have left her, and she breathed hard and fast, felt out of breath, panicking. The rain pattered down harder, and quite suddenly she felt faint and there was a pain in her neck that felt peculiarly warm. She heard Libby screaming, and managed to crane her head to see her as the umbrella pirouetted and was swallowed by the watching crowd. She looked so upset, her hand to her mouth and her face screwed up into a mess of agony.

Libby turned and ran, and Maureen's vision faded.

"Mother."

That was Norton. "Nor..." She felt hot liquid – blood, she thought, it must be my blood, land on her as she lay quietly, fearfully, on the wet pavement waiting for something. Waiting for rescue or death, whichever. She thought death might come first. The bag had gone, she could feel it was missing, and all hope for her children's future fled too; and then she heard a scream. It was Libby. She'd recognise Libby's voice anywhere. She heard Libby scream. Then she saw and heard nothing again.

Chapter Two

How it Ended

Today

EVEN THOUGH NORTON BAILEY was fifty-three he still cried each time he killed someone.

He cried not because he felt bad for killing them, but rather he always hoped it would ease his pain. It never did. It was like an addiction, hoping the next cigarette would be enough to satiate his desire, but it never was; it was a stepping stone to the next and the next. Never ending, smoking and killing. Killing and smoking.

Norton lived in perpetual pain. But he had one thing going for him – he had hope, and he believed in persistence. He believed in persistence because his father had beaten it into him with a cricket bat. "You have so much debt to pay; more debt than you could pay off in three lifetimes, boy. Never stop until you've made it right." Norton wouldn't stop until the pain went away. He was convinced that soon, one of them would set him free.

He stood on the corner of Harehills Lane and Beaumont Drive and hopped from one foot to the other. The rain was like his mood, cold and stinging. His wide eyes were never still, always flitting around, searching for the next one. It didn't always go his way; it was often weeks and quite often months before he found one. One time, he went three years without spotting one. During those three years, he'd changed routines, changed locale, times, days, but he still didn't get a bite.

He hopped and he put his hands under his armpits to keep the chill away from his fingers. His grey beard, complete with two long plaits, swung around his neck in the wind, and his hat almost blew away again. It was a bad night to be out. Litter tumbled down the street, rainwater chased it down the gutters, cars splashed water, and Norton squinted into the wind, gritted his teeth against the cold and against the noise. Wednesday was the night the youth came out to play – drinks were half-price in most—

Screams erupted behind him. By the cash machine, a trendy young woman wearing gold-coloured trainers was punched in the stomach. She hit the wet pavement groaning, and the youths snatched her money and spat on her before running away laughing. Norton ignored her cries; she looked directly at him, watery blood dripping from her lips, eyes pleading. He watched the robbers and hopped faster, the excitement building.

Harehills was busy despite the weather. Wherever in Leeds you lived, Wednesday meant party night. It meant getting pissed, getting laid, or getting glassed. Sometimes it meant all three.

Music thumped from passing cars, and from the open doorways of clubs up and down Harehills Lane, and for a moment, Norton's mind threatened to let go. As if suffering an episode of vertigo, he began to spin, and in a panic clutched onto the wall for support as dizziness rolled through his mind and blurred his vision. His mouth watered and he thought he would be sick, but the knife at his throat quickly put an end to it.

His old man's eyes swivelled and settled on a youth who had teeth missing. He smiled up at Norton through the rain. "'Ello, Granddad. Giz your money."

Norton took his hands away from the wall, and slowly raised his arms; cold water ran up his sleeves. That's what they did in the movies, lifting one's arms in a sign of compliance. "My dear young man, there is no need for the knife; I am quite unarmed, and I am more than a little fragile."

The youth looked to his accomplices, unsure if the old man was taking the piss out of him – obviously. His smile teetered on the edge of uncertainty, lingered for a moment, and then returned, happy, it seemed, that this was just the old man's way, and that he wasn't being ridiculed. The knife twitched, and one of the others hit Norton in the belly hard enough to double him up. He coughed and sank to the ground, his happy hopping a long way behind him. He put a hand up, fighting the pain as he tried to breathe. "I have money," he groaned. "Please... no more." He wondered if this was how his mother felt; he wondered it every time this happened, and each time it did he tried to keep hold of the feeling, to package it for later inspection, to savour it, but it was always fleeting and escaped into the night like the robbers tended to do. Bravado and the ability to act took over and Norton allowed them to pull him to his feet.

"Do we have to put you on the floor again?"

"No, no, no," the hand outstretched again, palm towards them. "Please, come with me, I'll get you the money."

He noticed a look pass between the three youths. He wondered if he'd made it too easy for them, he wondered if they would see through his charade, but if they did they were too greedy to acknowledge it. "Get a move on, you old fucker, we ain't got all night."

"Got other young women to rob?" Norton nodded across Harehills Lane to the sobbing girl leaning against the cash machine spitting blood.

The youth moved in, grinning, "A bit sassy for an old-timer staring death in the face, eh?"

Norton dared to smile. "I'm not afraid of death. I see it as a friend I've yet to meet."

"Keep this shit up and you'll be meeting it sooner than you thought."

Rarely did Norton venture this far from home, but he'd hit the streets closer to home so often that it had become dangerous, and despite his mind being preoccupied with other things, it never forgot the basics of staying free. The basics, in his case, started with not being seen. He hobbled along, feeling the rainwater and puddle he'd just been sitting in, running down his legs and into his sandals. His socks were sloppy tongues slapping the pavement. He ignored the kids' laughter, concentrating instead on walking as fast as he dare down streets he knew well, streets that didn't have CCTV.

Without notice, someone punched Norton in the ribs and he hit the ground again, his head almost colliding with a brick wall too. He squinted up into the rain and a finger jabbed him in the face, "You fucking us about, old man?"

"What? No, no. I have two thousand pounds at home."

A brief pause before, "How much further?"

"Two hundred yards, literally. We're five minutes away."

"I think he's full of shit," said one of the youths.

"I am not!" Norton made it to his feet, and through the rain he shouted, "I am a man of my word, sir, and I said I had money, and by George, I have money!"

The three youths took a step back, laughing at the show. One of them said, "Fair enough, granddad. We believe you."

"Well, I should hope you do. Our generation were not scoundrels, sir; our word was our bond, and indeed," he pointed a finger, "my word is my bond."

"And my word says you got five minutes left before we stop being so kind to the elderly, yeah?"

The door opened with barely a sound, and Norton staggered inside. Behind him, two of the three youths yelled at him to get a move on, the third stayed out on the street keeping a watchful eye and smoking beneath the shelter of a twisted little tree.

They shoved him in the back, and Norton almost tripped along the hallway.

"Wow, granddad, you got some shit in here."

"And it fucking stinks. When was the last time you cleaned up? You mucky old bastard."

"You are in my home. I ask that you treat it and me with the respect it deserves. We have both been through a lot."

A chubby youth grabbed Norton by the beard and rammed him into the hall wall. He was snarling. Through the snarl, he whispered, "No one gives a shit about you or your stinking shithole of a house. No one gives a shit about what you've been through. You should be wiped from the earth; you're redundant, you're useless. So do us all a favour, old man, hurry up and die. In the meantime, you owe me two grand."

There was something frightening about today's youth. It wasn't even the 'no respect' thing – kids had always been rebellious like that, right from his own youth back in the seventies – not so bad as today, granted, but his peers could be defiant when the need arose. No, today's youth were a violent generation, and a greedy one; not a good combination. "In here," he said. Shuffling feet followed him into the darkness of his parlour. His hand brushed the wall, and one long-nailed finger tripped the light switch. "Did you know that the Romans gave us decimation?"

"Not interested. Get the money."

"Seriously, if there was dissention in the ranks, then every tenth man was slaughtered in front of his comrades. Decimating them. Deci as in ten, see?"

The angry one spun Norton around and put his forearm against his throat. "My patience has gone now. Get the money or I'll put you on the floor so hard you'll break a hip. And then I'll break the other one for you as a bonus, see?"

Struggling to speak, Norton croaked, "I was setting it aside for new carpets."

"Where. Is. It."

He nodded to the mantelpiece. "What do you intend spending it on?"

"None of your business."

Norton looked at the greed in their eyes, and almost rubbed his hands together. "Did you know that Romans also gave us murex ferreus, sometimes known as a caltrop, which you'll find..." His words were ignored as the leader of the three stepped onto an old rag rug near the hearth. He reached out for a fat envelope sitting on the mantelpiece but before his fingers could touch it the floor gave way, and he disappeared. He screamed as he fell. It was a short scream followed by a thick warped kind of silence.

Norton stared at the second youth through the corner of his eye, and tried not to smile.

The youth stared back with a wide-open mouth and shock in his eyes. "What the fuck?" He rushed forward to peer into the hole, only to get a shove from behind. He too screamed for a moment, but somehow managed to avoid falling into the pit, keeping his balance by pinwheeling his arms, and threw himself to one side, landing hard on his back. Norton was beside him in seconds and just as the youth was getting to his feet, he thrust the bayonet into his chest.

They stared at each other again; fear on the youth's face, amusement, accomplishment, and pride on Norton's as he nudged the kid through the hole with the side of his wet sandal. There was a satisfying thud as the youth ended his short journey. Norton went to the corner of the room and hit a button. The trapdoors closed again with a solid thump, sucked into place by heavy-duty magnets. The doors were almost invisible, and rendered so by the rag rug favoured by so many people of his parents' generation, the make-do-and-mend set. It was cut in half, following the cut in the floorboards, and it was held in place by nothing more elaborate than a line of staples. Only a few droplets of blood needed cleaning away.

Full of triumph, he ducked back outside, holding the wet hat to his head, and called to the last youth out there under the tree. "Hello? I say, you there."

The kid looked over, flicked away his cigarette.

"You're to come inside."

"What?"

"You're to come inside, I said."

"Chubby said I was to come in?"

Norton shrugged, "If that's his name, then yes. He said you're to come in right now. Just mind your footing, those steps are jolly slippery when they're wet."

The third youth hitched his hoodie up tighter and ran from the cover of the tree through the rain and through the grabbing thorns and stinging nettles, up the steps and into the hallway.

"Go on through into the parlour."

"The what?"

"First right, dear boy, first right."

Norton slammed the front door, hurried into the room after the lad, and from the side of the doorframe, grabbed the rifle just as the lad turned around to face him. He didn't give the kid a chance to curse before he thrust the bayonet and was rewarded with a confused grunt and some healthy resistance. The lad fell to the ground, but was far from dead. Norton was disheartened to find he had only wounded him. He tutted as the lad rolled around on the floor spilling blood all over it, groaning and cursing.

He took aim, but the lad kicked the blade away and quickly clambered to his feet again. He lunged awkwardly at Norton, who just stood aside as the youth blundered past him and out of the parlour. Shocked, not knowing what to do because he'd never faced this before, never had to rehearse it before, Norton turned as the lad opened the front door. In the hallway, distant traffic noise, and a cold blast of rain-sodden wind, hit him in the face – as did the realisation that the lad was on his way to freedom.

It kickstarted Norton's heart, and he rushed forward, out of the front door and immediately slipped on the steps he'd warned the youth about, just as the kid stumbled through the gate and turned left towards Regent Street and towards people.

The old man shrieked at the pain in his back and the sharp yet dull throb of hitting his head on the top step. It made him dizzy, but determination – no, panic – made him lurch forward after the escaping prisoner. There was no room for failure – he simply had to catch him.

Chapter Three

The Robbery

THE RAIN FELL HEAVILY. Norton could see the youth, badly injured it seemed, staggering on towards the brightness of lights out there on Regent Street. Traffic thundered by, spraying a cold red mist in its wake. Up ahead, maybe fifty yards away, the kid stumbled and went down. Norton followed, one agonising step after another, hand out in front of him for balance, his other hand on his burning chest. His legs almost buckled but he forced them on, painful feet screaming at him.

Traffic seemed to slow as though it were looking at the fallen kid but it was a jam across in the other lane. Norton was less than twenty yards away, and for a moment he thought his heart would give out before he made it there. But he forced himself on and was at the lad's side, staring down at him, panting. The lad looked up and began screaming – short quiet bursts that were almost pitiful.

Norton dropped to his knees beside him, and easily pushed aside the protesting arm that tried to keep him at bay. There was a siren, and it wiped away the smile that was developing on Norton's face, a smile of victory that could yet turn sour if he wasn't quick. He could hear someone calling from across the road and maybe thirty yards downhill. Norton acted fast, stared at the kid, and leaned over him, putting his arm over the kid's mouth and nose.

Oh how he wanted to smile at him, how he wanted to tell him how he felt at killing another street robber – the joy he felt, the euphoria, the happiness it would bring to his mother and father. He had no time, though. Instead he stared into the kid's wide eyes and willed death upon him. All he could say to him was, "You deserve me." Blood flowed onto the pavement and the rain took it away almost immediately.

The kid's legs kicked a little, his arms flayed and then he went still. Dead.

Norton could see the kid's knuckles from here. Strange – 'hate' on the left knuckles and 'hate' on the right knuckles too. This kid didn't like people very much.

The siren was almost deafening now and the woman who'd cried out from the other side of the road was there, her streetlamp shadow growing darker the closer she came, and Norton was holding the kid's head in an embrace, a final squeeze to make sure the little bastard was dead. And he did this while crying into the night, sobbing in great bursts as rainwater trickled through his thin old man's hair. He looked up slightly, squinting through the rain as he had done all evening, and he saw a pair of gold-coloured trainers. His eyes raced to the trendy young woman.

"I'm a nurse," she whispered into the rain.

Norton could see blood at the side of her nostril, how it looked like a swipe as she'd wiped it away. "You..."

"Is he dead?"

Norton looked back down at the youth and found he was happy to say, "Yes. He's dead."

The woman in the golden trainers let out a sigh and she rested a hand on Norton's shoulder as the tears came.

"Come on, come on, sir," someone said, and Norton reluctantly let go, allowed himself to be pulled away, trying to reach out to the poor boy.

The ambulance crew got to work on him, and the woman held Norton as they did. He refused to move from the spot until they had confirmed the lad was dead. The woman seemed unsure if the old man's wailing was full of sorrow or full of laughter.

In all the commotion, the old man just walked away and disappeared into the night.

"And then there were none," he said.

When the police arrived, there was the girl in the golden trainers and two gawpers next to the body. The old man had just disappeared, the girl said during interview later. Oh, she had added, and I'm sure he was crying.

The police moved them all back and one of the officers took their details as the other watched the ambulance crew working on the kid. The rain didn't even have the decency to ease up a bit, and it wasn't long before the light green of the crew's uniform was dark green with rainwater and was beginning to shine in the pressure spots like shoulders as the water was forced out.

"I'll get the circus," the officer shouted over the noise of a busy street. Around him kids on the bikes and boards laughed, drivers slowed as soon as they clocked the blue lights, and partygoers shielded by umbrellas hovered as they gathered a new story for their drunken friends and for their Facebook followers.

Chapter Four

One Last Kiss

HE STARED AT IT, propped on his dashboard like a trophy. It was a full, sealed, half-bottle of Metaxa brandy, the good stuff. The best. His favourite. And if he listened closely he could hear it calling him. "Eddie," it said, "crack the seal, man. Have a drink, come on, you'll feel so much better. Things'll start to make sense, you'll see. Haven't they always made sense before? Huh? Have I ever let you down? Haven't I always been truthful? You deserve me."

Being a CSI meant lots of paperwork. After each job – a burglary, a rape, a sudden death, whatever, there was paperwork galore; the scene report notes and lists of exhibits. It was a long time to sit in the van, and it got pretty wearing at times. Your constant companions were neck ache, back ache, arse ache, and hand ache. This job was just a lot of aches, really.

To write up the latest job he'd travelled a few hundred yards away from the address and found somewhere pleasant to park up, a nice park with a small pond in the near distance, supped a cool coffee and smacked his lips. It was another late shift, and it was coming up to his meal time, about eight o'clock, the sun skimming the horizon through sycamores and their spinning seeds, glistening off the water like a million flickering lamps.

And here by the bench only fifty yards away were a couple walking along holding hands without a care to share between them. They looked so happy, and Eddie bit his lip in something he assumed approached jealousy. Kelly and he had been the best of friends at one point in their past. Now they were two enemies sharing a house, a child, and an acute distrust of each other.

He went back to the report and resumed writing. His eyes were focused on the words unravelling across the paper behind his pen, but his mind was eyeing the couple and wondering how his own relationship had free-fallen twenty-thousand feet through frigid skies, had missed the safety net that love was supposed to offer, and was at this moment heading for a bit of a rough landing on concrete, and a makeshift grave six foot beneath it.

His eyes were drawn to the couple kissing, embracing like they were the world to each other – like they meant it and it wasn't just something mentioned in the rule book on the back page. Hint: kiss each day like you mean it. Hint: tell her how much she means to you instead of assuming she knows. Question: she does mean something to you, doesn't she?

Eddie involuntarily shrugged, and said, "Don't know."

The couple parted, holding hands still, and they began walking towards the car park as Eddie tried to list the fingerprints and footwear marks he'd found at the last burglary he'd been to.

The couple had one last kiss and separated, went to their own cars.

Eddie saw her quite clearly as she drove by, still flushed with the heat of her encounter, the anticipation of a future encounter, the longing, the special feelings in her chest and the tingling feelings in her thighs.

Washed in autumnal sunlight as she drove past Eddie was Kelly, his wife.

Inside, Eddie was screaming.

Chapter Five

Back in the Tent

His heart was still on fire when the male party drove past Eddie's van seemingly averting his eyes, pretending to be busy looking for traffic or pedestrians – anything, rather than look at the police van. Eddie made a note of the registration number. He knew coppers who would search it for him. It was amazing to note the extent people went to in order to avoid eye contact with coppers.

"Bravo Seven-Two."

Eddie jumped. He hated that bastard radio! Every time he drifted away into some thought or another, it would smash its way in and drag him back here again – it was worse than the damned Tannoy announcements at Sainsbury's. He took a breath, pressed the button, and seethed, "Go ahead."

"Suspicious death on Regent Street in Mabgate if you're ready to take details."

"Pass them." He scribbled the address and log number down, and ignored the rest. He liked to be prepared of course – who wouldn't? But he also liked to enter a scene blind, sometimes, without having his mind pre-programmed by third party reports: get it from the horse's mouth. Once the transmission was concluded, his mind began to drift back to Kelly.

"Bravo Seven-Two, did you receive my last?"

"Yes, yes, show me code five."

He took another deep breath and pushed Kelly and her fucking boyfriend out of sight. Right now he had a job to do and there was no point muddying the waters with homelife shit which he could do nothing about from the seat of his van or from the side of a body in Mabgate.

If he were to think of Kelly, which he wouldn't, but if he were, he would consider himself lucky that she had taken the initiative in effectively ending the relationship. Eddie couldn't do that; being content to just drift along until the end of the world presented itself in the form of a catastrophic fall off its edge. At least this way, he thought, there might still be a chance of life.

As if by magic, and knowing that the young lovers had left the stage, the skies opened and Eddie put his windscreen wipers on the fastest speed. The nearer to Mabgate he drove, the darker the sky became until, when he arrived, it was night black and overcast too. The rain was heavy, the night punctured by flashing blue lights, yet despite the rain a small crowd had gathered because there was nothing more exciting on television just then.

Besides getting wet, the very first thing Eddie did after he slid from the van seat was to erect the tent and shuffle it over the slumped body of a young man on the pavement. One might argue that the tent was redundant since the weather was so bad that any evidence would surely have been compromised by now. But it was there to allow Eddie to work without getting even wetter, it was there to prevent prying eyes and the press seeing and publishing things of a delicate nature. But most of all, it was there to offer some decorum to the deceased and his family, and that's all Eddie cared about right now.

And just thinking that brought Kelly and Becca to mind. Eddie stopped everything and had a word with himself as the rain beat upon his head: just leave it, will you? You're here; do this and think of this and only this, and you'll get through it. Deal with Kelly later.

Once the tent was in place, he returned to the van, and in the shelter provided by its tailgate, put on a scene suit over his wet clothes. He saw plenty of blood on the body so it made sense to wear PPE; because it was bright white, it was a good way of not getting run over by drivers whose attention was not where it should be. He had the attending officers close the road temporarily as he fired off some long-exposure location shots.

He was about to get back inside the tent with the camera on its tripod, and armfuls of other gear, when a plain car stopped behind his van and a man stepped out. He flashed some ID card at the scene guard and ducked under the tape, and followed the scene guard's pointing finger. Eddie muttered into the darkness. "Why me?" he whispered.

He was a big man who squinted against the noise and the rain, and he hid under a small pink umbrella as he approached Eddie. "Are you Eddie Collins?"

Eddie looked at the umbrella. "Sounds like you already know. Do you already know?"

"You're famous throughout the force."

Eddie pulled back. "How do you work that one out?"

"They said to look for a knobhead." Benson almost smiled.

Eddie squinted at him. Didn't look like PSD – not smart enough, and they weren't allowed to swear – it turned them to stone. "You must be very strong."

The man shook his head. "What?" he said. "Why?"

"To come in here throwing your weight around like that."

The big man only tutted. "Are you Eddie—"

"Yes, yes! What the hell do you want? I'm trying to look cool for the press and you turn up with a pink brolly."

He came closer. "It was in the car," he said, moving even closer. "I'm Tom Benson."

Eddie looked at him, blinked. "Erm, so."

"I'm a DS at the Major Crime Unit."

"Woohoo, really? Can I have your autograph?"

"What? Look, I'm trying to introduce myself."

"I'm happy for you. If you could get to the point before bedtime I'd appreciate it."

Benson stared at Eddie. "Are you always this rude?"

"Aw come on; I'm wet through, I'm doing my best!" Eddie began to feel uncomfortable, like there might be a complaint coming his way by the end of the evening. They knew better than to send out people he didn't know to his scenes. Eddie did not like new people, they unbalanced him, they annoyed him, and they took away his focus from the scene – and that was the worst part by far. He looked at the big man, this Tom Benson, and looked at the scene tent, trying to decide which body he preferred the company of right now. "Look, I just want to do my job. I don't want to spend an hour talking about the fucking weather and wondering what your favourite colour is or generally getting to know new people, okay? It's not me. I just want to..." He pointed to the tent. "Do my best for him."

"That's good to hear. We should get along fine, then."

Eddie shook his head and stared at the pavement and the water rushing down the drain, probably taking a load of his evidence with it. He sighed and turned around to face him. "I thought divisional CID were dealing with this?"

Benson winked, "So did they. But it's your lucky night – the Major Crime Unit is well and truly on line and ready to serve the people of West Yorkshire."

"And what about CSI?"

"What about them?"

"You recruiting or just going to keep plundering divisional resources? We are finite, you know."

Benson whispered, "It's pissing it down and you want to talk Major Crime structure?"

"I'm already wet and you have your funky brolly." Eddie shrugged. "Just interested."

"Yeah, well it'll have to wait. I'll be back in ten minutes."

"There's a dead man in this tent dying to meet you! Where are you going? I feel like you're abandoning me. Benson? I say, Benson!"

Benson shook his head. "They weren't wrong about you." He pointed to a marked car further down the road. "There's a young woman in there who saw it all, apparently. I'm off to speak with her. Back in ten."

"Oh, no rush," Eddie said.

The noise of rain on the tent roof was loud enough to have them shouting to each other across a body and four yards of wet pavement. Benson stood rigidly in one corner wearing the largest scene suit Eddie had in his van, and even then it looked like it had been sprayed on. Every time he breathed in his eyes bulged a little.

Eddie put the camera aside and knelt next to the body. The kid was maybe twenty-five years old, shoulder length brown hair, tattoos on his knuckles: left was 'love', right was also 'love'. He loved everyone, apparently. Eddie acknowledged that, and asked, "Do we know who he is yet?"

"I asked him. He ignored me."

"I'll do that too if you don't treat this with some respect."

Benson coloured up and cleared his throat. "No. We don't know who he is yet."

Eddie fished in the kid's jacket and jeans pockets and came up with a fistful of items that needed photographing and seizing either because they were personal effects and the family would later want them, or because they were – or had the potential to be – evidence. The cigarettes and the lighter, the small amount of loose change, and the lottery tickets were all personal, and went straight into a bag. The mobile phone was evidence and could potentially provide further information. It went into a Faraday bag and then into an evidence bag.

"A Faraday bag? What's that for?" Benson asked.

"It's to prevent signals getting in or getting out. We want it arriving at the technical evidence centre untampered with by those who could access it remotely."

"And the bag does that?"

"You're sharp as a tack, Benson. I like that in a DS." Eddie fanned out a couple of debit and credit cards. "Michael Fogg." He looked to Benson, and Benson wrote it down in a small notepad using a pencil stolen from Ikea. "That girl have anything to do with him?"

"No, I don't think so. We've taken her in for a quick interview, but I'm pretty sure she's clean; seems a decent lass if a little worse for wear."

"What about house-to-house—"

Benson looked up from his little pad. "I've got cops doing house-to-house, and we're pulling together CCTV, so my guess is CCTV will clear her. She already told the cops she just happened to be here when he keeled over."

Eddie said. "Anyone else present?"

Benson looked ready to pop. He gave in, unzipped the suit, and breathed all the way out. "I was about to pass out. Leave me alone." He sighed and pulled the hood down too. "She said there was an old man here when she arrived. Said he was crying; when she turned around, he'd disappeared."

"Disappeared?"

"Well, I assume she meant he just got up and walked away, Eddie. Pretty sure he didn't take out a wand and… poof!"

"Since he has no licence or anything like that, you'll have to wait for his post-mortem to get an ID, unless you can get an officer with a Lantern Device down here." Eddie set to unpacking a body bag. He and Benson took a side each and stretched it out next to the body. "Do you have a PM arranged?"

"I asked for the Lantern, and it's dead apparently. Traffic car ran over it. Anyway, his PM will be tomorrow. You up for it?"

"Me?"

Benson stared around him, searching for someone else.

"Sarcasm," Eddie smiled. "I love sarcasm."

"Good."

"When it's done correctly. And no, I'm not up for his PM."

"Why not. It's better to have the original scene examiner."

"It is, but PMs bore me to tears, I'm afraid. Tedious things. Three hours breathing someone else's stench, and then there's the body stinking the place out, too. They ought to force CID to shower at least weekly. No, not really my cup of tea, but I appreciate the offer."

"I'm surprised you get to choose."

Eddie smiled. "I have an arrangement. My boss doesn't make me do PMs and I don't rant and scream around the office for a week. It works well. A win-win for all concerned."

Again Benson raised his eyebrows. "It wouldn't work like that at MCU."

"Then I'm glad I won't be joining you there."

"We wouldn't want you, I'm sure."

Eddie straightened up, felt the clicking in his back. "What do you mean you wouldn't want me?"

"We're keen to get the best of the best."

"I see they weren't so choosy when it came to picking their detective sergeants."

Benson nodded, touché. "Shall we get on? I have a lot of work to do after this."

"No need for you to stay. I'm going to strip him, lay him in the bag and zip him up."

"Strip him? Why?"

"Listen, Benson; I can either get on with it and finish at midnight, or I can explain everything—"

Benson held out his hand. "Shut up. Just explain to me why you have to strip him."

Eddie pointed to the body. "Have you seen this hole in his back?"

"Yes."

"Blood comes out of it, have you noticed?"

"So."

Eddie took a breath and sighed it out, stared at Benson as though he were four. "When the blood trickles out as he's in transit, it goes everywhere. Any blood pattern on his clothing is lost forever, any trace evidence is gone too. The clothing is a separate exhibit. Okay?"

"Come on, I'll give you a hand."

"Must you?"

"Yes, I must."

"Zip up first." Eddie had something to show Benson.

Chapter Six

Use Your Eyes

It was weird how the kid had ended up. Eddie suggested he'd been standing still, and then he'd sunk to the floor straight down as though his feet had been crossed, and so he'd ended up sitting on the ground with his legs crossed, like you would in assembly in primary school. "And then he's just kind of half rolled to his left side." The left shoulder and the kid's long straggly hair were in contact with the ground, and his right lower back was perfectly exposed so the wound was on full display.

Eddie knelt, brought the camera and scale in close and fired off some shots. The skin surrounding the wound was as white as Benson's suit and just as tight and shiny. He got in even closer, brought his torch up and wrestled a small magnifying glass from his kit nearby.

"What is it?"

Eddie held out the glass. "A magnifying glass. It makes things appear larger than—"

"I thought you had a lot to get through."

"I heard CID use them in their IQ tests."

"Oi."

"And in bed."

"Enough!"

Eddie grinned. "Now that's sarcasm. Amateur."

"Oh do get on with it."

"Hold on," Eddie said, getting close and holding his breath. "Orange. Browny orange."

"What?"

"There's a browny-orange stain around the wound – just around the uppermost part where the flowing blood hasn't washed it away."

"So how come the rain didn't wash it away?"

Eddie shrugged. "Don't know, really, unless the clothing bowed out and protected the wound. Or the rain was coming in at a different angle."

"So what's the stain?"

"I'll lick it, shall I? That should give us a starting point."

"What? You're not serious."

Eddie straightened and looked directly at Benson. "You are shit at sarcasm, aren't you? Come back to me when you've matured a bit." Eddie climbed back up onto his knees and put aside his equipment. "Let's see if we can tape that before we disturb it by taking off his clothing."

"Can't tape wet skin."

"We can try; it's only the stain I want. Anyway, if it does get wet, I'll just swab it; doesn't matter." He pulled out a roll of tape, tore a length off, and dabbed it across the upper part of the wound. He smiled. "See, we got some." Now we take off the clothes, see if we can see more."

Eddie and Benson laid out the jacket and t-shirt on sheets of brown paper and Eddie got the torch out and knelt at the stab site on both. Nothing on the t-shirt, but there was more browny-orange stain on the leather jacket, especially on the inner, suede, surface where it had acted as a squeegee and pulled this orangey substance off the blade as it was withdrawn from the body.

"It's rust." Eddie looked up at Benson.

"Rust?"

"You know what that means, don't you?"

"Is this more sarcasm?" Benson swallowed. "I haven't got time—"

"It's not your common or garden stainless steel bread knife, and it's not a thug's chrome-plated flick-knife, either. It means it's a different type of metal altogether, a different knife altogether."

Benson blinked.

"It means it'll be easier to find. It's more unusual, Benson, because it's a knife not made of stainless steel. What kind of knives are not made of stainless steel?"

Benson shrugged again. "I have no idea."

"Old knives. Older than 1913 – I think." Eddie scaled the hole in the leather jacket and photographed it, and then he closed in further, focusing on a white adhesive arrow he'd positioned next to the stain, and re-photographed it. He taped it, placed the tape onto an acetate sheet and put the whole lot into an evidence bag. He grinned up at Benson, "Not going to bag the jacket just yet, though."

"Good job. Erm, why older than 1913?"

"That's when stainless steel was invented. In Sheffield. Guy's name was Harry Brearley." He stared at Benson like that was common knowledge. "Still wouldn't have me in your little gang, then?" Eddie smiled. "Next we look."

"Look? What the hell are we looking for now. We know he's been stabbed; we have—"

"But that's not what killed him."

"What? I thought—"

"Yeah, better stop doing that; it's not healthy for your investigation, and you'll give CID a bad reputation. You don't know everything about this kid until you look, Benson. And you don't glance, and you don't allow your eyes to stray away; you look and you see – and it's harder than you think."

With the lower garments off and packed in brown paper sacks, ready to load into a forensic drying cabinet somewhere, Eddie got on his knees and took out his torch again. And he was quiet, busy looking and seeing, ignoring Benson's curious stare, ignoring his exasperation that Eddie should study something so closely when everything that was visible was there immediately on show, when everything that was important had already been discovered.

"Strange."

Benson stood up straight. "What is?"

"There's blood on him."

"Of course there's..." Benson unzipped. "I've had enough. You're just dicking about now. Well, dick about on your own time; I've got things to attend to."

"Fine. But there shouldn't be blood here."

Benson pulled aside a tent flap, preparing to leave when he paused. He licked his lips, obviously curious to know what Eddie had found. He dropped the flap and turned back to Eddie. "What have you found?"

"I need to swab this prior to transportation. Very important." He set up the camera and asked Benson to, "Hold this scale for me on the neck. Just there."

"Why is this very important?"

Eddie stared at him. "Hold the scale and then you can bugger off and pretend you're someone very important."

"Cheeky bastard, Collins. If I wasn't holding this scale, I'd—"

"Shush, will you. Hold still while I take the shot. Jesus, you're a chatty little DS tonight."

Benson ground his teeth.

Eddie laughed, but only to himself. He never wanted Benson to think he enjoyed his company.

"Why is this very important?"

Eddie fired a couple of shots, changing the flash angle to get the perfect image. "Because," he said, "it's not the kid's blood."

"It's not his blood?"

"Is there an echo in here?" Eddie looked up. "Seriously, are you fucking deaf?"

"No, but..." His face screwed up. "I don't get it—"

"Well of course you don't. You don't listen, and you don't look. No one could expect you to get it when you don't use the senses you were born with."

"That's not his blood?"

"Nope."

"And the stab wound didn't kill him?"

"It would have eventually, but... nope."

Benson sighed and clenched his fists all in one fluid movement. "So what killed him?"

"Look," Eddie said, "petechiae."

Benson sighed again. "I'm going to hit you in a minute."

"The tiny red dots on his face and around eyes. They look like small freckles but they're burst capillaries. It means someone strangled him to death."

Benson looked concerned – but it could have been confusion. "Who?"

"Go and get Sherlock Holmes; he'll sort it for you."

Chapter Seven

Late Again

EDDIE PARKED THE DISCOVERY next to Kelly's car, switched off the engine and lit a cigarette. Once the lighter's flame had died, a gentle darkness enveloped Eddie and he felt soothed by it.

Soothed or not, his hands were shaking and his heart rate was up, the beats were all over the place like a pissed up drummer. Maybe he should have kept the Metaxa. "No," he whispered. His heart rate would be through the roof if he'd drunk that now, and then his problems would end quite abruptly.

Eddie opened the car door...

...and closed the front door, hung up his coat and his keys, and stood in the hallway listening to silence. It was pleasant, like being soothed in the car. He could hear Watson, the German Shepherd, snoring in the kitchen – a great welcome home, Eddie thought, and a superb guard dog!

All the lights were off; Eddie had the entire floor to himself. He turned on the cooker hood light rather than the blazing kitchen overhead light, and made a strong coffee. Once in the lounge, he lit another cigarette and took a sip.

"You're late again."

Eddie jumped, almost threw the coffee across the room, and burnt his hand with the cigarette. "Fuck! I thought you'd be in bed," he said, mustering as much cool as he could. It wasn't a lot. She was slurring her words.

"If you're making a brew... bring a fresh bottle of wine in, would you?"

Eddie put down the coffee, slumped into the chair by the fire, and took off his boots before turning on the table lamp next to him. She was half sitting, half lying on the sofa scowling at him; tortured shadows lit her face like a clown. Eddie took a long drag on his cigarette. "Why are you sitting in the dark?"

She shrugged, stabbed out her own cigarette and hitched her legs further underneath her. "You're late again, Eddie."

"I'm never late. If there's work to do I finish when I finish—"

"My stars said I was in for a long day that ended with disappointment. Your shift was over at eleven. That's two hours ago. It happens all the time. You're never home when you should be home." She gulped her remaining wine. "How is that fair on me?"

It was his fault, then. It was all his fault. He thought of her in that man's arms by the pond and he wanted to smash that wine glass in her face. He could think of no decent reason why that wasn't a good idea right there and then, but he knew it wasn't going to happen. He'd never consider doing anything like that to—

"It's almost like you're having an affair, or something."

Eddie's hands gripped the chair arms so tightly that he almost pulled them off. For the briefest moment his weight came up off the cushion, and he was ready to race over to her and... what, exactly? Eddie was not that kind of man, never was and never would be, no matter what the provocation. He let the tension leak out of his hands, and for the moment at least, the chair arms were safe again.

He couldn't see a single decent reason to keep her indiscretion out of the conversation. And this conversation was only set to get deeper, louder, and more hurtful from here on. He had the nuclear device of all ammunition to throw at her, and he almost did. But then he saw the photo on the bookcase. "How's Becca?"

With a drunk's eyes, Kelly looked across at him, and though they were half closed it was easy to see how she despised him. He looked away and thought back to the days when they had kissed so passionately. It hurt to realise those days had crept away like fog in the morning sun, stealthily.

"She's fine, Eddie." Kelly sighed. "All this washes over her. But I'm not fine. I hate it."

Eddie opened his mouth, ready to begin the onslaught, ready to begin the shouting, that he knew she was having an affair.

And how could she, and didn't she know she was responsible for splitting up the family?

She stared at him, slow blinking.

Eddie closed his mouth. It was his fault. All of it. And if he wanted to stay Becca's dad, he needed to accept this situation for what it was, keep quiet, and move on. He stood, "I'm off to bed."

"I waited up for you," she hissed.

"I'm sorry. I said I was sorry, and I'm still fucking sorry, alright?"

"No, not alright. Start getting home on time. Becca needs you to do that."

"Becca does?"

Her eyes were suddenly alert, wary. "What's that supposed to mean?"

"You don't need me home on time?"

"Don't stir the pot, Eddie. You know what I mean."

Eddie stared down at her, still biting his tongue. "See you tomorrow." Turns out that after further thought he came to the conclusion that he was jealous of her. And he was jealous of the man she had been kissing, too. He wanted things to be like that between them again. But it would never be like that again, not after what he had seen.

And what had he seen?

He had seen his wife take what they once had and give it new life with someone else. It was awful. It was immoral. But it was natural, he supposed. Could he blame her for wanting that again? He wanted it, he just didn't have the balls to go out and get it, or the inclination to try and rekindle it with her.

His nostrils flared and his eyes stung. As he ascended the stairs, he almost wished her every happiness with her new man, and wondered what waited for him next.

Chapter Eight

The Promise

THE DARK ORANGE SKY was fading as daylight ran away from the approaching darkness; clouds gathered, armed and ready for their assault on the day's end.

Eddie looked out across Hyde Park on the northern tip of urban Leeds. Aside from the endless pubs and clubs around here, Hyde Park was famous for having a very high student population, and it was famous for its high degree of eccentricity too. The houses were beautiful – massive Victorian dwellings with high ceilings and picture rails. Usually landlords chopped them up and split them into bedsits to maximise the income; but occasionally one encountered an unspoilt house.

Though not split into bedsits, this was not such an example. This was more like a flat or an apartment. Small, it shared half the floor with another flat across the dim stairwell.

He stood on the balcony looking over the rail and into the back yard. He leaned further over, peering down at the twelve-foot drop to the top of the cellar steps; the void they created was crowned by a railing topped with ornate gold-painted spikes. Eddie gripped the balcony rail a little bit tighter.

From inside, the old man asked, "Do you like your job?"

Eddie came back into the lounge. "Nice view you've got from there." He shone light across the footwear mark on the balcony doorsill, spinning his brush through the pattern one more time. He reached past the old man and tore a label off the sheet, filled out the exhibit number and the CSI reference number and laid it on a scale by the mark. "Huh?"

"Uh-huh. Your job. You must enjoy it. Must be very satisfying, uh-huh."

Eddie took out his camera, locked the flash into place and gently pulled the old man to one side before firing off a couple of shots, changing lenses, and taking even more photographs close up this time.

"See that?"

"What?" the old man said.

Eddie pointed to the mark. "Adidas."

"Really?"

"Wince." The old man screwed his face up, and Eddie asked, "Are you alright?"

"Uh, you told me to wince."

"What? No, that's the... It's the name of the trainer – Adidas Wince."

"Really? Oh."

Eddie nodded. "It's a West Yorkshire Police naming thing; you wouldn't understand."

"Uh-huh. No. I suppose not."

Eddie took out a black gel lifter and laid it across the footwear mark.

"What's that, then?"

"I'm greedy. I want an image of the mark and I want to lift it too. I don't want to lose anything."

"You are very keen, uh-huh."

Eddie looked at the old man. "Of course I am." He tossed the footwear mark into his case. "You want someone keen," he said, "when you've been burgled. Don't you?"

The old man shrugged. "Well, yes, I suppose you do, uh-huh."

"What have they taken from you?" Eddie looked at the old guy. He stood there in the high-ceilinged lounge decorated sometime around forty years ago with burgundy fleur-de-lis flock wallpaper, and looked tiny and fragile, like a gust of wind would take the feet from under him and he'd shatter and turn to dust as he hit the floor.

The old man began to cry.

This was the worst part about this fucking job, Eddie thought, seeing what one human could do to another without even touching them, without being in the same room – not all crime was physical; psychological crime was just as painful. "Hey, come on," he said, patting him on the arm. "You want me to make you a brew?"

The old man held his breath, trying to be brave and stop the sobbing, but every now and then he'd hitch and a heart-breaking cry would burst out.

Eddie's eyes filled with tears, and he looked away. "Tea it is," he said. "Sugar?"

As Eddie headed out of the lounge, the old guy caught his arm. He dabbed a hanky at his eyes and sniffled, "I thought you'd just come here and... I don't know, do the bare minimum and go." He tried to smile. "Uh-huh. You know, just to get out."

"No."

"You must have more important jobs than this." He looked around, yanking up the sleeves of his torn blue woolly jumper to reveal tattoos all the way up his arms. "This is just a burglary," he said, fumbling with crooked fingers. "Uh-huh. There must be more important—"

"This is the most important job to me right now. Okay? I'll stay here all night if I have to. Whatever else is waiting for me can wait. Let's do a thorough job here first. Then we do a thorough job at whatever's next."

The old man coughed, "Thank you."

"Now, do you take sugar?"

There was something surprisingly refreshing about jobs like this where the most vulnerable in society had been screwed over. It was refreshing not because Eddie Collins was a bastard who hated the elderly – quite the opposite; it was refreshing because it gave him a chance to really work at a scene and do his best for those who had done their best for the country and for their own families for the last eighty-odd years – a chance to pay them back for all their hard work. A glance at the pictures of royalty on his walls said he was a patriot, and Eddie admired that.

The kettle switched off and Eddie poured as the old man wandered in, scuffing holed slippers against the worn lino floor.

"They nicked my bus pass. I can't get into town," he said, still hovering around the precipice of tears. "I can't go pick my pension up."

"Don't worry." Eddie looked across at the damp tracks down his aged face, and grew angry. "I'll get it back for you."

It was well after dark when Eddie left the old man's house. He'd been there three hours for a one-hour job, and had managed to ignore several calls over the radio – he was otherwise engaged doing this job. Sometimes talking to people helped more than anything else, and he deemed Walter worthy of those two extra hours.

A fiery cramp bit deep into Eddie's calf, and he growled and stretched out his foot. He was in his van, writing up the job sheet, writing up the yellow CJA labels and taping them to his footwear lifts. It all took time, and when he rubbed his tired eyes and looked up he wasn't entirely surprised to see it raining heavily.

He sighed, engaged gear, and pointed his van in the direction of Killingbeck Police Station. Once back in the office he endured his colleagues' banter for the last ninety minutes of his shift while he finalised the computer work for his day's efforts. He was the average arsehole sitting at the back of the office, away from the main group of people who were joking, comparing stories about idiot coppers they'd worked with and stupid complainants they'd dealt with – all the while unaware how idiotic and stupid they themselves were.

Eddie stayed out of it, wearing a pin-on generic smile and giving a knowing nod every time someone looked over to him just to affirm his solidarity with the group – it kept things simple.

"You joining up, Eddie?"

Eddie sighed. He thought it was too good to last, and looked up. "Joining up where?"

"They sent out an email. Didn't you get it?"

This was about the time Eddie would start to lose his shit, normally. He was trying to get his work done while they were engaged in idle chit-chat and throwing cryptic clues around, wasting time until the end of their shift. And if he had any emails, he didn't look at them, didn't want them, and would delete them without opening if he could. "No. Not looked."

"They're setting up a Major Crime Unit in Leeds. And they're creating a dedicated CSI department."

Eddie tutted, went back to his work.

"Not interested?"

"Bunch of egotistical arseholes," he growled. "I'd rather work with you lot."

"There's a pay rise, extra benefits." This came from his boss, Peter McCain, complete with knowing wink and flat smile.

"If I didn't know better, I'd think you were trying to get rid of me."

The office quietened; there was one or two badly muffled giggles. "Perish the fucking thought."

Eddie pushed his new keyboard away and propped his chin on his desk. "You see, I'm not bothered about a wage rise. I get by. I think enjoying your job is worth a lot more than a couple of percentage points on a pay scale. You wouldn't agree?"

McCain shrugged.

"I get a lot of satisfaction from my work out there. I know you lot are content to piss about in here while victims of crime are desperate for you to attend their property and do your fucking jobs!" He paused, watched the smirks drift off their faces. "And that's fine," he said. "just so long as you can sleep at night."

"You including me in that generalisation?"

Ros was standing behind him, and he felt like chucking his pen across the room. "Please, I just want to get on—"

"Are you?"

"No. I'm not. Now please piss off and let me finish this."

She smiled and squeezed his shoulder, popped a mug of coffee on his desk. "I should hope not." She emphasised the smile and went to join the rabble across the other side of the office.

"Thanks," he said, and she waved over her shoulder.

"But the worst part about it, Eddie, is they'll eventually steal away all the juicy murders you love so much."

Eddie stopped typing, looked at the screen with wide eyes that saw nothing. He didn't like the sound of that.

"It won't be long before their detectives take primacy over bodies from our divisional CID brethren. Thin end of the wedge, Eddie. Another few months, when they've recruited their super-CSIs, and all we'll be dealing with is the pleasant, non-smelly kinds of crime."

He turned, and noted the entire office staring at him. "You taking the piss?"

"Nope. Not even a little bit."

He swivelled so he could get a good look at Peter's face – always a good barometer for life in the office. If it were untrue, he'd be grinning – couldn't help himself, might even have been slavering. But no, he looked straight-faced and composed, all except that bit of dislike reserved especially for Eddie.

I wonder why they dislike me so much, he asked himself. But then he smiled – it didn't matter, he'd didn't care enough to ask.

He also wondered why no one seemed especially bothered that some other department would be stealing work from them, and good, interesting work, too. But he realised they were a volume-crime bunch – they liked domestic and commercial burglaries, street robberies, and vehicle crime, the easy stuff, the stuff that didn't take too much effort or too much thought. They could keep that; give Eddie a good murder any day.

Twenty minutes before the end of the shift, and Eddie found himself shunned by his colleagues; even McCain patted him on the head as he walked out – at last, Eddie thought, peace and quiet. He scrolled through West Yorkshire Police Personnel section and hit MCU jobs. He scooted right past the role profile and terms and conditions, and filled out an application form. It was sneaky, he knew that, and he didn't relish leaving Ros behind, but he could only stand this volume-crime shit for so long. Life for Eddie was all about the clues and the chase and all about sinking into the mind of a killer; he lived for those scenes. So to have MCU come into being and almost in their first breath snatch away the favourite aspects of his job meant this job was worthless to him. That left him one choice: he pressed send and forgot all about it.

His mind turned back to this evening's burglary, and he began searching for burglars who'd recently been released from prison. Eddie could not let this go, and he could not forget his promise to Walter. That the officer who dealt with the burglary earlier in the evening, the one who had put in a request for CSI, might want to investigate this crime first, didn't even enter Eddie's head. This was his crime, and he'd made someone a promise – a victim, and promises to victims were usually stupid things to hand out, but it was too late, he'd done it. And so now he had to keep it. He made a deal to pass on anything he found to the officer, and then decided it would be better for all parties if he did no such thing; making a promise to a victim was stupid, adding to it by telling an officer was downright reckless.

Chapter Nine

Making a Stand

Eddie closed his car door, sighing back into the seat, and feeling the hot tension leave his back and a cool relaxing sensation climb into its place. Every once in a while, a job came along that touched you. It might be a sudden death, or even a suicide – he'd known some horrific suicides in his time, like the kid who killed herself because she'd argued with her mum about a rock concert. That job always stuck in his throat, made him gasp each time it came to mind; how could you sacrifice a whole life for a slight argument over a rock concert? Really, potentially seventy good years of life thrown away over a pointless tiff. The ultimate spite or deathly sorrow?

Some jobs hurt – more than just the families.

But not all of them were death jobs. Some were mundane, like tonight's burglary for example. It was probably nothing special for the burglar; just one of many dozens of burglaries he'd committed over the last few years, just something else to get cash from instead of actually getting a fucking job and earning it – you know, like the old man had done. Sometimes these jobs bit deep too.

Eddie was becoming angry again.

It was just after eleven at night. Kelly would be expecting him home by half past.

Strictly speaking, this job had been nothing special for Eddie either. It was one of a thousand burglaries he'd examined over the last twelve months; another tick, another set of footwear marks lifted, or of fibres taped, or drop of blood swabbed. Just more evidence for the CPS to ignore or take to trial and lose through incompetence. A conveyor belt system that was geared perfectly for the offender and critically skewed against the victim.

Eddie lit a cigarette and started the car. All the way home he thought of the kid's body, the one that MCU would have stolen out from under him. And then he thought solely about MCU, and wondered if joining the place where all the suss bodies in Leeds pass through might not be such a bad idea after all.

Dogs barked. There were three kids smoking a joint up by the woods at Temple Newsam. One of the youths handed over money and was given a bag of weed in exchange. Laughing and letting bangers off. It was midnight, noted Eddie, and some people were up early for work, others were knackered after looking after babies or young kids or whatever.

These little bastards didn't give a shit about any of that. These little bastards loved being little bastards; they were tearaways just beyond the law, but just inside good people's lives, tormenting them, irritating like ticks under clothing, sucking blood and laughing about it.

And they were just outside the law because if there were ever any police available to come out and patrol around here – unlikely with all the 'proper' crime to attend to – these kids did one before the car even came to a halt, giving the coppers the middle finger as they ran, laughing into the woods.

This would be their life, too. They would live off petty crime their entire lives, sucking blood from the state to 'support' them as they claimed benefits and housing and took what they wanted from people who were dumb enough to go out and earn a living. They would be a constant irritation until they died of an overdose in their forties, and their final insult to society would be the price of a coffin. Except it wouldn't be the final insult to society – no, that would be the four kids they'd fathered who would go on to drain the country's wealth just like their dear old dad had done. And drugs would give them a Porsche by the time they were twenty and a dozen overdoses to chalk up by the time they hit twenty-four.

Eddie's hands curled into fists as these thoughts ricocheted through his mind. Anger lived in here.

But as well as anger, common sense was washing around somewhere too. It suggested it might be a good idea not to get mixed up with three stoned youths who would probably be carrying blades as well as drugs. But then, as though someone upstairs was listening, two of the three kids split off and walked away into the darkness after giving number three a brotherly fist pump – or whatever they fucking called it.

The last of the three lit up a cigarette and that was all Eddie needed to recognise him. In the brief time that an orange flame played on his features, Eddie could see that he had a finger missing and rings up the entire outer part of his right ear. His name was Sean Walker, and he was a complete wanker.

The Sean Walker Eddie knew had been released from Armley jail about three weeks ago. He also wore Adidas Wince – he knew this because he'd been caught wearing them during a previous burglary and was too dumb to think about changing them. His MO was burglary dwelling, usually with old people as the complainant – less likely to fight back, more likely to keep cash in the house, less likely to think about security and less able to afford it anyway. Sean Walker was a coward. All mouth, but a coward.

The streetlights were fractionally better than useless, and there was more shade than light, much more. Blackness ruled these streets.

Eddie Collins was sitting patiently in his car at the end of Wentworth Avenue in Halton Moor, tapping the steering wheel, letting smoke crawl up his face as he watched the darkness at the mouth of an alley between two houses. He'd been sitting here for fifteen minutes, and he reckoned Sean Walker would appear any second now, having walked from Temple Newsam woods.

Eddie reached up and clicked the switch by the dome light before opening the car door and getting out. He pulled up the collar of his coat, flicked away his cigarette, and walked towards Number 71, went straight down the garden path and parked himself around the corner out of the way. Complete darkness here. The smell of shit all around him; that, and cannabis – someone had a grow nearby. His heart sank another couple of degrees.

Less than a minute later, the sound of trainers squeaking on the pavement as they scampered down the three steps onto the garden path and then Eddie pulled his balaclava down and was on the move, quickly, pumped up, enraged. Seconds later he delivered a blow to the back of Walker's head and the kid hit the front door just as he turned the key, sinking to his knees on the concrete step and almost keeling over into the darkness beneath a privet hedge.

Eddie grabbed his hoodie and pulled him upright.

"What ya doing, man? You got the wrong dude, let me tell ya. You made a big fucking—"

"Shut up and get inside." Eddie pushed him through the front door. "Who else is here?"

"Fuck you."

"Who's here, Sean?"

"My missus. And my kids. I'm a father; don't you touch my kids."

Eddie twitched. How Sean sounded protective over his family was laudable, except it was bluster – every word wasn't worth the air it was breathed out on. He'd hide behind whatever little bastard he had upstairs if he thought it would save his arse.

"What you want, man?"

"You on the job again, Sean? Been out of Armley less than a month and already you're back to screwing old folk over."

"The fuck are you?"

"You stole from an old man tonight."

"Fuck you, I been here all night!"

"Really? I just walked in with you!"

"Who are you, man?"

"I want the stuff you took from him?"

"I ain't taken nothing from nobody, let me go, man. I'll fucking kill you; I swear I'll fucking slash you!"

Eddie shoved him through the hall door into the lounge. Over the fireplace was a fifty-five-inch television, and on the wall over the torn leather corner suite was an A3 canvas photograph of a baby wearing a teddy bear suit, grinning. It was an ugly baby. On the other wall by the kitchen were three large adhesive words: Live. Love. Laugh. There was no mention anywhere of steal.

There were cigarette ends across the bare floor, black stains under foot that were sticky, nappies in the corner, a clutch of used baby's bottles on the mantelpiece.

"Sean, give me his shit before I take it out of your face."

"Who the fuck are you, man?"

Eddie spun the kid around and punched him square in the nose. Sean cupped his face in both hands and went down straight on his backside, screaming.

"Give it to me. Now."

"I haven't done nothing. Leave me the fuck alone!" He was scrabbling back as fast as he could pedal with his Adidas Wince trainers, but was getting nowhere. He took his hands away and used them to propel him out of danger. Blood spilled down his face, bloody handprint on the floorboards. "Leave me alone!" He spat blood. "Chantelle, Chantelle, call the coppers!"

Eddie bent and punched him in the nose again, and this time there was a crunch like a walnut shell popping. The kid screamed and lay down on his side with hands over his face, crying, his whole body heaving with each sob. Upstairs a baby woke and began screaming too. Even its screams were ugly. "Oh for a fucking shotgun," Eddie said.

He looked around, on the mantlepiece was a passport and a bus pass in the name of Walter Cropper, and five credit cards, and a couple of antique rings. Eddie dropped the lot into his pocket and then pulled Sean's wallet out of his jeans pocket. There was just over a hundred quid in there. Eddie stuffed that in his pocket too, bent down and grabbed Sean's hoodie again. "If I ever hear of you burgling old folks again, I'll—"

Eddie fell sideways and the enormous pain in his head closed his eyes and stunned him; it knocked the senses out of him, and he could feel an ebbing blackness eager to envelop him; it took all his strength to resist it as Chantelle swung the baseball bat again. Eddie opened his eyes as the bat came towards his face, and jerked enough to take a glancing blow off his left shoulder. He got to his feet as Sean swung on his balaclava, pulling him backwards.

Now it was Eddie's turn to backpedal. He did and swung his right elbow into Sean's smashed nose. Sean went down again, joining the tumult with even more screaming.

"I'll fucking kill you!" Chantelle screamed.

She was a big girl, dressed in a loose t-shirt, hair tied up in a ponytail, and front teeth missing. She had nicotine stains running rampant across all the tattoos on her fingers, and a ring through her nostrils like you'd find on a bull. Eddie was shocked and couldn't take it all in at once. Part of him wanted to stop the show so he could appraise her more fully, because that strange part of him wanted to just stand there and laugh his bollocks off at her.

But with the bat on a return journey towards his jaw and throat, the appraisal had to give way to survival, and survival caught the swinging bat mid arc, and it thrust the handle of it into her face so her bottom teeth fell into her mouth. She shrieked and spat the denture out as Sean reached around Eddie's leg and clamped tight.

"Get 'im, Chantelle!"

"Fuck off, Sean," sounded like thuck oth, Thawn. Blood from her split lip trickled down her chin, and about now, thought Eddie, would be a great time for a family photograph. He took out the hundred quid and threw it at her, reluctant to take money from a mother with an ugly baby to feed – even though he knew it would go on drugs and the Sky subscription.

"That's more than you both deserve," he said, pointing at Chantelle. "Make sure he doesn't go burgling old folks again. If he does, I'll be back, okay?"

"And you can thuck oth, athwell!"

Eddie kicked Sean's arm away, and as he strode around her, she reached for his balaclava, and this time managed to pull it off his head. The first thing Eddie decided he must not do was look at her or Sean, and the first thing he did was look at them both. "Shit." He snatched back the balaclava.

"Who are you?"

Once back in the car, Eddie drove quickly away, only turning on the lights when he was well away from Wentworth Avenue and all the neighbours' CCTV.

Eventually he calmed down and dabbed the centre of the pain. His fingers came away from the side of his head with a thin smear of blood on them; just touching the wound seemed to bring the headache on two-fold.

Chapter Ten

The Dominance of Pigeons and How Life is Shit

Despite the trees at the foot of his garden being a majestic golden colour, the sun was just strong enough to prickle Eddie's skin. He slid a pair of shades back up his slick nose and took a swig of beer from a can. The noise in the street was a distraction – no, not a distraction, for he wasn't thinking about anything specific; it was a detriment to his overall enjoyment of an otherwise pleasant day. The wood pigeons didn't help; they had one of those calls that Eddie's mind latched onto and wouldn't let go of: infuriating, not just a detriment, but infuriating. Luckily, the kids kicking a ball about in between passing cars, squealing and screaming, broke the pigeon's monotonous call into manageable chunks.

Today was Friday, it was almost eleven o'clock, and Eddie didn't give a shit. This was his first day off, and he sank into it like a pig in shit, and decided he wasn't going to let anything or anyone bother him. For once he was going to go back to work on Sunday with lower blood pressure than when he left it yesterday – well, this morning at two o'clock to be more precise. He puffed on a cigarette and imagined living without Kelly, how idyllic it would be, how peaceful. And then the door opened and Kelly exploded into his serenity; he almost spilled his beer.

She began calmly enough. "Late finish?"

"Two o'clock."

She pointed to his head. "What happened?"

"Walked into a door."

She nodded, unconvinced, and folded her arms. Eddie sighed and took another mouthful of beer, bracing himself.

"It's noble, Eddie."

"Don't start."

"Start? You're at the wrong end of a long-dead argument. You love strangers in pain more than you love us."

He looked up at her, sighed and smoked, his fingers gripping the chair arms and his toes beginning to curl. He could feel the blood pressure rising. "How long have you been brewing that line up?" He took off the shades, squinted up at her, "I was three hours late. And you'd have been asleep—"

"Not the point."

"Well it fucking wouldn't be, would it? Come out with it, lay your demands on me, give me your ultimatum and then piss off indoors and watch Judge Judy and leave me in peace."

"You see, this is the Gemini in you!"

"No, this is the idiot in me for listening to this crap."

She smiled, but it was petulant, and Eddie could see she was trying to keep her voice level and calm, but failing. Or rather, preparing to fail. It was an old game of hers, exaggerating her anger and pretending to be rational. "I'm sick of you leaving me and Becca hanging just because someone got burgled or assaulted."

"It's my job—"

"Doesn't anyone else work there? Can't they take a share of the burden?"

He sighed again. "They're victims of crime, Kelly. They need—"

Her eyebrows rose, loving the battle, preparing the killer blow. "We need you!" She brought her voice back down, down far enough so that the pigeons were dominant again. "There will always be victims of crime, Eddie. We know that. But there won't always be a wife and daughter here waiting for you to join in; get that into your thick head, why don't you?"

Becca slid out between her mother and the door frame and leapt down the steps. Eddie took a last drag and flicked away the cigarette, glugged the beer and rolled the empty can under his deck chair. He grinned up at Becca and opened his arms.

She had a knack of smoothing down his ruffled feathers in one easy stroke and she sank into his embrace. "How you doing, sweet?" He kissed the top of her head. This was absolutely the best part of being home.

Becca smiled at him and whispered, "I brought you another beer."

Tears prickled Eddie's eyes then and he closed them just as the door slammed closed.

"What happened to your head?"

Eddie touched the lump on the side of his head, the epicentre of the headache he'd just realised had been there since he woke up. "I was looking to the side when I should have been looking forward," he smiled. "If I'd been looking forward, I'd have seen the lamp post."

Becca tutted, and then she laughed. They both laughed.

There was something almost comforting in watching him from afar. He couldn't hurt her and she could daydream. There, everyone was happy, then. She watched him sitting in a deck chair of all things, sipping beer from a can and smoking cigarettes.

She didn't like it when he smoked – but it was his life, his lungs; he was in charge of everything, and it was up to him how he lived. Anyway, Ros thought, it didn't really detract from her love of him. Ooof, there, she'd admitted it.

Would it be possible – would it be fair – she wondered, to coerce him into not smoking if she and Eddie were a couple? She gave the daydream some thought as Eddie's wife appeared on the doorstep, arms folded, face like a... what was it Eddie had said? Face like a bulldog licking piss off a nettle.

Ros smiled, suppressed the chuckle that wanted to escape.

She watched them, man and wife, and could tell just from their body language that they were on shaky ground as a couple. She was telling Eddie off for something or other – leaving the toilet seat up, perhaps. Eddie looked thoroughly depressed by it all – suffocated, that's what he looked like, suffocated. He puffed on the cigarette. It was a wonder his back wasn't bent double with all that his wife forced on him. Coercion by the truck load. He didn't need any more of that from me, she thought.

You could tell when two people gelled together, and these two were as far apart as the polar ice caps. That too made her smile.

Was there really a chance for Eddie and her, she wondered.
No, there was not. So stick with the plan.

The kid, Becca, ducked under her mother's arm and jumped down the step to land a couple of feet away from Eddie. Eddie flicked away his cigarette and put the can on the ground under his chair. He reached out for her, a smile glowing on his face like a candle in the darkness. And then Becca was smiling, and she fell into Eddie's arms. Eddie's wife, Kelly, shook her head and stormed off back inside. Ros could hear the door slam from here.

Eddie was a good man drowning in a river of despair. She saw the agony he was in, and she wanted to go to him now, to reach out to him. To be with him.

But she couldn't. It would be wrong. There was only one way to solve this conundrum.

Eddie was in the middle of a love triangle he didn't know existed. He was one third unhappy and one third unaware. Ros found the thought humorous and couldn't help smiling, even though there really was nothing funny about it at all. She'd always been the one standing on the side-lines watching Eddie, daydreaming, staring at him but unable to touch him.

A football hit her car and she woke from her reverie as the kids screamed past her. This would be the last time she would daydream about him, and the last time she'd sink this low.

Ros had tears in her eyes as she drove away.

He imagined Kelly standing in the front doorway with baggage at her feet, and Becca nearby holding her Kindle, distancing herself from it all, insulating herself. But it wasn't working; pretending it wasn't happening didn't mean it wasn't happening, and like everything in life, one has to lift one's head at some point and see the truth for once. Kelly left to pack their bags into her car, and Becca looked up at him.

It was like a nightmare, this whole leaving thing. It was like mourning without the death first. And though he thought he didn't love Kelly any longer, he cared for her. He was so sorry that he'd been so hard to live with that she couldn't love him either, and that he'd been so hard to live with that she'd decided being alone was the better option. Wow, he must've been a real bastard to live with, then.

Becca's cheeks were shiny, and just that sight made his chin tremble and his throat close up. He slid across to her and she fell into his arms. And though she made no sound, he could feel her sobbing as his tears dripped into her golden hair. She dropped the Kindle and she held him tightly, now full-on crying. Inside, Eddie was collapsing into a puddle of grief as his loved ones passed away right before his closed eyes.

He blinked and was almost surprised to find himself standing at Becca's bedroom doorway watching her sleep. It was the end of his first day off work, and he was suffering from insomnia. He sighed, it was almost eleven o'clock and he really should be asleep too, but he'd had a horrible dream and upon waking, the feeling of it, the flavour of it persisted like a dose of heartburn. Usually, once your dayshift-brain figured out that it had been hoodwinked, and everything had been a bit of a giggle played on it by the nightshift-brain, it would begin to reassert itself and put the world back into some kind of order. But that feeling, that heartburn type flavour, insisted it was not a prank at all, and that it was very real.

So he stood there at her doorframe and watched the light from the bathroom behind him pick out her duvet rising and falling. He was compelled to go to her and was shocked to find her eyes open as he neared her.

"Dad."

He smiled at her. "Didn't mean to wake you, sorry."

"I wasn't asleep." She pulled herself up and pulled at the fuzz of hair draped across her glistening face. "I was having a nightmare," she whispered. "Just recovering from it, actually."

Eddie sat on the edge of her bed, already feeling empathy. "What was it about?"

She rubbed her eyes. "Not sure. It was black, spiralling."

"Sounds like my computer screen at work."

"And I felt claustrophobic." She looked across at him. "And you were all by yourself."

That made Eddie's heart kick and he almost fell off the bed. It was the same flavour of dream he'd had. He almost snorted, and if it hadn't been for the similarity between their nightmares, would have dismissed it with a joke and wave of the hand, but... he didn't believe in superstition. "We're going through a bit of a shit time, right now. Your mum and me, I mean. I'm not very good at..." He looked around the room, as if searching for the right way to tell her, but in fact he was looking for the right way to lie to her. "I'm just not good at the whole husband thing, the family man kind of thing. I maybe spend too long at work looking after people who need a bit of a helping hand. And I think that upsets your mum, and rightly so. She deserves better than I can give her; you deserve better than I give you."

"You're not leaving us?"

"What? No. Good God, Becca, no, sweet."

Becca slid her hand over her dad's and squeezed, and Eddie was pleased the light was behind him so the shine in his eyes would remain hidden.

"I think you're a great dad."

He huffed, no words available right now, throat too narrow to speak anyway.

"You don't treat me like a fool, like a kid. You're honest with me."

"Well," he cleared his throat, and forced a smile. "Life is a piece of shit, dear, but if you forget everything else, remember this: your dad will never let you down, okay? And I'll always be here for you."

Chapter Eleven

Swilling the Leaves

Eddie knocked, a smile already planted in position – more in anticipation of what was to come than in any kind of public relations bollocks. He loved reuniting people with lost things. The door creaked open, and a face full of wrinkles looked up at him. "Mr Cropper."

"Uh-huh. The forensic man." The door opened wide and Walter stood aside. "I confess that I didn't expect to see you again. Please," he waved a hand, welcoming Eddie inside.

"Told you I'd find it."

"The bus pass?" Walter closed the door. "Yes, yes, you did, uh-huh."

Eddie handed it over. "Did you get the window boarded, okay?"

He examined the card. "Where did you get this? Have you caught the little bastard?"

"Ah, no not yet."

"He needs a good beating." Walter's chin wobbled. "So where did you find it?"

"Erm, let's just say I came across it in the line of my duty."

"Is that where the lump came from?" He nodded as though it was some kind of secret passing between them, but added, "Very cryptic. Uh-huh."

"I have to be circumspect; you understand."

"Yes, yes, uh-huh." He waved the pass. "Thank you, thank you for this."

"You're—"

"And thank you."

Eddie eyed him. "You're welcome. What for?"

"The twenty quid you left me."

Eddie rubbed the lump on the side of his head and seethed. "I didn't—"

"It was on the mantelpiece. I didn't leave money on the mantelpiece ever. Except if the Prudential was coming around but they haven't been around here for the better part of thirty years, yes uh-huh." He stepped closer, peered deeper into Eddie's eyes. "And if I had left a twenty there, don't you think the burglar would've snatched it? I do, yes yes. Uh."

Eddie replenished his personal distance. "Nothing to do with me. Now, I want to—"

"Did you find anything else? Uh."

Eddie studied the man's eyes – that question had hidden meaning; he was sure of it. "Like what?"

"Um, um." He shrugged, turned away. "I don't know, just... I was wondering, that's all."

"Credit cards?"

The old man froze.

"Did you lose some credit cards?"

"No." His shoulders slumped, and he turned to Eddie again. "No, credit cards. I don't like them. Uh."

"Then what?"

The wrinkles deepened in a smile, and he slid along the kitchen floor tiles in slippers through which his toes poked. "Tea?"

Although Eddie hadn't seen his father in years, the sight of Walter Cropper made him think of him now. Is this how he would look and behave? "I'm okay, thanks. But you get one. Do you good." He leaned against the doorframe and winced at the pain in his shoulder, "What were you hoping—"

"Jewellery." Walter stopped, and stared directly ahead, unblinking, not even breathing. His protruding teeth glistened in the overhead lamps, and he turned to Eddie. "Unique jewellery. Uh-huh."

"Wedding band?"

Walter shook his head and his wispy hair floated around his head as though he were underwater. "Pearl necklace. Tiara. Rings."

"Did you mention these items to the officer who took your crime details?"

"See, that's where things fell down. I'm not good with memory stuff, you know. And I forgot. And anyway, he didn't look as if he had the time. He was awful fretsome, like he wanted to leave. I didn't think it wise to keep him."

Eddie nodded, "Listen, Walter, you have to get those items—"

"It's alright, it's alright, uh-huh. Don't matter. I won't be seein' them again, anyway, will I?"

"But you might! I found this, didn't I?"

"There's a royal connection to it, I think. The jewellery. Queen Victoria." Walter put a finger to his lips, and shushed Eddie.

The eyebrows arched again, and Eddie folded his arms to accompany the look of astonishment on his face. "It'll be worth a few bob, then?"

"I expect so, yes, yes, uh-huh."

"I don't remember you telling me about missing jewellery when I came to examine your burglary."

The old man stopped again. Then, as though someone had wound him up, began moving. He put a strainer into the cup and poured hot water into the pot, swilling the leaves to make them stew quicker. "I need to sit down. I think…"

Eddie reached out and grabbed Walter just as he was reaching forty-five degrees. It was like catching a sack of table legs with a football balanced on top. It wasn't difficult for Eddie to imagine this old chap naked on a stainless steel table; translucent skin and pointy bones. And he wondered how long before it would come true. Shame. Eddie walked and semi-dragged Walter into the lounge, kicking up plumes of dust from the settee and the carpet. As the old man caught his breath, Eddie scraped spider's webs from his hair.

"Yes. Yes, uh-huh. There was a tiara and pearl necklace. Couple of brooches as well. And a few rings. They were tucked away nice and secure."

His eyes never made it above waist height, and so Eddie squatted nearby. "Hey," he said, "you okay? You need anything?"

Walter put his long nails to his smiling lips again. "No, you misunderstand; I'm holding them, that's all. And if the owner finds out I haven't got them… I mean, it's not as though I've got bloody receipts or anything, you know what I mean?"

Eddie bit his lip, confused by Walter's ramblings, and pushed out a sigh. "Listen," he said, "let me finish making you that brew; you'll feel loads better, I promise. And when you've calmed down a bit, maybe you'll remember more, eh? "

Walter nodded. "I'm messed up. I know it'll come back to me, though. I know it, uh-huh."

"Course it will. And when it does, we'll get that officer back to take full details." He saw the look of horror on Walter's face.

"No, better still, we'll get another officer down here, and you can tell them all about it, right?" There was still tension there. "Or we could get you down the nick and speak with CID. Up to you, whichever you fancy."

Walter nodded. "But if you're not here about the..."

"The crown jewels?"

"Yes, yes, quite." He smiled. "Then what are you here about?"

Eddie pulled out a plastic bag. "I found your bus pass, right? And I found these alongside them."

"Yes yes, uh-huh."

Eddie passed the credit cards over, five of them, all in different names. Walter shuffled them almost deftly, glancing at the names. Without expression, he passed them back to Eddie.

"You don't recognise them?"

"They're not from here."

"You've never seen them before?"

"No. I don't like—"

"So where did they come from?" It was a question asked out loud but not directed to the old man.

Walter said, "You should pop down the local nick and speak with CID."

"I was afraid you'd say that."

Chapter Twelve

Spinning Circles and The Baseball Bat

He RUBBED THE LUMP on the side of his head and swallowed another pair of painkillers.

It was the quietest part of the day: the early staff had gone home, and the late staff were all out at jobs. It was Eddie's favourite time of day in the office. If he had to do work in the office, this is when he'd choose to do it; much to Kelly's annoyance, he knew. Still, she didn't act so annoyed when the monthly overtime came in and floated her another expensive dress or a pair of shoes made of otter skin or whatever was fashionable to kill these days.

He stared at the spinning circle on the computer screen, and wanted to put his fist through it. But he didn't; instead his mind wandered, and he saw Kelly and some man in the local park kissing. How did she possibly think she could get away with being so... so public? If Eddie hadn't seen them, surely someone he knew would have.

And on top of that – if something that substantial could be topped – was this a prelude to Kelly walking out on him? Eddie's mind spun along with the spinning circle and it dived deep into what made Eddie Eddie: it saw him waving her goodbye and then dancing like a loon when she turned the corner; but it also saw him sitting in a darkened room sucking his thumb, rocking back and forth not knowing how to live life without her. She took care of everything for him. All Eddie had to do was get up, get showered, get his uniform on, and go to work. That was it. Everything else was taken care of by Kelly.

This is what he'd miss the most, he decided. At the moment, he could focus on his work, left alone to tend his professional life knowing the petty items were in hand and taken care of. And it suggested – not for the first time – that he was a selfish bastard. He'd left Kelly to do everything while he chased... while he chased? What exactly was he chasing?

The computer screen turned black, and then blue again, the spinning circle continued uninterrupted. The spinning circle eh; back in the day it was a spinning egg timer. That's progress, folks! Eddie kicked the tower under the desk. It fell over, the screen flickered and then resumed. Circle spinning as though sticking up the middle finger at him.

He wouldn't blame her for leaving. But neither would he fight for her to stay. She wasn't loyal or trustworthy; and Eddie began shrinking into himself, into safety, away from the danger of outside life – he began to withdraw. He almost began thinking about Becca, but he turned away from images of her because he didn't want to sink into a depression, and, like dreaming and knowing you're dreaming, he didn't want to wake up with snot trails down his chin and eyes red from crying.

"—Collins?"

Eddie looked up and someone was staring at him. He almost fell out of the chair in his haste to retreat. "Don't fucking creep up on people like that!"

"Creep up? I've been waving at you for twenty minutes. The only thing left to do was knock on your head."

"Twenty minutes?"

"Aye."

"In all that time, did it never cross your mind to put the kettle on?"

Benson was big, bigger than Eddie remembered; top button undone to let air get to his chins.

"It pays to give heart attack victims coffee, you know."

Benson sighed. "Have you finished dicking about?"

"What the hell do you want? I've got a spinning circle to watch here."

Benson came around to Eddie's side of the desk, "Those credit cards you found," he said. "Where are they now?"

"How do you know about them?"

"My DC does a daily trawl for those names."

"Does he find sudoku interesting, too?"

Benson tutted. "Those cards belong to missing people, Eddie. Some of them we believe to be dead."

"Ah."

"Indeed. Where are they?"

"The missing people?" He shrugged, "That's why—"

"The cards, Eddie."

"If your DC—"

"Please," Benson began, "no smart-arsed answer, eh? Just tell me where the hell they are."

"Storeroom."

"Thank you. And where did you get them?"

"The cards?"

"The cards. Where did you get them?"

Eddie's thumbs stopped mid-twirl. He found his fingers now tapping the edge of his desk. This was the kind of question that could lead somewhere distinctly unpleasant. He had a choice: lie and say he found them at the side of the road somewhere – and no one could disprove it. Or he could tell the truth, and—

"And be honest with me. There's a lot riding on this and I'll know if you're lying."

"How dare you. I found them at the side of the road."

Benson came closer, and just like Walter had earlier, he peered deeper into Eddie. "What happened to your head?"

Eddie touched the bulging, throbbing, lump and winced. "A baseball bat happened to it?"

Benson nodded as if he knew all about The Baseball Bat. "Where did you find them?"

"Selby Road."

"Bollocks. Listen, if you don't tell me right now, I'll get PSD in here faster than you can apologise for wasting my fucking time."

He could feel things growing distinctly unpleasant. "I erm, I relieved a local lad of them."

"Did you? Splendid, and it explains the baseball bat. Local lad's name, please?"

Chapter Thirteen

Common Sense and Spontaneity

"What do you want?"

"I walked into a doorframe?"

She looked up at him. "Uh?"

"My head. I thought you might ask about... the lump, the wound."

"Why are you here so late?"

"I know you've taken a few days off... I wondered if you fancied a natter before you went."

"Want a coffee?" Ros opened the door wider and nodded him inside.

The smile died when she asked him what the matter was.

"You going somewhere?" Eddie looked around the lounge; it was almost bare – no pictures on the wall – she liked pictures of the lakes, of rickety wooden jetties disappearing into the distance, that kind of thing. Only the walls were empty now, the light shades were missing, bare bulbs casting harsh light.

The question seemed to catch her off guard, and she stumbled before saying, "I'm having the place decorated, getting it ready for them."

Eddie nodded. "This coffee tastes like rat piss, you know that don't you?"

"As I recall, yours is shite so you've no room to talk."

"She's seeing someone else." He looked at the coffee table, but suddenly wanted to see her reaction but was too slow; she'd already looked away. "Ros?"

"I'm sorry." She stared at him, biting her bottom lip.

Eddie sat down, deflated. "I thought... You know, I expected more of a reaction. I'll be honest, I thought—"

"If you're looking for marriage guidance advice, I'm not—"

"I'm not looking for advice at all," he lied. "I'm unloading on my mate, that's all."

Ros put her fingers to her lips, trying to hide the smile.

"Not that kind of unloading, you dirty woman." But it worked; it broke the tension, and both relaxed a bit. "I don't know what to do. I don't want her to leave."

"Why the fuck not?"

"Eh?"

"Sorry," said Ros, "I mean why would you lie down for her to walk all over you again. Don't you think you deserve someone who won't betray you?"

"I was thinking of going for the MCU job; maybe the hours will be more reasonable."

"Which fairy-tale did you read that in? It'd be twice as bad."

"You not tempted to jump ship?"

"To MCU? No way," she said, "I like it where I am." She looked at him. "Is that why she's having an affair, do you think, because you spend a lot of time at work?"

He shrugged, then nodded. "She says I care for the pain of strangers more than I do my family."

"Bollocks."

This time he looked away.

"Eddie?"

He sighed. "I spend more time at work than I strictly need to, and I get more involved than perhaps I should."

"Grabbing overtime."

"Nah, it's just easier being at work than it is being with her."

Ros coughed, shook her head. "So what does that tell you? Listen to your voice."

"My voice speaks Gaelic; I have no idea what it's saying."

"Your gut, man. What's your gut saying?"

"It's saying I shouldn't have had that curry last night."

"Eddie!"

"I've got a ring piece like a dragon's nostril."

Ros sighed. "I don't believe you. How can you joke about this? Why don't you take anything seriously? This is your future."

"I find it hard to understand my own thoughts, let alone what I should or shouldn't do about anything." He sighed, played with his fingers. "I never know what's for the best. I should hit her. I should hit him! I should stop letting her dominate me. I should man-up." He sighed again, "That's a lot of shoulds, isn't it?"

"What about Becca?"

"She's my baby, and I adore her. But I'm pathetic as a father, too. So I'm torn. I want to spend time with her—"

"Then you should grow up and split up with Kelly." Ros's eyes opened wide and she sat back trying to distance herself from her own words. "Can't believe I just said that. Sorry."

"It's what I'm here for. A bit of unbiased advice."

"I thought you didn't want advice."

"I lied. Carry on."

A moment passed, and Ros said, "A friend of mine once said that it's better to come from a broken household than to live in one. No point in everyone being unhappy; I bet Becca would prefer that too if you could sit down and talk about it with her."

Eddie saw the tears in her eyes, waiting to fall, and he wanted to ask what the problem was. But he thought he knew. It was another problem dressed up as a gift; no point in adding... but she stared at him, and Eddie had to bite his lip until the pain made his own eyes glisten. She placed a hand on his and Eddie held his breath.

She leaned closer, and whispered, "Don't lose your little girl, Eddie. But don't let Kelly ruin your life." She looked away. "There're other options."

Eddie took his hand away slowly, hoping she wouldn't notice. He didn't want to hurt her feelings but he needed clarity right now not another lobotomy. "I should go."

"Of course you should. Just as you're making progress. It's what they say in the films: 'I should go'. Why should you go?"

"Ros. I can't—"

She smiled, but it was a shocking lie, as good as her coffee was. "It's okay; I know you've got to go."

"What are you doing on your leave days?"

"You'd make an excellent interviewer."

He couldn't tell if she was angry with him now, or taking the piss out of his subtle change of subject.

"Not much, driving to Scotland to see my folks." She stood. "Come on, out now, I need to sleep. I'll see you at work on Friday, yes?"

He flicked the cup. "I haven't finished my rat piss yet."

She laughed. "Go on, piss off, Eddie."

And he noticed something change in her. It was a sadness that seemed to deepen in her, to cling tighter, to smother her, and it frightened him to the point where he stopped on his way to the door. He turned, "Ros, are you—"

"I'm fine." She answered too quickly, a rehearsed line delivered with poor timing.

Eddie stood there a moment longer, and a smooth coldness seeped through him, and for the second time this evening he held his breath; it was one of those moments in life where there was a choice to be made, and although it said 'choice' on the label, it wasn't really up for debate. It was a simple right or wrong decision. Stay or go. But was stay the right choice or was it the wrong choice? Common sense screamed at him to go to the door and get the hell away, 'you're fucking married', it said, 'two wrongs don't make a right. Go home, sort it out!'

The door closed behind him and as he replayed the expression on her face, he knew he'd made the wrong choice. Common sense was an arsehole and he stood by with folded arms as spontaneity kicked the shit out of it. He was about to turn and knock on the door, to apologise, to make a move, to change the future, to... the hall light went off and Eddie's world turned dark as well as cold.

Chapter Fourteen

Blowing Smoke

BENSON AND KHAN STARED through the rain. "What a shithole," Khan said, crumbs falling from his mouth. Benson chewed on a Mars bar, and gave the faintest shake of his head, disgusted perhaps at Khan's observations, but more likely disgusted at the crumbs in his lap.

Benson put the empty wrapper into the centre console arm rest and pulled up his collar. "Come on. And let me chat to him, eh? No need for Mr Angry – leave him out of this."

"I'm cool."

"Make him out to be a kingpin, okay?"

Khan locked the car, and hurried after Benson who was already approaching the front door.

Benson knocked, and only moments passed before a smiling woman opened the door. When she saw them, the smile shot itself. "The fuck do you lot want? He ain't here, y'know. Why're you lot always pesterin' him, eh? He ain't done nothing." Her bottom teeth – a cracked denture – went wonky and almost fell out. She sucked them back in, and positioned them with a finger, all the time not taking her eyes off the coppers.

"Good afternoon, Mrs Walker. I'm DC Khan and this is DS Benson from MCU."

"Well I didn't think you was from British Gas, der."

"We'd like to speak to Sean, please."

"Must be serious," she said, "if they're sending a DS out." She smiled, folded her arms. "It's like an episode of Frost, is this."

"Where's Sean?"

She looked at Benson. "Not here, love. Haven't seen him in weeks."

From inside, someone yelled, "Hurry up with that bastard door, woman; I'm freezing my tits off here."

Any remaining bravado seeped away through the hole in her lies; she dropped her arms and stepped aside. "He's thick as pigshit," she whispered. "Through there."

Benson let himself into the lounge. A skinny runt of a kid wearing a backwards baseball cap, no top, and loose-fitting tracksuit bottoms, lay across the leather sofa, punching buttons on a remote. A bandage covered half his face, and smoke curled up it like a grey serpent. One lazy hand dropped the remote and picked up his phone, while the other rummaged down his tracksuit bottoms, massaging his balls, making sure they hadn't fallen off. "Who was it?" the side of his mouth said.

"It's the cops," Khan said.

Sean clutched a cushion to his chest, and shouted, "The fuck you let them in for?"

Chantelle stood in the doorway, her lips pursed tight. "When they leave," she snarled, "I'm going to smash your face in."

"Now, now, Mrs Walker," Benson said, "no need to wait till we leave."

Chantelle didn't even crack a smile, just glared at Sean and then went upstairs, leaving them to their own company, slamming the door behind her.

"We visited an old man last night. Walter. Salt of the earth."

Sean stared at them.

"You burgled him. Remember?"

"If you really thought that, you'd have me in chains by now. I ain't as thick as you think I am."

"Pretty soon you will be. In chains, I mean; we already think you're as thick as you are. We found your footwear mark inside his house."

Sean sat forward, know-it-all grin stretching a face that wasn't even regularly shaved yet. "This 'asn't got nothing to do with a burglary at an old fella's house, has it? Burglaries at old fellas' houses is for the monkeys to investigate, not the oily rag." Satisfied he'd cracked them wide open, Sean sat back, smug smile as rude as a rigid middle finger. "You'll have to try harder, lads."

Benson held his hands out, and nodded. "You got us, Sean. You nailed us."

Sean nodded. "I ain't thick as pigshit. I got you nailed, man. Fucking nailed."

"If you didn't burgle Walter, where did you burgle?"

"Nowhere. I ain't no burglar."

"Listen, Sean..." Benson sat down on the sofa and sank, swallowed by it. Sean squirmed away from him. "We know you're one of the top men around here—"

"It's why we came to see you," said Khan.

Sean nodded. "I get ya."

"If anyone knows about burglaries round here, it's you. No one does anything without your knowing about it."

"Or your say so."

Benson said, "Someone handed us five credit cards last night, and he thought you'd burgled Walter for them."

"But Walter doesn't know anything about credit cards," said Khan.

"So we thought you might know where they came from, which house. Obviously you didn't burgle the house yourself."

"But we're interested in knowing which house they came from."

"Not even bothered who the real burglar is? If you get my meaning."

Khan finished off, "We just want to know where they came from."

Sean eyed them both. "It's like watching the Two Ronnies, watching you. Got it all sorted out, eh, what you're going to ask me. Pretend like you know me, pretend that you even have street cred when you're both so far out of the way, man, you in a different zip code."

"Zip code?" asked Benson.

"It's street talk for post code," said Khan.

Benson nodded.

"Street talk? See, even you who thinks he knows street talk don't know shit, don't know street talk. Street talk is parlance, man. Okay? Free gift from me, free lesson for you. Every day's a school day, yeah?"

They stared at him.

Sean looked from one to the other, swallowed. Somehow his own street cred and his order in the hierarchy that existed only inside his own head wasn't an issue any more; his sanity was. He licked his lips. "I have a place in mind," he said.

"Great, where is it?"

Sean hugged the cushion tighter. "We doing a deal, here," he wagged a finger. "Me and yous two, right? We are dealing information. We are helping one another out, see?"

Benson sighed, and moved closer. "You know where those cards came from, Sean, yes? But you're refusing to tell us?"

Sean nodded. "That's about the size of it, man. I need something back, see? Back scratching innit."

"Innit?"

"Do you want to fucking know or you just gonna sit here taking the piss all day?"

Benson cleared his throat, "You're right, you're absolutely right. Sorry, Sean. You want us to forget all about Walter's burglary in exchange for the address where you found those cards."

"Wait, I didn't find no cards, man. You can't trap me like this, we in business together now. Right?"

"Didn't mean to trap you. Sorry."

"But yes. I'll give you an address, and you wipe that old guy's burglary, you wipe any connection you think I have to it off the computer systems, yes? I ain't had nothing to do with it, okay?"

"If you had nothing to do with it, why would there be a connection?"

"Because you're cops, innit. You make mistakes."

Benson nodded, looked at Khan, "I think we can arrange for any mistake to be erased, can't we?"

"It'll be tough, boss, getting division—"

"I know it'll be tough. But we're getting some reliable intel here. Isn't that right, Sean?"

"Bet your fat arse it is."

Benson winced, regained his poise, and looked at Khan. "Make that happen." He turned back to Sean and smiled his best smile. "Address where those credit cards came from."

"They're playing you."

Everyone turned to see Chantelle in the doorway.

"Are you so thick you can't tell when they're fucking playing you, Sean? They come in here with something dressed up as a deal and you're about to get their dicks out and teabag them. What the hell's wrong with you, you fucking moron!"

Sean leapt from the sofa and had his hands around Chantelle's neck before Khan could even get his arse in gear. "Oi, oi," shouted Benson, struggling to get up out of the sofa. "No need for this, Sean." Khan pulled him off her and Chantelle coughed, hands massaging the redness growing around her throat.

"You're a fucking lunatic, Sean, did you know that? You need sectioning."

From within Khan's strong embrace, Sean pointed at her, "You don't take the piss out of me, woman." Khan yanked him further away, and from somewhere a toddler began crying. "Go see to Abby, you bitch. And stay the fuck out of my business!"

Chantelle disappeared again and pretty soon the baby stopped crying. Khan released his grip.

Sean stared between the two. "That right? You playing me?"

"Sean, come on—"

"Who handed you those credit cards?"

"What?" Benson played for time to think.

"You said someone handed you some credit cards. Who was it?"

"They were just handed in at a counter," said Khan.

"Bollocks. It was a copper, wasn't it? Came in here last night and beat the crap out of me. It was a copper? Fucking Five-O come in here playing games with me, trying to get info out of me." He took a step towards Benson, his face now red, his swagger exaggerated, his snarl more prominent. "And all the while you sending coppers in. You planted fucking credit cards in my house, man, and then try to work me for them? Fuck off. Go on, get out of my house."

"We didn't send any officers in here."

"Fuck off. I'll be searching for listening devices too. If I find any, the press will be the first to hear about it, yeah? And then my solicitor. Got it?" Sean shuffled them towards the front door. "Like you said, Benson, I know them all 'round here, and I didn't recognise him; geezer emptied my wallet and then gave us the cash back? That ain't no Seacroft crowd, is it, that's one of you lot." The veins stood proud on Sean's forehead. "Try and do me for that old geezer's burglary if you like, go on. I ain't done nothing wrong." His mood was worsening, and Benson thought about the baby and how it had gone quiet because it was being fed, and he applied that to Sean too, how he needed a fix right now, and no amount of reasoning would calm him down – only the drugs would do that.

"Okay," Benson held out his palms. "We're going, no need for this."

Sean snarled and made to grab Benson but Khan pushed him into the wall and held him back. "You're one move from getting locked up."

Sean focused on Khan. "Get the fuck out of my house and don't come back."

Khan looked at Benson who already had the front door open. He released his grip on Sean and walked away.

When he closed the door, Benson heard Sean scream, "Get the fuck down here, woman!"

Chapter Fifteen

A Funny Taste

EDDIE LIVED WITH HIS family in Whitkirk, East Leeds. His house was on Barons Drive and he could see it for the better part of three hundred yards away as he approached. It was on the left, just before the road veered right and stopped at Selby Road and the access to the Temple Newsam estate.

He could see his house and if he had night vision, he'd be able to see the deck chair by the small apple tree on the lawn. But this evening, there was something different about it. He couldn't work out what, though. Eddie was the kind of person who knew instantly there was something different about a person, but he'd need it pointing out that someone had shaved off their moustache or had their hair cut.

And tonight was no different. He squinted, even put on the full beam as the Discovery clumped over the speedbumps. The moon was bright beyond the roofline, yet the full beam, right into his lounge window couldn't uncover what was different.

A prickle ran down Eddie's back and he took a longer drag on his cigarette. He reached for the stereo and turned Pink Floyd down.

A hundred yards away, he wound down his window, took a final drag, burnt his fingers and tossed the butt out of the window. Sparks in the mirror on the road behind him.

He worked it out.

Her car was missing.

Eddie drew up on the kerb just as he always did. He left the engine running and stared at the driveway where Kelly would leave her white Ford Focus. He stared at the place it would have been. He stared at an empty driveway and the spots of oil on it, as though willing the car to reappear. "What the fuck..." he turned off the motor and stepped out, glancing at his watch as he pressed the button and locked his car. It was one-thirty. Two hours late home again. It was quiet around here, eerily so.

He closed the black wrought iron gate across the driveway and readied the house key, all the while staring at the cleaner part of the drive where her car was usually parked.

The abandonment hit home when the door closed behind him with an echo he didn't remember hearing before. He felt compelled to call out, 'hello'. He almost did. But he refrained; the car might be in the repair garage having a fault looked at; it might be parked at Temple Newsam, having failed to start, broken down; recovery due at 9am. Who knew? It could be any of a thousand things, and shouting hello into the house might result in two grumpy women staring down the stairs at him.

But that echo?

"Hello?" he stood in the hallway holding his breath, heart tripping, feet twitching. "Hello!"

Nothing. No grumpy females; no lights coming on; no sound of bodies moving in beds, and no snoring. Ahead, he heard movement in the kitchen.

"Watson?"

Watson scratched at the door and whimpered. Eddie smiled a little and floated towards it on autopilot. Watson jumped up at him and the smell of urine stung Eddie's nose. This was not a good sign. He let the dog out, returned to the kitchen and turned on the light. On the worktop was a note that read, "You wouldn't listen. This is not au revoir." Eddie sighed. There was a PS. "Don't try to find us. We don't want finding."

The microwave oven was missing. He looked around, and the toaster was missing too.

A coldness fell across his shoulders, cloaked him, and he closed his eyes as Watson nudged his leg, hinting for food. After the dog had eaten, Eddie cleaned up the dog pee, and slid down the front of a cupboard until he was sitting on the kitchen floor. Watson draped his front paws over Eddie's crossed legs, looking up, ears swept back, feeling sorry for him. Eddie was feeling sorry for Eddie too. It was his right, and he picked up his phone, scrolled to Kelly's number and dialled. No reply, number non-existent.

"Fuck," Eddie whispered, and Watson whined in agreement. This was serious. He'd thought of this day many times over the last few months, especially since he'd discovered she had a bit on the side. It hurt much more than he'd thought it would. It burned. This was more than abandonment; it was a punishment too, a jab in the eye with a middle finger. And all the time he could imagine Kelly laughing at him, shouting, "This is what happens when you think of a stranger's pain more than you do your own fucking family, Eddie. I tried to tell you, I warned you, but you thought it was just a threat. See how wrong you were? Gerrup ow'da, now."

It was true. He had thought it was just a threat. But that feeling, the one of being alone very soon, grew sides and density when Mr Handsome Bastard appeared on the scene; it started to become real. But hold on, there was something else here, something that Eddie was missing. Was it the need to care for people without actually being aware of it? If a victim needed help, Eddie rolled up his sleeves and got stuck in. It was, as far as he was concerned, part of the job, the reason they paid him every month. It was the reason he climbed out of bed each day. Kelly didn't under—

"Oh, you bitch."

It hit him hard right between the eyes: her leaving had nothing to do with his working late; it had nothing to do with helping victims of crime, either. It had everything to do with Kelly. She wanted out and could find no better place to lay the blame than at Eddie's feet and label it 'Selfishness'. It had nothing to do with Eddie, Kelly just wanted out.

Eddie's stomach growled. "Can't believe she took the fucking toaster." But then he checked the bread bin and found she'd taken the bread as well. "Bitch!" Watson whimpered, and Eddie felt bad. He crouched and Watson buried his nose under Eddie's arm. "Fate and Luck," Eddie whispered. "These two words describe my life. They describe that feeling I get when I try my best and everything goes wrong anyway. It's the feeling of not only walking through treacle, but of walking through treacle that is flowing against you."

Eddie stroked Watson and eventually the dog peered up at him, eyes wider than normal. He knew something was wrong – something big.

"It is designed to piss you off, of course it is. You stub a toe, and then drop your toast, and the fuse in the kettle blows. All these things are designed to annoy the living shit out of you – but why? For the pleasure of the gods, that's why. Do you understand me, Watson?"

Watson whined, licked his nose and then butted Eddie in the face.

"This is The Law of Fate and Luck," he said. "Yes, the Law of Late." He considered it; didn't sound right. "No, this is The Law of Fuck." Eddie almost smiled – it sounded better already.

Watson looked at him as though worried he might do something silly.

There was plenty of silly Eddie could do right now, and he pulled the best silly out of his back pocket and read the name and address next to the registration number of the man Kelly had kissed in the car park last week. Watson barked and Eddie jumped. "What's up, boy?" Watson barked again. "If I didn't know any better, I'd say you knew what I was thinking and don't approve, right?" Watson whined. "Fucking pussy." Eddie lit a cigarette and strolled through into the lounge, turning on all the lights and noting how cold the place felt, how echoey it had become. The sofa and two chairs had gone. Half the DVDs were gone from the rack – the good ones, the standard lamp shade and the matching shade from the ceiling lamp had gone, all the abstract Baytree Interiors paintings that Eddie didn't understand, and he shook his head. "Must be serious," he whispered.

Upstairs, the story was pretty much the same: all her stuff had gone, and some of Eddie's too. She had left the TV in the lounge but had taken the one from the bedroom. For all he cared for TV, she could have taken them both. "I'd swap it for the toaster." He flicked ash and trod it in the carpet, not really caring any more. Becca's room was stripped bare. The bed was still there, but all her stuff – posters, even – had left the room as naked as when they'd moved in here four years ago, cold and unhomely.

"I'll always be here," he said, "because you can always count on your dad, Becca." Kind of ironic, he thought. Self-indulgent, even. "Prick."

Ah, there was something left, however.

Pinned to the wall was a piece of paper. It was a bank statement in the name of Mrs K Collins, a savings account. The closing balance for last month was a little under twenty-three thousand pounds. Eddie tore it off the wall, confused why it would even be there. He turned it over and in black pen was Becca's tall and thin handwriting: "Dad, Mum's been syphoning money from your joint account, I just found out tonight. Don't worry about us – she's made sure we'll be okay. None of this was your fault. She's taking us back to Dublin, ferry leaves 7pm on Sunday. I think she's putting us in a Holiday Inn until then, but she won't say which one. I love you, Dad. I'll visit when she lets me."

Eddie dialled Becca's phone and got the same result he'd got from Kelly's.

No mention of Mr Handsome Bastard. Was he along for the ride? Were they to meet him in Dublin? Did Handsome Bastard even know Kelly was leaving? Perhaps he'd been Kelly's shag for a few months, maybe helping to get the plans straight in between secret bedroom frolics?

"Why couldn't she just be straight with me?"

Watson walked into the room, curled up on the floor at Eddie's feet. Eddie patted him and fussed him while he contemplated his next move.

The next move involved getting the car keys, locking up the house and starting the Discovery's engine. Eddie lit another cigarette and selected drive.

There was a knock and Eddie came to and banged his head against the window. His eyes were stuck shut and his mouth was stuck shut and there was crusty snot around his nostrils. For a moment Eddie thought he was a two-year-old again.

He squinted through the fogged-up glass and saw a woman peering inside. She wound an imaginary handle. Eddie straightened in his seat and started the car, wound down the window. The cold air smacked him in the face and his squinting eyes widened.

"Eddie Collins?"

"Huh," was about all he could manage.

The woman smiled and held out a mug of brown liquid, possibly coffee. "I've been watching you for the last ninety minutes." She smiled again, a little unsure of how to proceed. "I have trouble sleeping these days," she nodded at his car, "unlike you it seems."

"How can I help... I'm sorry, who are you?"

"Phoebe. His wife. Timothy South, the man who's run off with your wife."

Eddie's eyes dropped away and settled on the steering wheel but a thousand miles through it, focused on nothing.

"Would you like to come inside? Bit nippy out here."

"What time is it?"

"Seven-thirty." She handed over the coffee and stepped back as though proud of her achievement.

He sipped and then drank; it was good. But then battery acid would be good after sleeping in the car all night and waking up to your tongue stuck to the roof of your mouth. "You don't sound surprised to see me here."

She shrugged, pulled her dressing gown a little tighter around her shoulders. "Third time he's run off with some tart." She closed her eyes, "I'm sorry; I mean it's the third time he's run away with some woman."

"I think you were right the first time. Why do you keep... how can you—"

"Put up with it?"

"Well, yes."

"Easy. I have very low self-esteem." She looked down at herself. "Have you seen me, Mr Collins? I'm not exactly a hot catch; I'm lucky to have him at all, really."

"You shouldn't be so hard on yourself."

"I don't like oral sex, you see. Never have."

Eddie spat out coffee and blushed.

"It tastes funny. And I think that's why he leaves; I really do. He finds it elsewhere, and when they get fed up of him – maybe it tastes funny to them, too – he comes back to me. Even though I refuse to perform fellatio. I won't, he knows I won't; I've told him as much."

An old woman walked past shaking her head. Eddie nodded at her politely.

A thought fell over in Eddie's mind and he focused on it before it could get up and walk off. "How do you know my name?"

She smiled. "Timothy told me, love. Well," she shrugged, "he talks in his sleep. We have no secrets," she laughed. "Well, he has no secrets. I have hundreds of the buggers."

Eddie grinned at her, there was something easy to like about her, and the thought of confrontation vanished. "I still don't understand—"

"Because..." Her eyes were downcast and although Eddie couldn't see her feet, he imagined them nudging little stones around on the ground; a distraction while the truth marched out of her mouth. "I... He's a good man. He really is. I know you don't want to hear that about the man who's... who's—"

"Shagging my wife?"

"Yes, yes. But he is a decent chap. He just has no self-confidence. He's so self-deprecating that he—"

"Self what?"

She sighed, "Stick with the low self-confidence, love, that'll do." She looked up and down the street as the sky began to lighten fully and then watched it darken up again with more approaching cloud. "I'm getting cold. So I'll leave you with this: he sleeps with your wife because he thinks he deserves better than me and because it makes him feel confident again – the old 'I've still got it' delusion. And your wife sleeps with him because she thinks you don't deserve her, and because she thinks she's punishing you."

"She doesn't know that I know."

"Oh, Mr Collins. Now who's being delusional?"

Eddie whispered, "Bollocks."

"But mostly, she's sleeping with him because it legitimises her dislike of you, and it allows her to leave without feeling guilty."

Eddie's mouth fell open. "Do you charge by the hour? I could come back and talk about my childhood."

"I could make a fortune." Phoebe smiled and held out her hand. "Good luck, Mr Collins."

Eddie went to shake.

"No, no, I want my cup back; I don't shake hands."

Eddie swigged the last of the cooling coffee and passed the cup back.

"Before you go, may I ask what you were hoping to achieve this morning. I expect you came here hoping to face up to him, and maybe even beat him up a little. Teach him a lesson, yes?"

"I wanted my fucking microwave back."

"Beg your pardon."

"Tell the truth, I don't know what I was going to do. My daughter—"

"He needs beating up, really. I told him as much; it'd ground him again, keep him close to home where he feels safe. I got someone lined up to beat him up once, paid him £250 and I never saw him again. You can't trust people, Mr Collins. Criminals, every last one of them."

Eddie nodded.

"Not interested in earning £250, Mr Collins?"

Chapter Sixteen

A Major Application

"Ooh, Ros, glad I caught you."

She stopped on the corridor, desperately trying to remember where the large open-plan office was – the one as big as a football pitch. How could you lose an office? Her arms ached because they were full of folders, head ached because of the turmoil living in there, and she tried to smile for Jeffery, to disguise how much she missed her comfort zone. "Living the dream."

"Wow, do people still say that?"

"I was being sarcastic, sorry." An image of Eddie Collins skipped across her mind.

Jeffery smiled, missing the point entirely. "Okay, so how's it going?"

"I keep getting lost."

"Cheaper. Modern design. Each floor looks the same, each room looks the same, too."

"And it's more work than I thought it would be. You'd think I could walk from one CSI job into another in the same force and carry on without missing a beat. Nope."

"Yeah," Jeffery said, "it's mostly a difference of procedures and blending the whole thing with MCU policies. Soon have you up and running."

Ros, doubtful of anything to do with 'soon', smiled again. Her arms were ready to fall off.

"Got another batch to interview on Friday. Some of them were colleagues of yours."

She raised her eyebrows, interested in who was applying, but aware that there was a data protection issue about to burp right in her face. If Jeffery told her, he'd be breaking the law. "Oh?"

"Eddie Collins, for one."

Had she been holding a bottle of booze, she'd have dropped it – because that's how clichés work – but she was holding files, and they slid from her grasp, bounced, and fanned across the modern, grey-flecked, carpet.

"Here, let me..." He bent and helped retrieve the files, and asked, "are you really okay?"

"Why did you tell me he'd applied?"

He looked confused, gave that familiar wonky smile that wanted to be genuine but all it did was inform you that the owner was missing something important. That smile was a snitch.

"You can't take him on," she said, almost gasping at the thought, and wrestling with the preamble of an anxiety attack.

"Really? I thought you'd be pleased." That smile was still there – he was still missing something.

"I moved here to get away from him!"

"I'm confused. I thought you got along well?"

She chewed her lip, still shuffling files, and didn't give her answer any thought before blurting out, "If he comes here, I'm handing my notice in. He's a drunk." Why on earth did she add that last bit? He'd been drunk twice since she'd met him, and both times were at Christmas parties – and for someone like Eddie being drunk at a party was almost obligatory, it was his way of being there without actually being there.

And would she hand her notice in? Yes, she decided on the spot, she would. It had been a hard enough decision to uproot her entire life to move house to the other side of Leeds and to come here so she wouldn't be near him, so she could remove all temptation. To have him follow her here would be infuriating, and it would be intolerable, and it would undo all her good work, and kick her resolve into the gutter.

When he'd called around to see her on Monday, she had almost caved in at the news of Eddie's marriage burning. She could have stepped in and embraced him; hell, she could have offered to let him stay the night. But she'd done the best-friend bit for seven years, and each time it was she who'd ended up in the burns unit. There was only so much regret one heart could take, and hers was overflowing.

Jeffery was stunned into a temporary silence. "Erm..." He shifted his weight and, as if realising his lack of judgement said, "I shouldn't really have mentioned his application to you in the first place."

"But you did."

"I did, yes." Jeffery stared at the carpet, lost for something to say, it seemed. "He was a superb examiner, though." And then, "A drunk, you say?"

She nodded, wishing the ground would swallow her whole.

"Okay," Jeffery began walking, "thanks for the info." After a few yards, he turned, "Ros, I expect you to keep our little conversation between us. Okay?"

Chapter Seventeen

A Need to Meet

CHANTELLE RANG THE BUZZER and sighed a nervous sigh, rocking the pushchair back and forth hoping Abby would keep quiet despite being an hour overdue for a feed. She didn't go into police stations, hated the coppers with something usually reserved for syphilis appointments at the clinic. There was just something, she shuddered, fundamentally wrong with the whole system that favoured the weak.

Chantelle had grown up in a tough household in a tough neighbourhood. If you were caught crying, you had the piss ripped out of you for months. No tears; it was a rule. No matter how much it hurt or how hard life was. No tears. If your life was hard, make it better, rob or thieve until you got what you wanted, until the beatings stopped.

She looked up and there was a copper staring right at her. He was leaning against a doorframe – seemed to be the door from the canteen – there was a microwave buzzing behind him, something like pasta groaning around on a plate inside. "What do you want, Chantelle? You come to make a complaint about him?"

"About who?"

The copper touched his face, mirroring where Chantelle's bruises were. "Sean."

She sniffed, embarrassed that they knew her and Sean by name, that they knew how bad things could be at home. This was stupid. At the very least she ought to have gone to another police station miles away where no one could possibly know her. "I want to see someone."

"About what?"

"None of your business. I need to speak to Sergeant Benson."

"Who?" The copper stood upright, confusion in his tone.
"Don't you know him?"
"Ten thousand people in West Yorkshire Police, love."

Chantelle sighed again, and a guilty prickle crept through her. Was this the only way? Surely anything would be better than this? She shook the pushchair harder.

"Where's he work?"

She eyed him, trying to work out if he was laughing at her inside. But she couldn't see, like there was a fog floating around him – an invisibility cloak.

"Do you know where he works?"

She shrugged. "Said sommat about Major Crime."

"Major Crime?"

"Look, I don't know, alright? That's what it fucking sounded like."

"Alright, alright. No need for that language in here." He sniffed and sat at the desk before her, nudged the mouse of an old computer. It groaned and creaked and almost coughed as it woke from its slumber. "Nothing I can help you with?"

Chantelle shook her head. Her heart pummelled, and a sick feeling chewed on her guts. "I want to speak to him, okay?" Abby was stirring, shuffling around. This was a bad idea.

The officer rested a pair of slack-fitting spectacles on the bridge of his nose, prodded keys with his two index fingers, and squinted at the screen as it lightened and coloured his face with each scroll of the mouse.

She checked her watch; it was getting too far past Abby's feed time; it was getting hotter in here, and she made up her mind to abandon it, to forget it ever happened. She made her way to the door, dry mouth, trembling fingertips.

"Here he is." He peered at Chantelle as she turned around. "Want me to ring him?"

She came back towards the counter and nodded. Nerves made her smile at him, but she wanted to stab him in the neck for making her feel the tinge of gratitude towards a copper pig bastard!

She could hear the dial tone and then the ringing sound. The copper held the handset between his ear and shoulder, eyes never leaving her.

"Morning," he said into the phone, "it's Colin Turnbull at Killingbeck... yeah, not bad, rain again they say. It's going to be a washout this season... I know." He looked up and saw Chantelle staring at him, less than impressed, and got down to business,

"Yeah, listen, I'm ringing to see if you have a DS Benson in your office. I was told... yes, that's him. Okay, thank you, cheers." He nodded at Chantelle, and Chantelle's heart missed so many beats that she almost hit the deck. She swallowed, eyes drilling into the copper's. "DS Benson. I have a Chantelle Walker here, wants to speak with you."

The officer held the phone up for Chantelle.

She took it, took a last look around to make sure no one she knew was listening. "Hello?"

"Chantelle? It's Tom Benson. How can I help you?"

She whispered, "I want to meet."

"Listen, Chantelle, you dicked me around—"

"I ain't messing about. I want a deal. You want this info or not?"

Chapter Eighteen

A Nasty Bastard

High up in the hills surrounding Temple Newsam house was a folly called The Little Temple. Capability Brown designed and built it in 1765 as a place to sit and admire the tumbling hillsides and enchanted woodlands, the lakes and the waterways. It was like a small Greek temple complete with leafy capitals atop the four grand columns, and in all the years since, it remained beautiful and free of modernity until the invention of two things: the aerosol can and the fuckwit.

Together, they, and entropy, have removed the grandeur and replaced it with shame. It stands now as a canvas to illiterate idiocy, and instead of people admiring the view from it, they use it as a clandestine meeting place for the exchange of bodily fluids and drugs for money.

"Nope, I like this coat and I'm not sitting there." Chantelle blinked at Benson, tutted at him, and sat down, crossed her legs and lit a rollup.

"Why did you have to choose here for a meeting? I can think of a least a dozen coffee shops within a few miles of your house."

"That's why," she said. "I don't want to be seen talking to no copper. You know what'd happen to me if anyone I knew saw me with the likes of you?" She had developed a slight whistle in her ill-repaired lower denture. There were some things, she realised, that superglue just could not fix properly.

Benson gave in and sat down a yard away. "Fair enough." He looked first at his shoes and the mud around the edge of the soles, and then out across the treetops down towards the house and the clusters of people enjoying the magnificent lawn in front of it. "I'm listening."

She didn't speak for a long time, content to savour the moment, perhaps, or shitting herself – one or the other, wondering what the outcome would be, wondering if she dare go through with this.

Benson waited.

"You were going to make a deal with him, not to press charges over that old man's burglary."

"I was."

"Is that deal still on the table?" She looked at him, holding her breath.

Benson sighed and drew his hands down stubbly grey cheeks. He shrugged, "I don't know now. They work pretty quick, the Identification Bureau. If they link him with that burglary through footwear, they'll produce a forensic hit. This goes through to division and it's allocated to research."

"And?"

"And they put together an arrest package."

Her shoulders slumped and she sat back, flicking away the cigarette. "Pointless being here, then."

Benson looked around at her. "Not entirely. I can try to put the brakes on if there's something in it for us – I mean if we can get to the greater good, the bigger picture."

Chantelle closed her eyes and breathed deeply.

"Where's your baby? Abby, is it?"

"She's being well looking after. Grandma Joyce has her, and Betty as well."

Benson nodded, tried to read the graffiti, the gouges in the wooden benches here proclaimed how 'Lucy Sucks Cock For A Fiver'. He raised his eyebrows, and considered the effects of inflation. "No offence, Chantelle, but you don't seem like a happily married couple. Some people might even think you'd be better off without him. I have no idea why you'd want to deal on his behalf and stay with a low-life, wife-beater bastard, anyway."

She took off the sunglasses and showed him the beautiful purple hue around the orbit of her right eye. "This is what happened after you lot left. It's because I showed him up; I embarrassed him. I expected it, Mr Benson; it wasn't no surprise. But I was worried you were just walking him into a trap."

"I was offering him the same deal you're here to get."

"He didn't do this himself. Paid twenty-five quid for some local Neanderthal to do it; he wouldn't risk me going to the police – not that I ever would, or ever had, for that matter."

Benson's mouth dropped open.

She nodded. "I'd beat the shit out of Sean if he ever laid a finger on me himself. And this way it keeps the threat alive, I suppose; never knowing how bad it'll be, how much he's paid them."

"I've never heard of domestic violence by proxy before." He shook his head again, aghast. "You could beat the shit out of him for paying someone to have you beaten up."

"He's got more money than my pride or my bones could handle." She looked away, hands fidgeting with another rollup. She eventually lit it, breathed out a grey cloud into the greying day and faced Benson again. "You were buttering him up. He's easily flattered, and despite being a macho man, he's easily fooled."

Benson spat a laugh into the temple and heard the echoes laugh back at him. "I was buttering him up so he'd talk. There was no trap. I just wanted the fucking information, Chantelle."

She held her hand up, "I know, I know."

"So, like I said, why are you doing this on his behalf if he's so gullible, and if he's so macho that he leaves his woman with eyes like plums? Eh? I don't get it, and I don't get you? In fact, I'm so perplexed by this meeting, that I wonder why the hell I came."

"This all started when that man barged in and stole stuff from us, beat us both up. And Sean thinks he was an undercover copper."

Another burst of laughter. "Trust me, he wasn't a copper."

"Then who was he?"

He hauled himself up short, put the cork back in the bottle, and said, "I have no idea. But what I mean is, if he was a copper, I would have known about it, there would have been a paper trail that I have access to, okay? There wasn't a paper trail, I checked. So can we put that side of things to bed and move on?"

"You said it like he wasn't a copper but you knew who—"

"Well I don't! Now let's move back onto the subject, shall we? Where did he get those credit cards?"

Chantelle's cheeks throbbed as she gave final consideration, nose in the air, still proud, and said, "He has a deal with some old guy in Mabgate. I don't know where he gets them from, but he sells them to Sean for a few quid and Sean knocks 'em out to some big crews in Chapeltown. Makes a good bit o' money from them."

"He the only supplier?"

"Nah, there's a handful more. But those cards came from that old geezer."

The pride she had collapsed, and she sounded meek and she looked deflated, and Benson still couldn't work her out. "That it?"

She looked at him. "What more do you want?"

"What more? How about an address or a name of this old man in Mabgate? Narrow it down a bit."

"Mabgate is all I know. Detached house."

He stared at her.

"Seriously!"

He turned to her, shimmied up the bench a little closer. "If you think that's going to buy Sean a Get Out of Jail Free card, you are sorely mistaken." He stood. "And now I have to clean my bastard shoes. The wife'll wonder what the hell I've been up to."

Benson began walking away and he'd got no further than twenty yards when she shouted at him.

"If he goes down, I'm finished."

Benson stopped, looked down at the muddy path, and at the view across to his left, over the treetops and up to the grand house. He planned on visiting that house one day, have a good look around it. He tutted, turned to her and trudged back to the bench.

"I have to say that if he goes down and you're finished, then you don't have an awful lot holding you up, do you? As a buoyancy aid I'd suggest he was more like a brick than a lump of Styrofoam, and that speaks volumes about your ability to choose right from wrong."

When she looked up, she had tears in her eyes.

"You're leaking."

"He's a knob. I know that; he's not a particularly good husband, and he won't win a Father of the Year award."

"You're not selling him to me."

"Abby is his. But I have Betty from a different father. Most men wouldn't touch me with a bargepole; Sean treats Betty like his own, you know? He's a good man trying to look tough in a housing estate that punishes weakness."

"Where on earth did you read that?"

"I'm trying to be honest here."

"And I'm trying to think of the name of the mental illness you're suffering from. Do you really think he wakes up with a fucking halo under his pillow? He's a nasty bastard, Chantelle. You might only see the good in him, but let me tell you about the night-time Sean Walker. The night-time Sean Walker breaks into war veterans' homes. Take old Walter, the last one your superhero 'borrowed' from. Walter is eighty-six and has been in the military all his life. He was a decorated hero in the Falklands Conflict; he's served his country – that includes misfits like you and Sean – all his life in places like Afghanistan and Yugoslavia, places you wouldn't visit if it was free, and he's seen things that'd make you vomit from sun up to sun set.

"Yet this bastard of a husband of yours breaks in, steals his money, all sixty-eight pounds of it, steals his fucking bus pass as well. Leaves him with nothing. Nothing! And dear old Walter can't rely on family because he doesn't have any, not even a wife since an illness took her a couple a years ago. He has to go begging to the state for his next fucking meal, and he has to pay for the damage to the window caused by knobhead Walker."

"I'm sorry."

"Tell old Walter, not me. But incidentally, what are you going to do with Walter's sixty-eight quid? Smoke it, buy food with it, shoot it up, pay a drugs debt, or buy some more X-Box games, you know, the essentials?"

She didn't cry because she had been programmed not to, but the tears fell.

"And guess what, you're asking for mercy for him? He's a waste of skin, and I've half a mind to let it be known on that hard-arsed estate that he's a police informant. See how he handles that."

"No, please!"

"You make me sick, Chantelle."

"Please, Mr Benson. If he goes to prison, I'll not cope alone again; my kids won't cope." She stared him in the eyes. "Please; we'll all suffer."

Benson stood silently contemplating not only her words but his own, too. He was hard on her, perhaps unnecessarily so, certainly unprofessionally so; Walter was no war hero so far as he knew, but it sounded good and added weight to his argument. But he was speaking from the heart rather than from a police manual. "Why do you stay with him? There really are more buoyancy aids in the sea."

She smiled. "I love him." And then she added, "Besides, who'd want me? After two kids I have to tuck my tits into my waistband, and my minge looks like a bag of Frazzles."

He almost snorted at that but restrained himself. He sat, and said, "Okay, I'll help keep his name out of Walter's burglary. But you have to turn him good. And let me say right now that I'm not being naïve; I know you'll try but you'll never succeed. Chantelle, turn him good because I will not save his arse a second time; if he's caught again he's going down for it."

She nodded, probably unable to believe her luck, but the gravity of the deal seemed to drag any residue of happiness from her. She knew there was no hope, not really. There was nothing more certain; just like water always flows downhill, someday Sean would end up back in prison or in a canal tied to a lump of rock. "Mr Benson?"

He looked across.

"Please don't tell anyone we met. No one, please."

"I won't, don't worry."

"Thank you."

"Stay under the radar, Chantelle."

"One last thing. The old man in Mabgate, he's a nutter. That's what Sean described him as. As a nutter."

"Well," said Benson, "that narrows it down a bit."

"Apparently, you need to be careful around him."

Chapter Nineteen

Climbing the Ladder

"Wʜᴀᴛ ʜᴀᴘᴘᴇɴᴇᴅ?"

Sean looked confused.

"The nose? Eyes are blackening up too."

"Just a skirmish with an idiot."

Ziggy appeared concerned at first, but when Sean didn't, he soon moved on. "If you're okay with it, then I'm okay with it too." He took out a small brown envelope and slapped it into Sean's sweaty hand. "That's three grand, man."

Sean stuck it into his inside jacket pocket along with feelings of achievement, satisfaction, and pride.

Ziggy watched Sean's right hand, and in particular the stump of a little finger. Sean curled the hand into a fist and the stump disappeared. Ziggy stopped looking, and smiled at him. "There's another three next week if you can get more cards and sell more coke, okay?"

"Cool," said Sean. "I'm on it; I'll have half a dozen by then."

The man nodded. "Make it a dozen, yes?"

"A dozen? I'm not sure—"

"We got eyes on you, bro, and we like what we see, eh? Remember that. You can piss a dozen. Can't you, Sean?"

Sean nodded. "Yep. I'll er, I'll make it a dozen."

"Everything okay with you?"

Sean looked confused, and took the chance to light a cigarette. "Yeah, man. I'm good, ta. You?"

"No problems from plod?"

"They come round my gaff last week saying I burgled some old twat."

The man raised his eyebrows. "And did you?"

"Yeah. I did." Sean smiled. "It's my trade, and I ain't stoppin', Ziggy, it's—"

"Whoa, boy, whoa. Ain't no one asking you stop, yeah? But get fucking better at it. We don't want the law floating around, know what I mean? You're climbing the ladder, dude, and we like what you're doing for us with the credit cards and the Special K and the coke. We don't want that to end, see?"

"To end?"

"By you getting locked up."

Sean breathed out. "Okay, cool."

"We not coming down on you heavy, Sean, you know. We don't work like that, really. Just remember where your future lies, and I very much doubt it lies breaking and entering, you catch me?"

"Yeah, I get it."

The man leaned in closer, just into Sean's space. He smiled, "Mind you do, Sean, yep. We like the credit card line, and we don't want that putting in harm's way, yeah?"

Sean moved back, smiled his best subservient smile, and said, "Sure, no problem. I get where you're coming from."

"Good. Well that's okay then, innit."

"I'm loyal, Ziggy, you know that." The smile stayed put, and Sean found himself stuck to the seat. "I'll do whatever it takes to keep moving up, you know."

"A dozen, then. That's settled. And enjoy the three-grand, man." He pressed a button unlocking the car doors, an invitation to piss off. "Oh shit, one more thing, dude." He locked the car again. He whispered, "You got a piece?"

"A piece?"

"Yeah, a piece. A gun. Have you got—"

"No, no I ain't got a gun."

"We think you should carry one. Safety an' all that. Can't be too careful out there, man."

He thought it over – very briefly – and was nodding his agreement before Ziggy had even finished his sentence. It was a chick magnet. And it was a fucking status symbol. No one would mess with him if he had a piece. No one. "If you think."

"Waa, man you's climbing the ladder. You gotta learn that the higher you get, the bigger the target is on yo back, yeah?"

Sean took the news like a newly promoted executive: stoically. "Yeah, you're right. Of course you're right. I've been giving my security some thought too—"

"Here."

There was a gun on the central armrest.

"It's yours. Take it."

He stared between Ziggy and the gun, licked his lips and didn't know whether to get a hard on or throw up. "Wow. I er, I ain't never fired one before."

Ziggy's eyebrows met in the middle. "Man, you a pussy. You seen John Wick, yeah? Played Call of Duty?" He shrugged, "Nothing to it, man. There's six or seven left in the clip, one in the breach, don't waste your time looking for a safety catch cos there ain't one, 'kay? Just point the fucker and shoot, like riding a bike. Simples."

Sean had a semi on and felt queasy. "What if I need more bullets?"

"You plannin' on cleaning up Leeds?"

He shrugged. "Seven bullets doesn't seem like a lot of self-defence, know what I mean?"

Ziggy tutted again, opened the armrest and took out a freezer bag with something like a dozen 9mm bullets inside. "Don't fucking waste them, yeah? They don't come cheap, and in future you'll be buying them from me."

Sean's eyes grew wide and the semi became embarrassingly obvious. "So cool."

When Sean took hold of the bullets, Ziggy slammed the armrest lid, stared directly at Sean and said, "And I have your first job."

The erection didn't embarrass him for long. In seconds it had evaporated to little more than a press-stud in his boxers. "First job?"

"Fuck yeah, man. What you think all this is about, huh? Grow the fuck up, Sean, and become a man. We don't let you in, see you climb the ladder, and tool you up just cos you'd look good for the women, geddit? You gotta earn your place and you gotta keep earning it. Make no mistake, man, there are others snapping at yo heels, and they'd take that piece and they'd do that job in a heartbeat. You gotta act, bro. As my old man would say, shit or get off the potty."

Sean watched him, looked up at him; Ziggy, a man to be feared, so cool, so intelligent... so fucking rich. He looked at the gold dripping from his wrists and the chains of it round his neck, a symbol of wealth, and dedication to the gang. He stared at it; all he had in the 'dripping with gold department' was a St Christopher Chantelle bought him for Christmas. Not really in the same league. Sean licked his lips again, ready to grasp the next rung and begin climbing. "I'm in, man."

"Good," Ziggy said. His eyes were cold and there was no camaraderie in them – just an instruction. "Your first job is to wipe out Chantelle."

Chapter Twenty

The Sixth Cigarette

HE REARRANGED THE TWO pairs of sunglasses on the passenger seat so they were square on with the edge. The rest of the car might be a shed, the exterior might be in need of its first wash in two years, but he liked things in here to be square.

Yesterday had rained all day. Eddie went out for a pizza about 8pm, and when he returned home an hour later, the front door was wide open. Despite a racing heart, and that bloated feeling he always got with a pepperoni, he'd run into the house to find it eerily empty, even more empty than it had been the day before when he'd come in from work to find his family had left him.

Turns out that while he'd been enjoying a stuffed crust, his bitch of a wife had come back and taken the fucking dog as well.

"Watson!" Eddie stood in the kitchen, looking at the floor where the dog's water and food bowls used to live, and his gaze was drawn to a note she'd left on the kitchen worktop. It said, "I forgot the dog. You can't look after him properly if you're out at work all those hours. We won't bother you no more. Bye."

Eddie wasn't a man to break down and shed tears much. He felt the pain that any reasonable person would under the circumstances. But he wasn't a wobbly wreck over it either. He could still function, he could still think, and he could still hate – and he could still get angry. So far, the only person he really cared for, Becca, had been taken away from him, and now Watson, his only companion was gone too. "Like twisting the fucking knife, Kelly, eh?"

The house was silent. It was huge, and it was his new prison cell – solitary confinement. And that's where the pain came from. He'd always preferred his own company, felt uncomfortable whenever he had to meet others, and even felt uncomfortable when he was with Kelly, like he wished she would go out for the evening so he could catch up with himself, so he could let his guard down and trust himself.

He didn't sleep much that night.

He lay awake in bed, staring at a crack in the ceiling and watching a tiny spider trying to cross over it. Pink Floyd ably came to his rescue and filled the background with auditory delights; insanity slid further down the slope, its grabbing fingers out of range for now. The forefront of his mind debated chasing after Kelly and Becca, at least wrestling Watson from Kelly's witch-like claws. But what was the point? If he'd dragged Watson back here, or even if he'd dragged his whole family back here, they'd be here under duress, and how could you live while trying to make others want to be with you? It was impossible. If people didn't like you, you were pretty much doomed to live in that territory all your life. So far as he knew, there was no love potion available at Boots yet. And anyway, did he really want her back? She was shagging around, and she was taking their money for herself. She wasn't trustworthy. She had no loyalty.

This morning he'd rushed downstairs to let Watson out before he peed all across the kitchen floor, only to realise that Watson didn't live here anymore. He came to a creaking halt, face drawn, eyes damp, and a reinvigorated sadness drowning an exhausted anger that had been pumping iron all night.

He drove to work and parked up without even realising it. He lit his customary third pre-work cigarette and stared out of the windscreen seeing nothing, mind as close to being blank as it was possible to get: it was in charge of the breathing, the smoking, and the sighing, and that was about all; everything else could go fuck itself. He didn't even have the energy to smash things up. "How very rock n roll," he whispered.

This joy of being alone didn't last long. His stupid blank mind coughed and woke up and wasted no time at all in immersing itself in his current dilemma again. And he discovered his cheeks were damp and his fingers were on fire. He tossed the burnt stub out of the window and automatically lit up another, wiping away the tears without giving them a second thought. This must be what being orphaned felt like – looking down the barrel of the rest of your life with no one but you for company, no one to annoy you, no one to laugh with, compare notes with, and as far as Becca went, no one to help grow up with.

He hated to admit it, but there was a possibility that this new status of his – separated – could open a door with Ros. Part of his mind chastised him for thinking about it so soon, giving no time for grief to settle in and do its thing before moving out again, and another part of his mind laughed and declared it had thought of it last night. Like it or not, he was available, and if he was reluctant to drag his family back home screaming, then what was wrong with becoming closer friends with Ros? She had a thing for him – it was obvious. Now, perhaps, they could do something about it. So what was wrong with becoming closer to her?

Nothing.

At the very least she'd be able to shake him by the neck and get him out of this melee his stupid mind endured. He locked the car and trudged through the gate into the back car park of Killingbeck Police Station, the courtyard. Minutes later, he punched his way through the office door.

It was still early; most of the other staff hadn't yet arrived and those who had were still comatose from their own 'first-shift-insomnia'. He fired the computer up, looking to snatch a job from the list and escape from the office before the rabble piled in and turned this comparative silence, this bliss, into an insufferable whirlwind. Getting out early on the first shift back had another advantage to it: the big boss, Chris Ashley – area forensic manager extraordinaire, liked to 'do the rounds' on the first shift back, and Eddie very much liked to avoid watching everyone suck up to him.

Staring right at him was a new email from the Personnel department. His mouth went dry. Did he really want to open it? Come to think of it, did he really want a job at MCU anyway? Surely it would be easier just to stay here – better the devil you know, and all that. Much less fuss than moving out, getting accustomed to all the new people he'd have to learn to avoid, and finding out where the coffee machine was. He stared out of the window into the courtyard below, a sight that didn't even register because it was so familiar to him. Familiar, right? This place, this office and the people in it, were about the only thing of familiarity in his life just now, and he drew a certain comfort from it.

He hovered the mouse over delete.

From outside he heard them: the rabble. They laughed and chattered their way across the courtyard car park and began climbing the stairs to the rear corridor. The whirlwind approached.

He clicked on open and hurriedly read the email. They'd granted him an interview. "Stupid people," Eddie said, smiling. And then he noticed the date of the interview. It was scheduled for Friday. Tomorrow. Eddie stopped smiling.

How was he supposed to read and memorise all that corporate bollocks and all the current buzzwords in one day? Adrenaline made his fingertips tingle. It wasn't adrenaline from the prospect of an interview, it was the adrenaline from knowing a crowd of people were about to bludgeon this pleasant morning to death, and he had to grab a job off the computer and run before they did.

Without even checking it thoroughly, he printed off a simple burglary scene up in Morley, snatched his van keys and radio, and bolted for the office door. If he was quick enough, he could avoid them by leaving the building via CID. He broke into daylight via their fire escape and slammed it closed behind him. "Perfect timing," he said, panting, and headed for his van.

He made it twenty-five yards.

"Eddie."

Eddie stopped, and continued to stare at his scuffed boots, reluctant to enter into a new thinking phase when he was still dealing with the old one.

"Eddie?"

He looked up, leaving behind the comfort of his boots, and there stood Peter McCain. "I'm early, Christ's sake. I'm nowhere near being late so you can't touch me."

"Come here."

Eddie checked his watch. "Shouldn't you still have your tongue up Chris Ashley's arse?"

"Please."

That was like a slap across the face. Police officers walked past them both, staring, and Eddie swallowed, definitely not wanting to enter this new phase. Peter was pale, his sickly smug-bastard smile was nowhere to be seen. Whatever was coming his way was life-changing. This wasn't Peter telling him that his van had been torched or the office windows had been put through again. The look in his eyes, the despair there, the overhanging brows all said you're not going to like this, and if I were you, I'd sit down and light up another cigarette in preparation.

"What is it?"

Peter swallowed, and seemed to shrivel away from it now that the time had come.

"Tell me."

He stepped forward, arms already outstretched, aiming for Eddie's shoulders. "It's Ros, mate."

Eddie died inside.

"Come over here and sit down."

"Just tell me before I rip your fucking head off!" Eddie's nostrils flared and he was sitting on a hot lungful of acidic breath that threatened to explode any second.

"She was driving up to her folks in Scotland Tuesday morning."

Eddie sat on a dwarf wall near the diesel pump. "She's dead, isn't she?"

Peter swallowed, tried to smile at officers walking past them.

"Did she die quickly?"

"What! Don't be a dick; she sent me a text last night to say she's not coming back." Now he did rest a hand on Eddie's shoulder as Eddie's vision blurred. "She specifically said you're not to try and contact her."

"Not coming back? What's that supposed to mean?"

Peter shrugged. "Dunno. I guess it means she's handed her notice in."

His boots were more scuffed than he realised. At one time he'd have kept them like a mirror – you could watch clouds floating by in them. Nowadays people didn't seem to care if your standards had dropped a bit, perhaps because their own had dropped too, or perhaps it was because no one wanted a mouthful of abuse from Eddie. He was going to polish them today, he decided; mirror shine, just like Ros's. "Specifically me? Why?"

"I know you were really close."

"Not close enough to warrant a goodbye, though, eh? No explanation. She's left her job and her home and... and me."

"Go home, Eddie. Spend a week with your family."

Tears hit the boots.

"Eddie?"

He didn't look up. "My family have left me. All I had was Ros."

It took several moments for Peter to reply, and he employed a tactic that Eddie had perfected and patented: avoidance. When that appeared a bit blunt, he tried man-tactic two: humour: "Are you noticing a bit of a theme?" There was a smile to accompany that little nugget, but it was like treating a cut finger by taking the arm off with a chainsaw. He cleared his throat. "Sorry, Eddie. Look, go home anyway, eh? I'll give you a bell in a week, see how you're doing."

"No."

Peter sighed. "Yes. Fuck off, Eddie. Let it sink in for a bit, get away from here."

"And do what? A week sitting at home next to a pile of empty Kleenex boxes – and not in a good way. Seriously, I'll go insane. I'm staying."

"You're not. I don't want you here, Eddie. You'll kill someone – possibly me. Go home. Watch Happy Valley or something. Final word." Peter patted him on the shoulder again, and it seemed to Eddie as though he was about to say, "There, there, there," as well, but couldn't quite muster that amount of sympathy. "Gimme your radio. And your—"

Eddie passed him the van keys and rubbed his temples only to feel the pain left by a baseball ball bat was still strong enough to make him wince.

Peter turned and walked towards the entrance and even managed to strike up a ditty that he whistled until the door closed behind him. He left Eddie sniffing diesel fumes.

Eddie didn't know what the hell to do. He climbed back into the Discovery, feeling the heat of the seats he'd vacated only minutes ago seeping into his back again. He lit another cigarette and dialled Ros's number. He got the familiar tone that told him the number didn't exist.

He'd heard that tone so fucking much over the last few days that he began to think this whole thing was getting mighty personal. How could so many people suddenly want nothing to do with him? How could so many people dislike him enough to summarily abandon him? What was wrong with him for people to feel so inclined? And then he remembered how bare Ros's house was the last he'd visited. "Decorating, my arse."

He swiped the sunglasses off the seat.

Chapter Twenty-one

A Circle of Shit

THE INTERVIEW HAD LASTED for an hour and twelve minutes. That was an hour and eleven minutes outside Eddie's comfort zone.

There had been two of them firing questions and scenarios at him: a Mr Jeffery Walker, the head of department, and a Mr Chris Ashley, the area forensic manager who bore Peter McCain's face impression on his arse cheeks. He knew them both and had almost no respect for them. They were pen-pushers, they were accountants who were as much removed from those at the sharp end as it was possible to get. They knew scene work inside out – but only anecdotally.

Sure, Jeffery Walker had done the job in the past, but he'd done it for the shortest possible time while keeping his eyes firmly focused on the end goal – head of department. Once he got out of uniform and into a suit, he seemed to forget all the troubles and strife surrounding the practical aspects of the job, and concentrated more on what computer was in vogue and how close his parking spot was to the building. He was dim but ruthless like that, nice but apathetic towards everyone around him, and especially towards those beneath him. He was the kind of man who polished his door plaque with the shirt off his minions' backs.

"Why do you want this job?"

This was one of the standard questions on any interview. It was a fucking ridiculous question because whatever answer the candidate gave, it would always sound patronising or trite:

"I want to better myself." Yes of course you do.

"I'm not doing it for the money." Bollocks!

Eddie's response was this: "I'm sick of wasting my time with volume crime when I could be put to much better use as a CSI on major crime, specifically murder. It's my thing, I'm good at it, and I enjoy it. I enjoy searching and I enjoy reasoning things out, working things out." He smiled with his eyes, "I love the challenge."

Jeffery Walker cleared his throat. "I hear your people skills are somewhat limited."

Didn't hinder your progress, you piece of fucking cardboard, eh? "You hear wrong." Eddie shrugged. "Anyway, who cares? The people I work for are mostly dead, and they don't seem to complain too much, do they? I work for them; I don't care whose toes I stand on or whose feelings I hurt – I work for them and their families. That's all that matters. If people don't like how blunt I am, that's their problem, not mine – my people skills are fine. Thank you for asking."

Later, people would advise Eddie that telling the truth in interviews is a very bad idea – especially when the truth is so… so truthful.

He knew there was a problem. He was sitting outside in the corridor – plush carpet, nice seats, paintings on the wall, that kind of thing. And he could hear raised voices from the interview room. Not a great sign.

Eventually the door opened, and Jeffery nodded him back in. "Please," he said, "sit down."

He did, and waited. They both had red faces and they both seemed reluctant to break the news. Eddie helped them out, "Am I wasting my time here? If you already have people lined up ready to go, then don't keep me here as filler, okay?"

"We don't work like that."

"Well, are you going to tell me, or is this like one of those tension-building pauses on The Chase before we find out if I've shit out or not?"

"On this occasion, Eddie, I'm afraid you have been unsuccessful in your application."

He thought about it for a moment and then stood. "Unsuccessful? I bought a fucking suit for this charade. That's a hundred quid you idiots owe me."

"Eddie," Jeffery warned.

"Shush. You've had your say, now sit back and enjoy the ride while I have mine." He slackened his tie, pulled it off and stuffed in his pocket, undid the top button. "People like you hurt this job; policing in general, I mean. You don't like me, you don't like how brusque I am, and that's fine. But if I got the job, you wouldn't be working with me, would you? No, you wouldn't. Your office is about twenty storeys above mine—"

"Actually—"

"Shush again. I'm still talking." He moved around the chair. "I am good at what I do – I'm one of those dedicated types who doesn't give in till he gets results. I was at a murder in Chapeltown once, and we were searching for a bullet. It had been fired at a female as she cowered in her bathroom. It had gone through her, gone through the floor and buried itself in the foundations. We needed that bullet.

"We searched for almost three hours. And when everyone else had got pissed off with it and left, I searched for another two hours. And I found it. And that bullet was matched to a weapon, and we got a good result.

"Now you're taking away jobs like that, the major jobs, leaving me with burglary sheds and theft from motor vehicles where my persistence isn't such a priority, and you're giving them to the people who might be very good in interviews, and they might give you super whizzo fucking answers to the pompous questions you dream up to throw at them… but how the hell does that little circle of shit you've created help the police investigation or help the victim or help their families? It doesn't. You're looking for someone who talks well, not someone who is a good examiner. Shame on you. I'll carry on with the volume crime, shall I?"

"Eddie, listen—"

"Piss off. Shove your job up your arse. I fucking hope this comes back to bite you on it because I will laugh my cock off. I hope you choose all those idiots who look great sitting in the office, chewing the shit about the status of being a CSI. They're the ones who shit themselves when the call goes out for someone who might have to work something out at a scene that'll take them way into overtime. You bought yourselves a sparkly shop front with no fucking stock."

Both men stared at Eddie as he opened the door.

Eddie turned back to them. "I bid you good day, gentlemen."

Eddie saw the fat dripping from Peter McCain's chin as soon as he walked through the doors at Killingbeck CSI office. In that one moment he hated Jeffery Walker and Chris Ashley for playing the game and giving the job or jobs to brown-tongued status-loving pricks.

McCain swallowed, licked at his shining lips and squinted at Eddie.

Eddie said nothing, just sat at his desk and hit the computer until it woke up. He logged in, listened to McCain's chair sigh as his colossal weight lifted from it. Within moments the smell of fried chicken announced McCain's presence at Eddie's side, that and his heavy breathing. Eddie looked up, focused on the grease shining in the crease of his chin. "Isn't your heart attack overdue?"

"Didn't get it, did you?"

Eddie logged in to the systems.

McCain laughed, and slapped Eddie on the back. "You're fucking useless. I knew you'd go for that job because you're so full of yourself and because the thought of normality scares the shit out of you. I should have known you wouldn't make it through the interview because your tongue is fastened to your stupid brain and your stupid brain is rude and arrogant!" He sighed and looked with disgust down at Eddie.

"Yesterday I gave you a week off to cool down, and yet here you are, back in my side like a bloody thorn. I'd hoped to have a week without you, just to see what it was like, just to dream of not having to worry what kind of mood you were in, just to relax knowing you couldn't bother me.

"I knew you'd applied, see? I even put in a good word for you – they must really dislike you if they turned you away after I portrayed you as a superman of the scene examination world. Wanker.

"I wanted you gone from here – I don't fucking like you, Collins. You're selfish, you don't fit in... and, did I tell you I didn't fucking like you? No one fucking likes you, actually. You're spiky, difficult to work with, and I wanted you out, but it's actually more fun seeing you here as the failure you are." He paused, grinning. "You're a piece of shit, Collins. You wouldn't have made it there anyway. Too tough for you, mentally I mean. You're better off here where you can relax, cruise through the day unchallenged..."

He leaned in, "Where you can roll along with a skinful and no one will bat an eye, eh?"

Eddie squeezed the mouse. A previous crack opened up, the tape holding it together split. "Where has this idea that I'm a piss-head come from?"

McCain, smile still on his greasy lips, stared at Eddie, and said, "Erm, that would be from you being pissed I suppose. Twice!"

Eddie punched the keyboard and letters danced across the desk, scattered onto the floor. McCain waddled back to his desk, laughing.

"I hate you, Collins." He tutted. "You're a waste of space. You know, if you had to apply for your own job again, there's no way you'd get it. You're a fucking liability, and you're selfish." He sat down, still muttering. "Waste of a salary, too. Certainly not worth your fucking salary."

"I'm not worth my salary? You fat turd. You could teach a monkey to do your job, but you need intuition to do mine. Now who's worth their salary?"

Chapter Twenty-two

Hopping Mad

It was like driving up to a Gothic country house, complete with threatening grey skies, something right out of the Rocky Horror Picture Show. It wouldn't have surprised PC Fiona Wright if she opened her window and heard The Time Warp playing as background music.

The only real difference – this was Leeds; Mabgate to be precise, and there was no elegant driveway to go with the Gothic house, no black wrought iron gates. There were cobbled roads, and weeds you could hide a decent-sized kid in. There was graffiti and there was rubbish blowing up and down what was left of the streets. And yet there was noise: traffic noise from the overpass a few hundred yards away. Leeds, like New York, never slept.

The house, Coulston House, seemed to loom over her as she slowly approached and parked twenty yards away. It seemed almost rude to park right outside the garden gate – an invasion of personal space.

The radio on the dashboard boomed and the same voice crackled in her earpiece. She took out a folder with a slim sheaf of papers inside – names, addresses, warning markers, that kind of thing. "What the hell was his name?" She searched through her tac vest pockets for the piece of paper she'd scribbled it down on last night. "Norton Bailey."

Lightning overexposed everything for a split second and it took a moment for her eyes to adjust to his profile picture printed in a 2" x 3" format black and white image next to a red box labelled Warning Markers. "Fuuuuck," she whispered. There was a long list, and though most of them seemed historic, it didn't make for easy reading. "Especially when you're on your own, Fiona, and there's a storm coming; it's raining, thunder and lightning, a creepy old man in a creepy old house on a creepy old road." Her fingers tapped against the steering wheel, and she thought of abandoning what was just a public relations exercise.

"He's the only one outstanding, that's all. No one's asking you to go down on him, Fiona. Why must you always turn the conversation to filth? Filthy Fiona." And then she was laughing again.

Ten minutes, five if you're quick, she said to herself, and then she could resume patrol – and choose somewhere less intimidating.

She stood at the gate, almost unaware of the spits of rain falling in her hair, coating it like tiny diamonds in the dimming light. Suddenly this didn't seem like such a fantastic idea any more. She looked back at the car, and thought of the tick – another tick to add to her collection; another job finished.

The walk up his garden path set her teeth on edge as she crunched snails and oozed slugs beneath her boots. She cringed. The flagstones were slick and green with freshly wetted moss.

All this was going through her mind, focusing on the big front door at the top of the steps, when her attention was dragged to the basement window to her right set in the bay of the lounge window above. Big windows with net curtains that were grey at the top but almost black with muck at the bottom.

The cellar must be quite substantial, she concluded, if the ground floor was another six feet above ground level. These old Victorian houses were massive inside and then she stopped thinking altogether – the basement window was ajar slightly. Had it been forced open? Had there been a burglary?

Norton hopped from one foot to the other, chewing at his bottom lip, peering at her from the lounge bay as she decided whether to walk up his garden path or not. She was a strange lass.

"Why the hell can't you just leave me alone? Coppers have never been interested in me before, so why start now?" A rush of coldness spiked inside his gut – she was staring at the cellar window. Norton rushed through the lounge along the hall and pulled open the front door. He shouted, "Hello!"

Fiona almost snapped her neck as she looked from the cellar window up to an old man standing at the top of his stone steps like a character from an amateur dramatic performance of Hamlet. In the second before she smiled and replied to him, she looked him over, at his clothes, his demeanour, his expression. From researching him a little before she left the office, it was obvious Mr Bailey suffered some form of mental illness, but she couldn't help wondering if there was a special shop that people with his mental illness shopped at: Nutters R Us, for example? His scruffy, tatty, trousers were three inches too short, and surely you didn't need mental prowess to know it, so why did he wear them? Maybe the play wasn't Hamlet after all, maybe it was Tom Sawyer.

He wore orange string – could have been baler twine – as a belt. To supplement the belt, he wore braces with the union flag all up and down them – dirty too, like they'd never been washed since they were bought for the 1966 world cup.

His green cardigan that had more holes than wool, and the braids in his beard marked him as... different. So did he know he was different? Why choose to stick a label on yourself if you didn't have to? When she got up a little closer, she could see that his beard had breakfast cereal in it and perhaps raisins – and not necessarily from this week – and the hat he wore was something an outback Aussie might tie corks to.

All of this was weird, including the frizzy grey hair, but perhaps the most weird was his constant hopping from one foot to the other; it was a placard: Hey, I'm a Fucking Nutjob! She tried smiling to herself but felt guilty. It's a 'stim', she thought – a stimulation that some mental disorder sufferers had as a coping mechanism.

He reminded her of sixties folk band, Jethro Tull, as she said, "Hello, Mr Bailey. How are you feeling today?"

He hopped; his face twitched. "Why are you here?"

Offering her most reassuring smile, she said, "It's nothing to worry about." She stepped closer, one foot on the bottom step. "We've been conducting house-to-house enquiries about an incident that happened a week last Wednesday—"

"A week last bloody Wednesday!"

More smiling. "We've tried repeatedly to contact you, just to tick you off our sheet as spoken to, that's all. But you've never answered the door when we've called 'round."

"Don't bother yourself. I know nothing about—"

"It's no bother." Fiona took the first couple of steps, keeping the revulsion from her face as she crushed more snails underfoot.

"Not for you, maybe, but it is for me."

"Oh. Did you have something planned?"

He shuffled, mumbled and then laughed. It wasn't a happy laugh. "Better come in," he said and turned away from her.

The hair at the back of his head looked like a block of shit. It was matted, clumped, dark brown and solid. And then she realised it was probably blood a long time ago. She imagined a nest of fly eggs in it. That thought made her a little bit sick in her mouth.

"Parlour. First right," he said, holding his back and grimacing.

She followed him along a dimly lit hallway, just the wedge of light from what she assumed was the lounge door off to their right, and when he opened it, the light fell against the paintings leaning against the hall wall to her left. There must have been half a dozen, all in all, each leaning against the other like giant dominos; some of them were taller than Norton himself. She stopped and waited until his shadow was out of the way and the topmost painting illuminated. "Wow," she said, "you paint?"

He turned in the doorway, sniffled and said, "A little, yes."

"A little? This one must be six feet tall."

"When I have to paint, miss, I have to paint."

"Does it help you?"

He twitched. "Help me?"

"You know," she said, "does it help you to relax?"

"I find it soothing, yes. And it helps with introspection. That is the subject matter of most of my works."

"Would you think me rude if I asked what it was?"

He stuck out his chest, chin up. "I would think you rude if you didn't." He pointed to the picture. "It's an abstract about love and loss. You can see the yin and the yang, the divide, between the loved and the loveless."

"Interesting," she said, not appreciating the subject matter and not really caring too much. She edged into the parlour, cursing because this job – this simple ten-minute house-to-house job – was turning into something more sinister. Bleak.

The parlour was dark; the walls covered with more artwork from chest height to the ceiling, with barely a few inches between their frames, dust gathering on the tops of them, and in the angles between frame and canvas, like painted-on snowdrifts in a thousand lounge windows at Christmas time. More dust, an inch thick, lay in the corners of the room, half an inch thick where traffic was infrequent and barely noticeable along a thin walkway from the door to the armchair by the old television set. It was like a cattle trail across a field. Also, the mantelpiece was clean – it stood out because it almost had a shine where the rest of the room didn't even reach dull. In the centre of the room was a rag rug, and it was big enough to fill her entire lounge. But here, it was merely a quarter the size of the parlour, occupying only the centre of the room.

Dangling precariously from the centre of the ceiling was a gas lamp with three dusty glass shades. The brass pull chains and the pilot light pipes had dulled and turned green. Wound around one of the gas supply pipes was an electrical cable that had given birth to a naked bulb. It looked like a teardrop; and yet it looked like electric light had strangled the old gas lamps to death, out with the ornate and in with utilitarian.

The black cobwebs that hung from the corners of the room like drapes, gently swayed in a breeze like a flag – the Jolly Roger, perhaps – but were not the worst thing to catch her eye; the rat droppings by the side of the armchair took the number one spot, closely followed by the stains in the crotch region of the armchair itself, and her stomach turned again. This was the kind of job you'd put a small dab of Vicks under your nose for. Pity she hadn't.

"You going to sit?"

She glanced again at the stains. "You sit, I'm fine. Thank you. We'll have a quick chat, Mr Bailey, and then I'll be out of your way, okay?"

"Back's not so good; I'll stand here." He stood in the doorway, a reluctance seemingly pulling him back to the painting and the explanation of it left unfinished. "I should ask if you'd like a drink."

His fingertips tapped his thumbs, getting faster and faster, and his feet hovered over the floor as he hopped from one to the other. His face was pale.

And I would decline. "Sit down, Mr Bailey. Please."

From upstairs came a noise, like a thud, but followed by a dragging kind of noise. If it were visual, that sound would have been a rat with a fat body and long tail. Fiona swallowed, and her stare swept down from the ceiling. "Is there someone upstairs?"

"God, you mean?" he smiled. "Can we get on with it?"

Fiona looked pensive, and said, "Last Wednesday a young man died not two hundred yards from here, just by the side of Regent Street."

His face was expressionless.

"About eight o'clock in the evening."

No reaction.

"Do you know anything about it, Mr Norton?"

"No," he said, and folded his arms.

"Did you hear anything unusual? Screaming, perhaps; shouting, that kind of thing?"

"No." Norton's hand reached across to the button.

Chapter Twenty-three

A Crying Shame

Norton ran a tongue over his rough lips, licking the edge of his moustache as he eyed the police officer. She was pleasant enough, just on the far side of middle-aged, he guessed, but they tended towards the pleasant ones, didn't they? No use sending out a horrible copper if they wanted to trap you, eh? No, they'd send out the grandmotherly kind. Like her.

He had her sussed.

It would be a shame if he had to do her in; a crying shame. She was a copper, supposedly one of the good guys... but he couldn't risk her discovering his secret. His hand slipped away from the button as another question gave rise to more eye contact. He swallowed and answered, but his mind was elsewhere – wondering how difficult it would be to stay out of any missing person enquiry should she not make it back to the station. How long would it take them to realise she'd been here before she went off the radar.

"Mr Bailey?"

"What?"

"Where are you going? We haven't finished the form yet."

"You might not want a drink, but I do." He left the parlour for the kitchen, and put the kettle on. While he waited for it to boil, he wiped out a dainty china cup with a cloth he found on the floor, and rested against the worktop, stroking his beard, thinking.

The kettle boiled and clicked off. He stared at it and woke up from a trance that was almost all-consuming, like waking from sleep. He blinked, and remembered why he was here.

As he carried the tea through into the parlour on a tray, teapot lid and china cup tinkling together as he went, he realised that she probably knew more than she was letting on. If this was just part of a house-to-house enquiry, she'd have asked if he'd seen anything that night, and just leave. Surely. Wouldn't she? Isn't that what they did?

He didn't know, but this visit seemed rather too intense for his liking. She had an ulterior motive; he was sure of it. The question was, what to do about it?

He paused by the painting, mouthing that it would be stupid of him to let her live. He could dump her body with the others, wait till it was properly dark and drive her car away somewhere and burn it. They'd never find her. Oh, they might visit him to ask questions, if he was on her job list – or whatever she kept as an appointment diary – but it would be a formality, that's all.

Did she call here? Yes, officer, she was very pleasant.

How long did she stay? Oh, twenty minutes. We were having a good old natter.

And... and she left okay? Didn't seem agitated? She left just fine, all smiles and handshakes.

Thank you for your time. You are most welcome.

Sounded good to Norton. After all, who'd suspect... wait, there were voices coming from the parlour.

He discovered she was on the phone to someone. When she saw him enter, she raised her hand – a kind of half apology, half wait your turn gesture. She'd already mentioned to whomever she was conversing with, that she was here. But wait, hold on.

"Just emailing my report through now, and then I'll be leaving. I'll grab a meal and then go on to the next one. Okay?"

Hmph, so after she was dead and lodged as missing, they'd definitely call here. "But that's alright," he whispered, "so long as they don't look too hard." I could distract her, use the bayonet if need be.

"So long as who doesn't look too hard?"

Norton gasped. She wasn't on the phone any longer, and she was staring at him, the concern on her face renewed. The button was just to his left. He licked his lips.

She put her pen away into a pouch on her hi-viz vest, and stepped forward. "Well, I'd like to thank you for your time, Mr Bailey. You've been very helpful."

Norton nodded, his hand slowly retracting from the button.

"Just one more thing, if I may."

He looked up at her, teeth bared.

"I notice the cellar window is open a bit. I can see marks on the frame, looks like it's been forced open. Have you been burgled?"

"What? No, no, it's always like that. Kids messing about. Nothing to worry about."

"Are you sure? I've requested CSI—"

"I'm positive. Now close the door on your way out."

"Mr—"

"Now. Before I..."

"Before what, Mr Bailey?"

Chapter Twenty-four

The Beginning of the Argument

IT HAD BEEN THREE days since he closed the car door and stood frozen to the spot as Ziggy drove away in a cloud of turbocharged smoke. The cloud, though, it turned out, was in Sean's head, and it still hadn't cleared. It was Sean's dream to be a part of the crew; the coppers called them an OCG – Organised Crime Group. He was in an organised crime group! He was practically mafia – practically a made man, untouchable. That status made him proud and angry all at the same time – it made him want to beat people up just because he could, just because he could and nobody would touch him for it. All he had to do was mention Ziggy's name, and anyone in the know would back off and run away with his tail between his legs.

Sean smiled.

Power.

That status made him want to shoot people. He had the power of a genie – of life and death. That was real power. But he'd been lying to himself about wanting to shoot people – he didn't want to do that. He sighed and lit a roll-up. Actually he did want to shoot people with it, but he just didn't want to shoot Chantelle with it.

He always remembered watching some movie or other where the guy said, 'Your mother would be proud of you'. Sean smiled again because yes, she would be very proud of him, to have actually become someone. "I just scored three-grand for doing nothing. Dad never managed anything like that. Neither did Mick, and he was older than me by two years."

But paying the price for being of such high status was the hardest thing he'd ever had to bear. Chantelle was everything to him; shit, she was the mother of his kid – and someone else's, granted, but still... And she was a good lass, he liked her. A lot. She was a good cook, mostly, and she was great in the sack, when she didn't have a migraine or a yeast infection. He could never understand what the hell bread had to do with her pussy, but still...

He swallowed and eventually sent his legs an instruction to walk before he got done for prostitution. He had no idea where he was walking to, just as he had no idea how he could kill Chantelle, or where he could kill her. If he could kill her. Those three days out with his mates, out on the town, and out of his mind, hadn't yielded any course of action at all. This would be one of those ad hoc moments in life you hear so much about; one of those unplanned events that turn out alright in the end.

She'd been seen talking to the law, Ziggy had said. A DS Benson. If the info had been that specific, he thought, then it must be true. Why had she spoken to them? Why? Silly bitch – it was like signing your own death warrant, man; well, she had signed hers, hadn't she? And she'd made life hard for him, now he had to go and kill her. Selfish bitch!

Of course, he began thinking of ways to escape this situation: put her on a train to Scotland and tell Ziggy the deed was done. He could even bail out with her and go on the run together, though it would mean looking over their shoulders all the time, and giving up his newfound and hard-earned status, something he'd rather not do.

Nor did he want to take on Ziggy head to head. The remains of his little finger – the stump, he called it, still hurt after all these years. Each time he saw it, he thought of Ziggy – Ziggy had smashed it with a hammer when they were fifteen or so – bitter enemies back then. That was the first and last time Sean played brave in Ziggy's face. Ziggy was always, always, prepared to go one step further than his opposition.

Surely, though, there was no need to kill his woman. Couldn't they come to some arrangement? Maybe slash her face, break an arm, something to teach her a lesson. Tut.

And say he did kill her, who the hell was gonna look after the kids? "Maybe Ziggy could get me a maid." Or maybe he could palm them off onto Social Services; yeah, he could do that, no problem.

He was not surprised to find that his autopilot legs had propelled him home. He felt the lump of metal in his hoodie pocket; a sharp bulge banging into his hip. Still, man, the power. There was another bulge too, slightly smaller, no sharp edges. It was the three-grand of course – now reduced to two grand – but even that didn't give him the same kind of buzz.

The three-day-old question nagged at him again. Where was he going to do it?

"Shut up," he said. "I ain't thought of nothing yet: where, when, or how." He closed the door behind him, and heard the kids playing in the lounge. He went in, saw that Chantelle was not there and wandered into the kitchen. She was wiping up after making the kids some lunch – spaghetti hoops on toast. In the background, the washing machine droned on. There were clothes draped across radiators and clothes horses. She'd been busy doing all the things Sean would have to do if he killed her. He bit his bottom lip. Nah, ditch the kids and get a new woman.

"If you want anything to eat, you can make yourself a ham sandwich. It's all there is." Chantelle stopped her fussing and her wiping up. "What's up?"

"Huh?"

"You look like you've seen a ghost. What's up?"

"Nowt. I'm okay."

She went to touch his face, and he swiped her hand away and the gun tumbled out of his pocket and hit the floor tiles with a solid thunk.

Both stared at it.

Everything paused while they both observed the gun.

"Sean? What the fuck—"

"It's nothing, girl. Don't get your knickers in a twist, man."

"It's a fucking gun!"

"I know it's a fucking gun."

"What are you doing with a fucking gun?"

"Listen, woman, I'm on the up, alright. Your man has been promoted. And because of that promotion, I have to protect myself."

Chantelle, despite the gun on her kitchen floor, laughed. "Seriously. They 'promoted' you? Most promotions come with a better car and a wage rise. Your lot give you a bastard gun? Kind of business they into, Sean?"

"You know."

"Yeah, I know, alright. And I know you shouldn't be walking around with a gun in your pocket. You are so fucking thick."

"Watch your mouth, bitch."

She snarled, her eyes reduced to slits, and she edged forward. "What did you call me?"

Sean backed off; hands outstretched. "I am the man of the house, Chantelle, and you'll do as I fucking say."

"Otherwise you'll get someone to beat me up again? Fucking coward." She slapped him hard across the face and by the time he looked at her again, his cheek was glowing like a three-bar fire.

"You fucking hit me?" He shouted, "You fucking hit me!" He shoved her aside and retrieved the gun, pointed it at her with a wildly shaking hand. Chantelle screamed and raised her hands to her face, tears spilling from her eyes.

"You been blabbing to the law."

"What, I never—"

"You were seen. DS Benfield."

"Benson, you prick!"

"Benson, then. You were caught. And they sent me to top you."

Chantelle stared, slack-jawed, seemingly unable to believe him. When his expression didn't change, she screwed up her face and bawled. Backing into a corner, she wiped her eyes, blew her nose into a piece of kitchen towel, and took a brave pace forward, stood staring at Sean with her hands on her hips. "Yes, I spoke to him. I got you off the old man's burglary charge."

Sean's head jerked like a pigeon's. "And you gave them what info to secure my freedom?"

She swallowed again, licked her lips and smiled as one of the kids entered the kitchen. Sean brought the gun close enough to his chest for it to be concealed. She plied Betty with biscuits and sent her back into the lounge to watch more TV. "He told me that there was people missing. They was presumed dead. And they had credit cards and ID and stuff. And—"

"And you told him where I got them from?"

"No, no I never, Sean. I promise I didn't. I told him I'd tell him if I ever found out, that's all. You have to believe me, honey, I wouldn't never sell you out to protect you."

Sean looked confused by that.

"I mean I'd never stab you in the back." She looked at the gun, held sideways in true gangster style. "And I'd never shoot you, neither."

"Yeah, well..."

"You and me, Sean, we was meant for each other. You know that. No need for any of this nonsense."

"They promoted me, Chantelle. I'm on the ladder. I deserve more than this, girl."

She closed her eyes, held them like that until she could think of some way of making him see the shit he was in. "You know when you're smashed and you start telling me you love me and all? How good things seem when you're out of it, and the next day when it's pissing it down and we ain't got no money for fags or gear and you have to go on the rob? It's a state of mind, Sean. It's something you choose to believe, that's all."

"You're making no fucking sense at all. Not even a bit."

"You choose to believe them. They're full of shit. They gave you a gun and they told you to knock off your old lady. And they dressed it up by saying you was promoted." There was a slight smile but she tried to hide it; panic made that easy to do. "And you believed them. As soon as you bump me off, they'll kick you to the kerb, or they'll give you someone else to slot. It'll never end, Sean, and one day you'll get caught and they'll bang you up as a serial killer or whatever. And for what?"

He thought it through, and the words 'serial killer' held a certain appeal. "I really have been promoted. They want more cards from me. I'm going to have to widen my net, Chantelle. I'm going to have to get more suppliers."

"And sell more coke."

"So what? It pays well. And we ain't never been skint since I've been dealing for 'em, have we? See, they're a good lot, put food on my table. I provide for my family, Chantelle."

"Until they tell you to kill your family."

He looked at her, and his eyes seemed hurt by her.

"Truth smacked you in the chops, Sean?"

"Shut it."

"Or what? You going to kill me? Eh? In the fucking kitchen, with the kids in the next room? Are you? Big hard man, Sean?"

"Mummy?"

Chantelle gasped. Sean tried to hide the gun again, and said, "Get back in the lounge. Now."

The smaller of their two girls, Abby, ran back into the lounge, her sagging nappy almost sliding down her dirty bare legs, bottom lip hanging out as she prepared to cry.

Chantelle was weeping when he turned back to face her.

Chapter Twenty-five

A Closed Throat

On his own doorstep, Bailey shouted at the officer, "Just go!"

"I'm going, Mr Bailey. There's no need to be so hostile."

"Hostile?" Norton's face was glowing red and his anger at being used by the local constabulary like this was a disgrace. "I have given you my time, and my hospitality, Miss. And you have sought to ridicule me over the phone to your colleagues, and you have been condescending towards me."

"I haven't—"

"I would like the contact information for your supervisor." He spat the last word out along with a mouthful of hot fury.

The copper stood halfway down the steps, and you could see from her face that she was more than a little shocked by his outburst.

He didn't care.

"Mr Bailey," she smiled, came back up a step or two, "I'm terribly sorry if I've somehow offended you."

"How on earth can you be terribly sorry if you have no idea what you're apologising for? That is a misnomer, my dear."

"Well," she said, a nervous laugh in her reply. "Forgive me for inadvertently offending you."

Norton clutched onto the door frame, chewing his bottom lip, heat still like a mini volcano in his chest. And he had to keep it there and he had to keep it hot. He needed this anger.

A curious smile swished onto her face, and she looked at him through squinting eyes. "Are you alright, Mr Bailey."

"No," he gasped. "No, I'm not."

"You don't look well." The curious smile gave way to concern, and Fiona ran back up the steps as quickly as the moss allowed. "What's wrong, Mr Bailey?"

"Throat," he croaked. "I need water."

"Is it your heart? Have you experienced this before?"

"Not my heart." He put his hands to his neck, and strained like he would if he were constipated, turning his face red, grimacing at the pain.

"Come sit down in the hall. I'll get you some water." She guided him in, dropped her paperwork on the floor inside the front door and then ushered him to the old telephone table and seated him next to it. "There, I'll get some water. Back in a sec." And she was off quickly along the hallway.

Norton paid no attention to her grunts of disgust as she sought a glass or a cup in the kitchen. Instead, he stood and removed the baler twine belt from his trousers. He quickly sat before she returned. And he waited.

Chapter Twenty-six

The End of the Argument

AND WHEN HE DID face her, Chantelle thrust the knife up under his ribcage, seeking his heart. She reckoned she only had one chance. If she only wounded him, he'd be furious and he'd shoot her just for the hell of it. She aimed well and though she put energy into the thrust, she was almost scared to push too hard for fear of hurting him – stupid, of course, because that was the whole point. But it made sense to her at the time, and then nothing made sense any more.

Abby was back in the kitchen, almost as though she'd never gone away. This time her nappy was around her ankles and she was screaming and Chantelle was trying to shush her and trying to reassure her even as Sean fired a single round in her direction as he slumped to the floor.

That one round entered her throat and followed the path of least resistance up through the soft palate and into her brain. She died instantly and the last thing she saw was Abby with her hands to her face, screaming.

From his kneeling position on the tiled floor, Sean saw it all in slow motion as the bullet took off the top of her skull and sent a thin shower of blood up onto the ceiling where it dripped back down on top of them both. Chantelle just dropped straight down like a carcass cut from a hook, and Sean moved aside just in time.

The pain in his ribs was enormous, white, jagged, sharp like a needle and cold as a dry ice infusion. He looked down and saw she'd pushed the blade under his skin but it glanced across the outer surface of his ribs until it had cut the skin, and the angle changed, and the blade went between two ribs. But how deeply? He coughed, expecting to see foamy blood bloom across the wall. No blood. It ran freely between his fingers, but it wasn't exactly a gush.

He looked down at her, and across at the gun. His mouth began watering and for a moment he thought he was going to hurl; Abby screamed in the background and then he screamed in the foreground. The nausea passed. Sean just wanted to cover his ears. The whole scene was pandemonium. He grabbed a tea towel, and took off his hoodie and t-shirt. He tossed aside the t-shirt and held the tea towel in place while he pulled on a clean t-shirt from the radiator by the back wall.

"Daddy."

Betty came in the kitchen too and she ran straight to her mummy, and lay across her, screaming into her face as though hoping she'd wake up and soothe her.

Abby screamed from the doorway, frozen to the spot, face wet, eyes puddles of grief, heartbroken.

Sean put on his hoodie and dropped the gun into a pocket. He looked at her one last time, and looked at the kids too, wondered what he could say to them. In the end he said nothing – what could explain it?

He left them to it.

As he reached the front door, he reconsidered. There really was no point in leaving this carnage as it now stood, was there? As soon as her body was discovered, the girls, certainly Betty, would tell the police who was responsible. Couldn't have that. Sean went back inside and closed the door behind him.

The screaming hadn't stopped, but it had reached the cacophony associated with someone running out of breath – it was a wail that died off and returned after about ten seconds, the scream of the exhausted. The whine of the baffled. "Abby, come here." Sean felt for the gun in his jacket pocket. He went into the kitchen where Betty still had her face buried in the bloody pit of her mother's neck. "Betty," he said. No reply. He went to her, tugged her arm. "Come with me, girl." He pulled Betty away, dragged her into the lounge. The girl's face was covered in her mother's blood, and her eyes were bloodshot from all the screaming, and she sobbed, hitching hot breath. She rolled fingertips against her thumbs, watching the blood leach into the creases of her flesh. Her hands trembled and her whole body shook as she sat on the sofa next to her sister.

"Girls," Sean smiled at them as behind him a new episode of SpongeBob burst into life. "I got a surprise for you both."

By now the front of his clean t-shirt was shiny and red with blood. It was leaking down his legs too until it looked like someone had thrown a tin of red gloss paint over him as a prank. His pale face, however, said it was no prank. Sean was becoming scared at the amount of blood he was losing, and a cooling wave of light-headedness almost made him fall, but he held onto a nearby car and gathered what few wits he had left.

From his pocket he took out his mobile phone, wiped the screen across a clean part of his jacket and dialled Ziggy.

"Yo, Sean, ma man."

"I need help," Sean whimpered. "I killed her, just like you said."

"Whoa, man, whoa, stop talking."

"But I need—"

"I said fucking stop. Meet me at our woods in Temple Newsam. Twenty minutes."

"Ziggy, I need..." But, almost predictably, the line was empty – a little bit like Sean's brain, he thought. "What the fuck have I done?" He walked on, aiming towards a meeting with the only person who could put things right.

And he needed fixing up; but they'll have doctors on the payroll, get me fixed up quick.

He reached the spot, and managed to sit on the bench a full five minutes before the meeting time. Sean lit a cigarette and coughed so much it hurt. He threw the stub to the ground and saw red fingerprints on the white cigarette paper. And he didn't care.

Ziggy approached quietly from behind. "You got the gun, Sean?"

Sean jumped. "Fuck, man, scared the shit out of me." And then he smiled. "I did it. Just like you asked. I take my role very seriously, and this proves my loyalty to you and the group. Right?"

"Gun, Sean. Here, drop it into this bag, man."

"Right, Ziggy? It shows my loyalty, right? You'll look after me now, won't you?"

"Drop the fucking gun, Sean. Of course we'll take care of you – what do you think we are?"

Sean relaxed, safe in the knowledge that his new organisation would carry him through this troubled spot. "I'm an asset, Ziggy," he said, dropping the gun into a Sainsbury's bag.

"Where did you do it? You buried her properly, yeah?"

Sean's eyes widened. "Buried her?"

"Yeah. You took her to some woodland, right? Or you disposed of her in a lake."

"Erm."

"Sean, tell me you did it properly. We don't need no police involvement, man."

"It got a bit heated." There was a red puddle in his lap. "She stabbed me."

"Too bad, put a fucking bandage on it. Now, where did you shoot her?"

"Through the head. Man, there was fucking blood—"

"Not where on her body!" Ziggy growled and came in close to Sean's right ear. "Tell me where you shot her."

"In the kitchen."

"The what? The kitchen? You shot her in the fucking kitchen."

"She was asking for it. Listen, Ziggy; I'm going to need patching up. You got a doctor who can stop me bleeding?"

"No."

"A vet, then?"

"A vet? What, you a fucking dog, now?"

"That's what they use in the movies when they don't have a doc, you know. A vet?"

"No. No vet."

"Then what do you do when—"

"Shut up. You a first-rate prick, Sean; you don't do something like that so close to home, man." Ziggy paused. "And where were your kids?"

"When I shot her?"

"Yes, when you fucking shot her!"

"They were there."

There was silence from Ziggy for a minute or even two. So much so that Sean began to think he'd run away.

"Ziggy?"

"Give me your phone, a minute, Sean, would you?"

"Sure. But why?" Sean took out his phone and handed it over.

"Just, drop it in the bag along with the gun there."

He did. "Why do you need my phone? You going to get me a replacement? I always fancied an iPhone, y'know."

"I want it because then all ties with you are cut."

The ever-present smile on Sean's face twitched and fell off. "I don't get it. I thought we were a team, you and me. I thought I was part of the gang."

"You're a fucking liability is what you are."

"But you told me to kill her, so I killed her. What's the big deal? I proved my loyalty."

"You proved what a fucking idiot you are. You were good with credit cards, but that's about all, yeah. You stick to them and to burgling, yeah. Stay the fuck away from me. And if we see you anywhere near the law, I'll take you out myself, okay?" And then Ziggy was gone.

Sean tried to turn but wasn't fast enough to see Ziggy disappear. "What? You can't do this to me. I'll get you, Ziggy. I'll fucking get you for this!"

Chapter Twenty-seven

Eyes Half Open

Norton didn't want to put the fear of God into her because then she'd shout up for an ambulance right away. It had to be something of concern without being something that needed urgent medical attention, and the closing throat – probably brought on by anxiety, she'd think – was the perfect ruse.

Norton was sitting in the telephone chair with his elbows on his knees, hunched over and when she approached with the glass and leaned over, he thrust himself and the glass up into her face. The shock and the pain made her scream and Norton grinned because he knew he had her. The glass shattered and water splashed, and he hit her in the face as hard as he could.

She went over backwards and hit the floor hard, blood already gushing from some quite nasty injury to her mouth that framed her remaining teeth red, and Norton was on her like a rabid lover, the baler twine around her throat.

Fiona put up a good struggle to survive, but it was nothing compared to the effort that Norton put into killing her. When she died, he fell off her panting, pulling at the cramp in his arms and the mess of his fingers caused by the twine digging in. He was exhausted and thought how well he'd sleep tonight because of that exertion.

She was a pretty lass – 'was' being the operative word. Bubbles popped between her partly open lips, and her eyes, still half open, looked dreadfully sad. For a moment he felt a little sorry for her, but it quickly passed. As he leaned back against the wall, trying to bring his heart rate back under control, he noticed something terrifying. He noticed the pulse in her neck.

Chapter Twenty-eight

An Innocent Corpse

Wentworth Avenue, Halton Moor. It was almost nine o'clock on Saturday evening. With this being England, it was raining – not heavily, but enough to have people grumbling. One of those grumblers was CSI Eddie Collins. He sat in his van wondering why he was even here. It was a murder, they said, and he had only two hours of his shift left to go; he could have passed it onto the night-shift CSI, or even just let someone else in the office put their fucking hand up for a change.

What did it matter?

He had no one to go home for anyway – not that having a wife and daughter was reason to ever go home in the past, eh, Eddie?

Eddie sighed and took another drag on his cigarette, wishing the guilt train would find another fucking station for a change. Couple of days ago, Eddie had arrived at work, been told that Ros had set sail – or was that abandoned ship? It was one of those analogies, couldn't remember which one, and so he was left with no one at all in his life. Not even Watson the fucking dog.

So no, he had no reason to go home; might as well be the only one with his hand in the air when the request came in.

Peter shook his head. "Absolutely not. Go home and watch Friends."

"Fuck off," Eddie had said. "You need someone at that scene."

"I need you to take a break from this."

"No, what I need is a break from life, mate. This shit I can handle; it's life that's a fucking mystery to me. I have no idea what the hell I'm doing outside of this shitty little world, so don't send me into it when I'm suffering as it is."

Peter slid his chair across to Eddie's, came in real close so that Eddie could see the pieces of chicken stuck between his teeth as he said, "I appreciate the offer, but... And I hate to sound blunt when you're so fragile, but I don't really—"

"Spit it out."

"I would rather come round to your house and find you dangling from the banister rail, than have you go ballistic at a scene and maybe take it out on me, or on a copper, or an innocent member of the public. Do you see what I mean? You shouldn't have come back, Eddie. I told you to fuck off on Thursday and take a week, so what on God's green earth you think you're doing here is beyond me."

"I've been here six hours. You kept this to yourself for six whole hours?"

"You came in with your fists clenched. Now, I'm not especially scared of you – your eyes frighten me a bit, I'll give you that – you're kind of mad, really – but with the stress of Ros and your missus doing one, I thought it better to let you lie, to let you catch up with emails and statement requests, yeah?

"But going out to a murder?" He pulled back, head shaking like a plumber giving a quote. "Not going to happen."

Eddie cut the gap between them back to breathing space only. "Look around you, oh wise one. How many volunteers do you have, exactly?"

Peter looked at his staff. Eight heads down, not one pair of eyes looking at him. He swallowed, turned back to Eddie, and gave it some thought. "If you fuck this up. If you go ballistic and hurt someone or kill yourself... I will..." He cleared his throat, pointed a finger, "Just... I mean it, be..."

"I will," Eddie said. "You can count on it."

"Do I make myself clear?"

"Crystal, mate."

And here he was sitting in his van listening to the rain on the roof and wondering if he should mention to the SIO that he was here a week ago having a bit of a punch-up with the occupants. If there was any of his blood in the scene... It would look bad. "If it was found," he whispered. He could check out the scene first, and determine if there was any likelihood of his own blood being found there. "Yeah, do that," he said and opened the door, grumbling about the rain.

One often hears the term 'bloodbath' when speaking of murders. This particular scene was more like a blood shower, thought Eddie as he stepped into the kitchen. Judging by where the deepest concentration of blood was – a putrid, dark brown sludge with slimy semi-solid lumps in there like red milk going sour – on the ceiling, she had collapsed like a sack of shit and just kind of sank backward a little against the back door.

Most of her face was still intact, and if you were to place a hat on her head, perhaps a beret, you could convince yourself that she was just a young woman with black eyes having a nap. Minus the beret, though, she was minus her skull cap and about fifty percent of her brain, clumps of which still dripped onto her bare legs from above.

"Nice," Eddie said, remembering how fiercely she fought him only a week and a bit ago. It was a shame. He envisioned her being a worthless crack whore, but she had the strength of a lion and a moral compass that kept her close to her family. In a twisted way, Eddie admired her.

He laid out a line of stepping plates so he could get close to her without destroying any footwear evidence on the kitchen tiles. And there was plenty of evidence to be had – a large proportion of those footwear marks were the bare feet of a couple of kids, one about two years old and the other about four or five. He imagined this room to have been very loud at some point.

Now it was as quiet as a dead person.

She wore a long t-shirt, the kind that many women wore as night attire, and he could see that she still wore her pants too, so that potentially took care of a handful of motives at least.

"Don't you think there's something peculiar about seeing so much of a person's blood on the outside of their body?"

Eddie closed his eyes and mouthed a curse beneath his mask.

"I do," Benson said. "It looks awful. I never get used to it."

"Nothing stopping you from leaving."

"How can you get used to it?"

A sigh the size of an elephant's fart blew out of Eddie's mouth. "Piss off and leave me alone, will you?"

Benson paused. "I know you're not one for engaging in social etiquette, but have I offended you anew? You're usually so polite."

"Since you ask." Eddie turned around to face Benson directly rather than strain his neck. "It galls me that this is a Major Crime Unit job, yet you're still leaching from divisional CSI when you must have some of your own staff by now."

Benson cleared his throat. "I sense bitterness."

"Fucking damned right you do. I went for an interview with your mob yesterday and they knocked me back, yet I am still doing an MCU CSI job. I was basically told to stick to burglary sheds." Eddie folded his arms.

Benson nodded slowly. "I see."

"Oh good, glad that's cleared up."

"I wish I'd known you'd applied."

"You'd have put in a good word, right?" Beneath the mask Eddie's lips were pressed tightly together, and the anger inside was steadily growing hotter.

"I would, actually, yes. I think you're good at your job. You're still a dick, but you're good at your job." He pointed at Eddie. "I wonder if that's why you didn't get it? You didn't tell the interviewers to go fuck themselves, did you? That could've had an adverse effect."

"Yeah," Eddie whispered, clicking his fingers, "that'll be it."

"Seriously, I'll have a word."

"Don't put yourself out on my part."

"Okay." The stepping plates creaked as Benson stopped behind Eddie. He nodded at the corpse. "She came to see me on Tuesday, just four days ago. Wanted to cut a deal so her piece of shit boyfriend could stay out of jail."

"No one talks to coppers round here. Don't you know that?"

"She was trying to break the cycle."

"It cost her dearly. I hope it was worth it." Eddie stood, searching for something more prophetic to come back at him with, and failed. Instead, he asked, "Where are the kids?"

"With their Grandma round the corner."

"Were they present when she was shot?"

"They're not talking."

"They're going to need specialist care."

"We're on with it. You don't need to worry about her kids, okay? You need to worry about getting me something I can use to catch a killer."

"Sean Walker. There, go catch him."

"Come on. I know he's a penis, but he's the kind who paid someone to beat her up so he wouldn't have to do it himself."

"Still guilty."

Benson sighed. "Please. Name of the shooter. Okay?"

"Yes, boss. Right away, boss."

Benson turned, heading back out of the kitchen. "Oh, Eddie. Make sure you don't find anything from any of your previous visits here. Okay? PSD would get such a hard-on if you did." Benson had indeed reached the door, but thought about something and came back. "I just wanted to add that I'm mighty pissed off with you."

"Makes a change from always kissing my arse, I suppose."

"How can you go into someone's home and beat them up? And beat their wife up as well?"

"She beat me up first. Anyway, kind of saved him a job there – or a few quid if he subcontracts out."

"Not funny."

Eddie took a long breath in through the nose and then faced Benson. "I did that because I wanted answers right away. You lot are hog-tied when it comes to real police work. I wanted answers there and then, and I want to get that old fella his gear back. Do you know they even nicked his fucking bus pass? His bus pass! I got it back for him, straight away. It would have taken coppers a fortnight to do that, if they could do it at all. That is serving the public."

"That is breaking the fucking law! I don't care about his bus pass, you cannot—"

"Well summed up; you don't care. And yet, in the same breath you appreciate me getting the credit cards for you. Perhaps if your lot weren't so hog-tied, we could actually make a difference to people's lives. What do you say?" Eddie's nostrils were flared, and his anger was on simmer, just ticking along ready to blow.

Eventually, the front door closed, and Eddie was alone with her again. Irrespective of who she was or what she'd done, she was now an innocent corpse – any debt she had in life was paid in full in death. As such, she commanded respect. He made himself calm down and forget the confrontation. He was here to do a job and that's what he would do with no distractions.

And of course she would get respect. But Eddie put that, and other feelings that contemplated showing themselves, firmly to one side and stared at her objectively. Now was the time to begin a scene examination, and that examination began like all of Eddie's examinations – by looking at it.

It took only a couple of minutes to conclude that the kids had been present – either in the lounge or here in the kitchen when it happened. And 'it' started life as a stabbing.

Near her feet, about three feet away and close to the sink, were splashes of blood that did not belong to her. These were splashes straight down from a person; the ceiling above was clean. They could not have come from her, and more compelling than that was a partial palm print in blood on the edge of the sink. This person was stabbed.

Only minutes later did Eddie grow even more confident in his hypothesis: on the floor by the washing machine was a knife, and the blade of the knife was smeared with a mixture of fat and thin blood. Those images in films where the knife is literally dripping blood always made him smile – one of the few things that could – before he turned off the TV in disgust; they were on the whole wrong; the skin acts like a squeegee and takes most of the liquid away as the blade is withdrawn from the body.

That knife pointed directly at something else which might just back up the theory even more. It pointed to a t-shirt, balled up against the wall, a t-shirt too small for Chantelle, but maybe the right size for someone like Sean Walker, and the t-shirt was covered in blood. "Covered in Sean Walker's blood." Let's hope you bleed to death before long.

Eddie was only eighty percent sure of this. It wasn't inconceivable that she'd been stabbed before being shot, but he doubted it. A look over her torso would soon put that 20 percent doubt to bed with no supper. And it was also possible that the killer was someone on Sean's payroll rather than the slimy little bastard himself.

"Oh come on! Give me some good news!"

Chapter Twenty-nine

Life's a Drag

For a moment, Norton couldn't quite grasp what he was seeing. He leaned forward, studied her neck and sure enough, there was a pulse there. She wasn't dead.

All at once her eyes opened and she took a huge breath. She used that breath for screaming with, and began scrabbling backwards away from Norton, who was still getting over the shock of finding the stupid bitch alive. He got to his feet while she was still reeling from being almost dead, and grabbed her hair by the ponytail and dragged her through the doorway into the parlour.

Fiona was screaming and screaming, but in her panic, she had the brains to search for the orange panic button on her radio set. One hand was all over the place, her screaming mouth was open, streaming eyes seeing nothing, fingers frantically searching for the radio and the small, recessed button on the top, and her other hand was trying to pry his fingers from around her hair.

Norton hadn't taken a breath since he began dragging her; he was creating an oxygen debt that he might not be able to repay, such was his focus and determination. He had no choice now, and there hadn't been any for some time. He had to succeed – failure was not possible.

He saw her fidgeting with her radio and dropped her on the parlour carpet, and then dived onto the button by the side of his chair.

Something clicked, but the trap doors remained closed.

He took a breath, and it scraped down his throat, cold and harsh. One corner of the doors had released, but the other was stuck. He hit the button again and it dropped half an inch but then stuck fast.

Fiona had found the radio, and her fingers were scrambling over its surface like insects on a dead man's face, searching... finding. She looked over at Norton and pressed her button at the same moment that Norton pressed his again.

This time the doors opened, and she fell.

There was a boom as she hit the spiked plate, and the doors swung shut with a bang. Norton lay on his front by the chair, panting, clouds of dust sent airborne, and he wondered if the alarm on her radio would sound.

Of course, it shouldn't – she and her radio were now inside a Faraday cage. No, there was no alarm from her radio, but there was grunting, and it developed into crying, and then escalated into screaming.

Chapter Thirty

Ridge Detail

THREE HOURS INTO THE scene exam and Eddie had processed the body, and taken his examination as far as the borders of a post mortem. He'd taped the exposed areas of skin; he'd bagged the hands and feet, and even slipped a bag over the head and tied it tighter than he usually would do – there was a lot of mush to keep from leaking out.

He'd pulled Chantelle away from the door, and managed to remove her nightie, and inch by inch, slid her into a body bag. Once in there he photographed her torso to prove there were no stab wounds front or back. At that moment Eddie silently congratulated her for having the courage to stab the bastard.

Eddie zipped her into the bag, tied an orange tag through the two zipper loops and photographed it – proof she was sealed up before she left the scene.

The good news Eddie had asked for came a little later, after he'd photographed the adult footwear marks that still had enough detail in them to be useful. The most predominant of those useful marks were Adidas Wince. He was waiting for the body snatchers and thought he could kill the time by photographing the bloody t-shirt front and back, maybe measure the stab wound. He picked up the t-shirt and saw a shell casing underneath it – miraculously free of blood, not contaminated by it.

Eddie's relief was immediate, and if it had a weight, it would be something colossal – maybe something Benson-sized. He smiled, and then he grinned. Benson would be pleased.

So far, there were lots of things to put Sean Walker here in this house. But 'here in this house' evidence was weak simply because he lived here. And evidence putting him in the kitchen was similarly weak. But when you start getting his blood on knives and his blood on t-shirts with stab holes in them, the evidence suddenly ramped up into 'interesting' territory.

When you found his DNA on the shell casing of the bullet that took off the top of her head and spilled her brains across the room, then you were talking life-changing evidence. Even if you had a mixed DNA profile, you should be able to pull Sean's out of the mix, and what you'd probably be left with is the guy who sold him the gun or the ammo. Either way, it was all valuable info.

Eddie swabbed the inside of the shell for GSR before he dropped it into a slim universal container – the same kind people handed in urine samples to the doctor – and jammed it in tightly using a snapped-off swab under the lid. He'd instruct the lab to swab the exterior of the casing for DNA.

Lastly, at least for now, was photographing the ridge detail in blood on the worktop. He took a location shot with a fairly wide-angle lens, then changed to his regular 60mm lens to get the image as close as possible to life-size. With a label and scale alongside, he fired off several shots and was pleased with the result. These marks were good enough for an ident, easily.

In this instance, photography was a much better prospect for that ident than using powders and lifting the mark. Sometimes if the mark was heavily saturated in blood, the powder brush would smear through that still-wet blood and ruin the ridge detail. And the bureau was less than happy to receive marks in blood – which were technically a biohazard – than a good image of it.

The net curtains across the back window billowed as someone opened the front door.

"Eddie, body removers are here. You ready for them?"

"Send 'em in."

With not much left to do, he followed the snatchers out of the house, having held open the doors for them as they went, and at last pulled off the nitrile gloves – pale, wrinkly fingers waved at him.

It was full-on night when he finally felt the familiar tickle of light rain against his cheek. To his right was a commotion of sorts but it didn't fully enter Eddie's field of vision until a few seconds later when he allowed the gate to close after everyone was out of the property. He was standing on a wide pavement with the snatchers positioning themselves and Chantelle at the entrance to their black van, when something like an Exocet missile broke through the cordon.

There was a lot of shouting. Eddie turned in time to see a youngster running straight at him. He could see the kid's eyes were focused beyond him, on the white bag with zips and grab handles teetering on a gurney half a dozen yards away. The adult's necklace she wore streamed in her wake.

Eddie caught her and dissipated her energy by taking her head right in the stomach, and the pearl necklace whipped Eddie across the face. He grabbed her and they hit the pavement together, Eddie providing a nice soft landing for her. He could hear her screaming – it sounded horrible like a bird caught in a wire trap or something equally painful and horrific, but her voice was lost, it was almost worn away, thin and wispy like a parent's promise to its child to always be there. The kid was squirming, throwing punches, pushing Eddie away, but he held on.

"Lemme go. I want my mammy. Mammy!"

The snatchers pushed Chantelle into the van and closed the tailgate. A pair of coppers grabbed the kid's arms, but Eddie held her tightly, and shook his head at the coppers. They let go and stood unobtrusively in front of the gate.

Eddie stroked the girl's head as she cried.

She was four years old, and her hair was wet and freshly combed. She smelled of Vosene shampoo. She was the kid who'd laid across her mother, crying into her dead body, and now she was crying into Eddie Collins' scene suit as Eddie rocked with her on the pavement while sitting on his arse in the rain. "Are you Betty?"

On the lounge wall nearest the kitchen were three large words: Live. Love. Laugh. And next to them were pictures of two blonde-haired girls, not much more than toddlers. In hand-painted silver letters below each was a name, Betty and Abby.

The kid didn't answer, just collapsed against him, the tension seeping away like heat from her mother's body.

"Your mum is in a good place," Eddie whispered. "You have to believe that."

The sobbing, faint now, weak, lingered. But eventually, a small voice asked, "Do you believe in heaven?"

"Sort of," Eddie said. "I don't believe in God or anything like that. I'm not religious. But I do believe there's a place we all go when we've finished our time here."

The kid pulled back, stared at Eddie.

"No one spends very long here. Have you noticed? That's why people always say that life is too short. It is, Betty."

"So where is she?"

Eddie stared at the tears in her eyes, her bottom lip jutting out. He watched as rain fell into Betty's hair and landed on the shoulders of a pair of pyjamas that were two sizes too big for her.

He could feel himself crumbling. What with Kelly and Becca leaving, with Ros leaving, Eddie had never felt so isolated. It was a condition he'd often dreamed of, but now it was here, it felt colder and darker than he'd thought it would. He stared at the kid and wondered if her world was cold and dark now. She was essentially an orphan who'd go through life dragging her little sister behind her like dragging a reluctant dog.

"She's in another place like this. Except the sun is shining all the time, and everyone is happy. They smile at you, and you know they mean it; they're friendly. No one is out to hurt you; you can relax and put down your guard. You can enjoy the sunshine, and you can enjoy life. But only your mind lives there, the soul if you like. There's no messy body to bother with and to feed and clean up after; it's just your thoughts. It's peaceful, Betty.

"And I know that once she gets used to being there, she'll enjoy looking down at you."

"Really?"

"Absolutely, kid. Don't worry about your mummy, okay? In many many years from now when it's your turn to leave," he paused with a reassuring smile, but really it gave him a few seconds to compose himself and speak without bursting into tears as well. "Your mum will be there to welcome you, and you'll have lots to tell her, and you'll laugh at Abby and what she gets up to." Eddie held her close again and said, "This is a trial run for a better life. But you must be good, and you must enjoy it, don't fear it. Don't hold onto the past so tightly that you forget to live for the future, okay?"

"Betty?" An officer stood next to an old lady, a grandmotherly figure. She bent and scooped her up in her arms, and the kid let go only reluctantly. "Come on, girl, let's get you to bed." And to Eddie, "Sorry, officer."

Eddie waved the apology aside. "Don't be. She's a wonderful girl, and she's going to have a wonderful life."

When they'd gone one of the scene guards across the gate said to him, "Lovely words. But you know she's only four, don't you?"

"Yep, I do. But they'll stick." He looked after the kid as she was being walked away, and he whispered, "Don't waste your life, your precious life, with silly regrets."

Chapter Thirty-one

The Hammer

He peered down the hole at her, but there was precious little light down there and what with the cloudy skies and the rain, there was precious little light up here too. One thing was for sure – she wasn't yet dead. That was the first thing to put right, and Norton gathered himself together, slapped the dust from his clothes and his face, and left the parlour.

On his way down into the cellar, he found he was not alone and when he turned on the light at the foot of the steps, two things greeted him almost simultaneously: the first was his mother sitting in her rocking chair, newspaper in her lap and cup of tea on a small wooden table to her right. The table cloth and the doily on it wafted in the breeze from the hole and she had to shake out her newspaper to stop that breeze folding the pages over.

She looked at him, tight-lipped, and gave her customary shake of her head.

"What?" he asked.

She looked directly at him. "I beg your pardon."

Norton looked at the ground, fingers fidgeting. "Evening, Mother. How are you?"

She folded the paper in her lap and took a sip of tea. "When will you learn, child? It is jolly bad practice to kill police officers."

"But—"

"But nothing! This is the very last one."

"She knows about—"

"Stop interrupting, Norton!"

He stared at his sandals again. "Sorry, Mother."

"She knows because you were sloppy with that youth, Mojo." She tutted. "Might as well have put an announcement in The

Yorkshire Post. Dreadful. Get your act together, Norton; I will not tolerate these constant errors of yours. Sort this out, child, and let's hear no more about it. And no more police officers."

"No, Mother."

The second thing to greet him in the cellar was anger. It took his hand and pulled him towards the machine, and the closer he got the faster his breathing became, and the faster his heart pummelled the more he hated the creature trapped inside there.

She was snivelling. Bitch!

She was on her back, and the stab vest she wore had stopped the spikes dead. Her head was an inch from its very own spike, and if you looked closely you could see a bit of hair and a drop of blood on the very tip of it. She was keeping her head off it and Norton could imagine how her neck muscles must ache terribly, how heavy her head must feel. Her right arm hadn't been so lucky; it was pinned by two spikes – one above and one below the elbow. And her legs... ooh, her legs were a bit of a mess. There was a bit of blood on the plate but not much. If she moved about and broke the seals formed between flesh and spike, then of course, blood would gush out, but for now, there wasn't much cleaning up needed doing.

On her radio was a plain red light. The 'no signal' light. Norton grinned and mimed 'phew'. Her left arm had been in the process of reaching across and pressing the panic button. It hadn't been injured at all.

She was mewing like a cat, her chin wobbling, tears tracked down her cheeks. Her eyes were pleading. It was sad to see such a fall from superiority to... to this. "Please," she said. "I need help."

Norton smiled at her. "Yes," he said, "you certainly do." He slid the cage door open and reached in, swivelled her radio around so it would pop out of its holder, and withdrew it. He took off the battery and dropped both parts down the hole, and rewarded himself with a sigh and a smile from his mother. She even clapped, and nodded her approval. "Thanks, Mother."

"Have you calmed down now, Norton?"

"No, Mother. Not at all."

She tipped her teacup towards him, and said, "Good boy."

"Please..." Fiona croaked.

"Shut up, there's a dear."

"Why did you... Why would you..." She was running out of breath. It was the shock, and Norton was surprised she had lasted this long. Shock was a superb killer – at least as efficient as the spikes, although not quite so visually appealing.

"Ssshhh, now." He moved around to a large wheel with a handle attached, and began to wind. "Let's get you out of there, shall we?"

The spikes slowly retracted, disappearing back through the holes in the lower plate, pulling free of her legs and her arms, each one feeling like its own form of torture, and Fiona's hands curled into fists and her face screwed up in agony. Her screams echoed around the cellar and Norton had to turn his head away. She was incredibly loud.

Once the spikes were clear, she laid her head down, sobbing still, and the amount of blood that came from her arm and legs was impressive; a steady outpouring that dripped into a tray beneath the machine.

Norton put his hands on his hips and stared at the underside of the doors, wondering why they'd stuck like that. They'd almost cost him a kill, and there was the possibility they could have cost him his freedom too. "Expansion," he whispered. "Water has made them damp. Need to wind them away from the sides a bit."

"Help me, please!"

He looked back at Fiona, annoyance clouding his face. "I dislike being interrupted."

"Please, get me some help."

"Please, get me some help," he mocked in a whiny voice. He opened the copper cage up fully and dragged her off the holed bed and onto a stainless-steel table to the machine's side – a healthy drop of two or three feet. As expected, this movement induced another screaming fit from her.

"I don't have to put up with this, you know. Stop your silly noise before I get really cross with you, young lady."

She tried to stem the screams by clamping her mouth shut, but there was nothing she could do about her hitching chest and so the screams were still there, just blocked by her lips. Her eyes pleaded still, and her body was leaking blood all over the place. More to clean up.

"Stop it now, this is silly."

"Why," she gasped. "Why are you doing this?"

"I'm going to get a whiteboard with all these questions answered so I don't need to keep repeating myself. Honestly, the amount of people who... no originality left in the world. It breaks my heart, it really does. And it breaks Mother's too." He broke her jaw with the first swing of the lump hammer.

She screamed and tried to move her head, but the second blow smashed the mandible until there were broken teeth running in a smooth rivulet of blood down her neck. And still Norton's anger raged. Her head was a mushy red pulp after another six or seven blows, and it became largely indistinguishable as human just a few blows later. A splinter of bone caught him in the eye and he had to pause while he made sure there was no damage.

When he'd finished, he dropped the hammer, rested against the table for a few minutes while he caught his breath. This kind of work was getting harder and harder the older he got.

He unzipped and pulled off her hi-viz vest, licking the splashed blood from his fingertips and rubbing it out of his eyes so he could see what he was doing. And what he was doing was removing any identifiable item that marked this body as a police officer. If this body, wearing its hi-viz stab vest and shiny epaulettes, bobbed to the surface in the River Aire, Norton would start twitching all over, because the force wouldn't stop looking until they found him.

That said, if she just disappeared, especially after declaring to her colleague over the phone that she was heading off for a meal, he could expect a quick chat from a detective and 'thanks for your time' nod of the head.

As he worked, he spoke to her. "You mustn't hate yourself. None of this is your fault; you were just too inquisitive by far." He looked up again at the failed trapdoors and smiled – it would be an easy fix. "Why do I do this? Well, seeing as you asked so politely. It began as a way of getting robbers off the street. I have a horrible disposition towards robbers, by the way. I hate them, and if I can kill them I will. But," he looked around to see if Mother was listening, and whispered, "I actually enjoy it. The more people I kill, the more alive I feel; it's like a therapy for me. Of course it's a very sad event, and I can't help crying over them – all of them; after all, it's an end to their life, no matter how awful that life might be. So, know this, I am grateful to you for keeping me sane."

Norton laughed as he created a small bonfire behind the house, and put her car keys in his pocket for later. He knew of a good spot for a decent car fire.

Chapter Thirty-two

A Friendly Visit

Sean still felt sick. The smell of it was in his nostrils and no matter how often he blew his nose, he could not shift it – it was vile, and it made him retch.

Since killing Chantelle and meeting with Ziggy, Sean had weighed up his options and it turned out that they didn't take a lot of weighing. He had no options at all, really. He headed through the dark Harehills streets on his way to Mabgate and old man Bailey, hoping for a bed for the night. He knew getting a bed for the night from him would be tough, but they went back a fair way and had a certain professional trust for each other – that trust would get him a bed. Bailey was also known as the Madman of Mabgate; it didn't make this rather slim option any more appealing, but it was that, or get the shit kicked out of him on a park bench somewhere.

The thought of spending the night in A&E appealed because he'd get the wound fixed up, he could gawp at the nurses, and he'd get a comfy bed with all meals provided. But the downsides outweighed those positives by about seven tonnes: the staff would report a stab wound to the police – game over; there were always coppers hanging about in A&E so the chances of being spotted by one of them were high – game over; the consequences of any OCG colleague or any of Chantelle's family members finding out where he was, were too severe to consider – also game over.

The wound hurt like crazy; it was a dull throb with a sharp, needle-like pain running through it. It was apt to bleed if he knocked it or if he even thought about stretching or yawning, and he wasn't sure how much blood he'd lost, but he could feel his boxer shorts getting crusty – something he was used to but never before because he'd been stabbed in the chest.

Sean was lost in thought and didn't notice the black Overfinch Range Rover pull up just behind him. The door opened and within moments, Sean had an audience of one. He stood there puzzled for a moment until he recognised the man. "'S up, Wes?" he asked.

Wes replied, "Ziggy wants to see you. Get in the car."

"Yeah?"

Wes nodded to the Range Rover.

"Had a change of heart, eh?" A smirk lifted the immature hair of what Sean liked to call his muff-tickler moustache. "I knew he'd see sense." He reached out to Wes, friendly, a tap on the arm, and Wes knocked it aside with more force than was strictly necessary. The muff-tickler straightened out and Sean climbed aboard and headbutted the black hole of a Glock.

"Don't make me ruin the upholstery," Ziggy said as the door closed behind Sean. "Wes would go nuts. I mean it. I saw some kid scratch the back door once, and Wes grabbed him, pulled the kid's fingers back until three of 'em snapped. Ha, I can still hear that sound of tearing cartilage. Creepy noise, man."

Sean's hands hit the ceiling and his bladder almost let go. He cringed.

Ziggy put the gun away. "That's so you don't get the wrong impression, know what I mean? We ain't buddies and we never will be again, 'kay? You don't work for me no more."

Sean nodded, hands still aloft, one knee on the seat, one foot on the floor.

"Sit down, man." Ziggy said, and then sniffed the air. "Wait a minute." He glared at Sean.

"I was scared, alright!"

"Dirty twat, Sean. You figuring on ruining the upholstery by pissing on it! Stay kneeling, man, I say stay kneeling."

"Sorry! Sorry, man."

"You disgust me." He turned to the driver. "Stick the AC on, Wes – full blast, man; the dirty bastard pissed himself." Wes said nothing, just flicked a switch, shook his head.

"You here to help me, Ziggy?"

Ziggy looked suitably confused. "I just told you we have no partnership no more, Sean. You killed your woman in front of your kids—"

"That should prove to you that I'd do anything for the crew."

Ziggy shook his head. "I was after intelligence, you imbecile, not brutality. In this game you got to know when to act tough and when to act smart, and you're shit at both. So anyway, listen up—"

"I did this—"

The coldness of the Glock in the centre of Sean's forehead stopped him talking instantly. "Take me to Bailey."

"What?"

"What's up with yo? Why must I repeat myself, eh? Take me to Bailey, you prick."

"Okay, okay. But why?"

Ziggy pulled the Glock back. "Wes saw him leaning over a kid by the side of the road last week, and that kid didn't make it. That kid was Mojo. Mojo is my cousin. And Mojo was out with Chubs and Starky. No one has heard nothing from any of them since that night. We think the MadMan of Mabgate knows what happened. And he's your man, right, your contact? You introduce us, yeah?"

Sean saw the very thin option of cadging a bed for the night from Bailey disappear like a politician's bribe - quickly. "I er... Look, he didn't have nothing to do with anyone's death, man. He's fucking senile and mental, he's crooked with arthritis, ain't no way he left his home."

"Cool. Let's meet him and he can tell me himself. Now take me to him."

Chapter Thirty-three

Tea and Biscuits with an Iron Maiden

The noises were terrible.

Had he taken one last night? He was supposed to have, yes, but that didn't help right now, did it? Had he taken one or not?

He couldn't bloody remember!

Norton smacked the worktop. He decided to take one now to make up for forgetting one last night. "I know!" They say you shouldn't take one if you forget a dose, but he had missed more than one. Or so he thought. He put his head in his hands and tried to remember, but couldn't. He was in tears when he took away his hands, and just swallowed another with water. These things always made him shudder; they left a horrid metallic taste in his mouth. Lithium. Hated it. And that made him wonder if he'd taken the other tablets too. The ones for mania and depression. It was no good, he'd simply have to start keeping records. He popped another couple of tablets, and waited for something to happen.

The noises stopped. And the images began.

He could picture it now as clearly as he could the day he built it.

It shone like silver. It was stainless steel. It was something not too dissimilar to an iron maiden, but on its side. And there was no door. Okay, it was nothing like an iron maiden. But it was beautiful. It was a metal plate about five feet square, and it had 225 holes in it. The holes were three-quarters of an inch in diameter. This was the fixed plate and it was bolted rigidly to a framework, and sat precisely nine feet below the lounge floor. Beneath it, and on a large screw thread like a scissor jack – something that many cars carried in order that a competent owner might change a flat tyre – was another plate. This plate had 225 spikes welded to it. The spikes were only about four inches tall, but they were jolly sharp.

The spikes coincided with the holes in the plate above. When the two plates were brought together, the spikes protruded. When the plates were wound apart, the spikes dropped through the holes until only the holes were visible.

The holes were great for draining away the blood.

But there was another, better, reason for having this dual plate mechanism. Indeed, when he first started out, Norton had only the plate with spikes in. It was extremely effective at killing people who fell onto them. But it was a nightmare getting their impaled bodies back off again. If a spike happened to go through the skull, for example, they seemed to get stuck there, and yanking on the head to get the spike back out could be backbreaking work, not to mention dangerous – those spikes were sharp, remember.

So the mother of invention gave birth to the two-plate method. When someone was impaled on the spikes, rather than spend an hour pulling them back off, he simply wound a handle and the spiked plate dropped away, leaving the hapless victim lying on the table with the holes in. Then all he needed to do was slide them off onto what he called 'the waiting table' where he would remove jewellery, wallets, and the like. Easy. The waiting table, as the name suggested, was also where he stockpiled the bodies until there'd been a good solid downpour or two, until Ladywell Beck was in full flow another fourteen yards below the basement. The bodies always went into the river when she was flowing fast. Always. And the floor of the river was littered with boulders sharp enough to tear a body and its clothing to shreds and even rip off limbs during the mile-long journey to the River Aire.

To reactivate the plates, he had a switch set into a small plastic box. One press of the button not only changed a small LED from green to red, but also shot the retaining bolt from the winding mechanism and allowed the spikes to explode through the holes again. As the plates came together, they made a booming sound that reverberated through the house; it was such a satisfying noise, so solid. It turned out to be very useful. One time he'd operated the trapdoors and had left the spikes retracted by mistake. Initially, he'd been angry at himself, but as the young lady in his metal pit came to, she began pleading, and offered all kinds of recompense to Norton in exchange for her freedom, and of course she would never mention this place to anyone, she'd said.

He'd smiled at that. When she got annoying, he pressed the spike-release button, and when the thunderous boom died away, she was totally silent.

He never accepted anything from anyone down in that pit, but loved hearing about some of the things on offer.

Nine feet above the plates was a pair of trap doors operated by solenoids. They were quick in operation, too; the touch of a button, a whoosh, a nine-foot drop onto four-inch spikes was but a blink away. Less than a second of sheer surprise followed by… well, nothing much really. Just the end. The doors were held closed by a very strong electromagnet, the kind of magnet that keeps closed many an office door, until that is, someone with a swipe card touches it to a card reader on the wall.

These particular doors opened instantly – assisted by two powerful springs mounted at the hinge sides so as not to rely solely on gravity and the weight of the intended victim. The switches were placed on the wall behind the lounge door, and a second was by the defunct television set. He kept a third by his chair; it too was set into a box alongside the spike-release button, and a casual glance might mistake the buttons as recliner buttons for his chair.

One never knew where one might be in any given situation, so it paid to think ahead and try to accommodate any eventuality. So far, for Norton, all three buttons had worked well. The whole contraption had been almost faultless for more than a dozen years; up until then he had relied heavily on the bayonet and some rather less sophisticated trap doors.

He'd had to replace one of the electromagnetic coils every now and then because they had a tendency to burn out if one kept one's finger on the switch – and when someone is falling through the floor screaming, one is liable to keep one's finger on the switch until, at least, the screaming has ceased. "I'm only human," he said. And the doors had swollen a touch, which meant he'd have to wind them out of the hinges a couple of millimetres per side. He made a note to re-waterproof them come the summer months.

Daydreaming about the machine was always fascinating, and reliving those special killings passed hours sometimes, but now he snapped out of it, and concentrated on his evening meal.

He stared at them. They were black and had tiny legs. They swam about in his cereal milk. Norton shoved them around the bowl with his spoon, nudging them with cornflakes until they sank. A moment later they bobbed back to the surface of the milk and swam on, oblivious.

He shrugged and scooped a spoonful into his mouth. When the bowl was empty he put it on the floor and stared at the wall. An hour later he was still staring at the wall when there was a knock at the front door. His eyes widened and his heart kicked him in the ribs; his fingers tingled, and he immediately wondered where he could run that was safe. The cellar, of course.

He gathered his tea, and shuffled through the parlour, and turned right along the hallway when someone shouted him. He froze and the voice came again.

"Norton. It's Sean. I got some snow for you, man."

He stopped, his breathing hitched on each inlet stroke and that little hitch echoed around the hall like a tick from an old clock. He licked his dry lips and turned around. A moment later, tea still in his hand, he clanked the bolts aside and opened the door. Sean was there, and Norton said, "I'm glad you've called, I have some more—" Sean was there, yes, but so too was someone else. Sean almost fell as that someone shoved him aside. The front door frame was suddenly filled by a stranger who rushed in and shoved Norton hard.

The teapot and cup smashed upon contact with the floor and the tray bounced on top of them, cracking under the feet of this uninvited monster. Norton screamed.

Half way along the hallway towards the kitchen, he collided with a small wooden stool and fell backwards, knocking his head on the floor and reopening the wound that was just beginning to heal, just beginning to itch. To his right, an elbow had punctured his latest work, a six-foot canvas leached with colour that represented what was happening inside his own mind. It had taken him eight months and now that work was destroyed.

"Get the fuck up!" The stranger reached down for him with rough hands.

"Be careful, Ziggy, he's an old man; you're gonna break him!"

"Shut the fuck up."

The man, Ziggy, snarled like some crazed animal, and before Norton could take a proper breath, he was hauled upright and punched in the guts. That part breath he'd snatched exploded out, and his diaphragm spasmed. Norton gasped for air reaching out with clawed fingers, eyes bursting, veins standing out on his forehead. He thought he was going to die.

"Leave him alone, you idiot, you'll fucking—"

Norton shrank away into the corner, snivelling.

And Sean was silenced as Ziggy smacked him around the face. "Any idea how difficult it is to speak without lips, Sean? Looks disgusting but it's funny as fuck, let me tell you. So keep yours shut."

Ziggy came back to Norton, sat him on the wooden stool, and held him still by the scruff of his neck, fist poised a couple of feet away, ready to strike again. Norton swallowed hard, hands on knees, air rasping down his throat.

"I don't know who you are, sir, but you've got the wrong—"

Ziggy slapped him, pointed a finger in his face. "Speak when I ask you a question, old man, yeah?"

"But—"

Ziggy's finger came closer, and he said, "Ah! Shush now if you know what's good for you. Yeah?"

Eyes downcast, Norton recoiled and nodded. His head began to buzz and from somewhere his mother spoke to him, "Are you going to let him get away with that?" She put her fingertips to her mouth in shock, and shook her head. She was disappointed in him, and he hated it when she was disappointed in him, because it was as though she was sharing the moment – the disappointment – with someone sitting beside her, embarrassed by his lack of action.

He chose to ignore her.

"Good old man." Ziggy stood, took a look around, stared at the newly damaged work and feigned shock. "You did this?" He looked at Norton.

Norton nodded.

"God, it's fucking shit, man." From nowhere the knife he produced sliced through the canvas top to bottom, and Norton just sat there and cried out as though he'd lost a loved one. Ziggy laughed at him, having got the response he wanted. "Got more of these?" He pushed aside the slashed painting and peered at the stack beneath it. "You'd think with the amount of practice you've had they'd be pretty decent. But I see they're all equally shite." He turned to face Norton. "Is this modern art, then?"

Norton nodded and looked away, fearing the worst. Mother just tutted.

"Sean here tells me you and him are close."

Norton's eyes watered as he peered along the hall to Sean and the blood smeared across his face. Sean was in a shocking state – blood all down his front, leaning against the wall, shaking. It was a kind gesture that Sean tried to dissuade this man from beating him up – he'd try to remember that, but not so good he brought him here in the first place. He'd remember that too.

"He gets some of his credit cards from you. You take a bit of coke from him." He stood, nose in the air. "Sounds like a fair exchange, a good way of doing business. I like it. It's entrepreneurial. And we like to nurture that kind of relationship – it's a mutually beneficial one, and less likely to end in distrust and violence. Know what I mean?"

"I don't think—"

"It was a rhetorical question, Bailey – no need to respond."

Behind them, Sean groaned and slid down the hallway wall, head in hands waiting for the games to begin.

Norton sat with his back against the wall wishing it was all over. He breathed hard, and asked, "What do you want?"

"Answers."

"Hurry up with your questions then, I have a fearsome headache."

Ziggy fired a fist into Norton's face and more pain exploded from the back of his head, and more blood sprayed across the wall like a starburst on fireworks night. "Wow, man, that's a lot of blood. Hope you don't bleed out before you give me what I want."

Norton cradled his nose. "What do you... want?"

"Okay, Bailey, last Wednesday you were seen in the company of my dearest cousin, a lad by the name of Fogg – but known locally as Mojo. He was a good kid. Very spiritual, y'know. Nice boy, sorely missed, yeah? He was found dead at the side of Regent Street, and you were seen with him."

"I know nothing—"

"Stop right there, old man." Ziggy squatted down before him. "I'm only going to offer this warning once, and then you take your chances, yeah? I know what I know, see, and if I think you're lying to me I'll take my little slashing blade to your face rather than your shite paintings, yeah? Do you follow me, old timer? Am I making sense? Do you fucking understand me?"

Norton closed his eyes. "I understand you."

"Did you see him that night?"

Norton looked Ziggy in the eyes and really didn't like what he saw there. This man wasn't especially interested in his answers or perhaps even the truth – he was interested in inflicting injury on him, that's all. "Went to see what was wrong with the lad. That's all."

"You're telling me you seen this kid kneeling at the side of the road and you were kind enough to go and see what the matter was? That right?"

Norton nodded. "He looked in trouble. I wanted to help."

"I'm nominating you for a good citizen award, Bailey." He patted Norton on the shoulder. "You are my fucking hero, man. A hero!" He closed back in on him. "Was anyone else with him?"

Norton stuttered, looked him in the eye, "I didn't see anyone else."

Ziggy considered this, and stood. "Coppers been round?"

"What?"

"Have the police been to see you?"

"They've knocked on my door a few times. I don't have anything to say to them."

Just as the words left Norton's mouth, someone knocked on the door again. Everyone froze.

Chapter Thirty-four

The Knock

Ziggy nodded at Sean. Sean got up like a man made of rubber, made his way to the front door and peered through the spyhole. He gasped, laid his back flat against the wall and whisper-shouted, "Benson."

Norton tried to stand but Ziggy held him firmly. "The detective sergeant your Chantelle was feeding juice to?" Ziggy asked.

Sean only nodded.

Ziggy had Norton by the collar again, and asked him, "What's he doing here?"

"How should I know? I haven't answered the door yet." Norton took control then, pushed Ziggy's hand away and stood. He ushered them into the parlour's darkness, silenced them with a hush, and closed the parlour door, nodding at Ziggy's hushed threats, agreeing to abide by rules he couldn't hear. Inside his mind he was already behind bars wishing he'd had the guts to do away with himself. This was the situation for which the saying 'stuck between a rock and a hard place' was invented. From a seat by the defunct telephone table inside the front door, mother appeared concerned.

His palms were wet with sweat, and the buzzing thrummed throughout his body. This was a customary reaction whenever something unexpected happened. Norton liked his life full of no surprises at all; he liked predictability, he liked routine. He did not like people knocking on his door at this ungodly hour.

He slid the chain on and cautiously opened the front door a couple of inches – if only he'd been this cautious the last time, he thought. Behind him the hall light spilled out onto the top step and illuminated a man standing there with his collar pulled up against the wind. He didn't look at all like a criminal, and that made Norton relax slightly. Relax enough to say, "Yes? Can I help you?"

"Mr Bailey?"

"You are?"

"Sorry to disturb you so late in the evening. My name is Tom Benson, I'm a detective sergeant with West Yorkshire Police."

Norton stiffened; Sean was right, then. This was one of those moments he'd thought about for the last thirty years or so. And the conclusion to all those thoughts was simple: bugger! Trying to talk one's way out of trouble, especially when there was probably still enough evidence in the fabric of this old house to put him in prison for the better part of three hundred years, seemed ludicrous.

He'd decided that when 'The Knock' came, he would have two choices: surrender or die. And by die, he meant use The Great Flaps of Justice, as he'd come to know them. It would be much more palatable than surrender – it would be quicker for one thing; he could imagine the hours of tedium at the hands of some police officer – perhaps even this DS Benson here – as they probed each death going back God-knew how far. And as if that wouldn't be purgatory enough, there'd be a two-month-long court case to endure, and there really was not enough cocaine in the world to get a man through that. And afterwards? Prison. For ever. Well, until the final breath.

So all in all, there wasn't a lot to look forward to.

"Are you okay? You look very pale."

Norton's eyes eventually focused on DS Benson, shocked to find himself here after his mind had wandered so far. "Sorry?"

"I asked if you were okay. You're very pale."

"Am I? I had a little fall." Norton took off the chain. Without even looking at the detective, he stepped aside and waved him in with a hand that shook rather more than he felt comfortable with. It would be a sad ending to what had been a fruitful life, and... Oh what's the point? The only thing he cared about any more was catching The Bad Man and getting the jewellery back again. And so far that hadn't gone terribly well, he reasoned, so what made him think he would be able to do it before the police finally caught up with him? And it turned out that 'finally caught up with him' was tonight. Seemed unfair, really; no notice at all, just a knock at the door and Goodnight Vienna.

Norton checked outside, expecting to see a partner at least, and a dozen cars with blue flashing lights at most. There were none. Confused, he closed the door and followed DS Benson along the hallway wondering if the line, "It's a fair cop," was appropriate now. Was it worth holding his wrists forward ready to accept the cuffs?

"Christ," Benson said, peering at the blood on the wall. "You need that looking at. It'll need stitches, Mr Bailey."

"It healed before; it'll heal again." Norton's eyes widened ever so slightly as a thought occurred to him, a way out of this predicament that meant he'd be able to carry on his search for The Bad Man. He licked his lips, knowing the solution was but a room away, just the other side of the parlour door, actually. He stopped, looked at the door handle and considered the initial commotion of letting Benson into a room where armed men hid. There was something almost beautiful about that meeting, almost poetic; something exciting. An emotion worthy of a new painting, perhaps.

Norton licked his lips, and reached out for the door handle.

"It healed before? What happened before?"

"Ah," Norton said. "Slipped on those bloody steps. They're mossy, and when they get wet... Hurt my back, and cracked the back of my head open. It had almost healed."

"Sorry to hear that," Benson said. "I need to apologise to you again."

Norton pulled his hand back. "What?"

"I am working on a case that features several missing persons, and I'm getting nowhere fast with it." His smile was friendly, but cold.

He was lying. Or he was embarrassed. Embarrassed by the lack of progress? Norton was confused, why would someone knock on his door and confess to a lack of progress? He moved from foot to foot, and his fingers curled in and out of one another. "And you're telling me this because?"

Benson said, "I've been told that you play nicely with the local mob by handing them stolen credit cards."

"What? How prepos—"

"Tell me why?"

"Why what?"

"Tell me why it's preposterous."

Norton looked at the parlour door knob. "I like a quiet existence where I am my own company. I don't think I'd fit the profile for that kind of criminal."

Benson smiled. "There is a profile, but people can be surprising, people—"

Norton's heart fluttered. "I don't trust you, Sergeant Benson. Don't take that personally because I don't trust anyone. I detest what lies beyond that front door and feel more anxious each time I am forced to step outside it." He paused, gathered his thoughts, and let his hands wring themselves into painful knots – it was somehow grounding, it was reassuring, familiar. "The world is a hateful place."

Benson nodded. "I agree with you; there's no argument from me, Norton. That profile you mentioned would certainly exclude you from playing out with the mob. Have I been misinformed?"

Norton bowed his head. "I interact with people infrequently, and I certainly don't interact with any mobster, as you say. Indeed, I doubt very much I have anything that could help in your missing persons enquiry." He moved towards the front door. "So allow me to show you out."

"So you don't interact with the local mob?"

"I made myself clear, Mr Benson."

"No credit cards and no connection with criminality?"

"No, Mr Benson. Now if that's all, I'll bid you goodnight."

Benson began moving back up the hallway, letting Norton shepherd him there. "You'll forgive me asking this of you, then. Our house-to-house team repeatedly tried to contact you. When they finally caught you in, the officer wondered if you had been burgled. Her report said the front bay window appeared to have been forced open. She's no expert, I grant you, but still, we like to be thorough."

The sweating palms and fingertips were wrinkled now; his legs felt like they belonged to someone else and the noise his heart made in his ears sounded like it did the night he chased an injured youth up the road towards Regent Street – ready for popping. "I told your officer that her concern, and now yours, was superfluous; kids forced that window months ago, but didn't—"

"So you were burgled."

Norton closed his eyes again and the muscles in his cheeks pulsed. "I do not wish to pursue the matter."

Benson said nothing for a few moments, and an uneasy quietness settled between them, like a row of barbed wire between two enemies – not dangerous if you just stood still and looked at it, but likely to inflict injury if you reached over it. "I'll leave you in peace. But if you think of anything else... please get in touch." Benson handed over a card and waited by the door to be let out. In the moment it took Norton to open it, both heard a cough from the parlour. "Visitors?"

Norton smiled. "Coronation Street, Sergeant."

Once the front door closed, Norton stood with his back to it, resting his throbbing head against the cold wood, knowing he'd leave another red bloom there. He blew upwards through his moustache for now he must open another door and this one was equally as terrifying to him. More so considering a pile of credit cards on the mantelpiece in full view. Some of the credit cards belonged to a plump man by the name Mr Andrew Chubb, and more to a Mr Robert Starky. There were eighteen cards in total – three nice piles on the mantelpiece that he'd gathered over the last few weeks.

This was going to end and it was going to end soon – Norton could feel it rising to a climax that no one would expect, and a climax that no one would walk away from either. It was not going to be pleasant. He swallowed and opened the door.

"Thought you'd fucked off with your copper buddy."

Norton stepped into the room, closed the door. To his right, Sean sat in Norton's chair, feet up on a pouffe dabbing at his nose with a bloody tissue, while Ziggy was by the window, keeping a lookout and steaming up the glass.

He turned to Norton, smiled, and said, "I think you were with Mojo when he died. I think you knew there were two others with him: Starky and Chubs." He stepped closer, "I think you're an old man who's full of shit, an old man who's not as frail as he makes out to be. And I think this is your very last night."

"Listen," Norton held out a hand, palm towards Ziggy, "I've had an awful day, and I'd like you to leave. Please, just go. You're not going to listen to me so you might as well leave now."

Ziggy stopped smiling. From inside his jacket he took out a gun and pointed it at Norton. He walked forward with a determination on his face that scared the crap out of him.

"Ziggy, there ain't no need—"

"Shut it, Sean." To Norton he said, "No one fucks me over."

Norton hit the button on the wall to his left. The trap doors opened with a bang and Ziggy screamed as he fell, letting off a shot that tugged at Norton's left forearm and left it stinging. The scream lasted seconds and then there was a curious silence, just gasps from Norton and an awful tingling feeling in his fingers.

Sean's face was blank, blood still leaking from his nose. He blinked as the doors closed up again, not a sign that they even existed. He looked across at Norton. "What the fuck was that?"

"Get me a tea towel, Sean," he held up his arm. "And then get me some coke."

Chapter Thirty-five

Sleeping With a Madman

"When I was at school, I considered suicide. I felt low and had no self-esteem – before you say that I don't even know what that word means, let me tell you that I looked it up, and it means that I don't value myself. It was true, I didn't value myself, and neither did anyone else."

"Wait," said Norton, "there's a violin around here somewhere."

Sean stared at him. "I thought you, out of everyone, would take this seriously."

"Amazing how wrong you can be."

"Sorry to have troubled you with it." Sean's eyes watered, but here in the basement, no one could see them shine.

"And that's your excuse, is it, for killing your wife?"

"That's it, I've had enough, if you're not going to listen, then just get on and get it done." Sean folded his arms, looked away from Norton with a certain petulance that only babies and teenagers possessed. And Sean Walker, it seemed.

Norton leaned forward. "Killing yourself is no easy task. I have contemplated it myself every day since 1987, and each time I conclude that I am not up to the job, and I wouldn't have the nerve to face my mother should we meet on the other side."

"The other side?"

"After death, Sean. After death."

"Oh, I see. I thought you already spoke—"

"That's different!"

"Oh. Sorry."

"So why didn't you go through with it?"

"Suicide?"

Norton nodded.

"It looked painful, for one thing. And for the other, it seemed so... so final, you know?"

Norton nodded again. "How do you mean, it 'looked painful'?"

Sean closed his eyes and let his head flop against the wall behind him. He drew on the cigarette, coughed, and said, "My fucking brother beat me to it."

"Your brother?"

"At first I thought my dad had actually carried out his threat – he was always threatening to kill us because we was so bad. He kept telling us how he'd make it look like suicide so the coppers wouldn't arrest him."

"And it wasn't your dad who killed him?"

"Nah, definitely no. My dad had been arrested the night before, and we— I didn't find out about it until my auntie told me. So it was definitely suicide." He sniffled. "Never seen a dead body till I saw Mick. It was fucking gross, and now I can't think of him without seeing his bulging eyes and tongue and how deep the rope had bitten into his neck. Coppers everywhere, man."

"It's not nice. Death... I used to think it was almost romantic. It was just a shell inhabited by those who'd finished living here and gone off to live somewhere else, like old clothes that didn't fit any more. Death truly is a mirror of life – it's full of horror and waste, and despair, and as you say, finality. And no matter how a person dies, it always looks painful, and it always looks sad. They never look happy that they were here or excited to see what was coming next."

"Maybe they weren't. And maybe they're frightened of what comes next."

"Is that what stopped you killing yourself?"

"I saw my brother and that's what stopped me. I didn't want to be him—"

"He'd beaten you to the glory, and the first of your family's tears. Tears for the second are never shed with such despondency."

Sean looked at Norton, but kept quiet because he didn't understand the statement.

"But what made you contemplate it in the first place?"

"I was bullied—"

"That's a wonderful excuse these days for doing anything you like. I stole from the shops but I was bullied at school; I raped a girl because I was bullied at school." Norton glared at him. "You make me sick; grow a thicker skin and move on."

Sean blew smoke out through his nose, lit another cigarette, and let the tears roll down his cheeks. "I was beaten most days. I had my clothes stolen and was forced to walk home in just my socks." He took another drag. "And mostly it was by one kid and his gang."

"Reprobates."

"And no matter how hard I tried to fit in, I just couldn't. One time I tried to fight back. His cronies took hold of my right hand and held it around a gate post. This kid smashed my finger with a hammer. His name was Ziggy, and he was a bastard to me my whole life."

"Ziggy? That Ziggy?"

Sean nodded, coughed out a cloud of smoke. "I've been trying to impress that bastard since I was twelve years old. I thought I was one of the gang last week, thought I'd finally made it. I was king of the fucking castle, Norton, let me tell you. I was up there with him; I was his right-hand man. He made me a member at last – no more teasing, no more beatings, no more humiliation." He smiled, but it waned quickly. "He gave me a promotion. And he gave me a gun, said my old lady had been speaking to coppers – that DS Benson, actually. Told me to sort it."

"He's had you round his little finger since your schooldays – if you'll pardon the connection with your own disability. You yearned to please him so much that you would have done anything to be in his gang, anything to be on his team instead of the focus of it, ridiculed by it. And you did do anything, you did something; you committed the ultimate crime so you could join in his penis-measuring competition. You killed your wife for the sake of your own status." Norton shook his head. "He told you to sort it and you did?"

"I lost my temper with her and did her in the kitchen with the kids in the lounge watching Peppa Pig. I should've taken her somewhere discreet—"

"Or you shouldn't have killed her at all, you idiot with low self-esteem. You're a loser, Sean Walker, and you should have followed your brother."

Sean snapped his head around to glare at Norton.

"But instead you'll use his suicide and your being bullied to get through life like they are crutches, and you deserve sympathy like charity. You are an evil little bastard, and you should be put to death."

Sean was silently crying. In the dim light down here in the cellar, tears glistened on his cheek and a bubble of snot blew out through his nose.

"Yeah," Norton said, "go on and cry about it, you piece of filth."

"I was on my way here to see you when Ziggy picked me up."

Norton pulled up a line of coke and took it straight up the nostril. He sighed, and all the tension seemed to evaporate; his shoulders rounded, and he put his chin on his chest and breathed shallow, peacefully. "Don't care."

"I want to stay with you a while till the heat dies down."

Norton lifted his head. "The heat will never die down, are you mad? You're more doolally than I am, boy. Your kids will tell the police who killed their mother, for one thing."

Sean shook his head. "They won't say anything to anyone."

Norton sighed out, "Please tell me you didn't kill your children as well."

"What? No, I gave them a Kinder Egg each. What do you take me for?"

"Subhuman is what I take you for. And rest assured, the heat will follow you."

"No way."

"Seriously, what happens when Ziggy's driver gets bored and comes knocking?"

Sean remained silent for a minute.

"Hadn't thought of it, had you?"

"It had slipped my mind, yes." He grinned, "You could—"

"No I couldn't! This isn't a garbage disposal machine, Sean. This is designed to get rid of street robbers, not just anyone I don't like. Otherwise you'd be in it."

Sean pointed to the machine, and shouted, "Ziggy!"

"An exception because he was about to kill me."

"So you get to choose who you use that machine on and who not, eh?"

Norton stood and held onto the rafters for support until the apparent dizziness subsided. "My machine, my rules, and I don't have to justify anything about it, me, or my fucking life to you, Sean Walker. But I will add this: when that driver comes here wondering where Ziggy is, you can take Ziggy's gun and kill him with it, okay? And then you can drive his car far away from here."

"I'll get to him before he comes here. But I need somewhere to stay, Norton!"

Norton's cheeks throbbed. "You stood up for me against that Ziggy chap. You bought yourself a week. But annoy me and I'll let you see how it feels to be impaled like your friend, okay?"

"Thanks, man."

Norton turned to face him, and asked, "Benson. How did you know he was Benson?"

"He's been to my gaff, asking questions about a burglary at an old geezer's place."

"You're a burglar as well?" Norton nodded in contemplation. "My, there is no end to your nefarious talents. You are a thoroughly hateful little man."

Sean thought about this for a moment, and his response caused Norton to smile at his ignorance. "At least I don't work in no bank, eh? I don't serve on tables at Frankie & Benny's. I am my own fucking man."

Norton slapped him. "You're your own man who's begging for lodging for a week! You're as intelligent as a baby's used nappy, and as useful as a chocolate fireguard. I suggest you stop bragging about how wonderful you are and concentrate on reality, and how fucking useless at anything you actually are. You need to understand that, and you need to accept it, and you need to learn from it and escape it. You will be thoroughly useless your entire life if you do not accept there is a fundamental problem with yourself. You must study, Sean, and learn to escape this circular rut you're trapped inside."

Sean was watching him, and there was nothing but confusion in his eyes. Nothing at all. "He had a strange little house. It was in a shithole but it had a balcony looking out over Hyde Park."

Norton blinked, "Who had a strange little house?"

"The old geezer, Walter they call him." Sean stood and flicked his cigarette into the hole. He leaned over but could see nothing in the darkness below. He could hear rushing water and he could even feel a drop in the temperature, but he could see nothing. "Where's it go?"

The glow stood out in the darkness like a beacon. Wes was playing on his phone in the Range Rover. Surrounding the car was nothing but darkness.

The big man jumped when Sean knocked on the window and gave the universal sign for wind down the window.

"What do you want?"

"Why the hell didn't you warn us when that copper showed up?"

"What? What copper? And who the hell are you, you piece of shit—"

"Alright, alright, keep a lid on it, Wes." Sean climbed into the seat behind him. "I suppose you can't really see the entrance from this far away."

"I ain't parking no closer; you has to keep a distance. And I'll ask again, what—"

"I'm only passing on a message. Ziggy's driving, move over."

"What?"

"Are you fucking deaf?"

Wes turned in the seat, "Watch your mouth, Sean before I have it plugged."

"Listen, I'm passing on a message, yeah. He says he's driving, and you're to move over."

"But I always drive the Range Rover." Wes narrowed his eyes. "Where is he?"

"He's enjoying a line with our new business partner and then he's on his way out. And he's very keen to drive home."

"Look, he's always nuts when he's done a line or two. Gonna get us killed."

"Orders, man."

"You're pullin' my chain."

Sean shrugged. "Suit yourself, but when he gets here and finds you in the driver's seat, I'm going to let him know I told you – like four times, man. Four fucking times!"

Wes climbed out, slammed the door and got in the front passenger side. He slammed that door as well and looked over at Sean. "If you're—"

Sean shot him in the face and cringed at the mess it made, and then he shuddered as Wes slumped against the door. Sean got behind the wheel, adjusted the still-warm seat and rear-view mirrors and then set off to a place he knew that would take the Overfinch and turn it into parts within a week. They wouldn't be too fussy that the upholstery was a shade red, and they'd probably perform body disposal duties for five hundred knocking off the price of the vehicle.

Chapter Thirty-six

Flattery but no Quality Street

They'd probably been hiding out all week in some cheap bed and breakfast until things were ready for them over in Dublin. They could have gone over sooner than now – they could have gone over that night, but Eddie guessed they were shedding skin: the new boyfriend. He'd served his purpose, got them away, protected them, offered Kelly some hot flesh for a while, and now she was getting ready to peel him off like a dose of sunburn. Mrs Whatsherface would doubtless welcome him back and still refuse him fellatio.

He'd had a text message from Kelly on Thursday asking him for a meeting today. Yes, he was shocked. He wondered if there was a chance for them to get back together, or was it the kind of meeting where they discussed money and access?

He had every intention of attending that meeting – he wanted them back; he wanted to be a part of a family unit again or he wanted to formally establish maintenance payments.

But today was looking bad for getting away on time. The list was full of burglaries and assaults. And then he looked out of the window and imagined Kelly saying it was just his fall-back excuse, and when are you going to sacrifice the job for your family for once.

Eddie's mind though, kept wandering further into the distance, to when Becca was tiny, lying in a cot next to their bed. He smiled as he remembered saying to Kelly that sleeping babies were like grenades, and how you'd sneak past them trying not to disturb them. And if they opened their eyes, you ducked and held your breath.

The smile didn't last long; it was cold and distant, like the memories of the happy days. Another thought blundered onto the stage and pushed baby Becca off into the wings: Perhaps she was giving Eddie time to live alone and see what it was like without her. Maybe she was hoping he couldn't do it, that he'd be a crying lump of shit in the corner without her around, tearing his hair out because he couldn't work the oven or the dishwasher.

She'd made Becca leave a note giving a date and time for the ferry departure so he could rush there to meet her and talk her out of leaving. How she'd take the high ground if he was daft enough to fall for that one. He'd never be allowed out of the house; he'd never be allowed a beer out in the garden. He was about to add that she'd never let him go out with his friends for a pint or to watch some live music down The Beehive in town – but he never went out with his friends anyway. He didn't have any friends.

His last friend turned her nose up and walked away to join the rest of them in ignoring him, in loathing him, perhaps. It didn't matter, really. Eddie never was a cuddly sort, preferring family over friends any day. But of course even family had deserted him.

The emails in the long list on the screen before him were a mix of good and bad. The good concerned the palm print in blood he'd found at Chantelle's scene, on the kitchen worktop. There was no offer of a prize for guessing it had come back as Sean Walker – inside his head Eddie popped a cork and greedily drank on a bottle marked Success.

At the other end of the scale was the horror of a missing police officer. Her name was Fiona Wright, PC 966, and she hadn't been seen since yesterday lunchtime. Her vehicle, a plain car used by the Neighbourhood Policing Team, hadn't been seen since. Her radio and the radio in the vehicle, both of which used sophisticated technology and GPS to ensure neither could ever be lost, had, it seemed, malfunctioned. To Eddie, that meant she and the car went into deep water, and the electrics shorted out and no longer worked. Poor lass, he thought.

Eddie's mood deepened further and hit bedrock when the phone on his desk rang. He'd unplugged it only yesterday and some bastard had plugged it back in again. Next time he'd create a wiring fault with his knife – fucking phones. He picked up the handset, and said, "Eddie Collins, blah, blah."

"Collins, it's me, Benson."

"Who?"

"Ben... Stop dicking about, you moron."

Eddie wagged his head and pulled a face. "What do you want?"

"Meet me at Coulston House on Mabgate at ten for a Section 18 search, would you?"

"What? Why on earth would I do that?"

"Because I'm asking you."

"I only take orders from my line manager." He looked across the office at Peter.

Peter laughed, and said, "You don't even take fucking orders from me. Lying imbecile."

"I heard that," Benson said.

"Who is that?" Peter shouted.

"I think it's a wrong number," Eddie was about to hang up.

"Will you answer me for a change, Eddie?"

Eddie sighed. "It's that DS from Major Crime."

Peter nodded. "Go and do what he wants. I might need a favour from him one day."

"I heard that too," Benson said. "Don't be late," and then the line died.

Eddie stared at the phone. "I hate it when people don't say goodbye. It's so rude."

And here he was sitting in his van outside Coulston House playing that last line over in his head like an old and very annoying song. It reminded him of Ros; he didn't get a goodbye from her, either. In fact, he got lies: just clearing the walls for when I decorate. Next day she'd moved out and quit her job. "I wonder if I have leprosy. Or just bad body odour, maybe."

He waited for Benson, put his foot on the dash and rested his head back against the seat, cigarette poised between flicking it out of the cracked window and bringing it to his lips for another drag. It started to rain, and Eddie wondered when global warming would finally reach Leeds. He flicked the cigarette and closed the window, and was about to close his eyes when he saw the rotund figure that could only be Benson waddle along the side of his van, knocking knuckles at the ready.

Eddie opened the door and climbed out into the rain. A sigh fell out of his mouth, and then another one followed it.

"Slight change of plan," Benson said, and closed in so as to keep the conversation private. "I'm arresting him on suspicion of murder."

Eddie's eyebrows nearly fell off the back of his head. "What have you got on him?"

"Never mind all that, I haven't got time. He's probably clocked that we're here already, and I don't want him dumping evidence."

"What evidence?"

"Shut up and listen, Eddie."

"Well get on with it, then, this rain is ruining my hair."

Benson shook his head. "Listen, that rust you found on the dead kid, see if you can find a weapon in there that'll match it."

"What?"

"I know. Just try."

"That it?"

"That's it."

"What about what Chantelle mentioned?"

"That Norton Bailey is the credit card kingpin responsible for all those mispers?"

Eddie folded his arms. "Exactly that."

"The warrant covers a blood and weapon search in relation to—"

"So I'm supposed to ignore—"

"Eddie, listen to me. I work by the book, okay? We have a warrant to look for evidence that Norton is involved in Mojo's death. Nothing more. You can't go snooping." He twitched his head, the new way of asking questions. "Understand?"

"No, not really."

"Start working outside the warrant and you're working outside the law. Work outside the law and you start losing cases that you shouldn't lose. Understand now?"

"Okay, okay, I get your point even though it's stupid. What else?"

Benson bit his lip, and then whispered, "I've been in there, I went in on a recce last night, and there's plenty of blood in the hallway – and I think that's from Bailey himself, he has a nasty scalp wound. Try to find blood belonging to Mojo." He looked around, as though searching for something that might help, but found only more problems. "I don't know; I just want to put that kid in that house or find his blood on a weapon."

"Oh wow. You think Mojo has different colour blood to everyone else to make it easy to spot? Blue, maybe?"

"No need to get flippant."

"How can you stand there and tell me the hallway blood is Norton Whateverhisnameis, and you don't want that, you just want Mofo's blood."

"Mojo's."

"Whatever."

Benson's smile was on upside down. "Okay. Well, you're the blood pattern specialist—"

"Whoa. No, I'm not. I'm a CSI, Benson. I'm a Jack of all crime trades and master of none. If you want BPA, you'll need a biologist or a BPA specialist."

Benson thought about it.

"Not keen on spending money, are you? Do it on the cheap."

"It's not like that."

"No? How about this then: use dear old Eddie Collins, and we can blame him if he gets the blood analysis wrong."

Benson was colouring up; his little fat hands were balled into… balls. "It's not like that, either. I don't work like that."

"Perfect, aren't you? You work by the book, but you work on the cheap. You won't screw me over, except when you have to. All gaffers work like that. I don't trust any one of you. Not a single fucking one of you." Eddie had grown aggressive, using sarcasm as a launching platform, and he didn't realise it until he was in Benson's face.

Benson didn't step away, though. He remained standing firm, and he whispered. "I got you here because I like how you work. I like how thorough you are, how you see things instead of just looking, which is what most of you lot seem to do. I could have asked for anyone in that office and Peter would have handed them over." He blinked, and said, "I chose you."

"That supposed to impress me, eh? A bit of flattery."

Benson shrugged, "I hoped it would, yes."

"Well it didn't."

"Okay, next time I'll buy you a box of Quality Street."

Eddie thought about it. "That would probably work, actually."

Just as he was almost done, Benson asked, "Why do you have such problems with authority?"

"Really, you want to get into this now?"

Benson shrugged, "Just curious."

"Yes, you are. But anyway, I don't have anything against authority. I'm against arseholes. And I think it's such a shame that so many arseholes get into positions of authority. Do you see what I'm getting at?"

"Fair point."

Eddie's cheeks throbbed as he gritted his teeth. He climbed down, and he cooled down, and he took that all important step back, away from confrontation, and somewhere towards civility. If he'd had the balls, he'd have apologised for his outburst; but men seldom do that, they just carry on, and they pretend it never happened. "Seriously, how the hell did you get a Section 18 warrant on that basis?"

"I just need him out of the house for a bit so you can do your stuff."

"If you're arresting him for the kid's murder, he'll be out of the house for a few years."

Benson smiled. "If I have my way, yes; but a half-decent brief will get him off my hook pretty fast, so you need to get your skates on, okay?"

"Ready when you are, Kemosabe."

"One last thing."

"Knew there would be."

"The cop who finally managed to speak with him, a house-to-house chat if you like, reported that the cellar window looked as though it had been forced. Check it out, would you? Burglary is an interesting proposition for a young lad, and murdering a burglar is an interesting diversion for someone slightly unbalanced."

Eddie snorted. "Don't have to be unbalanced to murder a burglar. It's sound socioeconomic sense in my book."

"Good job we're not using your book then, isn't it? See you soon."

Chapter Thirty-seven

The Punk and the Pianist's Finger

SEAN WALKER ALMOST FORGOT the gnawing pain in his chest, and stared at the kitchen, his mouth open. Aside from the fact it was very dark, what held his attention were the dozen slugs creeping along the worktop next to the sink, up the walls and across the drainer. They were ginger, fat as sausages and as long as a pianist's finger.

A dismal grey daylight crawled through gaps in the back door that a slug as fat as a sausage could crawl through – with headroom to spare – and resentfully threw itself on the remains of a small animal; could have been a kitten or a rat. Maggots rippled through its fur and played hide-and-seek in and out of its eye sockets and mouth. So even though his stomach rumbled like a little cloud of thunder under his sweater, the fear of throwing up whatever food was put in front of him made him reach instead for his cigarettes again.

"Not hungry?" Norton opened a packet of bread and pulled out a couple of slices edged with blue mould, popped them in the toaster and filled the kettle.

Sean didn't know whether to bring all the health and safety issues to light or act like they didn't exist – as Norton himself seemingly did. How could he not see the slugs? If he saw them, didn't he mind them being there? "You know there are slugs on the worktop, right?"

Norton stopped, and squinted. "You can see them?"

"Huh? They're there. Course I can see them. What's up with you?"

Norton shook his head as if trying to eject the fog from inside his brain. "Thought I was hallucinating." He turned to Sean, "Never mind. They won't get in your way. It's just nature."

Sean's face wrinkled with revulsion.

"Tut, if it bothers you that much..." Norton picked up a couple and chucked them across the kitchen. No one knew where they landed. He sniffed his fingers, then rubbed his hands down his trousers. "Now, you want toast or not?"

Sean gipped. "I'll pass."

Norton reached for a mug, swilled it out under the tap. He took tablets from three or four blister packs and gulped them down with four mugs of water, then dropped a teabag into the empty mug.

"What are those?"

"What? The tablets?"

Sean nodded.

"They er... they help with what goes on up here," he tapped his head. "They calm me down, numb me, if you like."

"What condition do you have?"

"Although we're still business partners, in a loose sense, and although you're my guest for the next week or so, I feel as though our relationship isn't close enough yet to begin discussing my private medical matters. If you don't mind."

"Didn't mean to pry." There was a considerably long pause, almost painfully so, before Sean said, "I never finished telling you about that old geezer's house what I burgled."

"Lithium."

"What do they do? Get you high?"

"The lithium is for my mood and for treating mania, others are anticonvulsant meds but they really screw with your memory. I mean, I was," he looked up at Sean who was back studying the remaining slugs. "Blah. Blah, blah, who gives a shit anyway."

"Okay, I was just making, you know, conversation. But thanks for telling me, man." He nodded at Norton. "So, Walter, this old guy I burgled—"

"I was waiting for that joy to recommence." Norton looked to the ceiling and then closed his eyes.

"It was covered in photos and paintings of the royal family, right back to olden times, you know when everything was in black and white."

"Wait. What? When everything—"

"There was photos of Victoria and Albert."

Norton stopped, and turned to appraise him. That Sean knew about past British monarchs was indeed—

"They was all labelled, like. Prince Henry, The Duke of York, they was all there, each with their own bit of space on the wall, see."

"Wonderful, I'm sure."

"He was a punk."

Norton tutted. "Who was a punk?"

"Walter. Riddled with arthritis, now, but he ain't much older than you. He used to be a skinhead. Back in the day. Tattoos everywhere. There was this one photo showing a tattoo on the back of—"

"How did you sleep?"

"Eh?"

"Last night. How did you sleep?"

Sean paused, brought abruptly to a halt by a question that was usually small talk, but here in this house, was a major topic. How did I sleep? The house is alive with insects and rodents; the mattress moves on its own under you, the windows fit as well as the back door does so the wind, and rain, and noise make it feel like you're outside in the fucking street! "Not bad. Some odd noises—"

"Do you miss her?"

Sean's mind put the brakes on. It was a subject he had avoided since it happened; it was too dangerous to probe it, it was too painful to look at.

"And the children. Who has them now?"

"Our relationship isn't close enough to begin—"

"Yes, yes, very droll. But you must miss her. Surely?"

Sean opened the back door and leaned against the frame and groaned at the pain in his chest. He looked down and saw the redness was now blackness and brownness; the blood was solidifying, and it was beginning to smell bad. But the pain was the worst; it was constantly there like someone squeezing his chest, tighter and tighter, hotter.

He avoided looking at the dead rat/kitten and its inhabitants. Instead he smoked and tried to put the pain to one side – if you didn't think about it, didn't allow it air time in your mind, then the pain faded. He stared out the back where a few dogs barked incessantly and a group of stray kids played football, even in the rain, because their parents didn't want them in the house.

Despite avoiding the topic of Chantelle as though it were a slice of mouldy bread, the very fact that he was actively avoiding something, made him think of it anyway. And of course he thought about her constantly – whenever he wasn't fighting for his life or taking the life of others, and whenever he wasn't listening to noises coming from the other side of the bath panel while he was on the loo – he thought about her so much. Tears began to gather in his lower lids, and he coughed, straightened up and took another drag.

"I do miss her. And to answer your next question, I wish I hadn't done her in. It didn't get me as far as I thought it would."

Norton sniffled. "Interesting. You regret killing her because it meant you were ousted from the gang you'd recently signed up to, rather than you miss her company and thought killing her was essentially wrong?"

Sean turned. "Wait, we're not talking about killing being wrong, are we?"

The toast popped and Norton found some butter, shooed away the flies and scooped off yesterday's crumbs. "I take your point." He stared at the window, at the sagging black net curtains hanging by rusty nails, lost in thought. "It's just that your dear wife had done nothing wrong, had she? She what, tried to prevent you returning to prison, in fact? So she'd done you a favour."

"I never finished telling you about that fella's tattoo, did I?" He shuffled along, unsticking his feet from the floor. "Right on the back of his neck, a big smiley face with sharpened teeth—"

"Stop, stop, stop!"

"Eh? What's up with—"

Norton slowly turned around to face Sean, and for the first time since being in his company, Sean felt scared. His face was still, his eyes were unblinking, wet with the remnants of tears or the beginnings of new ones, and his hands were clenched tightly into fists, so tight that his fingers were white. "The smiley face." His voice was low and shaky, held in check. "What colour was it?"

Sean laughed, the nerves he felt made him back away. "It was yellow," he said, licking his dry lips. "And the teeth was red."

Norton stood motionless. His eyes closed and the tears rolled into his beard.

"You, er. You okay?"

"Where does he live, this old geezer of yours? This Walter."

Sean swallowed. "Why? Why do you want to know? He's just someone—"

Norton's eyes rolled open and settled on him like a lizard's would. "Where does he live?"

"Do you know him?"

Norton screamed, and came at him with a butter knife. "Where does he fucking live?"

"Why are you so interested all of a sudden?" As he turned away from Norton, Sean did a double take. He peered out of the back door again, up and down the road that had suddenly become quiet. The kids playing football had gone. The barking dogs had gone, too. "I think there's coppers around here." He turned to Norton, "There's coppers—"

Just then there was a knock at the front door, and Sean's eyes widened.

"Quick, get in the cellar."

Sean stood anchored to the floor, heart pounding, everything throbbing, panic rising. "Where's the fucking door? I don't see the door!"

"Calm down. It's here." Norton slid aside a chair draped with cobwebs and pushed at the wall. A door opened, and darkness welcomed him as Sean slid inside it, shoved by Norton. "Same place it was the last time." Once inside, he searched the wall for a light switch as Norton pulled the door closed and scraped the chair back into place.

"What the hell was I thinking, coming here?"

He stood there holding his breath, refusing to allow the spiders and rats and dead things that surely existed here to enter his thoughts or mess with his head, and telling himself that the things touching his face were nothing to be afraid of. He listened.

This place seemed normal while Norton's company. But now, afraid, alone... Now it felt horrifying.

Chapter Thirty-eight

The Gothic Behemoth's Scullery

Eddie stood at the foot of the steps in the front garden and looked up. It was a huge old Victorian house with elegant attic dormers embellished with ornate wooden decorations, spires like stalagmites and others like stalactites. It had most of its original cast iron fall pipes left, with only a couple of those around this side of the house being broken, replaced by plastic ones, or cracked near the ground, with poor repairs allowing water to spew onto paving slabs and thick mossy grass. The windows were wooden framed and opaque with years of muck on the insides and years of spiderwebs and grime on the outside.

This whole ensemble was a gothic behemoth.

He took a step back as Benson and a couple of his detectives huddled in front of the massive front door under a tiled porch that leaked. They knocked and waited and got wet.

The cellar bay was an extension of the lounge bay above it and the bedroom bay above that. To the far side of the front door was another bay running top to bottom, and it was probably where the dining room was. The cellar might have been a scullery in days gone by, or there might have been a separate kitchen in the back of the house.

The bay window for the cellar was partially hidden from view of the main house by a void that had its own set of stone steps down to the basement level. Had the garden been anything but overgrown bushes and weeds, it could be splendid, and the basement void hidden totally from view, as was the designer's original plan.

Eddie took high steps over tall wet weeds and grass to get a closer look at the damaged cellar window. He crouched and saw old screwdriver marks in the wood, cracked glass, and missing panes. So maybe Benson had been right about the burglary. But no, this was very old damage. Though the window was insecure... When he crouched and shone his torch through into the room beyond, he could see nothing – no light came back to him. He looked puzzled, and put the cellar on his list of places to visit.

Above him the front door opened, and Eddie could hear subdued voices. A minute or two later and a man, wearing the most ridiculous clothing, accompanied the detectives, and Benson, down the slippery stone steps and was led away to a car.

Eddie looked at the open front door.

He had two or three hours. Benson would call when Mr Bailey had been released and was on his way back here.

Eddie dumped his kit and camera in the hallway and just looked, staggered by what he saw. There were paintings that must have been over six feet tall just stacked lazily against the wall near what he assumed was the dining room or kitchen entrance. Some appeared slashed or cut somehow. To his right was a closed door with ornate plasterwork above it – the other side of that door would be a grand room, no doubt.

But even here, just standing in the hallway, he had a feeling of dread. The floor was naked wood and up its centre was a shiny raised mound of uneven trodden-in muck, maybe decades old, and something you'd need a sharp-edged spade to scrape up. To the sides were scallops of dust, some rigid where water vapour had solidified them, and others floating like wafers on air currents. The doors, grand though they were, had muck adhering to those parts frequently handled. It was cringeworthy.

The sense with the most points so far, though, was smell. This was like an overload. There was the cutting stench of body odour, the underlying foundation of tobacco smoke and possibly a tinge of cannabis too. But there was something else that wouldn't immediately come to mind. In time, he was sure it would. The smell came straight from a nineteenth century doss house.

On that naked, compacted muck floor, were indeed splashes and small pools of blood. Eddie crouched and saw that some were fresher than others. For instance, just this side of the lounge doorframe was a three- or four-inch shallow pool of blood that had dried and crusted over around the edges but was still glossy and damp in the centre. And there was another such pool up by the far doorway. These were the pools of blood Benson had said belonged to Norton.

The first anomaly showed itself after only a few minutes of staring. To his right was the filthy and ornate lounge door. The strange thing about it was the hole in it. Straight through, maybe half an inch across, ragged edges to the hard wood that pointed to the hallway side, rather than the lounge side. Eddie brought his nose close and inhaled, and there was the undercurrent that had eluded labelling before. A metallic flavour, sooty almost. He looked across the hallway to the left-hand wall opposite the hole in the door and saw precisely nothing. Just wallpaper from the 1980s: large floral displays in the colour of last night's curry sauce. Though there was no hole in the wall that corresponded to the height of the hole in the door, there was a hole a little higher up, maybe fourteen inches higher. Through the wallpaper and lining paper, Eddie could see grey plaster dust and that was about all. Doubtless there would be a bullet in there somewhere or perhaps in the room behind it, but it wasn't on the surface.

Casting his eye downward, trying to replicate the angle of the two holes, he opened the lounge door and let out a smell of shit that caught in the back of his throat for a moment. He coughed and shoved the door open. More bare floorboards, more cobwebs the size of table cloths, more muck and dust. Just a shitty old rug on the floor – one of those rag rugs with bare patches where the hessian was poking through. There were alcove shelves overflowing with books and magazines, long dead plants, withered stalks in mourning. More shelves full of bottles and toby jugs and long vines of twisted webs that were black with dust and soot.

Across the window were strips of duct tape to keep it from rattling in the wind, he guessed, and taking pride of place opposite a TV that was topped in an inch of dust was an old armchair with what he hoped were gravy stains on the seat. On the floor next to it was a box with buttons to operate the reclining chair, and partly avalanched over it was a mound of cigarette butts easily eight inches deep and a couple of feet across. This lounge, probably called a parlour in the old days, brought gross to a whole new level.

And speaking of levels, it didn't really answer the question Eddie had: where was the shooter? The angle from the hallway wall through the lounge door meant the firer had to be lying in here on the floor.

It was a question Eddie would file away and ponder on when he had a moment to spare.

Sean held his breath as the knock rattled around the hallway again. By the time the noise reached him in the cellar head, it was dull and lifeless.

After a couple of moments he could hear muffled voices, and then it went strangely quiet, but the scariest of all was the silence. It was oppressive.

When he was younger, he'd go fishing with his big brother down to some private lake not too far away. He borrowed waders and loved how the water pressed them against his legs more and more the deeper he got. This silence was like those waders – he could feel his body being crushed by it, or by the anxiety the silence caused. It was comforting to begin with, but then it pressed in on his chest, harder and harder, until he forced himself to take a breath and hold it – pushing out his ribs, and then exhaling into the blackness like an explosion dissipating dregs of fear like torn strips of flesh. The wound in his chest was on fire and it took all his reserves not to scream out in pain.

A few more minutes drifted by – they could have been tens of minutes, though, he really wasn't sure. By now, his eyes should have become accustomed to the dark and given him something to see. But no, everything was just as black as ever, just as black as having your eyes closed and putting your hands over them too. He heard something faint, thudding. Footsteps on the hall floor again. Was Norton back already? Or was someone else in the house? Did he risk opening the cellar door, or wait, standing here, not moving, getting cramp in his legs and his back?

After prodding the walls for what seemed like hours, and ignoring the crawling things his fingertips met, he discovered a light switch. He knew there was a risk of it being seen from the kitchen – and eventually decided against turning it on. Hopefully, there'd be another light at the bottom.

Slowly, he descended the steps and felt the decrease in temperature along the way. By the time he hit the bottom step he could feel his hot breath against his face. The next thing he noticed was the noise – a constant rush, like putting a conch shell up to each ear. But louder. He found a waterproof light switch, something one might see in the garden, and the darkness evaporated to reveal a huge cellar probably fifty yards square with brick pillars every ten yards or so.

Within it he found a shelf with dozens of dusty carrier bags on it. In those bags were wrist watches, wallets, rolls of cash, spectacles, finger rings, earrings, gold teeth, but most interestingly, he found a bag of knives and another with a couple of guns. He recognised Ziggy's gun from last night straight away, and there were his credit cards and golden rings – even a couple of half sovereigns.

Sean licked his lips and remembered the trouble guns had already got him into, but he also remembered the power they had given him, and reached out for it – because this time he really needed one for self-defence. He really did.

Towards what he assumed was the front of the house was a raised plinth with pulleys and ropes and strings of electrical cable running around from a small distribution box screwed to a rafter. The rushing noise was loud now; and as he dragged his feet over the wet cobbles, he saw the metal plates over what he termed the Wishing Well.

For some reason those plates, one on top with holes in it, and one below with spikes poking through those holes, reminded him of Kyle, that crazy dog from the Minions movies, the one with long sharp teeth. And though Norton had done a reasonable job of hosing those plates down after Ziggy fell on them, he'd missed a lot of blood and hair that clung to the wishing well's walls. From the well rose a fine cooling mist like something you'd see at the foot of a waterfall. It was perpetually wet in here because of the mist, and the only time that mist wasn't around was during a drought, Norton had told him.

For this kind of work, he'd said, it needs to be raining, and preferably it needs to have been raining for several days, and raining hard. If you chose a dryish day, the chances of the body making it down to the River Aire in one fast gulp were slim, and he did not want to risk jamming the culvert up with dead bodies and have some nosey inspector finding them.

As he watched the spray bloom across the cellar, he heard the squeal of the lounge door directly above. And then he heard footfalls on the boards right over his head, maybe nine or ten feet up. Sean swallowed, and held his breath. There was no chance of being detected down here, but he held it anyway, watching as dust fell through the gaps of the boards above.

Who was up there?

He walked around the wishing well, eyes on the parlour floor above, and when he tripped and fell, the gun skittered across the floor into the darkness, and Sean got a mouthful of Ziggy's bloody face. He actually had to put a hand over his mouth to stop the scream escaping. And then he almost screamed again when he realised his hand was covered in Ziggy's blood.

He remembered Norton saying he stored the bodies until it was dark. No point sending something down Ladywell Beck – with its few exposed lengths – and into the Aire that passers-by might take to be a human being! Better to do it while it's dark, he said.

Chapter Thirty-nine

The Scene Examination

Eddie's tour of the lounge paused at the mantelpiece. There was something odd about it. It was clean. Every other surface in here was covered in dust, but the mantelpiece was clean. He stepped up closer, onto the rag rug, and inspected it. Other than its contrast with the rest of the room, there was nothing that stood out for him. Eddie took a step back and peered around both sides of the chimney breast alcoves, at the bookcases stuffed with books and anything that needed a home. Among the trails of dead plants was something that made him gasp.

It was a long rifle with a bayonet fitted at the business end. It looked old – very old – perhaps even WW2 old.

He took out his torch and shone light up and down the barrel and the stock and discovered that it too was lacking in the dust department – had it been recently used, perhaps? He couldn't tell if this rifle would leave the same kind of hole he'd found in the door or the wall because, for now, he didn't want to touch it – that was a job for a firearms officer, and only after consulting with stroppy-git Benson.

He felt sure that Benson would be interested in the bayonet. It was rusty, and it had a single edge to it, much like the wound in Mojo's back. And he was sure that the tiny red smear across the blade was blood. This was enough evidence for Eddie to move along to other parts of the house without breaking Benson's love affair with the conditions of the warrant and PACE codes.

As his gaze was drawn down the stock and back towards the floorboards, his eyes scooted along the rag rug and found the floorboards beyond it bore swirl marks. On closer inspection, the swirl marks were red – possibly blood, and this was possibly a bad attempt at cleaning it up. Eddie made a mental note to grab the KM kit from the van: that stain needed testing to see if it was blood, and if it was, it was a red-hot candidate for swabbing. Eddie would bet Benson's mortgage payment that the DNA would come back to someone other than Norton Bailey, perhaps even to Mojo himself. Eddie felt good.

From here, he looked up and saw the hole in the lounge door, and the shadow of the hole in the hallway wall. "No way," he whispered. "The shooter would have to have been below ground level...Unless the round took a deflection?" He stood and booted the floor but it didn't sound any different to the other parts of the floor. "Hell of a deflection, though." And then Eddie remembered how the basement looked black when he'd shone the torch inside the damaged window from outside. "Let's go take a look."

Back outside, what had been a light drizzle had turned into light rain threatening to get heavier. He peered through the broken window again into the basement void, but saw nothing at all. Only when he climbed into the cellar did he understand the lack of information. The entire bay had been walled off using big blocks of stone. The wall had then been painted matt black.

After climbing back out, Eddie strode through the hallway and into what turned out to be the kitchen, and wasn't surprised to find out how shitty this place was, too. It was the kind of place where you'd need galoshes or scene-suit overshoes unless you didn't mind sticking to the floor. It smelled of burnt toast and of something rotting. It also smelled of cigarette smoke; a good strong torch beam showed him two fresh cigarette butts on the floor – different brands.

Despite the cool temperature down here, Sean was sweating, and he began to feel short of breath. Even though it was autumn, there were flies all over Ziggy. For a moment this amused him until he noticed how many of the little bastards had landed on the black blood of his own chest wound. It smelled bad and he would have been screaming in pain or screaming because he was crawling with flies had he been alone in the house.

Sean crept back up the stone cellar steps using the light from the lamp back there by the wishing well to navigate by. He slowed his breathing and made no sound at all on the final two steps, just settled on his knees and brought his eye up to a knothole in the cellar head door, and peered out into the dimly lit kitchen. Only moments passed before a figure walked into the kitchen. He was sniffing the air like a dog, flicking torchlight left and right.

The man stopped and crouched down to look at something on the floor that Sean couldn't see. He then crouched down by the back door where he'd been standing for his breakfast only half an hour ago. "Cig ends," he whispered. He'd found our cigarette ends! Don't mean nothing, keep cool, man.

And he did. He took slow, shallow breaths and, despite the tremble, tried to relax.

The man stood and shone his torch around again, this time sending a direct spear of light through the hole and into Sean's eye, rendering him temporarily blind. He brought the other eye to the hole but couldn't see the man at all now.

He could hear him, though. Inches away. Right against the door, and probably not even knowing it was there. He's looking for a way in, Sean told himself. He wants to get into the cellar.

His heart boomed and he felt the man would be able to hear it from there. He almost dropped the gun. His dry mouth clacked, and his hands shook.

Then the man crouched and seemed to look right at him.

Sean recognised him and bit down on his tongue.

Chapter Forty

The Thumbscrews and the Samaritan

"Please take a seat, Mr Bailey. Can I offer you a drink? Tea, coffee?"

"Water, please."

Drinks provided, Benson sat down opposite Norton and took a sip of water from a plastic cup before opening a folder in front of him. The folder was empty. He looked up at Norton, smiled, and said, "I understand you suffer with mental health issues, and before we begin, I'd like to offer you an assessment, and access to a professional to make sure you are in no danger, and that this procedure is unlikely to cause you any harm or distress." He folded his arms and waited.

"Thank you. I am fine, and you may proceed."

"You'll note that we have supplied you with counsel today."

Norton looked across at her. She did one of those stuttering blinks that tries not to be aloof, but fails totally. Her nose was high, and she moved as far away as the bolted-down plastic seat would allow. She frequently held her fingers under her nose, for Norton was especially ripe today. "This is Mrs Cross, and you have the right to spend a reasonable amount of time with her alone so that you may apprise her of your case and so that she might offer—"

"My case?"

"Yes, Mr Bailey."

"But I don't know why I've been arrested."

"I told you why you'd been arrested while still in your house not an hour ago. You were arrested on suspicion of the murder of Colin Fogg, otherwise known as Mojo."

"Ah, yes. Forgive me, you did mention that. Carry on, Sergeant Benson."

"Do you want to consult with your counsel, or do you want to appoint your own counsel?"

"I'm fine. Please," he said, waving a hand, "let's just get on and get this thing over with. I want to get back to my house." His feet tapped on the floor, driven by impatience.

Benson nodded across the desk. "For the record, this interview is being recorded; your counsel will be allowed a copy of the recording. Present are myself, Detective Sergeant Thomas Benson, Detective Constable Ram Khan, Mrs Irene Cross and Mr Norton Bailey. The time is thirteen-twenty-three." Benson looked around the table, saw no disapproving looks, and continued. "Eleven days ago a young man died a few hundred yards from your front door."

Norton nodded, "Sad news indeed."

Benson sat up. "There were reports of an elderly man leaving the scene minutes before the police arrived. I wondered if that elderly man might be you?"

Norton's eyebrows arched through the creases on his forehead. "I assure you that I had nothing to do with anyone's death, Sergeant. And further, I did not venture out that evening, and rarely do when dark."

"I believe you, of course." He offered a flat smile, complemented with his own raised eyebrows that were an indication that he thought Norton was lying. "Just like I believe you have nothing to do with any stolen credit cards or association with any criminal gang."

"Sergeant Benson," said Mrs Cross, "this isn't going to turn into one of those interviews, is it? If so—"

Benson held out his hand, "I apologise. I'll keep it relevant, okay?"

"Well I hope you do. Let me assure you that I am conversant with the complaints procedure here, and to whom to address that complaint. Please keep your questions specific to the charge."

"Can we, please," they all looked at Norton, "just get on with it?"

"Desperate to get home, Mr Bailey?"

"Desperate to get out of here. Next question if you please."

Benson bowed his head at Cross, and looked up at Norton. "How's your head?" Benson watched blood that had travelled down the dirty creases behind Norton's right ear, disappearing into the mess of beard he not so much wore as allowed to grow rampant. And then it had reappeared some twelve inches further south through the beard where it had congealed and hardened into a thick red rope. "Looks like the wound bled quite a bit." He nodded to the cascade of dried blood down Norton's jacket.

Norton felt the lumpy painful clot of hair and blood, winced slightly, and nodded. "A bit," he said.

For a moment, Benson looked pensive, and then said, "Did he burgle you, Mr Bailey?"

Norton sat back and became rigid, jaw locked shut.

"Did he?"

"Don't know what you mean."

"That's why you were there, isn't it? At the roadside when he died."

"You saying I killed him? That's preposterous."

"I'm saying no such thing. Listen to me – it makes sense, that's all. If he'd burgled you, and you try to give chase and slipped on your steps, but were still within sight of him... you know, when he died."

"I don't—"

"I think it's very noble of you to help the lad as he was dying."

Norton blinked; a huff blew past his slack lips. He swallowed, took his time in answering as though picking up a script and reciting the words he'd tried to memorise. "He wasn't burgling me, Mr Benson. He'd been stabbed, see, and he made it to my house in desperation. My house is the only dwelling nearby – all the rest are businesses that close at five o'clock, see?"

Benson nodded, exchanged a glance with Khan, biting his lip the whole time. "Ah, I see. How do you know he'd been stabbed? Who stabbed him, then?"

"No idea." He shook his head. "I couldn't see anyone nearby, certainly no one was chasing him. And how did I know he'd been stabbed? Because he told me, that's how I knew."

"So you were," Benson paused, looking at him, "you were a good Samaritan?"

"I would have done the same for anyone."

"Then why did he run from you?"

Norton held up a finger. "He wasn't running from me; he was running to someone." He sniffled and allowed his eyes to drift out of focus. "I think he knew he wasn't long for this world; he told me he wanted to be back with his girlfriend when his life ended. It was very emotional."

Benson's mouth opened but for a time nothing came out. "That's so sad," he said at last. "And it's so brave of you to be there for him at the end."

Norton nodded slowly. "You can't kill community spirit."

"Indeed. It was very honourable of you."

"Thank you. Might I leave now?"

"Earlier you told me you had nothing to do with the kid at all. You lied to me."

"Regrettable. Yes, I did."

"Why?"

Norton snorted. "Why? I have a mental disability, Sergeant. The police are not known for their caring attitude towards people who suffer mental health issues – my being locked up here is proof of that. I chose to keep out of your investigation because I do not trust you to make the right decision."

Benson considered this for a while, pushed a pen back and forth across the table. "This file is empty," he said quietly. "It's empty because I want to fill it with your version of what happened that night. I came here with no preconceptions, ready to be convinced by your version of events. So tell them to me. Truthfully, please."

Norton looked at Mrs Cross. She nodded, and he began, "He banged on my door and I allowed him in because he seemed so distressed. He asked how bad it was, the wound in his back, and I took a quick look. But I'm not good with blood, and... well, I didn't tell him how bad it appeared to me, just that it was bleeding a lot."

"Did you go into the lounge with him?"

"The parlour, Mr Benson. Yes, we went into the parlour."

"And then what?"

"And then he left, and I followed him, telling him to come back and I would call an ambulance for him."

"Did he?"

"No. He was found by the roadside, so it's unlikely, don't you think?"

"So you went with him?"

"Yes, I already told you."

"You consoled him while you waited for an ambulance?"

"Well, I stood with him, but alas I had not phoned for help. I don't own a mobile phone, and I didn't get the chance to telephone for an ambulance while we were in my house."

"Okay, so you hoped someone else might make the call?"

"Yes, I was beckoning passers-by, signalling those in cars."

"No one took any notice? That's awful."

"I know," Norton said, hands soothing hands on the desk. "I felt very sad about it. Still do."

"Did you embrace him, you know, to reassure him, to be there for him as he passed away? You just said that you stood with him."

Norton took his time to answer. "I stood with him, yes. I waited with him, and when I saw blue flashing lights, I left. He didn't need me any more; I left him alone."

"Was he still alive when you left him?"

Norton shrugged. "So far as I know, yes, still alive."

"If you never embraced him, can you explain why your blood was found soaking his jacket collar and the back of his t-shirt."

Mrs Cross snatched a look at Norton.

Norton's hands stopped on the table. "It might have dripped from me as I stood over him."

"Really?"

He shook his head. "I don't know. I suppose it's not beyond imagination to accept that I might have knelt beside him as he passed over. I don't recall. Yes, I suppose I could have knelt by him; it would have been the kind thing to do."

"Seriously, you don't remember hugging a dying man?"

"Obviously, I don't."

"You lied about knowing the lad, you tried to avoid the police investigation into his death, you lied about him running from you, and you lied about holding him as he died."

Norton pointed his finger, "I did not lie about him leaving my house."

"Yes, you did!"

Norton folded his arms and clamped his mouth shut. He turned to Mrs Cross and asked, "Are you going to let him speak to me like that?"

"Like what?" she answered. "He's asking you questions about a man's death. So far I don't see any thumbscrews, Mr Bailey. But rest assured that if I do, I'll call foul, okay?"

Norton looked front again. "I didn't lie."

"You said that Mr Fogg wanted to get home to his girlfriend before he died?"

Norton nodded.

"You stand by that?"

He shrugged. "It's what he told me."

Benson rubbed his temples, eyes closed, almost meditating. And then he rubbed the file. "I was wrong about this file. It's not empty at all; it's full of bullshit that pours from your mouth in a sickening wave."

"Mr Benson."

"Apologies, Mrs Cross." He looked back at Norton. "Mojo was gay. He was in a long-standing relationship with someone called Mr Chubb – who has also gone missing. He went missing the same night Mojo died." He stared intently at Norton until Norton's eyes found something less intimidating to look at.

"I can't help you, Sergeant. That's what he told me." He leaned forward. "A lot of these gay boys are embarrassed to be gay, or embarrassed to admit it." Palms out, Norton stared at those present. "Come on. He told me he wanted to be with his girlfriend probably because he didn't want an old homophobe like me preaching at him. Simple. Anyone would have done the same."

Benson's clenched teeth relaxed and the ache in his jaw subsided. He looked at Khan, and Khan gave the merest hint of a shrug. He even looked at Mrs Cross, the lilt across her lips and her drooping eyes said it.

Benson closed the empty file and Norton saw the smiley-face sticker on the front cover. Back in the basement, and later in the kitchen, stupid boy Sean had talked about the time he'd burgled a house, and the chap living in that house had a smiley face on the back of... he didn't get around to furnishing him with an address. Norton's toes curled.

He drifted away into thoughts of the distant past where he was giving chase to a man who had a smiley face tattoo on the back of his neck. Well, the big, exaggerated mouth, full of big goofy teeth, was on the back of his neck. The eyes, also big and goofy, were on the back of his head – easily seen back then because the thief was a punk. He was a skinhead.

Norton's mouth dropped open, and he gasped.

Chapter Forty-one

An Honourable Arsehole

Eddie heard it quite plainly. From somewhere nearby was a gasp. It wasn't the old house settling, it wasn't a loaf of bread moving because a mouse was nibbling at one corner. It wasn't anything other than a gasp.

It took a second to register, like it would if you'd woken up at night to hear footsteps on the stairs outside your room. You'd need a moment to process that information, and in that moment, Eddie turned off the torch and moved. As he moved, he tripped over something and, as he went down, there was a loud crack and an orange flash. He almost screamed – someone had just tried to shoot him. His arm hurt and his hip was sore where it had collided with the floor, but otherwise the shooter had missed, and Eddie lived to realise that.

His heart tripped up over itself trying to get out, and for a moment he thought he was going to be sick. But he kept it together, and held his breath, feeling the thumping of his heartbeat through his ears.

He stared at the wall, from where he'd seen a flash and from where he had heard the gasp. And for a moment he thought about saying something, but only 'come out' came to mind, and he was pretty sure that wouldn't do the trick. But his red-hot mind kicked him in the shins and shouted, 'Do you really want a man with a gun to... come out? Really?'

Good point.

Eddie reached into his pocket and took out his phone. It didn't take him long to work out that the phone had been rendered a slab of broken plastic in the fall and that it was responsible for the pain in his hip. His thumb moved across the screen that now felt like a cheese grater. He said nothing, didn't scream or curse. He just stared as a growing sliver of weak orange light appeared on the wall where the gasp had come from.

His breath sighed out quietly and he tried to move on his backside towards where he knew the doorway to the hall was. His hand slid in something, and he pictured a big healthy dog turd squelching up between his fingers, and almost vomited again. This was not the kind of afternoon he'd had in mind when Benson first called him up this morning.

The hole in the wall grew into a full door, and opened all the way on shuddering hinges. The gunman crept forward, and so far as Eddie could tell was hampered by the same thing that stalled Eddie's retreat: darkness.

The silence was alive. It had the same kind of weight, the same kind of atmosphere an approaching thunder storm generated.

He swallowed.

His broken mobile phone wasn't broken when he truly needed it to be. This was destiny dicking him about again as usual. This was another example of The Law of Fuck in action. It rang like a church organ and the screen shone like someone had turned on the sun.

The gunman aimed again.

Benson followed Norton out into the public foyer. "Wait here, Mr Bailey. I'll give you a lift home." He handed him a slim sheaf of paperwork that basically said Norton had been de-arrested and no further action would be taken so long as no new evidence into the same crime came to light.

Norton made no reply, and Benson swiped his card to get back into the glass-ceilinged atrium, the growing darkness countered by large white, cold, LEDs. He settled himself into a plush armchair – one of five in a semicircle next to a water dispenser, and watched Norton sink his stinking old arse into a plastic and tubular-metal seat that was as uncomfortable a thing that one human could make for another's misery. They had those in waiting rooms up and down the country. Norton stared at the carpet, and his face had changed since he first came here. It was always serious, of course, Benson knew, but now it was verging on grotesque. He was thinking about something so deep it was almost painful.

Benson didn't give a shit. This old bastard was a wrong-un, and he was convinced of it. And he was convinced he'd find out one day what his particular seam of evil was. One day, he'd lock him up for a very long time.

Right now, he wondered if letting him walk was such a bright idea. He didn't confront Bailey with the petechiae – the burst blood vessels – across Mojo's face and chest indicating strangulation. He was hoping for CCTV footage to come to light, and although it had been ten days, there were still premises who needed a nudge to check and supply theirs.

He made a mental note to get Khan cracking on the court orders, the DP7s, needed to get people to cooperate with the police and hand over their CCTV coverage. And not for the first time did he wonder how someone like Mojo, young, fit, and healthy, could fall prey to Norton Bailey – for fall prey he surely did.

Benson took out his phone and a Mars bar, set the chocolate aside and hit a previously dialled number. That number belonged to CSI Eddie Collins, the strangest man he had ever met – without a shadow of a doubt – and he'd met a few, and was indeed looking at one right now.

Eddie Collins was like a man who had accepted a bet to get to the end of each day without murdering anyone. And each day he came closer and closer to losing that bet. Benson laughed to himself. Yes, Collins was an arsehole, but there was something about him, a kind of honour that Benson liked – it marked him as someone you could rely on to get the job done no matter how shitty that job was or who he had to piss off to get it done. "It's the Eddie Collins way," he whispered.

Benson opened the Mars bar and sank his teeth into it, eyes watching the phone on the seat arm. It rang for thirty seconds, not even long enough to chew, before it rang off.

The room lit up and the ring tone – Who Are You, by The Who – vibrated through the walls. Eddie closed his eyes and a shot thumped into the floorboards somewhere close by. His eyes snapped open again, and his feet back-pedalled against the shitty kitchen floor, his hands scooting backwards, depositing slime, heading somewhere in the region of the hall doorway.

"Benson said you wasn't a copper." There was a considerable pause. "I fucking knew you was."

Eddie slowly closed his mouth and tried to pop his eyes back into his skull. The gunman was Sean Walker! The same Sean Walker who'd shot his own wife dead in the kitchen with her kids sharing front row seats with popcorn and 3D glasses. "Put the gun down, Sean."

Sean fired another shot into the darkness.

It was deafening and it was scary. This man was already a killer. Eddie knew better than to piss this guy off. He swallowed, wondered if he could make it to the hall, and then maybe leap out through the still-open front door. He decided the odds were very much stacked against him.

The only thing he had in his favour was the dim light behind Sean Walker – it silhouetted him, made him into a target. Even if he were to stand right now, there was no light behind Eddie, he'd be a black shadow in a black room.

You're not seriously considering that, are you? What if he has a torch? What if he's a better shot next time? What if he's lucky, Eddie? Remember The Law of Fuck?

Chapter Forty-two

Dry-humping Cynthia

SOMETIMES PEOPLE MAKE RASH decisions. Take the Land Rover Discovery that Eddie drove around in, for instance. He spent less than a minute looking it over before signing the paperwork. That car was a V6 diesel – the dodgy model that everyone had warned him about; the model with the weak front prop shaft joints that were liable to break. But he bought the car anyway and he'd already run it for four years. Never a moment's bother with it. His house: he and Kelly walked around each room in that house twice. Twenty minutes maximum – and they bought the place for one-hundred and twenty-five thousand pounds. It was a big investment to make considering the amount of time they'd spent looking at it and imagined living in it.

People made rash decisions. And when Eddie leapt at Sean Walker, his predominant thoughts were: What the fuck are you doing? Have you really thought this through? And, I preferred it when you were a coward.

It was a decision taken in a split second that could have ramifications for the rest of his life – potentially extremely short.

The car had always performed well; the turbo hadn't let him down and the front prop joints were rock solid. The house was still in great shape. The neighbourhood was ideal for them, the school for Becca was excellent. Good decisions made after very little thought. Sometimes spontaneity worked well.

It didn't look quite so good for Eddie this time around.

As Eddie leapt, Sean lifted the gun. Eddie could see Sean beginning to squint against the inevitable recoil and the sharp crack; he thought he could see, in the pathetic light from the open door behind him, Sean's index finger turning white as he increased the pressure on the trigger.

And still as he leapt, it felt like an hour's flight from Leeds Bradford airport down to Heathrow, it was so slow. It was slow enough for him to realise that the squint in Sean's eye was nothing to do with the inevitable recoil at all. No, Sean was squinting because dangling from Eddie's outstretched hands, hands that were heading towards Sean's stunned face, were two of the largest ginger slugs he'd ever seen.

Maybe Eddie had it wrong. It now didn't feel as slow as a flight down to Heathrow. Now it felt quick again, and he thudded into Sean's midriff with enough force to send them both crashing back through the cellar-head door. The gun rattled down the stone steps, hit the wall opposite, and for the second time today, skittered away into the darkness.

Sean screamed louder than a simple tackle would warrant, Eddie thought; and then he saw and smelled the wound in his chest and realised he'd been right about Chantelle stabbing the bastard in her kitchen before the bastard quite literally blew her brains out.

Eddie smacked the side of his head against a whitewashed wall and Sean landed awkwardly on his upper back on the edge of a stone step. He groaned but moved quickly enough as the adrenaline must have propelled him to smash Eddie in the guts and begin his lurching descent into the cellar on a hunt for the gun.

The world swayed slightly when Eddie stood, and he realised he could only see out of one eye. The other was filled with blood and the side of his face was awash with redness that seemed initially hot but which cooled rapidly against his cheek.

Sean tripped down the bottom step and slumped against the wall, his hand frantically searching in the shadows for the gun. The light from the wishing well didn't reach everywhere, and one place it didn't reach was the place where the gun had come to a halt. That was always going to be a fingertip search if ever there was one.

But that look was back on his face, the one where he feared recoil – no wait, thought Eddie, it wasn't anything to do with recoil again; it was just fear, plain and simple. He grunted and then screamed at Eddie, "Why won't you die?"

Eddie continued his descent and he realised he must look like a zombie or something. He yelled, "Because you're a lousy shot."

Sean's fear, and the realisation that soon Eddie Collins would be upon him, and he was doomed, fled screaming, and in its place was shock, hope, and the upper hand. The fingertip search bore fruit. He dragged the gun into his lap, turned it so his bloody fingers could grip it properly and then raised it, and pointed it at Eddie.

Eddie stopped, this time allowing common sense a brief strut across the stage as it auditioned for the part of spontaneity. He sighed, no smiles on his face, no quip to lighten the load, just Eddie and an idiot with a gun pointing at him. He slid his hands in his pockets and leaned against the wall. "So, you waiting for an invitation, then?"

"What? What do you mean?"

"Are you going to shoot?" In his right pocket was loose change. He grabbed it. "What's up, not enough children around?" He threw the coins at Sean.

Sean raised his arms to protect himself, screamed as Eddie jumped the last few steps and landed right in front of him. Eddie grabbed his wrist and punched Sean in the face, right on his already broken nose. Sean yelled in pain and then let the gun go.

He stared up at Eddie, tears catching in the smooth downy hair he dared to call a moustache. His bottom lip quivered. "It hurts."

"What hurts?" Eddie took the gun and placed it on the step behind him, wiped more blood out of his eye, and cursed the cut on his head.

"My chest. Feels like it's on fire."

"It smells like it's rotting. I wonder if Chantelle got her revenge on you, you spineless piece of shit."

Sean blubbed but stared through reddening wet eyes at Eddie, and said, "Just who the fuck are you? Benson said you weren't a copper."

"I'm not. I'm a CSI."

"What the hell were you doing in my house!"

"Getting some brave old man his belongings back from you, you scum."

Sean stared at Eddie, and then belched a laugh into the conversation. "Pretty sure that's not very policey. Illegal, maybe?"

"My illegal and your illegal are very different animals."

"Except they both have the word 'illegal' in them."

"Shut up."

"You started all this, you dickhead!"

Eddie stood, asked, "I did what?"

"You. You started all this. You got Sergeant Benson involved, and then Chantelle tried to deal with him, and the gang spotted it, the meeting between them, and they told me to do her in, man!" Sean smacked his knuckles into the concrete floor and didn't even blink as the skin peeled back and fresh blood oozed out. He just sat there and cried, "You made me kill her."

"Don't pass all your bullshit guilt on to me. No one forced you to kill the mother of your children, no one forced you to burgle that old fella for everything he was worth."

Sean stopped crying and brought his face up out of the crook of his arm. "Rewind a bit, man. Brave old man? Burgled him for all he was worth? Are you having a fucking laugh?"

Eddie looked confused. He folded his arms and sat on the steps again, aware the gun was right behind him on the next step up. "I'm listening. This should be hilarious."

"His name is Walter Cropper and he's the biggest and best thief in West Yorkshire. And me, I'm his fence. I take the stuff he nicks and I get good money for it. And he's not as old as he looks."

Eddie was silent for a time. "Nah," he eventually said. "Walter Cropper? He's a decent old man. Led a good life. An honest life."

"Hmph, you are so gullible. You're a shit judge of character, man."

"And to think, I felt sorry for him and gave him twenty quid." Eddie blinked. "You're shitting me?"

"Oh yeah, I make these stories up for kids at the local park."

"Well not for your own kids, obviously."

Sean growled.

"Well go on, Enid Blyton, I'm listening."

"I paid him for some coins he got; unique stuff, top dollar stuff, know what I mean? Sovereigns, some of 'em. I paid him well – I mean like twenty big ones."

"Where the hell did you get twenty grand from?"

Sean struggled to catch his breath, and he rubbed sweat from his face. "You want to go into my finances or shall I tell you the story?"

"Twenty grand?"

"Twenty grand!"

"Fuck me."

"Chicken feed, man. You civil servants think you're so high 'n mighty. But when you see what we pull in, you always say shit like crime doesn't pay, and it'll catch up with you... all that bollocks. Let me tell you, crime pays better than you think. Moron. I sleep well on my silk sheets."

"Yeah, well let's see how well you sleep on polyester prison bedding with a thirty-stone tranny called Cynthia dry-humping you at four in the morning, sticking his tongue in your ear and his finger up your bum. Now get on with it."

Sean sniffed, spat across the floor, and gripped his chest again. "I need something for this."

"An axe?"

"You should be on the stage."

"I'll get you some paracetamol."

"No paracetamol. I need some coke, man. I know where he keeps it."

"What? Where who keeps what?"

"Keep up, man, I know that Norton has a stash."

"And how do you know that?"

Sean shrugged, surprised, "Really? I sold it to him. What's wrong with you?"

"You got a serious number of pies for only ten fingers, boy. Seriously, my flabber is ghasted. Carry on Pablo Escobar, I'm listening again."

"Who's Pablo—"

"Never mind," Eddie said. "Just get on with it before my piles flare up again."

"I'd paid him twenty grand for some coins, and he didn't deliver, kept on saying they was hidden somewhere, and he couldn't get to them."

"Why didn't he tell you where—"

"They was hidden? Exactly, man. Ex-fucking-zackly. But he wouldn't; said he had other stuff hidden with them and I'd take that stuff too."

"And would you?"

"What do you take me for? Of course I would. I'm a tea leaf, ain't I? I'm not stupid."

Eddie shook his head.

"Anyway, I wanted my cash back and so I broke in for it. Found his coins. Took some other gear while I was there, and like a penis he reported the burglary to you lot." He rubbed a shaking hand down his face and his hand came away wet with sweat, eyes half-closed as though he was on something. "He should've kept it in-house, man, shouldn't have blabbed to the law. Now look where we all are."

"Did you find your cash?"

Sean shook his head. "He still owes me."

Eddie looked at him, saw the sweat glistening on his forehead just as a cold shiver wound up his back. "I can't believe it," he whispered. "Walter Cropper is a fucking criminal. I thought he was a war hero."

"Not all old folks are nice folks, you know. You see a wrinkly and automatically think they're the backbone of England. Idiot." Sean kind of laughed, and said, "And if he was ever in a uniform, he was trying to nick something, you mark my words."

Eddie was shocked. "I did my best for him."

"Bet he loved you for it, too." Sean's words were slurred, like he'd glugged a few pints and a large whisky chaser.

"I found you, didn't I?" Eddie stared up at the dark ceilings and saw an army of tiny-bodied spiders with long spindly legs as they built a latticework of untidy webs. It sent a shiver running through Eddie.

"Yeah. You did. Well done, you. Here's a fucking gold star."

Eddie's eyes wandered as far as the weak ceiling light a few yards away would permit. But the noises down here, like gushing water, were intriguing, and there were some dark shadows that Eddie wanted to make sure were safe before he went upstairs and tried to get an ambulance for the kid there.

He stood, and stared down at Sean. Sean's eyes were closed and his hands were in his lap. Eddie nudged him with his boot.

"Leave me alone," Sean said.

Chapter Forty-three

The Faraday Cage

Eddie picked up the gun – he couldn't recall ever holding a gun without wearing examination gloves, and it felt weird, but the alternative was slightly more scary than weird: the alternative was leaving a loaded weapon in easy reach of a killer. Hmm, no prizes for guessing the outcome if Sean got hold of the gun.

He took a torch from a pouch on his belt, turned it on and found himself at the source of the noise. It was a rectangular stone wall about four feet high. From it vented a thin mist of cold water, almost a vapour that wafted on invisible air currents, dissipated across the entire cellar, and turned walls moss green and wood rotten and metal rusty. Eddie leaned over the wall and squinted through the vapour to see nothing but darkness. Even the torchlight couldn't give him any answers. It was just rushing water. "In Leeds?" Eddie asked himself. "An underground river?"

And what the hell was this house doing with a wishing well giving onto a fast-flowing underground river? The equipment above the well more or less gave the game away. Upon approaching it, Eddie had thought it was some kind of water treatment apparatus, but now, the two independent stainless-steel beds told him otherwise. He walked slowly around inspecting it, his torchlight crawling all over the wires and cables, loitering on the iron spikes for longer than it really needed to.

The spikes were welded to the base, and in the welds, it was possible to see redness – blood. "Probably blood," Eddie corrected himself. "Definitely blood," he corrected himself again.

Eddie was stunned by it.

Only when he shone light at the ceiling another seven or eight feet above the spikes did he fully understand what the hell this contraption was. It was a killing trap. The ceiling was the floor in a room in the house above. And he could see how the joists had been cut away so that the floorboards – which had been converted to two solid flaps, two solid doors, could drop open unobstructed, allowing whatever or whoever to come through the floor into the cellar and land on the spikes.

And if there was any way those unfortunates survived, they were encased in a copper mesh cage. He nodded, he knew what that was, it was a big, "Faraday cage," he said. No chance of getting a phone signal. The copper mesh had the green tinge of corrosion all over it.

Eddie backed away from the machine and stopped when something or someone poked him in the back. Over the sound of rushing water, he could hear buzzing, like flies or wasps, and when he turned, bringing the torch with him, he realised why the flies were here. A man laid on his side, legs not resting on the stainless sheet, but raised from it as though he'd been running or walking and had been turned to stone and then laid on his side.

His jeans pockets had been turned out, and there were marks on his fingers where rings used to be, and another on his wrist where his watch had been. "Who the fuck are you?" Eddie asked. The most startling point, though, were the wounds. There were wounds that had bled roughly every four inches across the entire side of his body, from his head to his feet.

The opening floor explained the lower-than-ground-level shot through the lounge door and into the hall wall, Eddie realised.

"His name's Ziggy." Behind him the kid groaned. "Used to be my boss. He gave me the gun..."

"That you used on Chantelle?"

"Yep." The reply was like a dying whisper, almost too quiet to hear.

Eddie turned away from Ziggy and looked again at the machine. There were powerful magnets holding the doors closed and some kind of pulley system above the metal beds. There was a wheel with a handle on it, like the brake wheel on an old tram or something. Eddie wondered what the wheel did. "Stay with me, Sean," he said. "I'll be there in a minute."

Chapter Forty-four

It Could be Beautiful

"Mr Bailey," Benson said. "We're here." Benson turned off the lights and the windscreen wipers, and climbed out of the car. He nodded at the scene guard who was sitting in her car outside the front of the house.

She got out quickly and approached them as Norton and Benson closed their doors. "Sir," she said.

"Who's inside?" Benson asked.

"Just the CSI." She unfolded a scene log and quickly scanned it, before nodding. "Yep, he's still in there, an Edwin Clusterfuck." She looked at Benson, unsure. "Clusterf...? He signed in as... Is that right?"

"Close enough," Benson said, pulling his coat tighter – it was growing cold, and the rain still hadn't stopped. "I'll be as quick as I can, okay?" The darkness was almost complete.

A car drew up behind them and from inside Khan waved at Benson.

"Who's that?" asked Norton.

"My colleague. Give me a moment, will you?" Benson ignored the obvious tut coming from Bailey and walked over to Khan, intrigue as well as the rain hurrying his steps. "What have you got?" Benson stood at Khan's side and soaked up the story, a smile widening on his dour face. They turned to see Norton leaning against Benson's car. The wind caught his beard and pulled it around his neck. He looked like something off The Lord of the Rings, only not quite as graceful. His too-short trousers clung to his skinny legs and his long, dirty toenails poked out through the socks and the sandals. The scene guard gipped.

"You did well, Khan. Would you like to break the news to him?"

Regret furrowed Khan's forehead. "I need to finish on time tonight. She'll pull my balls off if I'm late for another anniversary."

Benson shook his head. "I had mine pulled off years ago. Now there's nothing she can hurt me with." Benson walked away.

"Good luck," Khan called after him.

"Shall we pop inside, Mr Bailey? And then we can get back to doing something more interesting than this."

"Amen."

Both men shuffled along the wet garden path and up the stone steps to the hallway. It was well beyond twilight now, but in the hall, it was black. Surely, thought Benson, if you're a CSI working alone in darkness, in some big old house like this, you'd have every available light turned on. And Benson knew the hallway light worked because he'd seen it last night.

"Where's your CSI man?"

Benson stood still as Norton turned on the light and closed the door behind him. He heard the police car's engine start up, and wasn't surprised – it was getting cold out there. Benson stepped forward. "I wanted to ask you something else, Mr Bailey, before we finally part company."

There was a bang from upstairs. It wasn't especially loud and it wasn't something breaking; it was just a sharp thud. "Someone else here?"

"It's probably your CSI chap."

Benson nodded.

Norton said, "I'm very tired, Sergeant. And I'm in no mood for humouring you as you live your fantasy about playing one of Columbo's lines. 'Just one more thing'." He almost smiled, "I bid you farewell."

"I was hoping you'd be able to help me with the missing people."

In frustration, Norton closed his eyes and gritted his teeth. "And I was hoping to get something to eat, catch up on my medication and avoid killing someone!" Regret shone in his eyes, and he said, "I'm sorry; I'm just stressed, and I want to relax a bit, okay?" He blew out a sigh. "How might I be able to help you?"

"I'll be as—"

"Quick as you can? Yes, you keep saying that."

"Tell me where you've put them?"

"Let's sit at least while I pander to your inadequacies and indulge your fantasies," Norton opened the door and turned on the parlour light. "Would you like a drink, Sergeant, to accompany this informal interview?"

"I'm fine. You go ahead, though."

"What makes you think I have any knowledge about any missing persons?"

"Chantelle Walker told me about you. The day before she was shot dead."

"I read about that. Such a shame."

Benson wandered into the cold room as Norton sank into his chair and reached around the arm for something. He approached the mantelpiece, hands gathered behind him as he thought of his next question. "How do you come by the credit cards?"

"Sergeant. I don't come by any credit cards."

"She was wrong?"

"That or she lied."

"She didn't lie. She was basing her husband's freedom on that information. It was true." There was no reaction from Norton, so Benson engaged in the long game. "How do you afford to live here?"

Norton laughed, pulled at a thread on the chair's arm. "It's not exactly Grand Designs, is it, but I'm happy here. I've put my mark on it, you might say. It was worth a good amount of money in its day. Now I'm afraid it would cost more than it's worth to put it right. Age doesn't agree with some houses."

"It could be beautiful again."

"Not with me at the helm, I'm afraid." He looked around the lounge, sniffed at the air, and smiled at Benson. "This used to be one of the owners' houses. The manager lived in it, and took care of the factory right next door. It was a shoe factory, Sergeant, and it was world famous. The Empire Shoe Works employed over 2000 people, second only to Burton's as a large Leeds employer, but much longer in the tooth. So you see, this house was high status in the latter part of the nineteenth century. Servants for a manager was something out of the ordinary back then. Servants for the owner, sure. But the manager in his on-site home? A luxury."

"Has it been in your family all this time?"

"Yes. It has. My great-grandfather, Ernest Bailey, bought it a hundred years ago. Very well to do." Benson came closer to the rug. Norton licked his lips and searched for the hidden switch. "He made shoes for the gentry as well as the commoner. He made shoes, it is reputed, for royalty."

Benson stared at him. "Fascinating." He walked towards him.

Norton fumbled for the switch, grabbed it and dropped it again, and Benson stood before him on the wooden floor with the faint red swirls.

"He was gifted a couple of pieces of jewellery from the royal estate not long after Queen Victoria passed away." Norton looked away.

That raised one of Benson's eyebrows. "Even more fascinating. Where is it?"

Melancholy softened his face. "I don't know. It was stolen from us decades ago. Thirty years... the blink of an eye. It's very sad," he said, looking at Benson with no hint of madness in his eyes. Only a hint of loss. And more than a hint of regret.

"Mr Bailey, help me with those missing people. It will go very well for you after you've confessed to killing Mojo."

"What? And why would I confess to killing him?"

Benson waited a moment before bending slightly, peering into Norton's eyes, and saying, "My CSI found petechiae on his face, little red spots under his eyes that are indicative of strangulation."

Norton laughed, grabbed the button. "So someone else strangled him after I left."

"I knew you'd say that." Benson squatted down in front of him. "But I'm giving you one last chance to provide details of what you did to those missing people before I arrest you again for the murder of Michael Fogg. And this time, there won't be any de-arrest. Do you understand?"

Norton took a long breath in and sighed it out across the room. "I know nothing of any missing people, nor do I know who killed Michael bloody Fogg."

Benson stood again, laced his fingers behind his back. "We found a car earlier today; well, actually someone at a local chop-shop had an attack of conscience, and gave us a shout. But anyway, it was one of those big black Range Rover things. It used to belong to a local man called Zigolo Khatri; a well-known criminal whose nickname was Ziggy. In it was a dead man—"

"Oh come on, Sergeant, you can't seriously want to hold me responsible—"

Benson held up his hand. "Listen to me, you'll enjoy this story, okay? Just listen. Ziggy's car had a dead man inside it – his name's not important to this tale, but what is," he pointed a finger, "is the dash cam footage we found."

Norton's mouth fell open slightly, and the loose skin around his eyelids fluttered and twitched.

"Yes, it was very interesting. It showed you – not a man who looked like you, incidentally. No, it showed you on your knees behind a kid who was busy dying at the side of a road. It showed you with your arm around his neck, and it showed you squeezing him. Apparently, you can plainly see the kid's hands attempt to pull you away from him just before he flopped forward, dead."

"But I—"

"I told you it was interesting."

Norton stared at the floor for some considerable time. "He tried to rob me, Sergeant. Him and his two friends – and no," he said quickly, pointing a finger, "before you ask, I have not seen them since that night." He pulled himself up and out of the chair. "Perhaps I will have that drink after all."

Benson, not a trace of smugness, stood back, arms folded. He was surprised Norton had jumped on board with his story. The dashcam footage had been blurry and fleetingly quick – maddeningly so. It showed a man that was probably Norton Bailey at the side of a kneeling man – vehicle lights illuminating them, flashing over them. It had been like watching a short documentary on zebras lit by a strobe. But that's more or less all it showed, Khan had said. Wes's car was in slow moving traffic and the image of the two men was right in the extreme edge of the frame, so very warped, fish-eyed, he thought they called it. But anyway, none of that really mattered now, the little white lie had done its job nicely. "Make it a quick one, Mr Bailey, I have a lot to get through tonight and I don't like keeping Mrs Benson waiting. She'll pull my balls off if I'm late again." He smiled to himself.

Chapter Forty-five

Norton Bailey and the Great Flaps of Justice

THE DOOR MUST HAVE latched itself closed and in the near darkness, Eddie shouldered it but it didn't budge. He was certain he heard voices just above him and was equally certain one of those voices belonged to Sergeant Benson, and so, gun in hand, he'd scrabbled his way up the steep stone steps and was now kicking the door to get out.

He could feel Benson walking into a trap and was determined to prevent it.

The door gave out and the darkness of the kitchen smothered him like a blindfold. He fought his way out, not caring about the banging and clattering of things around him as he struggled to make his way to the hallway and the parlour.

Eddie barged into the room and pointed at Norton. "He's a killer!"

Norton pointed the bayonet at Benson and hit the button on the wall.

With a bang, the floor below Benson opened and he fell for what must have been a second or two, screaming as he fell. Eddie had lurched forward, hands outstretched to make a grab for Benson, but he was way too late; there was a metallic bang, almost like a gong but dull and without the reverberations, and the screaming stopped. The look of fear on Benson's face, the look of panic, of knowing his time was actually over, was just horrific.

Eddie held his breath, looked up at Norton, wide-eyed. Norton was grinning; a near full array of yellow and brown teeth showed themselves.

"Never get tired of hearing that special combination of sounds. I'll have to record it one of these days. Screambang. Screambang!" He laughed, licked his lips and said to Eddie. "Are you a betting man?"

The floor creaked and the doors closed back up with a solid click as the magnets grabbed them.

Eddie could almost taste the water vapour. He stared at the floor and then up at Norton Bailey. "You fucking killed him."

"It was a quick death, no need to fret."

Eddie marched around the carpet, teeth gritted, fists ready but the bayonet did not move aside. With a voice trembling with rage, Eddie said, "Save yourself a lot of grief, and put that thing down. Get out of the house now."

Norton grinned still. "No."

"Last chance."

Norton cocked the rifle. "Do you think this is loaded?" He jabbed the rifle forward and the bayonet caught Eddie on the back of his hand. "It might be rusty, but it's sharp, isn't it?"

Eddie looked down for the gun in his pocket and found – without any signs of surprise – that it wasn't there any more. Undoubtedly it was one of the things that clattered to the kitchen floor as he'd scrambled his way out. Fuck, was all he could think; The Law of Fuck.

"Why did you kill him? He was a good man."

Norton stared blankly at Eddie. "The two statements are totally unrelated. I don't care if he was a good man or not. I killed him because he just got in the way. And I can't abide people who get in my way. Do you understand?"

Eddie stared back, but blankly. He was trying to see inside the man; he was trying to get a fix on what the hell made him like this. "How could you kill someone and feel nothing at all for their death? Nothing at all."

"Be a good lad and go get Sean for me. I expect you overpowered him and tied him up in the cellar? In the kitchen?" He moved forward and Eddie reversed. "It would be easy to overpower him, both mentally and physically, I should think. Not the sharpest bayonet in the drawer, is he?"

"He's dead."

Bailey stopped. "Dead?" He stared at the ceiling, and his eyes squeezed shut, forcing dampness out into the corners. "I was away for two hours," he mumbled. "That's all, just two lousy hours, and he couldn't hold on."

Eddie nodded. "I reckon sepsis got him. The chest wound," he said, "started to smell bad. Worse in fact, than your breath. Still, no need to fret."

The eyelid twitched again. "You're very brave or very stupid."

"There's a difference?"

Norton swallowed, thinking it through.

"I don't know why you're so upset; it's not like he was a decent man."

"No, he wasn't. Quite the worst little swine I've ever met."

Eddie slapped his leg, perplexed by Bailey. "Then why so upset he's gone?"

"He had some information I wanted. It was the closest I've been to getting it in thirty-five years. You any idea how it feels to want something so long and then have it snatched away at the very last second?"

"I can see you're mourning for him already. Such compassion. It's very moving."

"Did he say anything before he died?"

Eddie tapped his bottom lip, thinking. "Now you mention it, he did."

"Well?"

"Ouch."

"Come on! What did he say; it's important?"

"He said you still owe him for the coke, or something like that; it was quite touching."

"What's your name?"

"I'm not in the habit of giving out my name to murderers."

Norton stared, jerked the bayonet at him.

Eddie sighed. "Eddie Collins. You can call me Edwin Clusterfuck."

"Did he say anything before he died?"

"I'm not interested in helping you, you fucking—" Eddie lunged for the rifle and managed to get a hand on it before Bailey yanked it free and smacked the stock into the side of Eddie's head, it seemed the favourite place for murderers and criminals in general to hit him, and Eddie was getting annoyed. He hit the floor inches from the rug, panting, hand raised in submission "You'd get on well with my wife," he said.

Norton panted too, but he did it through a smile. "Almost funny, Eddie."

Eddie scraped backwards along the floor and bought himself enough free space to get back to his feet again. "Why don't you put that down, it's time you and me went for a walk; there's a pair of cuffs waiting for you and some sludge they call tea back at the nick."

"I can make it out of here. Even if there were fifty officers out front and fifty officers out back. I could still walk out of here. And I'd like to take you as some kind of bargaining chip if things should go wrong. But I think things would go wrong for me a lot quicker if I did take you." He tightened his grip on the rifle. "Step onto the rug."

"Fuck off."

"Beg your pardon."

"Listen," Eddie palmed Norton away, "I've had the worst week on record, mate; you can't hurt me. My wife left me and took my daughter with her, oh and then she even came back for the fucking dog! Then my best mate at work abandons me and floats off to God knows where to rediscover herself."

"I... Look, I really don't care."

Eddie brought his hands up and curled them into fists. "Some lowlife bastard burgled an old fella of everything he owned. Guess who the burglar was? Your slimy little pal, Sean bastard Walker. But not to worry because I got some of his stuff back for him, an action which, Sean Walker says, caused him to shoot his wife!" Eddie was growing more and more angry. "And on top of all that, you killed a fucking sergeant I didn't hate yet! So go ahead and shoot me with your antique, you crazy old fucker; they'll be in here inside ten seconds. And how far will you get..."

"Shut up a minute."

"...by then?"

"Just shut up a minute. Please."

Eddie coughed, dropped his fists and stood there stalled like a chastened child wondering what to do next.

"You have had a bad week, haven't you?" The smile crawled back onto Norton's face.

"I've had better."

"I want his address."

"Sean's?"

"The old man he burgled. Walter. The one you fought for to get his stuff back."

"This is what you wanted from Sean? Has he been telling you about Walter? You want the twenty grand?" Eddie was confused. "Let me get this straight," he said. "You've killed Christ-knows how many people using those trap doors and that contraption downstairs, and now you've just killed a police sergeant, and you want me to give you information so you can go and... So you can go and do what, exactly?"

Chapter Forty-six

To Want Something Too Much

"What if I just say no?" Eddie stood and resisted putting his hands on his hips – this all sounded camp enough as it was, without adding to it.

Norton was ten- or fifteen-years Eddie's senior, and it pissed Eddie off no end to find he was so much more agile, spritely, even. So when Norton found and retrieved in a matter of seconds the gun Eddie had dropped in the kitchen, Eddie wanted to scream to those bastard gods again. Norton, it seemed, wasn't startled by slugs, ants, or rodents running amok. He simply checked the magazine, decided it had enough bullets in to serve his purpose and then pointed it at Eddie.

"The rifle, which incidentally is a 1913 Lee-Enfield Mk1, and fitted with a mild steel Pattern bayonet, was not loaded after all. I find getting the ammunition very difficult. You should bet more often."

"What do you want from him?"

"None of your business."

"Then I'm not going with you; find him yourself."

Norton stopped what he was doing, looked at Eddie and sighed. "Okay," he said. "Let's put our cards on the table, shall we?"

Eddie said nothing, just folded his arms, and tried not to look intimidated.

"I've heard dozens and dozens of people hit those spikes beneath the parlour floorboards. Dozens of them. And equally,

I've heard lots of people hit the holed sheet rather than the spikes." He came up to Eddie, and offered some cold hard words. "I know he hit the plate with the holes in it – it makes a different sound entirely. I know he's still alive. I wondered how you'd managed to separate the plates, but you found the wheel and worked it out. Thrilled for you. So, he's still alive, yes." He pulled in close, eyes glaring at Eddie's. "But only for as long as I allow it."

"What?"

"He dies when I get fed up of your whining. He dies if you pull any fast moves on me. Eddie, he dies if you refuse to get me to Walter's house. Okay? Is that clear?"

"Not entirely, no. What's the copper cage for?"

"To stop any trapped individual ringing for assistance."

"A Faraday cage."

"Correct." Norton nodded. "You wound the plates apart, and I applaud your ingenuity. But I have on my person a button that trumps your ingenuity. If I press the button, the solenoids snap closed, and with great force, the spikes rocket through the holes." He turned away from Eddie. "Need I paint you a picture of the consequence for anyone lying – or even standing – on that plate when I press the button?"

"I get the idea."

"Thought you might." He turned again, ready to leave. "Shall we?"

"But what happens when you meet Walter?"

Norton looked upwards towards the cobweb-infested ceiling, and he seemed to think for a moment or just to pause. "Don't really know yet."

"You haven't thought about it?"

"Can we just leave? All this... all this conversation is bringing me out in a rash."

"You don't seem very excited for someone whose lifelong dream is only an hour away."

"Please. Can we just—"

"I'm only asking. I'm interested, that's all. You have a chance to meet with someone from years ago – someone who affected your life very much – as much as anyone's life could be affected. And you have no idea what—"

"I'm very nervous."

"Why?"

"You can want something too much, Eddie. I think the more you want something, the more likely it is never to come true, or for something to go wrong. Or even more probable still, for you to get your dream and find out it is rotten and not what you expected at all."

Eddie gave this some thought; he could apply the same logic to his wife – how he longed for her, but how he knew she was poisonous. "This is called the Law of Fuck, and it is a real thing. It's fate and luck ganging up on you, sabotaging life."

"Better not get too excited." He picked up the torch, threw it to Eddie, and lit his own torch. "There," he pointed with the beam. "A side door. It just pushes open."

As with the hidden basement door, Eddie relied on touch rather than sight and felt the change in the wall, pushed and the door opened smoothly in front of him.

"There are steps down and they are likely to be slippery the further down you go. So watch your footing."

There grew a sound out of nowhere, a sound of rushing water, and it became cooler down here too, almost instantly like someone had flicked on the AC switch. Eddie called back over his shoulder, "What happens once you get your dream?"

Footsteps behind him stopped. Eddie turned, Norton was eight yards behind him, his torchlight pooling on the ground by his feet. Norton's face was white and wide, and his mouth was scary, eyes black and staring. It was fear. Eddie walked back, the sound of rushing water lulling like high-volume white noise into the background as he approached. There was an echo as he said, "What's up?"

Norton blinked, his face became animated again, and he looked at Eddie. "I hadn't thought of that for such a long time: what the hell happens if this comes true?" He cleared his throat, looked away again, and Eddie saw the bristles just under his lower lip, in that shallow dip before the chin, stuttering and wobbling a bit. Norton was holding back tears. He was human after all.

"If it comes true," he said, "then I can stop all this. And for the briefest of times I can realise what it is to be normal again, and not to have a burning in my chest and need in my mind that will not abate." He stared off into the invisible distance. "For the briefest of times." Only a moment or two lumbered past before the blackness took Norton's eyes again and he woke up, nudged Eddie, and said, "Get a move on. There's a door to your right in about fifty yards."

Eddie felt Norton's hand on his arm and stopped.

"We'll be outside then," he said. "And we'll be within hearing range of your colleagues. You could probably summon them," he said. "If you do that, Eddie, I will shoot you. Really, I will. Do you understand me?"

Eddie nodded.

"Say it."

"I get it, you'll shoot me in the back if I tell people you're a fucking nutjob."

Norton gave a squeeze and then his hand fell away. "Go on."

Chapter Forty-seven

And the Jaguar Purred Across Crumbling Bridges

Eddie looked over his shoulder, and following him was a mad orange hippy wearing sandals with socks flicking up water. The streetlamps threw a burnt-orange light across the wet cobbles, and you could see the rain falling through the night, and see the orange plume on the overpass a hundred yards away, hear the hiss of traffic on wet tarmac; everything had a sickly orange hue attached to it that looked like Fred Flintstone's shirt.

Eddie tramped past the site of a bonfire. He could have sworn that there were still wisps of smoke coming from it, but it was difficult to tell for sure with the wind being so strong. As he passed by, he thought he saw something bright yellow and stopped to get a closer look. As he crouched down, Norton, the mad orange hippy, nudged him.

"Come on," he said. "This has been driving me crazy all day. I want to—"

"Hey, there's some hi-viz garment here."

"Kids leave those blousons around here all the time. These days, everyone wears one. Come on, I want to get this finished tonight. One way or the other."

Eddie stood reluctantly, and accepted what Norton told him. Over his shoulder the big old house was disappearing into a background of slinky high-rise apartments, being swallowed by an encroaching city and the half-darkness that lived there. Headlights glowed outside it, faces inside the car illuminated by the glow from mobile phones. Eddie sighed, lit a cigarette, and took a very long drag. "You don't suggest we walk all the way to Weetwood, do you?"

"I have a motor car."

"Where?"

"See that petrol station up ahead? That's where."

Eddie kept putting one foot in front of another until he reached the forecourt of the Shell garage.

"Around the back of the kiosk. I have an arrangement with the owner. Eighty quid a month. He keeps it clean and roadworthy, and he keeps the local youths off it."

Eddie rounded the corner and the wind-driven rain smacked him in the face, took the cigarette right out of his mouth and scattered sparks along the street. Squinting through the rain he saw a black Jaguar.

"4.2 V8. Supercharged. Floats; it's like driving on a blancmange."

"Nice."

"Here." Norton handed a set of keys to Eddie. "You're driving."

Once inside the car and buckled up, Norton faced Eddie. "We can drive this journey with me pointing a gun at you to make sure you don't abscond. Or I can trust you and hope you'll repay that trust by not running away. And don't forget the little bit of persuasion in my pocket."

Eddie turned the key and listened to the motor burbling. "Even if your dream comes true, you're going to prison. You know that don't you?"

Norton just smiled. "It doesn't matter. Now, do we have a deal?"

"Put your silly gun away. I'm not going to run, but I want to know why we're going to see Walter. I used to think he was a decorated war hero until I mentioned him to Sean not two hours ago."

Norton moved closer in his seat, intrigued. "What did he say?"

"He's not a fucking war hero – not old enough, for one thing. And he only looks old because arthritis has crippled him. He's a villain, and Sean was his fence—"

"Wait, wait. Fence? What's a fence?"

Eddie laughed. "You deal in dead people, you're a coke addict, and you're..." he stopped short of calling him a maniac. "You're... well I find it strange that you don't know what a fence is."

"I might be all those things and more, but there is no need to become a cliché. I'm not interested in being down with today's youth."

"A fence is someone who'll get rid of stolen gear for a price."

"Sean did that?"

"Sean was a man of many talents. Still a twat, though."

"Go on with what you learned of Walter."

The Jag blew through the wet streets, its occupants insulated from the cold and the wet, enjoying instead the leather, the warmth, and the gentle supercharged V8 backing track. Eddie felt right at home and right at ease. And he knew he should have been on an edge that could see him land in a vat of acid on one side or see him fall twenty-thousand-feet the other. But he didn't care – today, all of it, had been like living life on a precipice.

He was watching something unfold that caused his fingertips to itch; it was something tense, something that had kept old Norton there ripping the heart out of the Leeds underworld for the last thirty years while evading capture as a murderer along the way. Fascinating. Grizzly and cruel but fascinating.

"Sean told me that he paid Walter twenty-grand for some coins he had. But then Walter pulled out of the deal and didn't give the cash back."

"Why did he pull out?"

"Said he changed his mind. There was something special among the coins, but he couldn't get to it easily – the hiding place, and didn't trust Sean to go without stealing whatever else was hidden along with it." Eddie saw Norton lick his lips.

"Didn't mention jewellery?"

"Nope." And then Eddie remembered that old Walter had mentioned specific jewellery to him. Sean had seemingly stolen a Victorian ring, a tiara, and a pearl necklace, but he had tucked away a couple of brooches or something. Yes, he remembered now, but decided to keep it to himself – it might come in useful.

The next ten minutes were spent in silence. It was, after all, a strange partnership – and then Eddie slapped himself for calling it a partnership. It was nothing of the sort. It was merely a collaboration, and performed under duress – he'd be sure to mention that when he was debriefed by the gaffers sometime later tonight – he hoped.

But there was an excitement attached to it, a treasure trove to find! It was a pirate's quest, and Eddie was getting swallowed up in it. Of course, he could have used Benson as his anchor, something sad to ground him and keep things real, precisely what he needed. He had to remember that sitting next to him was a serial killer – a bloody good one – who happened to have a loaded Glock tucked into his belt. Oh, and he was fucking mad, too. So all in all, not a great combination, and it alone suppressed his mood without having to bring Benson's predicament, and possible demise, into the equation, like having someone's foot on your head keeping you under the water.

Eddie stole a glance, and he saw Norton's eyes were out of focus, staring into nothing, his head rocking back and forth with the motion of the car over the potholed Leeds roads. Another twenty minutes and he'd be fast asleep, no doubt. Eddie asked, "How many?"

Norton's head came up and his eyes snapped into focus. He sniffled and shrugged his shoulders. "I don't know, really," he said. His voice was quiet, matter of fact. "If I had to guess, I'd say forty or forty-five, maybe. Something like that."

"And you tossed them into that underground river?"

Norton nodded. "Ladywell Beck, it's called. Been there centuries."

"I never heard of it."

"Most people haven't. They haven't a clue what goes on under their feet."

Eddie laughed, "But surely the bodies must all wash up in the same place, and they must all bear the same kinds of injuries. No one linked them and—"

"Traced them back upstream?"

"Exactly that."

"The answer to that is sitting next to you."

Eddie nodded, "Yeah, suppose you're right."

"And anyway, the river can be violent; it shreds people, dismembers them. There aren't many whole bodies that make it into the Aire."

"And when did you begin?"

"Ah, that's the question, isn't it? Would you be shocked to learn that I'm not really sure?" He smiled; it was almost demure. "I... to my shame, have indulged in cocaine these past twenty years or so. Large amounts. It's very good at doing what alcohol cannot – I know because I tried that avenue too. It's very good at blotting things out in a much more permanent fashion. With alcohol, the memories are never far away, are they? Booze sinks them for a while, takes them out of your field of view – out of sight, out of mind, I suppose. But the next day the memories bob back up to the surface again, washed all fresh and clean, ready to be inspected again. Bigger than ever, more painful.

"Cocaine really does dull them. It's like turning up the transparency on them." He smiled. "So when they bob up to the surface the next day, they're not quite so bright; they're almost see-through. Marvellous stuff. What you fail to realise as a cocaine user – I don't think I'm an addict, I could cease if I chose – is that it's not that particular memory that's disappearing, it's your entire memory! Everything in the brain attached to memories is slowly being turned down, being obliterated and dissolved until it just doesn't function any more.

"So, how many years have I been cleaning the streets?" He shrugged again, and fastened a smile to it this time. "Possibly fifteen, sixteen. But who cares? I never bothered keeping count. You see, everyone I killed was the last one. I never went out with the intention of killing a dozen, or killing twenty. I never went out thinking I'd get through four a month. For me, each time I killed one of the little bastards, it was THE one, it was the last one, at last.

"And when I killed again, I'd be ashamed of myself, and I'd cry for them. I was breaking a promise I'd made to myself after killing the one before: that I'd never kill again; that's it, an end to it all! But I'd go right out and do it all over again, and feel the shame that comes with taking someone's life. And with breaking a promise for the fortieth time. It's an addiction greater than that with the coke – even though I pretend not to be addicted to it." He paused. "But the killing, the pretence, the chase, if you like; I still find that very enjoyable."

Eddie shifted, feeling uncomfortable talking like this to a self-confessed killer – a multiple killer, too. "Do you recall how it all started? I mean, you didn't just wake up one morning and think, fuck it, I'm going to kill a street robber. Or did you?"

"Do you have a family?"

Eddie nodded. "Somewhere. I have parents, well a father, somewhere. Mother is dead. And I have a brother."

"You close to him, your brother?"

He snorted. "No. Not at all. Don't even know where he is. Malcolm was always just a twat I grew up with."

"Doesn't that bother you?"

It was Eddie's turn to shrug. "Not really."

"What if you were about to die? Wouldn't you want to reconnect, even if it was for the shortest of times?"

"What does this have—"

"Answer me? We're engaged in conversation here, and the art of conversing is to answer questions when set."

"I asked you one and you started talking about bastard families!"

Norton raised a finger, and opened his mouth. Only air came out. "I was answering you in a roundabout kind of way. So, indulge me, would you?"

"When I die, I'd want someone I knew there, yes. Not necessarily a brother I have a lot of issues with; it wouldn't be right trying to mend crumbling bridges while death is racing to claim you, know what I mean?"

"I see, yes."

"Death wouldn't wait. The Law of Fuck would come into play. It would allow you to get to the part where things begin to matter again, and then it would take you. Life – and so death too – is a bitch like that."

Norton nodded; eyebrows raised. He leaned forward. "I too had a loving family."

"I never said ours was a loving family."

"No, but mine was, so listen to me. The art, remember!"

"Your rules stink."

"We had it all. We were reasonably wealthy, we were all healthy, and we all got along well. I loved my parents and my little sister, Libby. I was preparing to step into business alongside my father in my third year at university studying electrical and mechanical engineering – they still preferred tangible courses back then, rather than something wispy like business studies, or whatever. Anyway, everything exploded."

As Norton's eyes blurred and he began staring off into the distance again, Eddie coughed loudly, suddenly interested in this murderer's past.

"Mother had taken Libby and me out into Leeds. We'd done the department stores: Lewis's, Debenhams, and Woolworth's. Mother was preparing to leave us for half an hour. I remember she kept checking her watch. Anyway, I was to look after Libby for that half an hour. She never said where she was heading off to, but I already knew. An antique jewellers called Cartwright and Minster; she had a Saturday appointment.

"It was 1980, August the 9th. At two o'clock we were waiting for mum to draw out some cash from the ATM outside The Midland Bank on George Street. I remember it was raining. I was going to take Libby into the market for a cup of tea and to buy flowers for the parlour at Rene's Flowers. Funny how you remember details like that.

"Libby waited with mother at the cash machine, and I was staring into the window of the shop next door. It was a model shop, you know, Airfix models, that kind of thing. She withdrew twenty pounds – quite a lot in 1980." He swallowed, and his breathing grew shallower and seemingly more laboured. His eyes saw further into the distance and on his face grew a layer of fear that Eddie could feel.

Chapter Forty-eight

The Tattoo with Pointy Teeth

As they drove, Norton continued. "And I sensed something to my left. I glanced and through the throng of people, I saw mother take money from the machine, and then quickly, like a flash of lightning almost, I saw a man running at her. I distinctly remember gasping because I knew something bad was about to happen. And it did. About as bad as it could have been. He grabbed the cash and handbag, and I lost sight momentarily, so I moved closer, shoving people aside, and mother was screaming, trying to grab this fellow, trying to get her bag back again.

"This man was suddenly the centre of attention for a gathering crowd. I saw him spinning around, wondering how he could possibly escape. He concluded that stabbing her in the neck would create such panic and confusion, that escape with four shiny five-pound notes and a dull leather handbag, would be a cinch. And so it proved.

"He lunged at her, and for a moment, no one knew what he was doing. As he withdrew his arm, I saw the blade, and then I saw the blood. It was horrid. There was such a lot, high pressure. It gushed over my arm as I got close. It was awful. The crowd screamed, men as well as children. It was so shocking for them too. Mother's eyes were enormous, and her hand was at her neck, and she was turning, looking for me, for Libby. Libby screamed like I've never heard anyone or anything scream since. It will live with me till I live no more, that scream like a dying animal.

"And then mother collapsed, and the robber fled through the disintegrating circle of onlookers. Who would venture to capture the thief now, huh? No one, Eddie. No one. Except for me. I ran after him, I ran across the road and I chased him down George Street towards the bus station and ironically, towards Millgarth Police Station. I ran for all I was worth. I watched him, a scraggy man with skinhead cut, skinny arms gradually exposed by his jacket slipping down his arms revealing a Celtic pattern on his left upper arm and an entwined rose wrapped around his right upper arm, but I could be wrong. I wanted to gather every piece of information about him as I could for when the police got involved, you see. On the back of his neck and scalp, I saw a large open smiling mouth with sharp red teeth.

"He carried mother's black leather handbag in his left hand. There was a small silver chain dangling from one of the loops and fastened to the chain was a key fob that Libby had made for her, woven from strips of red and yellow silk." He took a long breath, trembling fingers fidgeting in his lap.

Eddie could see long hairs sticking out of his ears, and more sticking out of his nostrils. They trembled.

"You understand I was under a great deal of pressure, stress so taut it was almost musical. I even recall his horrid Adidas trainers with frayed heels and dirty laces flicking into the puddles of recent rain. I recall hearing a screech of tyres and thought it must be because of this stupid idiot darting across the road in front of us. But in hindsight, there was nothing coming except for an old bus, and all it did was sound its horn. He disappeared from view over a grassy embankment and then into Quarry Hill flats.

"I almost collapsed. I was not at all fit, and I was entering territory that had a fearsome reputation. But mostly, I was fearing for mother. She, like you, Eddie, would not want to die without a familiar, friendly face, to reassure her. I needed to get back to her, I needed to run faster than I'd ever run before, because this moment would not come around again; I knew she must be dying, and I knew I must be there for her.

"I raced back across the road, back up the hill past Millgarth Police Station, and barged my way through a throng of people gathered around her. Except she wasn't even there."

Eddie stared at him, mesmerised.

"As the circle of people gave me room, I could hear them hush. They quietened so much that I remember hearing my own heavy breathing. In the centre of the circle was Libby. The shock of seeing mother killed like that had scared the poor girl half to death. And a speeding car had taken her the rest of the way there when she ran into the road. I looked at her, and she didn't move. Her eyes were open and her mouth... her jaw was partly detached. It was odd. There was a little blood but not much.

"But the strangest thing ever was that her chest was not moving. I had never before seen Libby without seeing her breathing too. Sounds ridiculous when you hear it out loud, but it was true, and it hit me hard. Eddie, she was dead. The crowd parted as police officers arrived, and through their legs, I could see more officers kneeling at mother's side, draping a brown woollen blanket over her. I wasn't there for her when she died. I feel so selfish. They slid cuffs on me, and I remember mother's blood dripping from them.

"I'm afraid I don't remember anything else of that day."

"He got away with it?"

Norton nodded. "There was no CCTV around back then. The coppers didn't give chase at all. It was just me. And this man was swallowed up by Quarry Hill flats, and they looked after their own well back in those days. No one saw anything. They blamed me. They assessed me; said I was mentally unstable – of all things! I am the smartest person in this neighbourhood – and I served seven years in Juniper Hill."

"Christ. No one believed you?"

"I can be difficult to deal with, Eddie. People don't see the real me, they see the nutter, the drug addict freak, and it's not too big a leap of the imagination to turn me into a killer."

"How did your father deal with it?"

Norton closed his eyes for a long time. Tears came through the lids and glistened on his dirty cheeks. When he opened them again his chin wobbled too, and Eddie thought the man was going to burst into tears, but he didn't. He gathered himself and straightened up his shoulders.

"When they released me home from Juniper Hill, Dad beat me to a pulp and left the house. I didn't see him for three days, and when he returned, he chose his favourite cricket bat, the one signed by the England team, and beat me again. I was unconscious when he broke it on me; I found the bits of it in a skip.

"He lasted almost a full year before I found him unconscious. He failed to wake up after a particularly heavy session one night.

Dad was bloody good at drinking, but I got him to hospital alright. I think he stayed alive after I was arrested just so he could make my life a misery when I got out." Norton smiled and examined his fingers, feet still tapping. "On each anniversary of that day, he bought me an Airfix model kit, and made me display it in my room. They're still there, because he was right: I should never forget that day and how those plastic models ruined our perfect family. Now I have no siblings, and I'm far from perfect.

"Though I try to be. And my contribution to society, you might say, is that I rid it of vermin. Street robbers – my favourite type of vermin. Really, though, I don't think my efforts even make a dent in the amount of criminals out there. But it's not society I think of when I catch them and kill them; it's me. Purely me. I'm very selfish, you see. I keep hoping that one of them might be that man, the tattooed man who killed my mother, but of course, he'd be my age, wouldn't he? And people my age tend not to be street robbers. I still looked out for those tattoos, though, hoping to see them on display one day."

"And that's what worries me."

"Why should it worry you? It has nothing to do with you."

Eddie sniffed, "That right? How 'bout you killed a million people, Norton. How 'bout the false imprisonment of a West Yorkshire Police sergeant; threats to kill. How 'bout kidnap and abduction? There's a shitload more. So don't fucking tell me this has nothing to do with me. Right now, my whole life revolves around you, you selfish bastard."

Norton reached for the gun.

Eddie pulled the car up at the side of the road. He put it in park and looked across. "What? Now you're going to pull your fucking gun on me? Shoot me, you old bastard, and you'll never find Walter. And I bet you finding Walter means more to you right now than anything else."

Norton hissed, and put the gun away again. He stared for a long time through the windscreen, listening as cars and trucks sped past, making the car sway.

Chapter Forty-nine

Hyde Park in the Rain

"I LOVE IT WHEN it rains."

Eddie took a glance across at Norton and the smile on his face didn't escape Eddie's attention. For an instant he looked almost normal. "You cooking something?"

"What? No, I just like the rain. I like the darkness too. I find it—"

"Comforting?"

"We're not so different."

"Cliché alert."

"We're not. Not really."

"I haven't killed forty-five people." He sniffled, "Dreamed of killing them, granted, but never got around to it."

"No, but you know what I mean? There's an underbelly of humanity that needs cutting out."

"And you're the one to do it, yeah?"

"Been pretty good at it so far."

Eddie lit a cigarette and guided the Jag through the ever-narrowing streets of Hyde Park, until they rode down cobbles barely wide enough to accommodate the car. Skies darkened, and the rain had begun to fall harder. The street lights glimmered off the wet road, flickered between trees, and the Jaguar's headlights shone on a couple of scurrying rats before they disappeared into a hedgerow. Night-time fell out of the sky like soot and smothered them. Their visible surroundings condensed into just a few yards; the valiant streetlights pushed it back with all their might but ultimately failed. This was as close

to Victorian England as you could get without it being a film set.
"What happens at the end?"

"The end?"

"When you've got what you came for. What happens to me, to Walter? What happens to Benson?"

Norton's face hardened again. "We'll have to wait and see. But I'll be honest: I don't much care."

Eddie's nerves chewed at his bravery until it was in shreds. They were almost there.

Slanted rain fell through the Jaguar's headlamp beams and collided with back-to-back houses, making the red brick walls shine and the graffiti come alive. The streets were throbbing with students running for cover under jackets held above their heads, squealing like the windscreen wipers as the rain got them anyway.

"Are we nearly there yet?"

Eddie blinked, sneaked another look, and said, "You sound like a seven-year-old."

Norton made no reply, but it was easy – even in this comparative darkness – to work out he was nervous. His face was a never-ending frenzy of twitches and it had probably gnawed its way through today's calorie intake all by itself. And then, "Pass me a cigarette, would you?"

Eddie handed the pack and the lighter over. "You're bricking it, aren't you?"

"Shut up."

"I thought you were hard as nails. You're good at pointing guns at people, good at shoving them into a pit of spikes, but when it comes—"

"I said shut up, Eddie."

"Fucking coward."

Norton backhanded Eddie across the face, and Eddie didn't even think about retaliation – it happened of its own accord. Eddie rammed a fist into Norton's twitching face and the car became the scene of two men slapping and blindly hitting each other with one hand, squinting, swearing, and shouting.

It all stopped when the car rolled into the side of a house. They were travelling slowly, maybe just a bit quicker than walking pace – four or five miles an hour – but it was a sufficiently large jolt to cause them to lurch forward, and grunt as the seat belts dug in.

Eddie took a final blind-sided punch at Norton and then stopped.

Norton had the gun at Eddie's temple. "Go on," he whispered, panting, "do it once more. I dare you."

"See. Coward."

"I'm not nervous about Walter, you imbecile. Now where does he live?"

Eddie didn't know whether to rub the pain in his neck first or his cheek where the muzzle had been. He peered through the windscreen, dazzled by the headlights being reflected by the graffiti on the wall, and reversed the car back onto the road. "We just crashed into it."

"Good." Norton unbuckled his seat belt. "Come on."

"Wait, wait, wait," Eddie said. "I get it now. I get why you're shitting yourself."

"I'm not in the mood for your amateur psychoanalysis; I can get that done by a professional any time I want. Now get out."

"Once tonight is over, it all changes, you'll have a new normal because you'll have nothing to be angry about any more."

Norton shook his head. "Having my family slaughtered is enough to keep me angry for a hundred lifetimes. So shut your silly mouth with your Freud nonsense and get out."

"When I've finished with that house of yours, you'll be living in an eight by six cell at HMP Armley. That'll be your new normal for every one of those hundred lifetimes."

"Will it?" Norton slapped Eddie across the face. "Have you forgotten Benson? After the meeting, I'll kill him just to annoy you, Eddie. And then I'll kill you too. Now get out."

Chapter Fifty

The Art of Delusion

"I haven't forgotten Benson at all. And now I've delivered you safely to your wet dream's conclusion, how about you give me the button, and let me go and get him out of that contraption?"

"I don't think so."

"Why? He might need medical treatment."

"And I might need you again, yet. I'm not finished with you."

"You're a selfish, twisted old man."

They stood at the door. "Never mind knocking, just open it and walk in."

There was still aluminium powder across the front door from when Eddie examined it a couple of weeks ago. Giving advice to people about how to clean this powder off was a waste of time; no one ever bothered. Eddie tried the handle and the door swung open to reveal a hallway freshly decorated in 1981, bathed in subdued light from a 60w bulb that was shaded by a shit-brown lamp shade. The wallpaper was similarly shit brown, and featured a garish flower design that was supposed to look pretty, but, when combined with the threadbare brown carpet, made Eddie want to hurl again.

From somewhere ahead of them came the sound of a very loud television set. As they crept along the hallway, past dark rooms left and right, into view came a stripe of brighter light. It was the lounge doorway, door ajar, some gameshow blaring out.

The smell of tobacco and piss, a sickly scent flavoured with tooth-rotting boiled sweets and sherbet dip brought back memories of sitting in this very hovel drinking tea with a sweet old man. Eddie couldn't believe it; not only was this man not a decorated war hero, but he was a lowlife scum bastard, the same as the man at his side who prodded a gun in his kidneys.

"His taste in décor is equally as shit as your own. Have you got an avocado bathroom suite, as well?"

"You can't help yourself, can you? You've got to open your stupid mouth."

From behind them, a voice said, "Uh-huh. Drop the gun and stand still before I spray your brains over my shit décor, okay?"

When Benson was younger, he kept goldfish. One summer, when he was about thirteen or fourteen, his parents had taken him away to Butlins at Bridlington for a week. And when he returned, he remembered the goldfish. One of them was floating on the surface of the tank and the other was in distress, huddled by a pirate ship in the corner suffering from anaphylactic shock. The water was foul, brown, and gloopy. It stank.

As Benson's eyes flickered open, that very same smell punched him in the face. It took him a full ten seconds to realise where he was and then a second or two later, the smell moved aside, and pain punched him in the face.

He screamed, and as he took a breath, thought he heard someone. The pain hit again.

His left femur was broken just above the knee and now that he was fully conscious of it, he couldn't bear it; it was so intense, so powerful that he thought he would have heart failure any minute. He didn't have heart failure, but he did pass out.

"Thanks for driving into my house, by the way, uh-huh. You know you've cracked the Artex in my kitchen. I'm not paying for it, either, you are."

Eddie, hands in the air, slowly turned. "He was hitting me at the time."

He squinted in the gloom. "Are you..? You're the forensic man, uh-huh; I recognise you now."

"Hello, Walter. Good to—"

Walter still looked like a sack of table legs with a greasy, long-haired football balanced on the top. He was a weak and feeble skeleton with eye sockets three times too big for the eyes that peered out of them. But those eyes were sharp, and they didn't miss a trick. The body might be decidedly second-hand, but the mind was an athlete.

He had large bony knuckles, and oversized hands – about two sizes too big for him. They looked comedic but they also looked like they meant business. He nudged the shotgun and Eddie's hands prodded the air even higher. "Who the hell is this?"

Norton seemed to grow from Eddie's side, and he stood perfectly still, eyes scraping every last bit of detail from Walter's face like a laser mapper. And when it had finished, a switch flipped over in Norton's head. "Time has been cruel to you."

A flash of recognition lit Walter's eyes.

"You used to have a skinhead haircut."

"So. I used to have teeth as well."

"What tattoo do you have on the nape of your neck?"

"Who the hell are you to walk into my house with a gun and start asking about tattoos? I was watching The Great British fucking Bake Off I'll have you know, uh-huh." And then a thought struck him. "Wait a minute, how the hell do you know about my neck tattoo?"

Eddie looked at the shotgun, and then he looked down at the pistol, and realised he was the only idiot here without a weapon. This is not going to end well, he thought. And then a second thought hit home right on the tail of the first – someone's going to get a shitload of overtime out of this scene and it won't be me.

"Where's my jewellery?"

"Wait, wait, wait," Eddie said. "If you think I'm standing in shithole alley with two demented old fuckers with loaded weapons, you need your bumps feeling. I'm off."

"Stay there." Norton put the pistol to Eddie's head.

Walter put the shotgun to Norton's. "Touché. Now leave the lad alone – he's done me well, so leave him be, uh-huh."

Norton swivelled and stared around the shotgun at Walter. Walter didn't so much as blink, and Norton sniffed, shrugged, and lowered the gun.

Eddie nearly fainted. "Mind if I smoke?"

"Catch fire for all I care," said Walter, and to Norton, he said, "Jewellery means more to you than your mother's life?"

"What's that supposed to mean?"

Walter snorted. "I recognise you, Norton Bailey, even after all these years, and even after you grew a beaver on your face and turned into a simpleton. But even you, you greedy bastard, must have felt something for your mother? Yet you enquire about the bloody jewellery first. That's callous, is that. Callous."

"I... But you were..." Norton stuttered to a grinding halt and for a moment it looked like he'd got stuck and couldn't get going again. "You stabbed her in the neck. I watched you do it. You snatched her handbag, and you took the money she got from the cash machine." His face creased up and tears turned his eyes watery and made them look a thousand years old. They rolled down the creases of his cheeks and glistened in his beard. "And then you ran." He looked away, the gun in his hand forgotten about as his arm relaxed and fell to his side. "I chased you," he looked into Walters eyes and said, "I chased you down past Millgarth and you fled into Quarry Hill never to be seen again."

Walter looked confused. "What?" He glanced at Eddie, and asked, "Is this some kind of joke?"

Eddie puffed on his cigarette, shrugged, and then nodded to Norton's dress sense.

"Is that seriously how you remember it?"

Norton cleared his throat. "Is that how I remember it? Of course, because that's how it happened."

Walter shook his head. "You're delusional."

"I am not, sir!" Norton pointed the gun at Walter and thrust it toward his face. "I am not! I remember it plain as day."

Chapter Fifty-one

A Tin of Biscuits and Dreams

"I'm in the lounge if you want me." Eddie left them to it in the hallway, went into the lounge and turned off the television. "It was shit, anyway, Walter." The silence hit them all not like a pressure wave, but more like a vacuum wave, and they all swayed, blinked at the realisation that they could hear things again, things other than adverts. "This stuff will wreck your head."

Eddie was assaulted by the décor again, only this time, as well as a floral wallpaper, there were framed photographs of the royal family, past and present. Everywhere, there was royal memorabilia: union flags, figurines, decorative wall-mounted plates, a rack of teaspoons with the royal crest on the handles, another collection of mugs and more of the royal guard and armoured knights. On the chimney breast were two images: Queen Victoria and Prince Albert on the left, and Queen Elizabeth and Prince Philip on the right. "Wow." Despite appearances, Walter was a devout royalist.

"Is that what happened to you, Norton?" Walter asked. "Too much TV? Addled your mind, uh-huh."

"Nonsense."

"No," Eddie called out. "Good old Norton there prefers cocaine, don't you, mate?"

"Shut up, Eddie."

Both old men joined Eddie in the lounge. Eddie was standing by the net curtains that swayed over the doorway to the balcony. He stood still, smoking, watching the rain falling into the night, and looking at the smear of streetlamps and the spots of light from people's windows.

"Can't you shut that?" Norton said, "I'm freezing."

"No," Eddie said. "Get arguing about how wonderful you are; that'll warm you right back up. Or do a quick line if you want the old cockles toastie."

"Is that why they locked you up, Norton?" Walter asked. "Because the naughty street robber stabbed your mam in the neck?"

Norton shot Walter a look, and Eddie peered at them over his shoulder.

"I was wrongly accused."

"Bollocks," Eddie said. He stepped through the curtains out onto the balcony and flicked away his cigarette end. "I read the report about you. You had arterial bleeding up the sleeve of your right arm."

"I cradled her, I—"

"No, you didn't."

"No, I remember now, she bled on me as I approached, as I held out my arms."

Walter said, "Don't you remember our arrangement?"

Mouth open ready to counter Eddie's allegation, Norton's eyes swivelled towards Walter. His mouth snapped shut. "Arrangement? What arrangement?" A nervous smile pulled at his face, a smile that was there in preparation to rebuff any nonsense that Walter... "What arrangement?"

"I bought this the day you chased me down past Millgarth." He lowered the shotgun, prepared, it seemed, to trust Norton with the news he was about to impart. "You were fucking crazy. You had a scary look in your eyes, kid, and I don't mind telling you that it sent a cold shiver running right through me and left me feeling exposed, uh-huh. Vulnerable, that's the word, vulnerable. I needed protection, and I bought this. Loaded it and it's been loaded ever since, uh-huh."

Norton swallowed. His voice was tiny and in it lived a tremble. "Go on."

"I knew you'd come back one day. Didn't know it would take a burglary and the events that followed to make it happen, though."

Norton looked from one man to the other. "I don't understand. What the hell happened?"

Walter took a breath. "Would you like to sit down? Cup of tea, maybe?"

"No I would not like to sit down, and nor would I like a cup of tea! I would like you to tell me what the bloody hell happened to me!" Norton panted almost to the point of falling over. But he didn't. He remained upright, closed his eyes and took shallow breaths, and even they, the breaths, trembled. "Please."

"You met me the week before. You saw me dip a wallet, and got me up against the wall just around the corner, uh-huh."

"Dip a wallet?"

"Pickpocketed it, right?"

"Right. I did?"

"I knew there and then you wasn't short of a bob or two, know what I mean? So I didn't feel at all bad when I dipped your wallet too in the scuffle." Walter smiled at the memory. "A man's gotta eat."

"Okay, get on with it," Eddie said. "Benson is still in this idiot's basement. Christ, might be dying for all we know."

Walter looked concerned, "Still in... who's Benson?"

"The detective who came and saw you, remember?"

"Oh, yeah, I remember him—"

"I am not an idiot!"

Eddie and Walter looked at each other.

"Will you get on with it?"

"You got him in your basement?"

"Yes. Now get on with it."

Walter coughed and lit his own cigarette. "You offered me a deal. You said the following Saturday, your mam and your sister would accompany you around Leeds centre, shopping and what-not. You said your mam was off to get something valued with a view to selling it, see, on account of her not getting along too well with the mister. Cartwright and Minster, that's the shop she was going to get it valued in."

"I said all that?"

"Most of it. I inferred the bit about her not getting along too well with Mr Bailey – made sense at the time. Anyway, you said the point at which she, your mam, gets cash out of the hole in the wall, is the time I should make my move. You paid me fifty quid to do this, and you said I could keep whatever money she withdrew. So long as I took the handbag and I made it look like a genuine street robbery."

Norton rubbed his face and looked like he was having a hard time accepting this, but allowed Walter to continue.

"You were looking in a shop window. She was standing at the cash machine, and I made my move. I snatched the money, and then I tried to grab the handbag from her shoulder. She shouted at me, and right then I knew this was going to be a shit job; I knew something was going to go wrong – I knew it. She was strong, she was mighty strong, and I was struggling to get it away from her. And then your sister started screaming and hitting me, attracting attention. Christ knows where you were while that was going on and then you were there, fighting me but not fighting me. You were pulling on the bag too, in my direction, against your mam.

"And then, events get a bit fuzzy; I mean, it was a long time ago, and it happened so quick, see, and... well. Well, sometimes when you remember things, you're not remembering them at all. Sometimes when you remember things, you're remembering what you thought happened or what you told yourself happened." Walter looked right at Norton, seemingly trying to decide if he could handle what was to follow. Sometimes the truth isn't easy to accept. Sometimes it's like swallowing acid from a barbed wire cup.

"You took out a knife and you stabbed her in the neck, you screamed at her to let go of the sodding bag.

"I mean, I was almost rooted to the spot. I was shocked, Norton, I really was."

"You stabbed your own mother?" Eddie gawped. "After all you said about street robbers and what scum they were. You stabbed her in the neck."

Norton was confused. Almost in a panic, he looked from Eddie to Walter, and backed away. "No, no, no, that can't be right. That's nonsense." He grinned, pointed a finger, "You're taking the piss, aren't you? This is a joke."

Walter's face remained stoical. "What have I got to gain by telling porkies, eh? I'm not making anything up; I couldn't be arsed, uh-huh. You stabbed her and I fucking ran, mate. I remember the first spatters of blood hitting the pavement, and I saw how crimson the droplets that bounced up looked in the sunlight. I realised just how wrong this one simple job had turned. I was shitting myself. I took that bag, and I ran like the wind. Behind me I heard people shrieking and screaming, and then I was gone, legs pumping, fear pushing me along."

"Fear?"

"Yes, fear! It turns out I hadn't made an easy fifty quid at all; Christ, I'd jumped into bed with the devil, and when I looked around he was chasing me. I screamed and ran faster."

"And you kept going."

"Yes, I bloody did. The blood, man. There was so much blood. And you did it, uh-huh."

Norton said nothing. He was looking at a montage of photographs in an old frame nailed to the wall. Sure, there were photographs and portraits of royalty going back hundreds of years, just as Sean had said. But this montage was from Walter's youth in the seventies and eighties, especially the punk days – black leather and chrome studs. In among the images was one of Walter's neck – it was a big smiley face with red teeth. It sent a prickle up Norton's back. It made him swallow.

Walter licked his lips, and whispered, "And then you ran back to her, didn't you?"

Norton's eyes were wet. He nodded. "She was dead. Obviously. But so too was Libby."

"Your sister?"

"She was fourteen years old. It freaked her out. And like a lot of people who'd just witnessed a lady being stabbed, she turned and ran. But she ran into the path of a car coming down George Street. I lost the two people I loved the most in the space of four minutes." He offered a wan smile, something to mask the steady flow of tears down his dirty cheeks. "The day my life changed forever."

"How long did they give you?"

Almost in a daze, Norton ignored the question. "She was going to sell them. They belonged to Queen Victoria. Two brooches, a small tiara designed for her by Prince Albert, and a pearl necklace. Beautiful. A couple of rings too."

"Was it that tiara?" Walter nodded to the chimney breast.

Norton approached the picture. His mouth fell open and his entire body went slack; the gun dropped from his hand, and he wasn't aware of any of it. And he cried.

"That's it. The sapphire coronet." He reached out, reverent fingertips inches from the painting, heart a million miles away from the memories. "I remember now." He looked up and smiled as he said, "It looks so like her, like Libby. I remember her wearing it. It was a secret that Libby and I shared, but when we were youngsters, we used to play with them when mother and father were out. We would play kings and queens. I was always a fair and just king, and Libby was always a majestic queen. She was very good with the commoners." He looked down at his dirty hands, and a tear fell onto them. "She would have been a wonderful woman. Out of everything that happened that day, I miss her the most. I miss seeing who she would have grown into; she'd be amazing, and I would be proud to know her." He sniffled, slid a sleeve under his nose.

"Why would she sell them?"

Norton was silent for a moment or two, and then whispered, "Because our perfect family wasn't perfect. What family is? All that glitters is not gold, gentlemen. I wasn't privy to their feelings, obviously, but Libby and I caught some of their arguments and it transpires mother and father were to divorce."

"She wanted financial security?"

Norton nodded. "Seems so."

"And you couldn't let her sell them?"

He shook his head. "She could sell anything but those. Anything. And really, father would have seen her right, I'm sure he would. The house was paid for, he had investments... there was no need to sell them except for her want of independence, perhaps." He looked Eddie in the eye, "Besides, they belonged to me. They were my inheritance. She had no right—"

"Wake up you idiot. Of course she had the right, they were hers, not yet yours."

"So how long did they send you away for?" Walter asked again.

Norton shook his head. He looked up, squared his shoulders and said, "Not long enough, it would seem." He swallowed, choked on his own tears and said, "I told them about you, I shouted about you to them. I told them you stabbed her, but I knew nothing about you, no details. I didn't tell them about our deal, of course, but I told them you were a street robber." Norton sat down clumsily into the first chair he saw. He looked frail, ancient, as though a strong wind would disintegrate him. "They didn't believe me, said the crowd had seen me stab her. I thought they were lying. Up until now, I thought they were lying. How could I stab my own mother? I loved her. I love her still."

Eddie blinked and scrubbed at his face, taking away any trace of dampness. "Are we all good, Norton? Is the past sorted out now?"

"Hmph." He looked up and shook his head. "I've based my present – that is the present over the last twenty years, on a falsehood. It's not easy discovering you're not who you thought you were; it's not easy knowing you lived your own lie." He sniffled and he looked broken. "It's not easy learning you killed your own mother."

"What about all the others?"

He eyed Eddie, shook his head. "What about them?"

"They might not have been as bad as you thought."

He snorted again. "Please," he said, "they're still scum. Street robbers – irrespective of who points a finger, be it police officer, be it vicar, even, or be it me, a man guilty of matricide... they're still street robbers bringing misery to commoners. They still deserved to die."

Eddie squatted down next to him. "How well did you know your victims?"

He shrugged. "Well enough to come to the right conclusion."

"You think?"

"Of course. I'm not in the habit of killing innocent people."

"The young lad you killed on Regent Street, Mojo?"

"I didn't kill—"

"Oi, you can lie to Benson and he's stupid enough to believe you, but don't insult me, okay? I know you strangled the poor fucker. And I don't give a shit whether you sit there and admit it or deny it. I know the truth, okay?"

Norton said nothing, his eyes drifted out of focus.

"He was a good kid." Eddie stood and both knees popped.

"He was a thieving little bastard. I saw him and his friends kick and punch a young lady and rob her of money she got from a hole in the wall, just like my mother had."

"That young lady was a nurse. She said she was blind drunk, and she fell over—"

"Of course she said that! Fool! They threatened to kill her."

Eddie was shaking his head. "She came to help the kid after you killed him and buggered off. I was there. She told us she was pissed and fell over. She said three youths stopped to help her, made sure she got her money from the cash machine. And she came over to help Mojo because she recognised him and wanted to help him in return."

"No... No, that's not right. They demanded money from me; they badgered me all the way home."

"Really?"

"Yes, bloody really! Now you listen to me," Norton grabbed the arm rests and pulled himself up and eventually stood facing Eddie, his cheeks red and his eyes screwed into slits, "no one died in my house at my hand who didn't deserve it. Every last one of them was like him," he pointed to Walter, "thieving bastards who should have been put down."

Walter stepped forward, "Put down? You paid me to do your dirty work and you've got the nerve to stand there—"

"He doesn't know what he's saying, Walter, back off."

"Of course I know what I'm bloody saying; I'm perfectly capable of speaking for myself, and as for you, you thieving bastard, where's my jewellery?" He picked up the gun and pointed it at Walter.

"Not again." Eddie sighed and shook his head. "Oh, come on!"

"Where is it?"

"I kept it all this time. It wasn't mine, see. I'd been paid to do a job and I did that job, and I kept that stuff ready for you to collect. But of course, you never kept your appointment with me, did you? But I still kept it for you, for today."

Norton's eyes remained slits, "So where is it?"

"You won't believe me."

"You thieving scum, you sold it, I should—"

Eddie said, "Calm down. He was burgled, remember. I told you all this; the burglar took it all."

"You can 'ave a look, if you don't believe me. I have a steel box, a biscuit tin, full of coins, sovereigns, and jewels and medals and Green Shield stamps and such. One of the brooches," he said, "and a couple of rings, they're still there. But the tiara, the pearl necklace, and a brooch, and a bunch of my coins, have gone. I'm sorry—"

"Sorry? Sorry!"

"Put the gun down, Norton."

Norton strutted across the lounge, a big wrong aiming to be put right.

"Norton!"

"Shut it. You're next, you lying thieving scum, both of you!" He waved the gun between them. And then he took out the switch, and grinned. It looked like a doorbell, maybe slightly bigger, and on the front, next to a shrouded button was a tiny light. It was green. For now. "Benson's life. Right here."

Eddie and Walter split up, hands in the air, and as Norton came closer, they went wide, one to his left and one to his right. Norton spun around, pointing the gun at them both, dribble and tears spilling into his beard. "You're traitors, both of you. You've taken everything I've ever loved." His bottom lip shone in the overhead light. "And now you won't return the jewellery. There was a tiara that Libby used to wear, and brooches, a pearl necklace." He sobbed then. "And there was mother's wedding ring. They belonged to Queen Victoria, and they were insured for eight hundred thousand."

"Here," Walter said. "Take this for now." He handed over a key fob woven from strips of red and yellow silk.

Norton stopped talking, and for a moment his venom subsided. "She made this. Libby made it for Mum." He clasped it tightly in his fist, and looked up at Walter with something that might have been mistaken for gratitude, but essentially was more akin to loathing.

Walter ruined the moment by pleading his innocence. "I swear, Norton, I haven't sold them, I promise." His hands were high, and they shook. His whole body shook, his clothing, loose on his thin body, trembled, and you could see his teeth chattering. "Please take a look in the box; most of it will still be there."

"Liar!" Norton fired the gun.

Chapter Fifty-two

Inside the Faraday Cage

When he opened his eyes this time, there was sweat across his face, and he was shivering because he felt so cold. He urgently needed to pee and already the pain was setting his chest on fire. He gritted his teeth against it all and pulled out his phone.

Christ, there were scene guards outside, there was Khan back in the office – oh, no Khan had abandoned ship, hadn't he? Gone home with his balls intact. But the rest were still there; all he needed to do was call them. The phone lit up and where the signal strength indicator was, there was a red circle with a line through it. Benson moved the phone around like someone trying to get a signal on a black and white TV in the '70s. Nothing.

He tried dialling anyway and only proved he had no signal.

His hand went to his leg, tentatively, touching the bulge above the knee in the darkness, and imagining the bone poking out, a lump of gristly meat on the end. He lit the little torch on his phone and dared to look at his leg.

There was no blood, so the bone hadn't punctured the skin; that was a little plus point, something to be celebrated. It didn't take away the pain though.

He shone the torch at his surroundings and understood why he had no signal. There was a copper-coloured cage all around him. It was like chicken wire only black with faint traces of copper-colour shining at him. Even the underside of the trap doors was covered by it. This was like a Faraday bag that Collins had spoken of. He never thought he'd get to experience it for real.

And the floor on which he lay was shiny metal, something like stainless steel. It wasn't solid metal, though; this plate had lots of orderly holes in it. Each was about an inch across and they were spaced about four inches apart.

He tried to lean in closer, shining the torch, but still couldn't make out what was in the holes.

Chantelle had mentioned this old fella in Mabgate. He's a nutter, she'd said, and you need to be careful. He'd seemed so helpless...

It was dark and bitterly cold down here in Norton's basement. There seemed to be something like a blowhole nearby, and coldness came from it, along with mists of water, every now and then. And he could hear the rushing noise of it. Benson was immediately scared; is that where Norton would put him? In the well?

And what the bloody hell was that smell? The rotting goldfish smell.

With shivering fingers, he pulled at the copper cage and saw a gap opening up. That alone cheered him, and he put extra effort in seeking latches or bolts, pulling himself across the metal floor with his fingers hooked through the holes in the cage. He saw it, a bolt that he might be able to get a fingertip to. Benson was buoyed; he had a plan, an objective, something positive to do – a way out of this! And then the phone battery died, and the torch went out.

Benson screamed.

Chapter Fifty-three

The Killer, the Thief, and the CSI

Spontaneously, Eddie rushed forward and knocked the gun out of Norton's hand, and it fell behind the chair. And like most fights between grown men, they hugged and grunted as they wrestled each other around the room. Eventually Eddie broke free, and Norton didn't waste the chance, he threw a punch into his guts. Eddie doubled up and coughed blood from a split lip. He looked up just as Norton kneed him in the face and Eddie hit the floor feeling dazed, bewildered that Norton had the strength of a Power Ranger and the fighting acumen of Jason Bourne.

"I'm getting pissed off with you," Eddie slurred. "I'm supposed to be at a reconciliation meeting with my wife."

"Don't care."

"If I lose her—"

"If you lose her," Norton paused, clawing back his breath. "If you're at the stage where you're having meetings, you've already lost her, and it has nothing to do with me." He panted hard, hands on his knees, button pincered between thumb and index finger, looked across to Walter.

Walter reached for the shotgun, fumbled it and attempted to catch it, but it dropped to the floor. At that moment, Norton took his hands off his knees and ran at Walter.

Eddie got to his feet and barged Norton out of the balcony doorway. Norton tripped and fell against the wrought iron railings running around the periphery of the balcony. Half running, half crabbing backwards under Eddie's momentum, he hit the railings and tipped over them.

He didn't scream.

And unlike in the movies, he made no sound as he fell onto the basement railings a storey below. The railings boomed, though, like a handful of tuning forks. Eddie got to his feet and peered over, the rain patting the back of his head, and was joined a moment later by Walter. Norton was stationary, pinned onto the top of the railings thanks to the decorative spikes that had pierced his body from the nape of the neck to the pelvis. He looked shocked, yet somehow he looked at peace. Rain bounced off his face and saturated his beard. For a moment he looked happy as watery blood dripped from the yellow and red silk strips in his fingertips. At last, Eddie thought, Norton had finally discovered his new normal. A peace he had spent a lifetime searching for.

"I wonder what happened to his jewellery?" asked Walter. "Sean would know."

"Yes, he would, but he's dead too."

"No. You're kidding?"

"Nope."

There was a pause, and Walter asked, "Wish I'd flogged that crown now. I'd give anything to know where it ended up. You got any idea?"

Eddie remembered the night he finished Chantelle's stabbing scene and one of her children, Betty, ran up to him as the body bag stuttered into the back of a shiny black van. He hadn't noticed at the time, but Betty wore a pearl necklace that came down to her navel, and a brooch too. He wouldn't mind betting she had a tiara at home. He hoped those trinkets would take those two kids to a better place, a place where they didn't live through horror daily, and with people who'd see them happier too, once the pain of loss had subsided. Eddie smiled, "I have no idea."

A few moments drifted past where nobody said anything, and where neither took their eyes off Norton. Walter then said, "That white box he had. Is that it over there? There's a red light on it, uh-huh."

"Red? Shit! Walter, do you have a phone?"

"What? I have no family, I don't make a habit of complaining about anything to anyone, I don't—"

"Just a simple 'no' would suffice."

"No. I don't, uh-huh. And what're you going to do about him?"

Eddie stared at Norton Bailey. He seemed such an angry man, a man who still wouldn't be happy if you took away all his problems. If you took away all his problems, he'd have nothing to complain about, and if he had nothing to complain about, that would make him angry. And he'd complain to you about it. "I don't know. For once I have no idea what the hell I'm going to do."

Walter was shaking his head in something approaching disgust as Eddie walked out of his house.

He stood in the rain and let it wash over him and let it wash through him too, let it cleanse him and wash the blood out of his hair and the remaining dried and cracked blood from his face. The decision he had to make now didn't concern Norton sodding Bailey at all as it happened. Eddie couldn't give a shit about him. But he could give a shit about Benson, and he could also give a shit about Kelly. It was time for their meeting.

If he hurried, he could still get there in time. And if he managed that it would score him some big points with Kelly. All he had to do was climb aboard Norton's old Jaguar and open her up on the way across to the ferry at Holyhead in the West.

Across there in the East, back the way they had come, was Norton's old house. In it was Detective Sergeant Benson, probably incapacitated, maybe unconscious. More than likely dead if that red light on the button box was anything to go by.

But he might not be.

He climbed aboard the Jaguar and started the engine. The windscreen fogged up almost immediately and he set the blower on full and punched the AC button for good measure. And while the screen cleared, his indecisiveness cleared too, and he could see what he needed to do.

He could try to find a phone box. One with a working phone. Or he could try to commandeer a stranger's mobile and try to explain that a Major Crime Unit sergeant was in danger. But even if he could commandeer a phone, there was no easy way to get hold of anyone at the scene – Eddie didn't know any of Benson's colleagues, and that made him think – hell, he didn't know any of his own colleagues. Had Ros still been around, he could have rung her mobile no problem, but as for anyone else...

It occurred to him to phone 999, but if he did that, he'd need to explain to the operator how important it was to get into the house urgently and find Benson in a copper cage over a plate full of holes without triggering the spikes. Don't touch any of the wall switches in the lounge – parlour – he'd have to say, and he'd have to tell them not to touch the switches by Norton's armchair, too. And once they find the machine, don't touch the winding mechanism.

He felt queasy just thinking about all the things that could go wrong, all the messages that Chinese whispers could really mess up. And that was considering things hadn't already gone wrong. Did he really want a house full of coppers stomping all over the place if Benson was already dead? He licked his lips and finally the windscreen cleared.

"Decision time. West to save my marriage, or East to save some fat copper?"

Chapter Fifty-four

Fire and Bluetooth

Eddie slammed the car door and got wet all over again, looking through the rain at the fucking ugly old house and the coppers in the steamed-up car parked out front. The house was old and it was falling to bits; its similarity with Norton Bailey, deceased, wasn't lost on Eddie as he knocked on the police car's window. He could have marched right past the coppers for all the notice they appeared to take of him, but he knew as soon as he started along the weed-riddled garden path, they'd be on him, so might as well play nice.

The window glided down, and music blared out. The scene guard squinted against the rain.

"Sign me back in the house, will you?"

"What?"

Eddie twisted an imaginary knob, mimed, "Turn it down."

She did, and looked back at him. "What?"

"Will you sign me back in the house?"

"Sign you in? I don't remember you coming out." The officer got out of the car, pulled her hood up and had to hold it there against the wind. "I thought you said you were going to be ten minutes."

"I know; it's amazing—"

"That was two hours ago. Clusterfuck."

"Ah," Eddie smiled. "Time runs away with me—"

"They don't have the staff available to replace me. I'm stuck here. I should have been home ages ago. My boyfriend'll kill me."

"Well if he does, give me a call. I'll do your scene free of charge." He grinned but the PCSO did not. "I just wanted to let you know there's another exit that needs guarding. It's just down the side."

The PCSO stared at him.

"Can't miss it," he continued. "Brings you out... down by the..."

"No staff. Remember?"

Eddie nodded, hooked a thumb over his shoulder. "I'll er... pop back inside then."

The PCSO got back in the car.

He stood in the wind and the rain staring at the light bar on top of the police car. He hoped Walter had stuck to his word and summoned the police for Norton's body, and wondered if he should make doubly sure by telling the PCSO to get the cavalry.

The PCSO wound her window down again. She looked up at Eddie. "What?"

He felt sure Walter would have called the police. "Nothing. All's good, thank you."

Although he hated being told off, Eddie put the grumbling PCSO behind him metaphorically and physically, and walked up that path as the weeds and the nettles brushed against his fingertips. Behind him he could hear the music again.

The house loomed over him. This was the part he'd been dreading ever since he set off from Walter's house. What was he going to find in there, and what was the protocol for telling an officer's wife that their husband was dead? Was that something he should leave to MCU or even to Peter McCain to do? Or should he knock on Mrs Benson's door himself and tell her what he found in the basement?

He swallowed, let the rain cascade down his face, and opened the front door. The gloom inside was still there but even thicker now. It was as though it had waited for him to return and welcomed him with a weight and sombreness that was almost physical. The house creaked in the wind like an old sailing ship in a force nine, all scrapes and groans.

He stepped inside and searched the wall to his right for a switch. He turned on the light and the gloom receded a little way, but reluctantly. He closed the front door behind him, and the silence embraced him like a second skin and slowly began to crush him; claustrophobia took his hand and led him along the hallway, but everything froze solid – including his heart – when Eddie heard a cough.

He wavered, eyes wide, heart packing its bags, guts cold, and a squirming feeling by his arse. There came the cough again, from the parlour. It didn't belong to Benson. "Why the fuck did I not just get the PCSO to call it in? Ah yes," he whispered, "no staff." He licked his dry lips with an equally dry tongue and said, "Benson?"

Eddie dripped water onto the floor.

For a long time there came no reply, and it was such a long time that he thought he'd imagined it, and was about to walk on through the kitchen to the cellar and on to Benson – whatever state he might be in, when the reply finally came.

"In here."

Eddie bit his lip and stared at the parlour door, summoning the courage to enter. He looked at the front door again, swallowed, and wondered if he shouldn't just leave. Thoughts of Benson kept him in the house, and made him turn the door knob to the parlour. "Who's there?"

"Come in and find out."

He was not in the least surprised when the hinges creaked. Sitting in almost total darkness was a man in Norton's chair. "Close it behind you, boy."

Next to Norton's chair was a slender black table with a fat old candle on it. The candle holder was straight out of a Dickens movie. In a flickering light the old man sat with a crooked back and long nose, long white hair tied in a loose bun. The light picked out nasal hairs an inch long and eyebrows that a Black and Decker hedge trimmer would struggle with. All he needed was a cloak and he'd look like Gandalf from The Lord of the Rings.

As it was, there was no staff across his lap, but instead something much more sinister.

"I prefer candle light." His voice was throaty, deep, and commanding. "There's something comforting about it. Electric light is so cold, uninviting. Clinical. It has no soul."

Eddie turned on the light. Both men blinked against it.

The old man brought the rifle up and pointed it at Eddie. With the bayonet attached it was a mighty long weapon, and Eddie was only just outside its arc. "This is my rifle. Had it since 1938. It was manufactured for the first world war, but it's still a good weapon. Still going strong." The old man wore a flimsy long-sleeved night-shirt that covered everything down to his knees. From there down to his feet was like bone spray-painted hearing-aid beige – not a bit of meat on them, twisted veins popping out like a bad wiring diagram, feet like talons.

Eddie asked, "Who are you?"

"What's happened to Norton? Where is he?"

"What? Are you his father?"

"And are you a burglar, sir? What the hell are you doing inside my house?"

"I'm with the police. I want to know if my colleague is alright. I'm going to turn around now, and leave this room, okay?"

"I know who you are; I watch, you know. But take a step in either direction, boy, and I'll pull this trigger."

"I thought you couldn't get bullets for it."

"Norton can't. I can. Would you like to inspect it, or do you trust me?"

Eddie put his hands up.

"Good."

"Is my colleague okay?"

"I know where some of my jewellery is, and I'm taking steps to get it back, but I want to know where the rest of it is. So where is it?"

"Taking steps? How are you taking steps?"

"And where is Norton?"

"Anyway, I thought it was Mrs Bailey's jewellery."

"And who do you suppose gave it to her? Me. And since she is no longer with us, it reverts to me. It is mine. I want it back."

"It's lost. It was stolen."

The old man cocked the rifle, elbow out, stock clamped into his armpit.

Eddie stiffened. "I can't make it un-stolen just because you threaten me." Eddie dropped his arms. "Who are you, anyway?"

"Dennis Bailey. You know my idiot son, I believe. And those jewels that Norton had stolen from my wife in 1980 were going to pay off debts, and were going to fund a restoration of this house. Instead we've lived from hand to mouth ever since; the house decays, like me. Entropy always wins in the end. You don't even get a chance to fight the blessed thing; entropy always wins."

"How's my colleague? I want to go to him."

"Greedy bitch. If it hadn't been for her greed, taking them out of the house… Bah!" The old man leaned back and his spine creaked and cracked. "I beat that stupid boy black and blue when I found out Airfix models were more important than… Than his mother's safety. And his sister's too. I should have killed him by rights, but then I've always been too soft on him." He laughed hard enough to shrivel Eddie's nerves. The laughter drifted away and Dennis' face grew serious again. "I should have killed him. I really should have."

"My colleague?"

The old man folded back the drooping skin of his eyelids and managed to bring Eddie into focus again. "What? Oh do stop going on. What a dreadful bore. He's in the cellar, isn't he?

"My great-grandfather, George, stole them from Queen Victoria when she visited Leeds in 1858. He broke into her chambers at the Mayor's residence. Took them off her dresser, whoosh, just like that. Would've loved to have met him." He smiled as though reminiscing. "Been in the family ever since. Well, until Maureen tried to sell them, that is. Greedy bitch! There was an outcry," he laughed. "She never returned here. The Queen, I mean. Queen Victoria, that is."

"That's just so interesting." Eddie turned and opened the door, and the old man raised the rifle and shot at him.

The bullet hit the door and travelled through it. Eddie stood motionless, grinding his teeth, clenching against that squirming feeling in his arse again. He wondered if the PCSO had heard the shot, but remembered her taste for loud music, and groaned.

"This rifle has a seven-round capacity."

Eddie hurried towards the old man as he squeezed the trigger again, and knocked the bayonet as the shot fired, deafening him. His fist stopped at Dennis' white whiskers. Dennis smiled at him.

"One more move and I press it." Dennis held a button in his crooked fingers, long yellow thumbnail poised.

"It's already been triggered by Norton."

"Where from?"

"Hyde Park."

"The other side of Leeds?" The grin widened. "I'm not as savvy with modernity as Norton is, but he talked me through his mechanical toys and the electrical toys that control them." Dennis shook the button. "These are all Bluetooth connections. There are four of them, and each would be useless forty yards from here."

"So he's not dead?"

The old man shrugged. "Don't know. But he will be for sure if I hit this. Now go and stand over there." He nodded to the rug.

Eddie's anger increased, but he felt frustrated as he took a couple of steps back. "Norton's dead, you know."

Dennis stared at him, his eyes milky with cataracts, his teeth brown and his cheeks sunken. He regained control of the rifle, raised it and held the button in his right hand, arm out at ninety degrees. "I don't care. He should have died a long time ago. Boy's bloody useless."

"Look," Eddie said. "This is ridiculous. What the hell do you want? Let me go and see my colleague."

"No."

"Why?"

He held the button aloft like some mighty offering to the gods.

Eddie stood still, studied the old man's features and deduced from the sickening, ever-present smile, that this was some kind of game, and a game Eddie knew nothing of. He only had one provocation to throw at him: "Did you know that Norton planned the robbery?"

Oooh, there it was; the smile hitched up at one side, the eyes cooled for a moment.

"What are you talking about, boy?"

"It's true. He hired a skinhead to rob his mother of the jewellery."

"Nonsense. Why would he do that?" His eyes flicked away sideways, not meeting Eddie's stare.

"Because she was going to sell them. And he wanted to keep them, saw them as his inheritance."

Dennis reinflated the smile. "Doesn't matter now, does it?"

Eddie shrugged. "No, it doesn't. But it's how you remember your history that matters, how your memories add up in your life, and if your memories are false, you're living under a lie, under a misunderstanding. See what I mean?"

"No, not really. You are quite the most absurd man I've ever met."

"Let me enlighten you, let me pull you out from under your naivety. Did you know that the robber did not kill your wife?"

The smile hitched again, and the eyes narrowed slightly. "What are you talking about, boy? Utter rubbish. Start making sense."

"Okay. The robber did not kill your wife. Norton stabbed her in the neck because she wouldn't let go of the bag containing the jewellery." Eddie peered into the old man's eyes. "Didn't you go to the inquest?"

"Well, I mean, I... It was a foregone conclusion. They've been searching for the robber ever since, and Norton went mad because of her death. And Libby's. He went mad, I say."

"They locked him in Juniper Hill for seven years because he killed his mother; but you were right about him being mad." Eddie watched the button, watched the thumb rubbing across its surface. If what he said was true, Benson might still be alive. One false move from Eddie could change that. "And when he returned home and you beat the shit out of him, what did he do? He began killing people."

"Robbers, he said. He said he was killing robbers."

"And you knew about it? Sanctioned it?"

"No, no, you've got it all wrong; stupid man. It was his way of making up for not saving his mother; he saw it as a civic duty, killing vermin. It was to be applauded! He was trying to right a wrong."

Eddie moved to his left, and the old man's aim followed him, arms swivelling. "Even if you kill my colleague, and even if you kill me," Eddie said, "there are other officers out there just waiting to come in." He moved further around and the outstretched arm followed him again. And then he waited, smiling a little. "The game is up, Dennis. No way are you ever going to live like lords again. Soon as this is over, you'll be in a cell, or on a mortuary table next to your sick fuck of a son."

"Believe whatever you want. It has no consequence."

Eddie tracked sideways again, and a thought so fierce grabbed his attention, that he shouted, "Did you put Norton up to it? The robbery? The whole thing; hiring a thief, and then... "Did you know he'd stab her?"

Dennis was growing angry too, but couldn't do anything because as soon as he opened his mouth a scream tore its way out. His sleeve was near the candle, and when Eddie had moved, the sleeve was right next to it. The garment was flimsy cotton, and it took to the fire like a petrol-soaked rag. Dennis screamed and the rifle fell as he tried to stand on shaking legs, tried to get away from the fire. But he fell on the floor by his walking frame. He kept a tight hold of the button, though.

Eddie watched, mesmerised. He whispered, "You wanted her dead, and you wanted the jewellery back..."

"Help me!"

Shocked awake, Eddie took off his jacket and beat at the flames. Eventually they lessened and died down, but so too did Dennis's thrashing around on the floor, and Eddie realised he was too late to do any real good. The shock had seen the old man perish quicker than the fire had. His breathing was shallow, fast, and his heart was fluttering – the pulse at the side of his neck was erratic and feeble.

The old man groaned, and Eddie watched as the trembling hand clamped tighter on the button; the exertion made him shake and before Eddie could reach it, the ragged old thumbnail pressed the button.

Eddie held his breath.

The green light turned red, and from below ground there came a solid bang that made Eddie jump.

Dennis's hand relaxed, he sighed, closed his eyes, and stopped breathing.

Eddie stood, and almost ironically, more rainwater fell from his hair. "Selfish old fuck."

Chapter Fifty-five

From Green to Red

THE CELLAR DOOR WAS still ajar and there was the hollow glow of light that stood out bright against the darkness of the kitchen. Eddie opened the door and held his breath against the stench coming from downstairs. Each footfall on the stone steps echoed until the sound of rushing water surpassed everything else and screamed at him the lower he got.

Off towards the centre of the room was the enormous copper cage and the bed of nails within it. Darkness surrounded it because the trap doors were closed and the glow from the ceiling bulbs seemed weaker here, somehow.

Around the far side of it was a black shape on the floor – Ziggy, a cloud of flies around him too, despite the coldness in here. The noise was very loud, and Eddie screwed up his face against it. Although light was very poor, when he looked up through the copper cage he could see the horrid spikes poking upwards, exposed and lethal. There was no Benson in there.

He sighed, closed his eyes in gratitude and then wondered where the hell he could be.

"Benson?" Eddie held on to the contraption tightly, and wondered if he'd got out somehow, only to fall down the hole into Ladywell Beck. He moved across to what would have been a picturesque wishing well in happier circumstances. "Benson, where are you, you fat fuck?" He peered over the edge where the noise of rushing water was deafening, and in the darkness there could make out the spray of white water.

"Shouldn't you be meeting your wife?"

Eddie spun around. The black shape he thought was Ziggy moved. And then it grunted, and then it screamed.

"Get me off this fucking thing!"

"Benson?"

"Yes, Benson."

Eddie took hold of him and helped him off Ziggy's body and gently down to the ground. "You know necrophilia is illegal in England, don't you?"

"Very good, Collins. And if you ever call me a fat fuck again, I'll bring you back here and throw you down that well myself. Got it?"

Eddie laughed. "You smell like death."

Benson smiled. "You look like death. Now go and see your wife."

The laughter stopped quite suddenly.

"You going or what? Get me an ambulance and then skedaddle."

"Shhhh."

"What?"

"Something's wrong."

The 'something wrong' was a distinct absence of certain dead people. Dead person, to be more accurate. Sean was an apprentice stiff when Eddie left this house two or three hours earlier. He should have been enrolled on the newbie course by now, being inducted to the afterlife, shown the best practices and being made aware of fire and trip hazards.

Instead there was a blank piece of ground where he had begun his decomposition. Indeed, Eddie remembered seeing flies alighting on his chest wound.

Sean was missing. Where the fuck was Sean?

And then it hit Eddie precisely where he would be. He could remember finishing Chantelle's scene, and leaving the house with the body. But the sharpest memory of that scene, the one with the most emotion attached to it, was when Betty Walker, Chantelle's four-year-old daughter had run up to him, crying, asking about her mum. One of the things he remembered the most, apart from her big round eyes full of tears, was the pearl necklace she wore. If he played the memory back but turned the sound right down to minimise distractions, that pearl necklace became one of the most vivid parts of the memory; he could see her running to him, and the necklace was bouncing around, casting curves that shone brightly.

And they shone brightly, it turned out, because of the television cameras – something he hadn't thought of before, because he was busy imagining her with her mother's high heels and lipstick on, filling in the scene, creating an ensemble daydream to match the reality of Becca when she had been that age.

The television cameras had high-powered lights, that's how he'd seen the pearls casting shining curves as she ran. And that's what Dennis meant when he said he was taking steps to recover some of 'his' missing jewellery. And that's where Sean had gone – to track down Betty and Abby.

It didn't take Eddie long to connect the dots – Sean was now working for or with – probably for – Dennis Bailey, recently deceased. And all he could think was that Sean had been a fucking good actor because Eddie was convinced he was dead as a dodo.

Back outside, Eddie wrenched the police car door open and the PCSO guarding the scene, dropped her phone in shock. She reached across and turned the music off.

"Do you mind," she said, "I was on a high score then!"

Eddie didn't apologise. He gave her short sharp instructions that consisted of getting an ambulance down here now for Benson, and getting units to Sean's house as soon as possible. He didn't wait for an acknowledgment, but instead slammed the door and rushed along to the Jag.

The PCSO picked up her phone, blew the dust off it and finished the game of solitaire she'd already begun. She was disappointed to finish it with the lowest score of the shift thanks to being interrupted like that. She then went on to call the ambulance as requested, before starting a new game, determined to beat her highest score without interruption.

On the journey through Leeds from Mabgate to Wentworth Avenue in Halton, Eddie had done some more remembering.

The remembering that put this whole shitshow into context was something Walter Cropper had said. He'd talked about the treasure he kept in his biscuit tin, the treasure he'd been afraid to let Sean see in case he swiped it. That treasure was the coins he kept, the coins and the sovereigns. Sovereigns were worth a lot of money, but they were worth nothing compared to the sapphire tiara and the other bits of Queen Victoria's missing jewellery collection.

Sean had indeed swiped the coins and the sovereigns, and he'd taken a handful of trinkets for his girls – he'd taken the shiny glass crown and the plastic necklace and a golden badge to stick on their cardigans, amazed by how real they looked. He'd taken what he assumed were toys, dress jewellery, worthless junk for the kids to play with.

When Dennis had seen the television news and seen those kids' toys, he'd become super excited – excited enough to get out of bed and bumble downstairs to where the human race was running. He'd been as excited to locate those missing pieces of jewellery as Norton had been – thirty-five years living without them; but the excitement was for entirely different reasons: sentiment for Norton, money for Dennis.

No doubt the news had broadcast an image of Sean as wanted, and also no doubt Sean had made his way up the steps into the kitchen or the parlour, and so began a business partnership forged in hell.

Chapter Fifty-six

No Room for Justice

EDDIE DROVE NORTON'S JAGUAR as fast as he dared. It was still raining hard and the very last thing he wanted to do was crash while on the way to...

To what?

Sean Walker was the last person in this saga who should have been granted anything like justice. For killing Chantelle and leaving those kids without their mother, death was about right, but somehow he'd sneaked away while the guy with the scythe was out having a smoke. He really did have the luck of the devil.

The Law of Fuck, Eddie thought once again.

He liked to think that at the end of a life, the dead chap could sit down with the scaly representatives of Luck and Fate departments, and have a frank discussion with them, and see a list of things those bastards had meddled with – not just the constant barrage of red traffic lights, but the death of a friend, say, the horror inflicted on a person for no good reason, the wayward wife... it would be good to punch those fuckers in the face for each time they meddled.

Eddie was convinced if they left him alone his life would be in a net black situation because he worked well, and he worked hard and he was always fair and he was kind when required. The Laws of Fuck had worked against him and knocked him into a net red situation. Unfair. Uncalled for. Unnecessary.

People like Sean Walker went through life bad. They went along killing people to better themselves without giving a second thought to others – his children, for example – and until recently, he had been pretty much in the black by a large margin. And it was wrong. Someone ought to have a word with Luck and Fate about him, and about others who went through life blinkered and happy and wealthy. It was so wrong. That he was a zombie, a soon-to-die, was not recompense enough – not by a long fucking way.

He drove the arse off the Jag not knowing exactly where those young girls were. Obviously, they were at a grandma's house or a friendly elderly neighbour's, but there was no way Eddie could find out that info. The only thing he dared to hope for was that Chantelle's house was still under scene guard. It was the site of a brutal murder only yesterday, so he'd be very surprised if MCU had released the scene yet. They usually kept important scenes like that guarded for a few days in case new evidence became known and a revisit required. If it needed to be kept on longer, they'd fit their own locks and alarms, because manpower was very expensive.

Anyway, if it were still under guard by officers, they might know where the girls were staying until foster care could be arranged. And if they didn't know, there might be some other means of detection.

As it turned out there were other means of detection. Before he even got to Chantelle's house, he saw commotion and heard shouting at another house nearby, just around the corner. There were people in the street yelling, and Eddie knew this was the kind of scene that followed Sean around like a tail on a dog. It wouldn't be long, he thought, before the police arrived to calm things down. But those little girls might not have that long – there was no telling what Sean would do for that tiara.

He stopped the Jag, locked it, and jogged across the road. He asked a woman what was happening. She told him someone had smashed an old lady's front door in and everyone came out of their homes when they heard the little girls screaming.

"Has someone called the police?" Eddie asked. She nodded, and Eddie wasted no more time. He ran to the garden gate and squeezed through the crowds.

The woman had forgotten to mention the knife.

The front door was wide open, spilling light from the hallway onto the small crowd of brave souls outside who wanted to get involved; yes, they really wish they could, but didn't want to miss

Coronation Street. Instead of rushing in, they had their phones out, thumbs poised on the red dot that would start recording if anything juicy happened – social media didn't feed itself, y'know.

If only he'd brought a huge bag of popcorn, he would be a hero to these people.

Eddie excused his way through them and ignored the 'how dare yous' of people who loved being offended by having their own inactivity pointed out to them. Eddie was no hero, having always described himself as an average arsehole, a coward of epic proportions. But this wasn't bravery; this was a man desperate to keep two little girls safe from a murderer.

Once in the hall, Eddie turned right into the lounge and stopped dead. An old man, mid-seventies had also stopped dead before him – face down, head against the hearth, blood soaking into the carpet. He wore braces, and one of them was loose over his arm; his hands were fists, his reading glasses twisted, lenses popped out next to a book he was enjoying.

On the chimney breast was a picture of the old man and presumably, his wife. Joyce and Bernard, the little label at the bottom declared.

As a professional, whenever Eddie was confronted by a body, he slipped easily, seamlessly, into CSI mode and put aside all thoughts of the human elements this body once possessed. To him, it was a job, and this was just meat in clothing.

But to walk in on a body when not expected, caught him off guard and left him exposed to the feelings normal people, people not desensitised, might feel. He stared at the old guy who, until Sean Walker arrived, was a granddad, someone's husband, someone loved, and now...

There was a scream from upstairs, and Eddie snapped out of it.

Without thinking, he turned, ran out of the lounge, past the open front door still filled with gawpers, and took the stairs two at a time.

To his immediate right was the master bedroom, light off, empty, and then there was the bathroom, also light off. But at the end of the landing was a room full of cacophony. The sorrow that dragged Eddie across the short distance was immense and it was deep. The room was a craft room of sorts and had been converted into a playroom for when the kiddies came around. And right now the kiddies were here but there was no laughter, there were no games being played.

On the floor was a farmhouse where the unicorns and the dinosaurs had been playing. They were smashed, in pieces, witness to a violence that was a prequel to the main act.

Eddie peered into the room; there was a grandmother lying on the floor nursing a cut to her face, and her other hand was reaching out to someone as yet unseen. And there was a toddler – her name was Abby – curled in the corner of the room screaming herself hoarse. He looked through the gap at the hinge side of the door, and there was daddy sitting on a low wooden desk, the chair to it knocked over and broken. His face was white. If he kept still long enough one would mistake him for a cadaver – something Eddie had already done and something he would like to turn him into again on a more permanent basis. His eyes were half closed and the red stain down his chest was like a curtain across his jeans too. When he slid across the desk, he left a smear of blood behind him.

In one arm, Sean held Betty. She was looking at the ceiling; her face was wet with tears, eyelashes clumped together, snot trailing down her quivering chin. Her lips were tight closed and her chin was dimpled as she tried hard not to scream and not to cry. Daddy didn't like it when she cried; it made him angry, thought Eddie. Her little chest hitched with each hidden sob, and Eddie could see her hair twitching as her heart thudded.

At her neck was a hunting knife, the kind with saw-teeth running along the flat edge like a stickleback. The blade shone and the hand holding it shook. He was filthy, he was covered in muck and dried blood – his hands were etched with it, his fingernails were circled by it, and his cracked lips were highlighted with it.

Eddie gasped and swallowed a lump of fear that made him gag. It attracted Sean's attention, and like a robot, his head juddered around to face Eddie, his mouth opened up and a smile spread like a disease as he slurred, "If it ain't Eddie Collins. Here at the beginning, and here at the end." He laughed, but it was the kind of laugh that sounds painful, the kind that made people cringe. It rattled.

"Thought you were dead," Eddie said, entering the room.

"Nearly was. Thanks to you. I'm allergic to paracetamol."

"Ah, sorry to hear that." Eddie nodded. "Can I get you some more?"

Sean smiled. "I want me stuff. And then I'll be on my way."

"What stuff?"

He reached across, kicked the old lady in the face. "Tell him!"

Eddie went to her, and helped her to sit up. He knelt in front of her, shielding her against further attacks from Sean, and inspected the cut across her face. "You'll be fine, Joyce," he whispered, and tried to reassure her. But how do you reassure someone when you have a deranged idiot like Sean Walker in your house, especially since this lady was now a widow. The poor woman was shaking, and Eddie didn't need his first aid training, which he mostly slept through, to work out that she was going into shock.

"Tell him!"

She jumped, and Eddie tried to soothe her. "What's he on about?"

She looked over his shoulder and then pointed. "He wants the toys – the crown thing and the jewellery. He wants the brooch that Abby's got on her t-shirt and the necklace that's fallen down the side of the bed." She rested a hand on Eddie's, "He's getting frustrated." She whispered, "He won't let anyone leave." Through tears she said, "He knows he's dying, and he wants to take his girls with him."

Eddie couldn't think of anything worse. He turned to Sean, but didn't stand up. He remained kneeling so as to reassure Sean he wasn't going to make a move on him; the height advantage, if he were to stand, might intimidate him. He tried to think of something diplomatic, and soothing to disarm the situation, and said to Sean, "You were a dick the first time I met you, and you haven't fucking changed."

Sean grinned. "I want me stuff, and then I'll be out of here."

"And how far do you think you'll get?"

Sean shrugged. "Betty here wants to come with me."

"Come on, Sean, she's petrified—"

"Don't offer to take her place, you're not welcome."

"Don't do this to your own daughter."

"She isn't my daughter." His face turned sour. "So shut up. This isn't about family, it's about money. I want my money. I want the crown and then I'll go. Okay? Simple. Why can't they fucking understand that? I'm in a new partnership. Once I'm out of here, you'll never lay eyes on me again."

"If you're talking about Dennis Bailey, he's dead. Burnt to death."

Sean eyed him. "You serious?"

Eddie nodded.

"People have a habit of dying around you, don't they?"

Eddie looked at Abby, almost comatose in the corner, just cranking out the same old screamy-whine on each breath, and Betty was sinking too. "These are young girls, Sean. Don't inflict yourself on them, don't give them nightmares forever; don't scare them!"

"You got a family?"

Eddie closed his eyes. "Don't do this shit; everyone does this shit. My family, your family – two different things, and none of your business! I don't put a knife to my kid's fucking throat!"

Sean grinned. "You're scaring my princess," he said. "Tip top negotiator, Eddie. Did you get a certificate for it?"

Eddie sighed. "Let her go. I'll get your crown and you can let yourself out."

"She comes with me, remember? Now, you curled up a bit when I mentioned your family; why did you do that?"

"What? We're not here to talk about—"

"I say we are. And right now, this knife makes me the boss, yeah? Get it?"

"What do you want to know?"

"Eddie Collins? Happily married with children."

"Separated. One daughter."

"Separated." He looked at the old woman, "Hear that, Joyce? Even the good citizens can't keep their shit together." Back to Eddie, he said, "She blames me for breaking the family up."

"Killing your wife might give that impression."

Sean stopped smiling. His eyes opened fully, and he pressed the blade into Betty's neck hard enough to draw blood. The kid screwed her eyes up and cringed, bracing herself. Eddie held his breath and tried to reach out but couldn't for fear of making it worse.

"I'm sorry I said that." Without taking a breath, he said, "My wife shagged around. She left me last week, actually. Took my daughter, and then came back for the bastard dog."

Sean relaxed, smiled at Eddie's misfortune.

"She said I was in love with a stranger's pain; that I spent too much time at work and not enough with the family."

"See, can't help but stick your nose in, eh. Look around you, Collins, see the devastation you caused? Do you think they'll give you an award for this, man?"

Eddie sighed, and he'd never felt so much like crying in his life – that's the coward part, he thought. He just wanted to nudge

Abby out of the way and sit in the corner crying. It was all too much. He was a scene examiner; he searched for fingerprints at burglary scenes, and he put dead people into white plastic bags with reinforced carry handles. He didn't do this; he didn't do playing with kids' lives.

"Turns out you're not much of a family man after all, eh Eddie. Bit like me. I'm not either, to be honest." Sean grinned at him. "Well, you are a family man, actually, just not your own family." He laughed. "You're fine pissing about with other people's lives and their families." He licked his lips, and there was a sparkle in his eye. "Just not right cracking when it comes to your own, eh? Pathetic piece of shit. I'm not right clever with words, me. I know that. But I know one that's reserved for you: patronising. You think you're better than everyone else." He sat up, teeth bared, anger making its way to the surface. "But let me tell you, Collins, if you were born into my family, you'd have turned out just like me; you'd have no choices, you'd live crime or die – you'd be a criminal or die."

Eddie replied, "And is that what you wanted for your girls? Huh, maybe they could have made you proud by starting off with a shoplifting? Then, if they made the grade – if they got the fucking certificate! – they could have progressed to a bit of robbery; no, no, how about prostitution, maybe?"

Sean leaned forward, snarling.

"Fetch a decent price for a fit little body. You'd make an excellent pimp, Sean. Set them off on the drugs scene – they could be superstars of Leeds, and their stage name could be Crack and Crack, eh – drugs and fanny all in two nice little parcels. And then you could afford your very own black Range Rover!"

Sean tightened his grip on the knife, took a breath.

"How does that sound? And before long they'd nominate you for Father of the Year awards! You'd be famous, you'd be a role model for all the shit dads out there like me – we could all fucking follow you on Twitter!"

Sean pushed Betty aside and lunged at Eddie. Eddie grabbed his wrist and twisted, and both corkscrewed to the floor. Eddie screamed, "Get them out!"

The old lady grabbed Abby's arm and yanked her out of the corner, and Betty ran out of the room after them, all three screaming.

Somehow Sean managed to get on top, and almost lay down on Eddie. The room was tiny, and there was no room to manoeuvre, despite Eddie trying, and the knife presented itself to Eddie's left eye with Sean's weight on it. Above the knife, Eddie saw his face, teeth on display, a snarl on his face, a growl in the air, scented with badness. Eddie writhed and the knife slid sideways and bit into his shoulder, as Sean tried to headbutt him. He lay there, having the breath squeezed out of him, pushing against the knife with both hands, his cheek against Sean's cheek. He could feel the exertion, the sweet-smelling sweat of death.

It should have been easy. Eddie should have been able to push this lad off him with his little finger, but for some reason, he couldn't. It was like Sean had sold his soul to the devil and had been rewarded with Herculean strength, but more likely he'd done a couple of lines of coke.

He turned his head slightly, and he bit Sean's ear. He bit it hard; he felt the skin tear and hot blood run into his mouth. He was reminded of Peter's KFC and the chicken fat running down his chin.

Sean screamed and he tried to pull free, but Eddie clung on. The knife receded slightly and Eddie bit harder. He felt the gristle between his teeth and he felt an earring snap. Sean froze. All the weight came off the knife and this time when Eddie shoved, Sean rolled off him like a man made of papier mâché, and his hand went to his ear. Blood seeped between his fingers. His eyes were closed and his teeth this time were on display thanks to a grimace.

Eddie sat up, and realised he was sitting in a pool of blood that had seeped from Sean's chest wound, and the smell was horrific. The wound opened and Eddie almost puked.

On the floor there in the corner where Abby had been sitting, was the tiara. He was going to stuff it down Sean's throat and watch him choke on it. There was no room in here for justice any more, there would be no trial, no jury and no prison sentence. It would end today, and it would end painfully for Sean. No amount of prison time could ever bring back their mother, or would ever erase their nightmares. No amount of prison beatings would give those girls their granddad back. Eddie raised his fist and stopped.

Someone touched his arm.

Shocked, he looked around, and the world fell out of chaos in that instant. It became quiet and tranquil and warm and peaceful. Betty put her arms around Eddie's neck, stood on tiptoes and kissed him on the cheek. "Thank you," was all she said.

Chapter Fifty-seven

When the Fire Went Out

EDDIE SCRUBBED BLOOD OFF his face with sterilising wipes, and then stuffed a rolled-up bandage under his t-shirt where the knife had caught him.

It was only after Eddie sat back in the Jag and lit another damp cigarette did it occur to him. And it only occurred to him when a couple of police officers began erecting cordon tape across the front of Joyce and Bernard's home. Their uniforms were like his – black. But coppers were different in that they wore bright day-glow body armour. To that body armour – which was supposed to be resistant to blade penetration – they attached all the gubbins they'd need throughout the day; pouches for this and that, water bottles, spare batteries, handcuffs, pocket notebooks – all kinds of stuff.

And those pouches were pretty much job specific. Sure, plenty of people wore day-glow garments these days for health and safety reasons and as part of their uniform. But there weren't many jobs that required people to carry pouches – just the police as far as he knew.

As he'd walked past Norton's house earlier tonight, he'd come across the smouldering remnants of an old fire. And in that fire...

"Oh, shit," Eddie said and started the van.

Beginning a scene examination at this time of night, in this kind of weather, and after the day he'd had was a stupendously poor idea. So Eddie elected not to do that. Instead, he'd scout the fire scene, have a poke around in it, and then declare this as a scene and leave it covered by a tent until someone fresher could examine it.

He found the fire scene again, dragged most of the way here by his nose. The torchlight worked wonders and it wasn't long before he found bits of pouch and the black stab-resistant plates that belonged inside a tac vest. And then the finds came thick and fast; the more he prodded and poked the less inclined he was to wrap the scene up and pass it on to someone else.

He found half an epaulette with the last number being six, and a pair of slash-resistant gloves nearby. This was all police officer's garb. This was the uniform belonging to a missing police officer. He would put money on it that the epaulette number once read 966. And the reason it was here was because Norton wouldn't want a day-glow jacket belonging to a missing officer to pop up on the River Aire and invoke a thorough search.

There was no way that Eddie would allow this little fire scene and that bastard house to be examined in his absence. He needed to be a part of this; he feared he would never reach full closure if all this went on behind his back. And everyone, no matter who they are, needed closure.

There were sometimes circumstances that warranted an absence, no matter how much one wanted to be there. It was the same for Eddie, and the mitigation in this case was his family. The house exam would wait for him, but there was one more thing he had to take care of first.

Chapter Fifty-eight

Promises, Promises

IT WAS BITTERLY COLD. Ireland was beautiful and it crossed Eddie's mind yet again about coming out here to live. It was gorgeous, but if he thought it rained a lot in Yorkshire, it was like a torrential downpour from sun-up to sun-down over here. And while he didn't mind the odd shower, he couldn't handle being soaked to the skin every day.

Eddie chose to fly from Leeds rather than drive across to Holyhead and endure a three-hour ferry crossing to Dublin. The Ryanair flight arrived at seven-thirty, giving him just under twelve hours in Ireland before he was due back on the plane home.

Twelve hours to fix something that broke twelve years ago. Or more. It didn't seem like it was possible.

Eddie glanced at his watch for the third time this minute, and it was still 12:05, and she was still five minutes late. No problem, five minutes was nothing compared to how late he was.

Last week, Kelly had sent a text message offering to talk about the relationship, and set a meeting time on her turf at roughly the same time Norton was sailing through the air outside Walter's house last night. Still, it couldn't be helped. And when Benson told him he was late for this meeting, he knew he'd blown any chance of getting back with her and claiming her and Becca as his family again. It was sad, but he'd mopped up enough tears without adding to them further. It was time to be grown up and it was time to put a stop to this, and become the family man he should have been all along.

Benson hadn't made a big thing of it, but Eddie could tell he'd been crying – big ugly tears, too. He said he'd heard voices upstairs and then he heard gunfire and shouting, and with him stuck down here by himself in utter darkness, he was afraid Norton had come back and was ready to finish the job off.

The last thing he remembered was falling for what seemed like a year and landing awkwardly, knocking the wind out of his lungs and breaking his femur too. When he woke up, the pain was agonising but thankfully he spent the first hour or two unconscious.

Of course, Norton by this point was dead, but prior to that, it had taken Benson about ten minutes to work out what the holes were in the metal plate he came to land on. By the light of his phone he could see ingrained blood in scratches in the metal, and the copper mesh he was enclosed in prevented him getting a signal. By the time he'd figured out how to get out of the net before the spikes came through the holes, his phone had died and left him in total darkness.

He had fumbled in that darkness for what must have seemed like hours, panicking that he would be impaled any second. And when he finally tumbled out of the cage and off the plate, and landed in something smelly and buzzy, he knew what it was. But when the spikes finally shot through the holes with a deafening bang, it rang on for a full five minutes like the reverb from a church bell. All this was ten minutes before Eddie arrived in the cellar, and he had all but pissed his pants with fear and pain. In the darkness he had elected to stay put on the body rather than risk getting down – because getting down might have meant falling into a well of some kind; the rushing water was overpoweringly loud. It had been uncomfortable there on the body, he'd said, but it was safe.

And when he'd heard someone say, "Benson, where are you, you fat fuck", he had laughed and cried all at the same time – they'd won.

"So you made it, then?"

Startled from his daydreaming, Eddie looked up at her. He stood. "Kelly. I... I didn't think you were coming."

"I know that feeling well, Eddie Collins. Over the years I've endured hours of it. And sure enough, if last night wasn't a replica of what we've endured over the last God-knows how many years."

"I'm—"

"Sorry?" She sat. "You always are."

"How's Becca?" She looked wonderful. Smart and glamorous all at the same time; eyes made up, hair tied up and her slender neck on full show. Eddie licked his lips.

"Fine. I think the slower pace of life here is doing her the world of good."

Eddie nodded, and the feelings of blame began accumulating, as if the pace of life was his fault now. "And Watson? How's he?"

She ignored him. "So what was so important you couldn't come to a reconciliation meeting with your wife?"

"Is that what this is? A reconciliation meeting?"

She sighed, forehead already a corrugation of frustration. "We'll see, Eddie. Small steps, okay?" She took a breath, "Why didn't you make the meeting last night?"

"Work."

"Yep, I got that, Eddie. It's always fucking work. But what work?"

He looked at the table just as the waitress arrived. "Just coffee for me, please." Kelly ordered tea and when the waitress thanked them and left, she resumed glaring at him.

"I can't tell you. I'm not allowed to tell you."

"Course you can. Was it a burglary? Oh, come on, I just want to know it was something explosive, something worth being fucking stood-up for, you know what I mean? I don't want to be stood up for a theft of a motor car."

Eddie smiled, she might have lipstick on, but behind it her teeth were just as sharp as ever. "Murder, robbery, kidnapping. There, and all in one day."

She sat forward, a tiny smile interrupting the carefully painted frown on her lips. She nodded, "If it's true, then I feel a simple text would have been in order."

"I broke my phone. Sorry."

"And you couldn't borrow one?" She folded her arms.

"I was a bit busy, I'm afraid." And there, just then, he could feel it. If he could remain seated and stay perfectly still, but get up and walk across the room and turn around and look at himself sitting here, he'd be able to see that his shoulders had become rounded, that they'd sunk, that his neck was crooked like a cartoon vulture, and he was already looking up at her, chin raised, eyes wide and shiny. And he was an awful shade of yellow. She did this to him; she turned him into a skulking creature, a Gollum, offering itself to her for another whipping.

The drinks arrived and Kelly didn't take her eyes off him, while Eddie didn't look at her once. If he'd had a tail, it would be between his legs.

"That has been your line for fifteen years, Eddie Collins. Too busy. I'm at work. Sorry I'm late. I'm sick of it. So sick of it that I moved back here."

"And you emptied the house."

"I did no such thing!"

"And you emptied my bank account."

"That money is legally mine." Her eyebrows were a perfect V and he noted how anger really suited her. She did her best performances when she was angry. "I had every right—"

"It was in my account."

She blew through slack lips. "Oh come on, Eddie. Don't you think I deserve that money for all the times you haven't been there, all the help I needed from you, and you were off somewhere else giving help to strangers instead? Don't you think that's a fair price?"

"Let me get this straight. You want my money because I left you alone – as a housewife with no job to go to – while I went out to work and earned our money the hard way. You want recompense because I was out at work, keeping you?"

"No need to wrap it up to sound like I'm the bad guy."

Eddie laughed. "But you are." He stared at her and realised something. "You never actually loved me, did you? You just wanted someone to support you while you went out and enjoyed yourself with your friends or your lovers." He watched her and she flinched. "You wanted some mug to keep you in idleness. And all you did was moan about it to make it sound like you were having a rough time of it."

"How dare you?"

"Easily, as it happens. Oh, and speaking of lovers, I spoke to his wife."

"Whose wife?"

"James Smarmy-pants. Otherwise known as Timothy South."

Kelly gasped.

"She said he always wanted blow-jobs from her but she refused him and so he sought them elsewhere. Tell me, Kelly, did you enjoy blowing him?"

"I don't have to stand for this."

"No, I expect you were on your knees most of the time." He pointed a finger. "Your incessant complaining about me being late and you being the victim all the time, about how I felt I was doing something worthwhile to help people, was a way of deflecting your own inadequacies onto someone else, was just a way to point the finger and blame me for your own life being a shallow shit show."

"A shallow shit show? And that's all because of you – you're so insensitive, so un-romantic—"

"Well, now you can find true romance with someone else. And with no one to blame but yourself."

"This is all bullshit. I worked my arse off keeping this family happy."

"Happy? You blamed me for working long hours and caring for strangers more than I cared for my family, but that was all a front, wasn't it? You wanted your freedom but didn't want to be seen as the bad guy by breaking us up. So you blamed me and turned yourself into a martyr. Plus, you get to divorce me on grounds of unreasonable behaviour, no doubt, and claim my pension. Whereas," he continued, "if we split up because you were shagging around, you'd get nothing. I hate you for turning us into a cliché."

"Eddie Collins, we're through."

Now Eddie folded his arms. "Yes," he said, "we certainly are."

She paused, searching his eyes, and then she smiled. "What did you say?"

"I'm filing for divorce."

"You haven't got the balls. You fucking need me. Without me your life would fall apart."

"Without me you'd run out of money inside a month."

No smile now. Just a swallow.

"You are a selfish egomaniac, and I think you're also a bit psychotic, maybe even a bit of a sociopath."

"How fucking dare you?"

"Again, easily. Truth is easy to speak and hard to receive. You suck the goodness out of everything, and you suck the enjoyment out of me until I hate everything, and you suck... well, I'll leave what else you suck to your imagination." Eddie stood, threw ten euros on the table. "Tell Becca she's always welcome back if she chooses, or she can settle with you over here. I just want what's best for her. I'll pay you an allowance for her if she decides to stay. Goodbye, Kelly."

"You hate everything anyway, you grumpy fucker. You shout at fucking traffic lights!" She stood, "Eddie? Eddie, you get back here right now!"

Eddie left the coffee shop and Kelly was out before the door had swung shut.

"Eddie, please."

He stopped and turned around, and lit up a cigarette. He took a drag and blew smoke into the air, all the while staring at her, wondering what bollocks would come next.

"Don't do this," she said, "please. We can make it work if we put in the effort. I won't complain if you're late home, really I won't. And I've already stopped seeing him. I won't do that again, I promise."

"Have a nice life, Kelly."

"Look, it was out of boredom. That's all; he meant nothing to me, nothing. I felt reduced to fucking him because I couldn't fuck you. I was demeaned by it all."

"You were bored? Ever heard of crochet? And anyway, darling, each time you fucked him you were fucking me too – only not in a nice way."

"But—"

"It might have meant nothing to you, but it did to me. It really did. You demeaned yourself, Kelly, but you killed us. Where's your self-esteem?"

"Stop," she whispered.

Eddie did stop, and he turned to her.

"I know why we don't get along, Eddie."

"Because I fart in bed and you leave hair in the bath plughole?"

"Stop it! We don't get along because you're a Gemini and I'm a Pisces."

"What? We don't get along because you're a fucking fruitloop." Eddie tutted and looked to the sky. "Why must you keep on with this astrology bullshit?"

She pleaded again, "It's the only way I can... it's the only thing that explains to me why you are like you are."

"We don't get along because you and I are two different substances. It's like beef Wellington and custard. It's like you're trifle and I'm gravy."

She offered, "Like I'm chalk and you're cheese?"

"Don't be daft, I can't stand cheese."

They stared at each other.

"Real families care for each other, and would do anything for each other. A real family wouldn't make ultimatums like you do."

"But—"

"I don't love you any more, Kelly. You're selfish in all aspects of your life." He held her hand, and said, "But I hope you find happiness."

"What are you going to do?"

Eddie stepped up and kissed her on the cheek. "Can't leave Dublin without sightseeing. But I want to see Becca first."

Chapter Fifty-nine

Epilogue

WALTER WALKED OUT OF the shop. He was grinning like he'd never grinned before. In his wallet was a cheque from Cartwright and Minster for twenty-three-thousand pounds. He'd swapped a brooch and gold ring for it.

When the cheque cleared, he bought everyone in his local their drinks for an entire evening. While he was out buying those drinks, two burglars broke into his house and stole almost the whole lot. They left him twenty quid on the mantelpiece.

All Walter had left in his collection were some old coins and some Green Shield stamps.

On the plus side, he thought, there were no fewer than sixteen drugs deaths in Leeds the following week, and old Walter hoped it was his money they'd blown killing themselves.

Across the other side of Leeds and nudging into North Yorkshire, Abby and Betty Walker were starting a new life with some wonderful foster parents. They were told that their future would be secure, and that future, consisting of over a million pounds, was in trust for them until they reached twenty-one.

Turned out someone saw Betty on the TV news speaking with a CSI outside her former home. And this person had noticed the brooch and pearl necklace she wore. An anonymous dealer with close royal connections paid the girls off, and the collections of the Victoria and Albert Museum in London grew by several pieces of jewellery that had been missing for over a hundred years, among them a priceless tiara designed for Victoria by Albert – the sapphire coronet.

Benson was promoted from sergeant to inspector, spent six months off work while his leg healed, and then tried to convince his bosses that Eddie Collins would make a great addition to the CSI family they were stealing. No matter how much he pleaded, the answer was always no, and he never knew why that was.

Eddie Collins contemplated buying another dog to replace Watson. He decided against it for several reasons: quite high on his list was how he hated picking up dog shit, and that he didn't have the time to dedicate to it was a close second. But what stopped him was this: he didn't ever want to get close enough to something or someone again. If he had feelings for something or someone then it was an odds-on guarantee those feelings would eventually get smashed, shredded, trampled on, and then burned.

And the way his luck went with The Laws of Fuck, that was always going to happen. It was better, he concluded, to live alone and please yourself about everything – that way, no one could intentionally or otherwise hurt you, and that way, you could focus on the job.

Waiting for Eddie when he returned to work the next day was an email from the Submissions Bureau telling him something that was immaterial now: the blood he found on Mojo's back belonged to Norton Bailey.

Over the coming weeks, more news filtered down from various scene examinations that had been carried out by Eddie's colleagues. The black Range Rover driven by Ziggy's man, Wes, had Sean Walker's prints all over it, and his prints in Wes's blood – which was everywhere – proving his involvement with Wes's death, or at least confirming he was there when it happened. But proving direct involvement in the killing was GSR on Sean's hands that matched GSR from the weapon, the weapon known to have killed Wes and known to have killed Chantelle.

Benson finally managed to wrap up his missing persons' file. There was direct evidence of eighteen victims in Bailey's cellar. There was a bag of credit cards on a shelf featuring many of the names he was interested in, and Eddie returned to the basement to work on the contraption. He managed to get mixed DNA profiles from another six people. It was highly probable that up to forty people went through Norton Bailey's machine but proving it was almost impossible.

The machine was dismantled and taken to a breaker's yard and cut up. The floor was covered in two layers of chipboard and the well was bricked over.

The house is currently for sale; offers in the region of £80,000.

Afterword

I found research into Leeds fascinating. And I found the little world I'd created, in a small part of it called Mabgate, strangely endearing. I thought I'd put Norton's house, and the world in which it existed, here for you to 'enjoy'. Some of what follows is true, some of it made up...

Charles Dickens said, "Leeds is a beastly place, one of the nastiest places I know."

It got nastier, Charles.

Leeds really came alive in the pre-Victorian times when the wool and textile industries exploded. It was as though a golden cloud had burst over the city and it rained sovereigns for years. Another reigning sovereign, Queen Victoria, visited Leeds in 1858 and opened the new Town Hall. She stayed overnight in a house owned by the then Mayor, Peter Fairburn, and made him a knight soon afterwards. It is thought that the Queen's entourage left Leeds slightly lighter than when it arrived. Though never proved, it was suspected a thief had entered the house and removed jewellery from Her Majesty's bed chamber – namely two brooches, a pearl necklace, an assortment of rings, and the famous sapphire coronet, a tiara designed for Victoria by Prince Albert.

Norton's great-great-Grandfather, George Bailey, was the thief. He stole them when he was only sixteen.

Those items stayed in the Bailey family for almost 130 years before The Great ATM Robbery of 1980. The robbery severely affected Norton – but not so much as it affected his poor mother.

Anyway, because of the Queen's visit, and because of the words of a certain Mr Dickens, that newfound wealth helped the city leaders combat future outbreaks of cholera that had plagued the city throughout the 19th century, killing over three thousand people. That investment consisted mostly of slum clearance, and designing and building a working sewage system. Part of that system involved taming a beck that flowed through what was to become a large expanse of industrial and urban regeneration that would never see greenery again.

Ladywell Beck ran under a new shoe factory. That factory was called The Empire Shoe Works and was complete with its owner's house – Coulston House, named after the founder, Benjamin Coulston Esq.

Work on the beck finished in 1939; it was hidden from view all the way from Mabgate to the River Aire over a mile away.

Halfway between the two, in the centre of Leeds at the foot of Eastgate, is the Arthur Aaron roundabout with a copper roof. Over the road from it used to be the Quarry Hill flats, and all 938 flats spewed their sewage into Ladywell Beck. That underground beck had grown into a tunnel some twenty-four feet across and fourteen feet high. And it was often full, especially after a heavy rainfall.

No one knew or calculated the speed of water travelling through it, but estimates put it somewhere between twelve and eighteen miles an hour thanks to an overall incline of twenty-four yards. It would take something dropped into the river here a little over four minutes to be ejected into the River Aire. And by the time it got there, the beck would make sure it was unrecognisable.

When they knocked down The Empire Shoe Works, the remaining slums and unhealthy tenements, the abandoned workhouses and almshouses, the only place left standing was Coulston House. After typhoid killed old Mr Coulston, Ernest Bailey – Norton's great-grandfather – snapped the house up for a mere £3,500 in the year in which the second world war broke out, and despite that, it was, at one point at least, a happy family home. How did he get the money to buy the house? Good question. He sold one of the stolen rings.

During the latter part of the war, and just afterwards, the area prospered, and the nearby Regent Street became the centre of a clothing industry spawned by supplying military uniforms. A few decades later, the clothing, leather, and shoe industries declined, thanks in part to cheap imports and in part to stubborn unions and greedy mill owners. They steered their industries towards a bleak future, powered by a greed that was highly commendable in Victorian times, but was totally unsuccessful in a post-war near-bankrupt England.

The underground tunnels of Ladywell Beck continued to carry the filth of Leeds out through the East Street Culverts and into the River Aire. And they still do today.

The house stood through it all.

These days it could use a little money spending on it to bring it back to life again; actually it could use a lot of money spending on it. If it was in good condition, it would be worth £1.4M. Right now, if it was for sale, you could probably grab it for £150,000. The land it occupied would be worth considerably more to developers. The roof failed to be water-tight twenty-five years ago, and some of the rooms in the attic and second floor became uninhabitable, several of them unsafe to enter. Oh for Victoria's jewellery now.

Most of the rooms on the first floor were safe, though damp, with mould sprouting from the walls and rot creeping through the floor boards, ceiling joists, and door frames, keeping the woodworm safe from dehydration.

Since the slums had gone, Coulston House sat in a couple of acres of mucky overgrowth with just a maze of weed-infested cobbled streets left to show it had neighbours at one time. New premises sprang up around here; a couple of hundred yards away was a petrol station, and then light industrial units claimed land back from encroaching nature, followed by chrome and glass apartment towers that made Coulston House look like a ruined hotel from a horror film.

The house sat fourteen yards above the fast-flowing Ladywell Beck, and if the traffic on the nearby overpass was light, it was possible to hear the echoes of gushing water as it raced beneath the building, heading towards the centre of Leeds and then onto the River Aire. If one were to remove the large wooden manhole cover in the basement below the house, one would feel something like a sea breeze, something like sea spray prickling one's face with icy coldness, and feel the rumble of water and hear the hiss of that spray and the boom of water cascading along brick and concrete tunnels, dark tunnels, violent and deadly tunnels.

If only this basement could speak.

Acknowledgments

This book took an exceptionally long time to come to you. You can blame the person to whom it's dedicated: Lottie Rose. She arrived at the back end of April, 2021, just as I was getting up a head of steam on this thing. As it turned out, the steam leaked out and my new daughter kind of took over.

Nevertheless, here we are setting the latest CSI Eddie Collins book afloat (or adrift, depending if you liked it or not) - it being, strangely, the first in the series. I've written lots about this anomaly, and you can read about it in lots of places. This place is here for me to thank those who've been kind enough to give their time and expertise making this book waterproof, for without them it would surely have sunk.

    Firstly, and as usual, I need to thank my wife, Sarah, for being so selfless. It's an honour to be married to someone who knows how important a person's dreams are, and allows them enough slack to chase them down. Did I catch any dreams? Well, I still work full time, so obviously I didn't catch them all, but hey, I'm sitting here writing this to you about another new book, so yes, if you look in the net, you'll find a couple of them flapping around in there.

    Kath Middleton is a woman you've probably heard me mention before - and with good reason; she's the one who turns a collection of ninety-thousand words into something that makes sense - yep, she waterproofs the hull - okay, enough with the sailing metaphor (I don't even like sailing, no idea where it came from). She is a very keen reader, and she's phenomenally generous to the indie-author community. I feel blessed to claim her as my best friend for over a decade. There's nothing she doesn't know about me, yet she still remains my friend - how strange! Thank you, Kath.

Emmy Ellis took my hand and led me through the turbulent waters... wait, wait, sorry. Enough of the water! She guided me through the process of creating and selecting a cover designer and a cover - and I think I struck it very lucky indeed. Thanks Emmy.

Thanks also to my Facebook friends in the UK Crime Book Club - really great support from everyone there, followers of my Andrew Barrett Page, and members of the Andrew Barrett Book Group for their encouragement, insight and constant giggles throughout the last year - all very welcome.

Thanks to all those people who are subscribed to my newsletter – that you participate, comment, and email me is not only very kind but very much appreciated.

A special thanks go out to my wonderful beta readers. For most of them, this is the second novel we've worked on together; once again, their input makes the book sparkle. And if you're one of my ARC readers, I bow to you. Your enthusiasm and your keen eye make this such a fun journey - it's one of the best parts of publishing a book.

Lastly, if you're one of those readers who care enough about the story, the character, and the time devoted to knitting them all together, to leave an honest review so that new readers might share your enjoyment, then I bow sincerely at your feet - you keep the world turning, and you keep me and my author friends tapping the keys.

Beta Readers, thank you...
Roxy Long
Richard Jackson
Barbara Woods
Fritzi Redgrave
Shari
Alex Mellor
Gail Ferguson
Mike Bailey
Patti Holycross
Dee Groocock

About the Author

Andrew Barrett has enjoyed variety in his professional life, from engine-builder to farmer, from oilfield service technician in Kuwait, to his current role of senior CSI in Yorkshire. He's been a CSI since 1996, and has worked on all scene types from terrorism to murder, suicide to rape, drugs manufacture to bomb scenes. One way or another, Andrew's life revolves around crime.

In 1997 he finished his first crime thriller, A Long Time Dead, and it's still a readers' favourite today, some 200,000 copies later, topping the Amazon charts several times. Two more books featuring SOCO Roger Conniston completed the trilogy.

Today, Andrew is still producing high-quality, authentic crime thrillers with a forensic flavour that attract attention from readers worldwide. He's also attracted attention from the Yorkshire media, having been featured in the Yorkshire Post, and twice interviewed on BBC Radio Leeds.

He's best known for his lead character, CSI Eddie Collins, and the acerbic way in which he roots out criminals and administers justice. Eddie's series is six books and four novellas in length, and there's still more to come.

Andrew is a proud Yorkshireman and sets all of his novels there, using his home city of Leeds as another major, and complementary, character in each of the stories.

You can find out more about him and his writing at - www.andrewbarrett.co.uk, where you can sign up for his Reader's Club, and claim your free starter library. He'd be delighted to hear your comments on Facebook (and so would Eddie Collins) and Twitter. Email him and say hello at - andrew@andrewbarrett.co.uk

Also by Andrew Barrett

The CSI Eddie Collins series:
The Pain of Strangers
Black by Rose
Sword of Damocles
Ledston Luck
The Death of Jessica Ripley
This Side of Death

Did you enjoy The Pain of Strangers? I hope you did. You'll need the next in the CSI Eddie Collins series; it's Black by Rose.

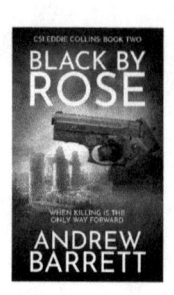

Try a CSI Eddie Collins short story or a novella. Read them from behind the couch!

The CSI Eddie Collins novellas

Have you tried the SOCO Roger Conniston trilogy?

Reader's Club

Sign up and Read

As a thank you for joining the Reader's Club, I want you to enjoy a couple of free books, a starter library - I call this Sign up and Read.

I'll make sure you get a brilliant thriller and a stunning CSI Eddie Collins novella written in first person.

The Reader's Club features a monthly newsletter with details of new releases, special offers, and other goodies, together with news and snippets of interesting items. How do you join the thousands of other crime-thriller fans there? Simply click this link to my website (or type it into your browser), www.andrewbarrett.co.uk, and sign up today.

CPSIA information can be obtained
at www.ICGtesting.com
Printed in the USA
BVHW030412020822
643544BV00013B/1082

9 781739 659301